THOSE WE COULDN'T BURN

WHITNEY L. SPRADLING

Midnight Tide
PUBLISHING

Those We Couldn't Burn

Copyright © 2023 by Whitney L. Spradling

All rights reserved. No part of this publication may be reproduced, stored in or introduced into a retrieval system, or transmitted, in any form, or by any means (electronic, mechanical, photocopying, recording, or otherwise) without the prior written permission of the author.

No part of this book may be used to create, feed, or refine artificial intelligence models, for any purpose, without written permission from the author.

First Edition

ISBN 978-1-958673-56-0 (paperback)

Published by Midnight Tide Publishing | Midnight Tide Publishing

Edited by Sara Coombes | Sara Coombes

Cover by The Cobs | The Cobs

Midnight Tide
PUBLISHING

This is a work of fiction. Names, characters, places, and incidents either are the product of the author's imagination or are used fictitiously. Any resemblance to actual persons, living or dead, events, or locales is entirely coincidental.

Content Warning

This book contains adult themes that may not be appropriate for all audiences. These themes include: on page graphic sex, drugs/alcohol, drug/alcohol addiction, violence, language, and fantasy racism.

National Drug and Alcohol Treatment Hotline

You never have to struggle alone. There is always help.

National Drug and Alcohol Treatment Hotline
1-800-662-HELP(4357)

The National Drug and Alcohol Treatment Hotline provides information on alcohol and drug abuse, local treatment options, support through hotline counselors to speak with about alcohol, drug or family problems.

To anyone who has ever experienced injustice.
To anyone who has ever had to hide their true self.
To anyone who has ever dealt with ignorant assholes.

Never let them win.

Who knows why we were taught to fear the witches, and not those who burned them alive?

-C. J. Cooke, The Lighthouse Witches

PROLOGUE

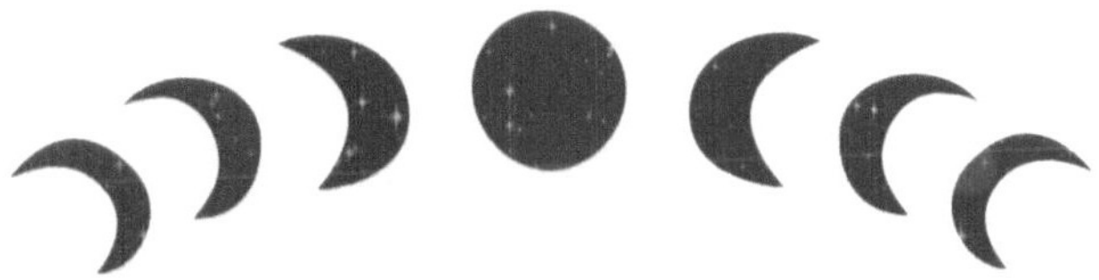

BLOOD. IT'S ALL OVER THE FLOOR. SO MUCH OF IT, IT'S A wonder it all fit inside his body. *His body.* A sob escapes me, and I clap a hand over my mouth. I can't help it. I loved him terribly, but I need his power. Without it, we will all die.

My fingers shake as I brush his blond hair from his eyes. Already, his skin is cooling. His beautiful tan turning a sickly shade of gray. I kiss his forehead, shuddering at the rubbery texture of his skin against my lips, no longer warm and inviting. A single tear slips down my cheek, but I wipe it away.

As I turn from him, my heart cracks. It splinters into millions of pieces; the pain piercing me to my soul. I bend over, clutching my chest and wail. How is this fair? Why do I have to be the one to do it? All my life, I've been grateful for my power. I've used it for good, helping the man I love. Helping his people. My people. But now? Now, I hate it. It's a curse I wish I could rid myself of.

I kneel in the pool of blood. It's cool against my skin as it soaks through my skirts. The knowledge of where the blood came from, of who it belonged to, tears me to pieces. No longer does it pump through the heart of the man who gave that very organ to me. He loved me, and this is what I did in return. I drained him of his life force.

But you had to. The voice whispering in my ear is my own. *Don't let the sacrifice be in vain.* I plant my hands in the blood, splattering it onto my arms and face. My vision goes white and I gasp. When it clears, I have only one thought in my head, but the symbols I draw in the blood mean nothing to me. My life means nothing to me. The words are all I know.

"She is coming. The one with the sight. She will save us. Only she can stop the threat."

Shouting and screaming erupt around me. But still, I say the words.

"She is coming. The one with the sight. She will save us. Only she can stop the threat."

Hands wrap around my arms, hauling me to my feet. But still I say the words.

"She is coming. The one with the sight. She will save us. Only she can stop the threat."

A fire lights under me. The flames spread to lick at my skin. Still, I say the words.

"She is coming. The one with the sight. She will save us. Only she can stop the threat."

She is coming. The one with the sight. She will save us. Only she can stop the threat.

No Warts, No Boils

Fire is a funny thing. Watching the undulating flames is mesmerizing. The oranges, reds, and yellows licking and dancing. Embers sparking and spitting as they rise into the air. The crackle and hiss as the wood chars and burns.

It's amazing to me how fire evokes such different feelings for each person. On a cold snowy night, the roaring of a fire in the hearth is romantic. Add to it a good book or the arms of someone you love, and it's the perfect picture of tranquility. In the outdoors with a marshmallow and some chocolate, you have the backdrop for a fun adventure with yummy treats.

However, for the witches who live in the country of Rossvale, fire is the stuff of nightmares. It haunts our dreams as well as our waking life. It's the weapon used to eradicate us. Innocent women who have done nothing wrong, except be born differently. And everyone knows what happens when people are different. They are feared, hated, and preyed upon. Because, goddess forbid, we can't live in a world where differences exist.

For me, as I watch the flames catch and spread, my heart races. A fine sweat breaks out over my skin, and bile climbs up my throat. I want to look away, but I can't. The two women currently burning at the stake deserve more than that. So I force myself to watch as Josie Goldron and her oldest daughter, Marley, burn alive. They don't scream. We're stronger than that, and we won't give them the satisfaction of seeing us break. But if you look closely, you can see the fear in their eyes. While we may not fear death, we certainly don't enjoy the process.

The taste of ash coats my tongue, and the stench of burning flesh assaults my nose. Even though we don't scream when we're burned, I always think I hear the cries of witches past as the flames eagerly devour the bodies of their sisters. It makes me shiver, goosebumps pimpling my arms that have nothing to do with the cold.

The eager crowd that came to watch slowly dissipates as the bodies on the stakes crisp and blacken—there's nothing exciting left to watch, so they might as well be on about their evening. I stay, though I move to a darkened alley where I'm less noticeable. No point in drawing attention to myself.

When the flames finally die down, the soft rub of a cat against my legs propels me into action. *Yeah, yeah. I'm going.*

One of these days, you're going to get caught.

The voice in my head makes me grit my teeth. When I turned sixteen, this damnable cat appeared on my doorstep and wouldn't leave. Of course, I'd end up stuck with a cat as a familiar. I fucking hate cats. And this one is the worst of the worst. It's pure white, except for the gray tipped ears and gray feather duster tail. Aren't witches supposed to have black cats? And he's mouthy. If I could get rid of him, I would. And I've tried. A lot. He won't leave.

If I get caught, at least I'll be free of you. I say to my familiar, in my head. I have to be careful not to talk to him out loud when we're in public. It's too dangerous if people see a female talking to an animal.

Jinx huffs inside my head and saunters off, his long white coat standing out in the rapidly darkening streets.

I make my way through the city, dodging cars and buses filled with people on their way home from work. As the nicer skyscrapers turn dingy and rundown, I pull my hood over my hair. Not only does this protect against the stiff wind blowing between the buildings, but it also helps me blend into the ghetto.

Trash and squishy things fill the streets, and it's best to not examine them too closely. No fancy cars here. Just the occasional bus and run down beater. Deciding to take the chance on the shortcut to my apartment, I dart inside an alley and hurry through the darkness. Puddles of unknown substances splash under my boots, but I do my best to ignore them. Rats squeal indignantly at me as I interrupt them feasting on something gross and rotten. I jump over them, shivering as their naked tails angrily swish across the concrete. Disgusting creatures.

Something moves in the darkness up ahead and I grit my teeth, hand dropping to the knife I keep on me at all times. A half-rotted crate falls from a stack and collapses into a pile of decayed wood. I jump, stifling a scream, and press my hand to my chest to keep my heart from pounding straight out. Picking up my pace, I dash the rest of the way through the alley, jumping over the broken pieces of wood, and emerge onto a street only slightly brighter.

Half the street lamps in this part of the city don't work, and the ones that do only work about half of the time. A neon sign from the local dive bar flickers to my left, and raucous laughter spills out from the open doorway. I turn right, hoping to avoid the drunken patrons of that seedy establishment and the disgusting offers they'd no doubt shout at me. Dealing with the aftermath of a dead body isn't something I feel like doing tonight.

My apartment building is up ahead. A tall skinny building with more windows broken than intact. I jump to grab hold of the fire escape and pull myself up to the landing. This is by far the best way to get to my apartment. Avoiding the creeper landlord has become a pastime for me. Taking the wrought-iron stairs two at a time, I make my way to the eleventh floor.

The golden shimmery veil of the spell I placed on my apartment is just barely visible. Humans wouldn't be able to see it, but if they tried to cross it, they would suddenly experience the intense stomach gurgles of someone who needs to use the bathroom immediately. I prick my finger and press the bloody tip to the window ledge to make the spell dissipate.

The window sticks like it always does when I haul it open, but at least it's winter. In the summer, I usually have to keep the damn thing open completely or else it gets stuck for good. Once inside, I shut the window as far as it will go. There's still a good one-inch gap at the bottom, but it's better than nothing. I pull the curtains to help keep the icy air from creeping through the rest of the space. It doesn't do much good, but again, it's better than nothing.

I shiver as I strip out of my clothes and step into the bathroom. Ash coats my skin and sticks in my hair. The thought of *who* that ash is makes my stomach roil. The handle for the shower squeaks as I turn it as hot as it will go—whether the water actually heats this time is to be determined.

Standing in front of the mirror, I stare at my reflection. There is nothing about me that stands out from any other person on the street. Light brown skin, dark brown eyes. No warts. No boils. No pointy, crooked nose. My hair is the only unnatural part of me. The dark plum strands fall just below my shoulders in a smooth, silky curtain. The good thing is, it goes well with my nose piercing and tattoos, so people just assume it's dyed.

I finger the golden arm cuff coiled around my bicep. It's simple, but it's definitely not normal. My mother gave it to me when I turned sixteen. It's adjusted itself as I got older, magically growing with me to always fit perfectly. If I were to take it off, etched on the inside, is the triple moon symbol. My mother said if I kept it on, it would help me control my powers. I don't know how true that is, but I haven't taken it off since she put it on eleven years ago.

Sighing, I turn away from my reflection and hold my hand under the spray of water. Cold. Ice cold. I could use my magic to heat it, but something about that seems wrong tonight. Two witches have been murdered, and their families are mourning their loss. Indulging in a magically induced hot shower doesn't sit right. Steeling myself, I hop in and suck in a ragged breath.

"Holy shit balls," I grit out between chattering teeth.

The icy needles stabbing my skin steal my breath and make my heart skip beats in my chest. I wash as quickly as I can, my muscles jerking from the intense shivering. When I've taken as much as I can handle, I turn off the water and wrap a towel around me. Rushing to my bedroom, I shove my legs into black and white plaid fleece bottoms, a Rossvale University hoodie, and the ugliest pea green fuzzy socks. They may look atrocious, but they're warm. I sigh as I climb into my bed and pull the pile of blankets over me.

When my skin finally thaws, I grab the journal from my nightstand.

January 3. Josie Goldron, 47, & Marley Goldron, 23. Burned alive.

I set the pen down and flip backward through the pages. It's filled with the names and dates of all the witches that have died since I turned seventeen. Most were from burnings, some straight up murdered. Very few had died by natural causes or old age. I glance up from the journal when Jinx hops on the bed.

It was Killian Rothchild. He settles at the foot of the bed and pierces me with his bright blue eyes. *He caught Marley using her magic to heal an injured bird.*

I sigh and pinch the bridge of my nose. She should have known better than to perform magic in public where she could get caught. Still, it isn't fair she got burned at the stake for healing an injured animal. What a fucked up world we live in. *Thank you, Jinx.* I pick the pen back up.

January 3. Josie Goldron, 47, & Marley Goldron, 23. Burned alive. Killian Rothchild.

This makes twenty-three murders by Killian. Second in number only to the one and only Tyberius Berkshire, prince of Rossvale, who has thirty-two. In ten years, I have taken revenge on twelve members of the Witch Guard, the elite force of men who are tasked with ridding our world of witches. Tyberius and Killian have been at the top of my list, but they are impossible to get to.

Jinx stretches out his front legs, his claws gripping the blanket. *It's happening more frequently. They've killed how many in the past two weeks?*

"Six," I reply. "And two of those have happened on days other than Wednesday."

You need to be careful.

I kick out my foot, knocking him to the floor. Of course I'll be careful. I'm always fucking careful.

Hag. Jinx hisses as he saunters out of my bedroom, tail swishing angrily back and forth.

"Rat." I settle down in my bed and close my eyes. But I don't sleep. All I can see are flames dancing behind my eyelids. Invisible heat scorches my skin until I'm sweating and have to kick off the blankets. Every time I watch a burning, I have to fight back the panic. My thoughts spiral until, in my mind, it's me on the stake. I can't help but imagine what it would be like. The heat, the smoke, the crackle. Even as sweat continues to coat my skin, I shiver.

One of these days, that will be me.

I PUSH open the door to the library, groaning as the heat warms my chilled skin.

"It's colder than the underside of a penguin's ballsack," I say as I rub my hands together to bring some warmth to them.

Moira, the librarian, cackles. "Why do you think I never leave this place in the winter? Got everything I need right here."

Moira lives in the little apartment above the library. And behind the library is a hidden space she uses for her herb practice. It's dangerous coming here, but we all risk it now and then.

"I'm looking for a specific book, Moira. It's about a trumpet player who falls from the grace of the conductor." I trail my slightly numb fingers over the spines of books displayed on the shelves.

"Hmm, I think I know which book you're talking about," she says with a nod. "Let me see if I have it."

While Moira disappears, I pull out my phone to check the time. Damn. It's already almost seven. I was supposed to get off work at five, but my last client got stuck in traffic, so I wasn't able to walk their dog until they got home. I asked them for the code to their garage, but they don't trust me enough for that yet.

Moira emerges from the back with a book covered in a plain leather binding. "I believe this is the one you were looking for."

I take it from her and open it, pretending to flip through the pages. Sitting inside the hollowed out middle of the book is a pouch of devil's trumpets. "This is it. Thank you." I shove the book and poison plant in my bag before heading back out into the frigid air. Moira will send an invoice later for me to pay. Less suspicious than paying her for a free library book.

The wind hits me immediately, sweeping my hair back from my face and making my eyes water. *Son of a bitch, it's cold.* I make my way through the city, ignoring my rumbling stomach. I can't afford to eat out. My last tattoo ended up costing more than I anticipated, and it set me back a few months. Another night of ramen and cheap wine for me.

Neave. Jinx jumps from a window ledge and lands on my shoulder. Curling under my hair to keep warm, he wraps his tail around my neck and covers his nose. *I have bad news. They caught Eloise.*

My steps falter. "When?" In my shock, I forget myself and speak to him out loud.

About ten minutes ago. They're taking her to the city center.

My heart skips a beat. *What? It's Thursday. They should be taking her to the cells.*

They don't seem to be following their own rules lately. It's too late, though, Neave. You can't save her.

I may not be able to save her, but I sure as hell won't let her die alone. And I sure as hell will mark whoever captured her. He won't live much longer.

I rush to the city center. The Witch Guard has been burning witches for thousands of years. The stone platform in the center of the city has been there since the very first burning. It's blackened and covered in soot and the ashes of my sisters. Every Wednesday evening, citizens of Rossvale gather in every city across the country to watch the murder of innocent women. Rossvale City is no different, except that it's the capital and the burnings have become more of a show than an execution. The past month, however, the Witch Guard has broken their rule of Wednesday burnings. This is the third one where they've dragged their captive to the stakes immediately.

Eloise is the closest thing I have to a friend. It's not safe to make friends with other witches. The more we gather together, the more likely we are to get caught. And making friends with non-witches is too problematic. It's too easy to slip up and show who you really are, so we live mostly solitary lives.

I met Eloise when I was twenty. She had just moved here with her mom and was talking with Moira in the library. We exchanged numbers and still text back and forth constantly. We meet up for drinks once a month. Guess that's all going to come to an end now. If only they weren't taking her straight to the stakes, I could risk a prison break.

Jinx jumps from my shoulders and disappears as the city center slowly fills with people excited to watch a human being burn alive. It's disgusting. Word of a burning spreads so fast in the city, and tonight is no different. The crowd fills the square before the guard arrives with Eloise. Usually, I remain near the back, close to an alley I can easily escape into. Not this time. For Eloise, I place myself front and center.

The crowd cheers and jostles me as the Witch Guard pushes Eloise onto the dais. My gaze lands on the man with his hand wrapped around her bicep. With his blond hair swept to the side and his chiseled jaw, he's not hard to recognize—Prince Tyberius

Berkshire. As the son of our king, Tyberius is a hero in the eyes of the citizens. He devotes his time and attention to hunting and killing witches. A real fucking hero.

His face is stern as he drags Eloise to the stake. The guards behind him smile and bump shoulders. Killian high-fives another guard with locs dyed the color of a firetruck. I haven't seen him before, but he just got added to my list as well. Tyberius shoves Eloise against the fresh wooden stake and binds her hands to the post behind her. When he steps away, her gaze lands on me.

Her bright green eyes widen slightly, and I see her suck in a breath. Tears shimmer on her lashes, but they don't fall. I hold her gaze and nod my head slightly. I'll be here for her. She won't die alone. The icy wind pulls strands of her black hair from her ponytail and they whip in the breeze like ropes. My eyes water, and I tell myself it's from the wind.

Killian hands Tyberius a torch, and my chest tightens as he walks to the stake, boots thumping on the ground. The torch lowers and the first piece of wood goes up in flames. The fire spreads quickly with a whoosh, fed by the fierce wind. Eloise holds my gaze as the first of the flames reaches her feet. Her jaw tightens and the tendons in her neck pop as she holds in her screams. Tears leak from her eyes, but the heat of the fire dries them instantly.

It's horrible to watch a person burn alive. It's even worse if it's someone you care about. I thought after seeing so many, I would be desensitized to it. But it only gets worse. The scent of roasting meat. The crackling of the flames. The hiss and pop of the wood. But it's the image of blackened flesh peeling from the bone while the victim is still alive that always gets me.

I try to shut down my emotions as I watch Eloise's flesh start to bubble and char. But each pop of wood reminds me of a nail slamming home into a coffin. One more witch, gone. A friend, as close as she could be. One more person in my life that I cared about, taken away by the angry flames of fire.

Behind me, I'm aware that people are leaving the city center.

Eloise is gone. There is no more reason to watch. I stay, though. Unable to make myself look away. Unable to make my feet move. It's dangerous, and I should really be going, but my body won't do what it needs to.

Movement to the left of the stakes pulls my eyes from Eloise's burned and disintegrating body. Tyberius approaches the flames, but he stops as his gaze lands on me. I meet him stare for stare.

Your time is limited, Prince. Enjoy your last few breaths.

Colder Than A Witch's Left Tit

Shouts of praise and congratulations, shoulder slaps, and fist bumps. They all greet me as I walk through the palace. I smile and nod, accepting their words. It's obnoxious really. The smile on my face is forced, but no one seems to notice. It's a fucking job. One I'm sick of already. But it's either this, or rule. There is no way in hell I'll ever take up the crown. So witch hunting it is.

I make my way to my dad's study, my boots thudding on the pale marble floor. This palace has been here for thousands of years. Well, not this one exactly. But the current palace stands where the old one did, before it burned to the ground. Ironic, really. The opulent wall hangings and glittering statues no longer snag my gaze. When I was younger, I used to marvel at the colorful tapestries depicting battles, burnings, and coronations. I guess thirty years of living in wealth has jaded me.

I push open the study door, not bothering to knock, and slump into the leather wingback chair before the massive mahogany desk. My dad, King Leander of Rossvale, glances up from his work, dark blue eyes weighing and judging, before turning his attention back to what he was doing. I cross my arms over my chest and resign myself to waiting. When he's ready to speak, he will.

"Sit up straight." He doesn't even look at me as he continues his work, but he has no problem chastising me.

Screw him. I slouch further in the chair, spreading my legs wide for extra emphasis. A lock of my blond hair falls forward, and I leave it, knowing it will drive him mad that I'm not as put together as he wants me to be.

He sighs and removes his glasses, pinching the bridge of his nose as he sets them on his desk. "How was the hunt?" he asks, instead of tearing me a new one—it's usually 50/50 with him.

"It wasn't her."

He nods and reaches for a piece of paper, scratching out a name. "Keep hunting." King Leander bends his head back over the desk, the golden crown on his head shifting with the movement. There's more silver in his brown hair than there was a few years ago. His neatly trimmed beard is now almost all gray.

"I have a lead, though," I say before I stand. I don't usually give him updates on my hunts until they turn out to be failures. But something in his expression, his posture, makes me do it.

He's worn down. Fraying at the edges. It's like there's a sword poised against his neck, and the clock is ticking. With each month that passes, he becomes more drawn in on himself. More focused on his work. More desperate.

When he looks up, a fire has been lit in his eyes. "What can you tell me?"

I shrug. "Not much. She was at the burning tonight. Front and center. It's not the first time I've seen her, but I never had a reason to think she was a witch until tonight." I run my hand through my hair, thinking back to the look she gave me, and I repress a shiver. "It was her eyes. They ... they didn't glow, per se, but they took on an unnatural light."

"Find her. Bring her in."

I nod, but he's already back to his work. Standing, I let myself out of the study and turn toward my room. I desperately need a shower. The stench of smoke clings to my clothes and hair. I fucking hate that smell. Rounding the corner, I run into the last person I want to deal with.

"Ty. I heard you had another failed hunt."

I snort and push around my little brother. "I don't see you taking up arms and going hunting."

"One of us has to learn to rule. Clearly, it won't be you." He follows me through the palace like a lost puppy.

That is exactly the picture I have of my little brother. Julian is the favorite child. The do-gooder. The brown-noser. He is always doing whatever my dad tells him to. During our childhood, when I showed no interest in learning the ways of ruling our lands, Julian took advantage of the opportunity to become next in line. I haven't officially given up my title yet, but it's coming.

I stop in my tracks and turn to face him. His blond hair is cut short, his ocean blue eyes the exact same as mine. That's where the similarities stop. Taking in his outrageous outfit—black dress pants, white button-up, and red dress coat with gold stitching— my lip curls in disgust. If I had to dress like that, I'd throw myself on the flames of the next burning.

Our relationship hasn't always been this strained, but since our mom's death twelve years ago, everything seems to have fallen apart. Mine and Julian's relationship, my dad's opinion of me, my life, my goals and dreams. Sometimes I think I don't even know who I am anymore.

"What would you do if I decided to not give up my title?" I ask, purely out of curiosity.

His eyes narrow on me. "Why are you asking that?"

I shrug and continue on my way, already bored with the conversation. "Nevermind."

He grabs my arm, forcing me to turn around and face him. A muscle ticks in his jaw as he stares at me. "You wouldn't dare." I raise one brow, and he continues, "You would be a horrible king."

Shaking out of his grasp, I turn back the way I was heading. He's not wrong. I would be a god awful king. Julian was made for the crown. I was ... I don't know what I was made for. I used to think the Witch Guard was my calling. But now, I'm not so sure. Sighing, I shut the door to my room in my brother's face. I'm going to shower and go to bed. Tomorrow, I will start planning how to find that purple haired witch.

"SERIOUSLY, Ty, we've been out here for three hours with zero leads."

I peer at Killian, my second-in-command, from the corner of my eye. It's not always a good thing to have your best friend under your command. This is one of those times. "Quit complaining and help. Or else go back to the palace."

"Wow, you're in a mood today," Killian grumbles under his breath, but not quiet enough that I don't hear it.

"Didn't sleep well last night." It's not a lie, but I don't know why I had such a hard time falling asleep. Something is bothering me, but I can't put my finger on what it is exactly. It's a crawling sensation under my skin, making me twitchy. I keep looking over my shoulder, expecting to see something there, something ominous.

The weight of my thoughts lately has been tiring, to say the least. I never wanted the crown, despite being the firstborn. When Julian stepped up to the plate, I gladly slunk into the shadows and poured everything I was into becoming a hunter. My uncle didn't take my training lightly, and he treated me no differently than the other trainees. It didn't take me long to work my way up the ranks until I took on the commanding role of the Witch Guard.

I have happily done my job. For the past eleven years, I have thrown myself into the role of hunting witches. I was able to ignore the disapproval from my dad and the judgment from my brother, nothing is good enough for them, and those thoughts have been burying into my bones and getting harder to ignore. Something has changed, and I'm not sure it's a good thing. The feeling of being lost and unsure is not something I want to experience again.

Twelve years ago after my mom died, I hit rock bottom. She was the bright spot in my life, and the only one to stand up for me to my dad. He always thought I was too weak to be king, but my mom instilled in me the idea that having a caring heart is what makes a great leader. When cancer took her, it might as well have taken me, too.

At seventeen years old, I turned to drugs and alcohol to get me through my depression. Killian and I hit up every night club, drinking, drugging, and fucking ourselves to oblivion. And because I'm the prince, we were never turned away. For Killian, it was merely a thrill. For me, it became an addiction, a way to numb the pain of my mom's loss and my dad's disappointment in me.

"Is the little princey-poo having bad dreams?" Killian reaches up to ruffle my hair, bringing me back to the present, and I slap his hand away.

"Seriously, asshole. Either help or leave." I don't mean to snap at him, but my nerves are raw, and I just can't help it.

He makes a noise in the back of his throat and slaps me on the back hard enough to make me stumble. "It's colder than a witch's left tit out here. You're on your own, dude. I'm out."

He flips me off as he walks away, and I curse. I'll have to deal with that later. It's fine for him to act like that in the palace. Everyone there has watched us grow up together. They see our antics every day. But out in public, I'm still the prince to the citizens of Rossvale. Killian can't be acting like that where people can see.

I sigh heavily and rub my eyes. The headache I had when I woke up has steadily gotten worse as the day has worn on with no clues as to the whereabouts of this purple haired witch. My usual sources all say they know who I'm talking about, but have no information on her. At this point, I'm tempted to have another burning tonight, just on the off chance she shows up. Actually, that's not a horrible idea. If I don't find her by dinner time, that's what I'll do.

I push open the door to a flower shop and step inside to the aroma of green things and dirt. It makes my nose itch, and I rub the back of my hand over it to aleve the growing sneeze. The shopkeeper, a middle-aged woman with black hair streaked with gray, is standing behind a counter covered with various flowers.

"Good afternoon, ma'am," I say, nodding my head toward her. "I was hoping you could answer a few questions for me."

The shopkeeper looks up from the bouquet she's tying with a ribbon, and her gray eyes pop wide in surprise. "Your Highness." She sets the flowers down and wipes her hands on her apron before awkwardly curtsying in a pair of loose brown pants. "What can I help you with?"

"I'm looking for someone, and I was wondering if you had ever encountered her before." I cringe inwardly at my words. Formality was never easy for me, and I feel like a pompous ass when I interact with my subjects.

"What's her name, Your Highness?"

"Well, I don't know. She has light brown skin, brown eyes, and purple hair that falls to about here." I indicate with my hand to just below my shoulders.

The shopkeeper's eyes scrunch as she thinks. "That doesn't ring a bell. Someone with purple hair would certainly stand out in my mind. I'm sorry, Your Highness."

"Not a problem. Thank you for your time." I nod in her direction again before heading back out into the cold.

It had been the same at every store I stopped by. Either they had never seen her, or had seen her, but knew nothing about her. It's like she doesn't even exist. Leaning against the brick wall of the flower shop, I dig my phone from my pocket and send a quick text to Killian to have a burning prepared for tonight. It's looking like that will be the only way to find this witch.

Shoving my hands in my coat pockets, I head for a pizza shop I know makes amazing pizza. If my dad knew that's what I was eating, he would flip his lid. Pizza is not food for a royal, according to him. Screw that.

Just as I turn down the little alley the pizzeria operates out of, I catch a glimpse of purple hair rounding the corner at the other end. My heart rate kicks up, and a smile spreads across my face. Bingo. Looks like I won't be getting any pizza after all.

Not My Kink

Belly full of delicious veggie pizza I truly shouldn't have spent the money on, I make my way back to my apartment. I've only been outside for a few moments and already my fingers are numb. *Why is it so fucking cold?* My breath fogs in front of my face as I hurry through the city, ignoring the honking horns blaring as I cut in front of traffic. *Selfish assholes. Honking in the warm comfort of their car while I freeze off my lady balls.*

It's too cold to take the long way home, so I cut through the alley with the rotten crates stacked against the side. A glimmer of white catches my eye, and I spot Jinx sitting precariously atop one of the unsteady stacks, washing his paw like a fucking king. I roll my eyes and hurry toward him, intent on kicking the crate at the bottom of the stack so he tumbles down.

Before I can take three steps, a footfall behind me and the press of a knife against the side of my neck freezes me in my tracks.

"Don't move. Don't even *think* of using magic." The voice is deep and smooth, ringing with authority.

A hunter found you. Jinx doesn't stop his bathing, but his blue eyes meet mine over his paw.

Gee, really? My heart stutters behind my ribs, and my mind empties like the tide receding from the shore. I need to get out of this situation. Now. *Isn't it your job to warn me of danger?*

Cats can't shrug, but I swear Jinx does. *Maybe next time you'll think twice before kicking me off the bed. Bitch.*

Fucking spineless rat bastard.

"Hands behind your back. And move slowly." The knife presses a little harder against my neck. Not enough to draw blood, but really fucking close.

I grit my teeth but obey. There is nothing living in this alley besides me and the hunter. Without a living thing to pull magic from, I'm powerless. And with my mind eerily blank, I don't know what else to do. It's like my brain has frozen in this frigid air, and I can't get a single rational thought to filter through. Slowly, I shift my hands to my back, kicking myself for not having my bookbag with me. If I did, I could grab the devil's trumpet, but no use dwelling on that now.

The hunter grasps my hands and roughly clasps handcuffs around my wrists, tightening them until they dig painfully into my skin. Without warning, he shoves me against the wall of the building to my left. I hiss as my cheek stings from scraping against the rough brick. His foot kicks my legs apart and the hand not pushing against my back roams over my torso and down my legs, removing my weapons. Clink after clink sounds through the alley as each of my knives joins the growing pile on the concrete. I try to see over my shoulder to see which hunter caught me, but I can't get a good look.

"You know," I drawl lazily, "Being tied up isn't really my kink. No shame to those who enjoy it, but it's just not for me." He doesn't respond, just pushes me harder against the wall until I grunt. "I do like it rough, though."

"Did I get them all?" he asks as he adds the knife hidden in my boot to the pile on the ground.

"You missed the one in my hair."

He grabs the slim hair pin and pulls it out, releasing the top half of my hair from the messy bun it was holding up. I sense him shuffling behind me a second before a sharp pinch in my neck makes me jerk. Burning spreads from the spot, racing down my neck and chest, outward to my arms, down to my feet. It sets my veins on fire and steals my breath. The heat vaporizes the magic inside me, and I gasp as emptiness takes its place. *Fucking hell.*

"Let's go." He yanks me around, and I get the first glimpse of my captor.

Blond hair swept to the side. Ocean blue eyes. Chiseled jaw. Kissable lips. Prince Tyberius Berkshire. Number one on my hit list.

"Oh dear," I say lightly. "If I had known you were the prince, I would have curtsied." He grunts and pushes me forward hard enough to make me stumble. "Awfully rude for a prince." He pushes me again, and I clamp my mouth shut, forcing the sarcastic tirade to the back of my mind. No point in getting myself in more trouble. Not to mention, there are no glittering threads connected to him. Whatever was in that needle blocked my ability to reach for magic completely.

I let him lead me through the city, ignoring the stares and cheers as people notice us. They congratulate Tyberius and curse me. I suppose I should be glad it's the prince who caught me. If it had been anyone else, the crowd would likely throw rocks, but it's too much of a risk to do that when they might accidentally hit their prince.

My feet turn to lead when I realize he's taking me to the city center. To the stake. *No. Not yet. I need time to escape!* Breathing becomes more difficult as my chest constricts painfully. When the platform comes into view, I can't help the whimper that climbs up my throat. I'm not ready to die. My vengeance isn't complete. I tug my arms, trying to free myself, but his grip is too strong.

Instead of leading me up the steps to the platform, Tyberius leads me around to the back. He takes a large metal key from around his neck and uses it to unlock a heavy metal door set into the ground. The hinges squeal as he pulls it open, revealing a dark set of concrete steps, lit by dim bulbs.

"Down." He gives me a shove into the opening, and I stumble down the first few steps. Tyberius stops me so he can close and lock the door behind us.

With the door closed, the lights along the wall barely give off enough illumination to see three feet ahead of me. At the bottom of the steps, a tunnel stretches as far as I can see with sporadic lights creating yellow pools at set intervals. Water drips down the stone walls, puddling along the edges. It's dank and musty, and it makes my nose itch. The chill seeps through my coat, pebbling my skin in goosebumps, but at least there's no wind. As we pass through the patches of light, my breath fogs in front of me.

The tunnel seems to last forever, and each step makes my heart race a little faster, but eventually, another set of steps appear ahead of us. Tyberius uses the key around his neck to unlock another door. When this door opens and he shoves me through, I find myself in a prison. A short hallway with rough stone floors is lined on either side with cells, the dark gray metal bars glinting dully from the overhead lights. The anxiety gripping my stomach eases slightly. I'll have an opportunity to escape. Somehow.

I'm led to a cell and shoved inside, and the cuffs binding my hands are removed. The door closes behind me with a clang that echoes through the space and makes my breathing hitch. I rub my arms absentmindedly as Tyberius locks the cell and leaves without a backward glance.

Locked up. Caged like an animal. Waiting for my time to burn.

I back up until I hit the cold stone wall and slide down, drawing my knees to my chest. My lungs ache as I force air into them, breathing deeply and holding it until my vision wavers, then releasing it. I repeat this until a semblance of calm settles within me. Resting my forehead on my knees, I close my eyes and try to think through options of escape. For some reason, though, I still can't get my brain to work properly. There are no thoughts in my head. It's eerily blank up there. Empty.

There isn't much to look at. The wall and floor are both dark gray stone. It looks old, and has probably been here since the original palace was built. The metal bars are thick and the space between them narrow, mostly obscuring the view to the hall. A cot with a single threadbare blanket sits in the corner, with a chamber pot tucked underneath. It's like I've been dropped into some ancient fantasy world. Replace the yellow fluorescent bulbs with torches, and it would look like a dungeon.

I've always known this was a possibility. I thought I had accepted the fact that one day I'd be burned alive, but nothing can truly prepare you for the time when it comes. And the lack of magic is almost worse. It leaves me cold inside. A cold so severe it makes my blood sluggish in my veins and my heart beat erratically.

I'm not sure how long I sit in this position, doing nothing, thinking nothing, when footsteps echo in the room. I look up to find an older man with gray hair and glasses perched on the end of his nose unlocking my cell. He steps in, carrying a black bag bulging at the sides. His khaki pants and white button up are slightly wrinkled, and his black loafers are scuffed and well-worn. Kindly brown eyes meet mine as he kneels in front of me.

"Hello. I'm Doctor Harmon." His smile crinkles his eyes and deepens the grooves lining his face. "How are you feeling?"

I gape at him for a moment before I find my words. "How am I feeling?" I ask incredulously. "Let me think about that. I was captured by a witch hunter, injected with something that wiped out my magic, and shoved into a cell to wait until I'm turned into a human marshmallow. How am I feeling? I'm feeling fucking great!"

The good doctor chuckles and opens his bag, pulling out a stethoscope. "Mind if I take a listen to your heart and lungs?"

I shrug. "Sure, why the hell not?" I cross my legs and sit up taller so he can reach me better. Closing my eyes, I lean my head against the wall while Doctor Harmon does his thing, breathing when he says to. What the hell is happening? Why is a doctor checking me out before I'm set on fire?

Doctor Harmon hums and jots down my stats on a pad of paper. Next, he puts his stethoscope back into his bag and pulls out a vial and needle. "I need to take a blood sample, if that's okay?"

"What the fuck for?" I reel back and tuck my arms against my middle. The last time a needle penetrated my body, it stole my magic. Why does he want a sample of blood?

"Just for scientific purposes." He shrugs and pulls out a tourniquet.

Oh, fuck no. Every witch knows not to give up any DNA. That's just asking for disaster. "I'm afraid I'll have to pass on this one."

His smile turns sad. "I'm sorry. It's not really an option. If I have to, I'll ask for a guard to hold you down. It's easier if you do it willingly."

I'm tempted to make a scene, to make him call for a guard, but in the end, what's the point? I'll be dead soon. Whatever they do with my blood won't affect me. Might be a selfish outlook on the situation, but I don't see much of a choice anyway. He'll get that blood sample either willingly or by force.

Sighing, I shrug out of my coat and roll up my sleeve, sticking out my right arm. I close my eyes as the tourniquet tightens around my bicep, and the pinch of a needle follows. Before I know it, the doctor is sticking a bandaid on it. Wouldn't want me to bleed out before they can burn me.

He puts everything away before digging through his bag once more. "We just have one more thing."

When he pulls out a vial of dark brown liquid, I recoil. What the hell is he going to do with that?

"I need you to drink this." He holds it out to me, but I don't take it.

I eye it like it's a massive, hairy black spider. "Fuck. No. If you think that is going anywhere near my mouth, you're insane."

He sighs. "Again, I'm sorry, but it isn't an option."

"Then you'll need to ask for a guard, because there is no way I'm drinking that willingly."

He nods like he expected that to be my response, and hollers to someone I can't see. A guard steps into view and enters my cell. His black hair is shorn to his scalp and a nasty scar cuts across his nose and through his top lip, giving him a permanent sneer.

He grabs my shoulders and pulls me to my feet. I fight back. I kick and thrash, but he leans against the wall, using one leg for balance and wrapping the other around my legs. One arm bands around my middle, while the other holds my head against his shoulder. The doctor steps forward and grabs my jaw, forcing it open. As the vial comes near my face, I catch a whiff of the putrid substance inside. It's like rotten blood and death. I gag before he ever tips the contents into my mouth.

When the liquid hits my tongue, I gag again. Doctor Harmon holds my jaw shut and pinches my nose closed. I thrash and try to free myself, but it's no use. The liquid slides down my tongue to the back of my throat and my swallow reflex kicks in. The liquid goes down, thick and slow, tasting of death and rot. Tears spring to my eyes, and I choke as vomit climbs up my throat. I don't have a choice but to keep swallowing.

When the liquid is finally down, they release me. I fall to the floor, limbs too shaky and weak to hold me. My stomach heaves and I retch, but nothing comes up. I shakily wipe the tears from my cheeks and glare at the doctor.

"What the fuck was that?" My voice is raspy and my throat raw. The taste of death still clings to my tongue and I heave again. Still, nothing comes up.

"A test." That's all Doctor Harmon says as he gathers his bag and follows the guard out.

I'm left sitting on the floor, shaking and gagging.

An hour later, the pain takes over.

I WAKE IN A DAZE. Sometime after that foul concoction was forced down my throat, I moved the cot, but I don't remember doing it. It's not much better than the floor. The rough, scratchy sheet doesn't keep me warm, and the chill seeps into my bones. I'm pretty sure I'm dying. And if I'm not, I wish I was.

My body shakes with teeth clacking shivers. Each jerk or twitch of my limbs sends stabbing pain shooting through them. I have never felt so awful. My stomach cramps alarmingly, and I barely have time to roll over before I vomit bile. The movement makes lights dance behind my eyes. I groan as pain shoots through my skull, like someone stabbed my brain with an ice pick.

Trying to sit up makes the pain in my body flare hotly, and I shiver so violently that I collapse back onto the cot. The darkness closes in, and I welcome it with open arms.

The next time I wake, I feel even worse, if that's possible. Bile climbs up my throat and I try to swallow it back down, but it keeps coming up. I lean over the side of the cot and add to the pile of sick on the floor. Breath rasping harshly out of my aching chest, I lay back down, shivering and moaning in agony.

I open my burning eyes, but my surroundings are blurry. If it weren't for the cot under my back, I wouldn't know if I was in the same place or not. More cramping in my stomach alerts me to another wave of nausea, and leaning over the edge of the cot again, my insides try to come up through my throat.

I lay back down, gasping, with tears streaming down my cheeks as the darkness claims me again.

More time passes. I have no idea how much. It's filled with random moments of alertness before I slip back into unconsciousness. Odd dreams plague me. Dreams of blood, cackling, and symbols. Dreams of fire. Dreams of death.

Each time I wake, I throw up. I'm past the point of anything coming up, so my body just heaves and shudders. I'm so cold I wouldn't be surprised to find hoarfrost splintering my bones, and I don't think I'll ever be warm again. If I even survive this. My body is so weak, I can barely move, which is probably a good thing. Each movement sends agony burning through me.

Each waking moment is spent praying to the goddess. Praying for her mercy. Praying for this to end. Praying for death. It doesn't come, though. Just more heaving, more shivering, more pain, more fever dreams.

More darkness.

You Got Anger Issues, Bro

My muscles quiver with exhaustion, but I push myself harder. I advance on Killian and throw a right hook. He ducks like I expect him to and meets my left uppercut in the process. His head snaps back, and he curses as he falls to the floor.

"Fuck, Ty. We're even. Can we call it?" He glares at me from his sprawled position on the sparring mat, chest heaving and blood dribbling down his chin. "I think you chipped my fucking tooth." He prods the tooth with his tongue and flinches. "Yeah. You did. Bastard."

I huff and shake out my arm, glancing at my skinned knuckles. "Yeah, we're done." Reaching down, I haul him to his feet.

While we were sparring, he lost his hair tie, and his locs came free and now frame his face. He pulls another tie from his wrist to wrangle half of the rogue locs back up. "You got anger issues, bro. Don't take them out on me."

I ignore his probably true statement and head for my bottle of water. "Quit whining. You landed as many on me as I did on you. As you said, we're even." Snagging a towel from the bench, I wipe the sweat from my face, then chug half the bottle. "You're off tonight, right?"

"Yeah. What's the plan?" he asks as he grabs his own towel and water.

I tug my lower lip between my teeth, debating. *Fuck it.* "Can you get some of that pixie shit?"

Killian's brows raise to his hairline, then a slow smile spreads across his face. "Yeah, I can. You sure you want to?"

Running my hand through my sweaty hair, I nod. "Fuck yeah. I need to forget who I am for a night."

He grins and slaps me on the back. "Hell yeah, princey boy. We can do that. I'll see you at eight."

I watch him leave the gym and check the time. Five hours. I have five hours to shower and finish paperwork. Then I can slip into oblivion for a bit. Throwing the towel into the dirty bin, I shove out of the gym and head down the hall.

"Your Highness!"

I turn around to find Doctor Harmon rushing toward me. "What is it?" There's a harried look in his eyes that sets excitement and fear swirling in my gut. He's got news—whether it's good or bad remains to be seen.

"The witch you brought back three days ago. The one with purple hair? I think she's the one."

My heart stops, and I have to shake myself to get it pumping again. "I'm sorry. Did you say you think she's the one?" I had to have heard him wrong. After eleven years of witch hunting, I have failed every fucking time. There is no way I finally found her.

"Yes, Your Highness." He bows his head, breath slightly uneven. Pushing his glasses back up his nose, he shifts on his feet. "She's having dreams. None of the others have. However, the blood is affecting her negatively. She hasn't recovered. She's still feverish. Not eating or drinking. Her body is wasting away. If we don't intervene, she won't last through the night."

"Take her to the infirmary. Do what you need to, but keep the equalizer in her system. We can't let her get control of her magic." He bows and turns to walk away, but I stop him. "Don't let her die, Doctor. I mean it, do whatever you have to do to keep her alive. And don't tell my dad yet. Let's make sure this is the real thing."

He bows again and takes off to follow my orders. Nervous energy has taken up residence in my body—little shocks of lightning making my heart skip beats. Could she really be the one? I don't even realize when I reach my office. I'm so lost in my thoughts, in the possibilities, that I zoned out the entire walk here. Now I just need to make myself focus long enough to get my work done.

IT TOOK an extreme amount of cursing and yelling at myself, but I finished my paperwork with an hour to spare. I don't know what to do with myself for that hour, so I head to the infirmary to check on Doctor Harmon's progress. On my way there, Killian texts me to let me know he got the goods, and I smile. The perfect way to celebrate.

My gaze lands on the figure laying in the hospital bed as soon as I push into the infirmary. A weird sensation hits me in the gut, something that makes me want to rush to her side. With her wrists and ankles cuffed to the bed frame, and a thin sheet covering her naked body, she looks so ... small. An IV line runs from her upper arm to the bag on the IV pole.

"What are you giving her?" I ask out of curiosity as I approach the witch.

Doctor Harmon jumps from where he was bent over his desk. "Your Highness! I didn't hear you come in." He bows low and pushes his glasses up his nose as he stands. "Fluids and an antibiotic. As well as something to reduce the fever." He shrugs slightly. "It's about all we can do."

I nod and walk closer to her. Already, her cheeks and eyes are sunken in. Her collarbones stand out sharply, as do the bones in her arms. It looks like she's been eaten from the inside out. I frown. "Is it normal for someone to lose so much weight in such a short amount of time?"

"No, Your Highness. It's very strange." He stands and moves to the opposite side of the bed, gaze traveling over the witch's emaciated frame. "It's another reason I believe she might be the one. None of the others have had this kind of reaction. I took a second sample of blood to compare to the first. I'm still waiting for those results."

Looking past the signs of illness, I can't help but think that she's a beautiful woman. *Witch. Not woman.* Shame, really. Her hair, dyed a dark shade of purple with a few light pink highlights, goes perfectly with her light brown skin. "What's her name?" I find myself asking, then start as I realize what I just did. I've never once wondered what their names were. It doesn't matter.

"Neave Parker," Doctor Harmon says as he returns to his desk. "Twenty-seven years old. Lives alone, as far as I can tell."

I shake myself. That is not information I need to know. "Keep me up to date on her health. When she wakes up, let me know."

I leave before Doctor Harmon has a chance to respond and hurry to the front of the palace, where I find Killian waiting with a grin.

"Ready, Princey?"

Rolling my eyes, I brush past him and into the frigid night air. "Fuck off with that shit."

We head to our favorite club, the one with the darkened corners and VIP section. The owner of the joint couldn't care less what we do while we're there, so it's our go to when we want to get into shit that most people frown upon. The entire walk in the freezing cold, Killian eyes me, studying me like I'm some kind of science experiment.

Eventually, I snap. "What are you staring at me for?"

"You okay?" he asks, more serious than he's been in a while.

"Fine. Why?" I shrug my shoulders, the leather jacket suddenly tighter than normal.

"I just want to make sure I'm not about to send you on

another bender. If you need to talk about something, you know you can talk to me."

"I'm fine. Really. Just been working too much. I need a break." It's not a lie. I have been working ridiculous hours lately, and I do need a break. But it's also not one hundred percent the truth, and by the look on Killian's face, he knows it. Thankfully, he says nothing else about it.

By the time we reach Club Eden, I can't feel my fingers and the tip of my nose is probably as red as a clown's. The bouncer lets us in, and we make our way across the busy dance floor to the VIP lounge. Bass vibrates deep in my bones from the speakers, and vibrant, colorful lights flash in my vision. The heat from the press of bodies is welcome after the blustery cold. For now, at least. Pretty soon, I'm sure I'll have sweat dripping down my spine and making my hair stick to my forehead.

I wave to the bartender as we pass the bar, knowing our drinks will be at our usual table in minutes. Behind the waterfall wall is a small section of booths, sectioned off by curtains of vines. The dim lighting and the privacy of the vines and waterfall wall invite all kinds of rogue behavior. I slip behind the hanging vines and claim my usual bench, with Killian sliding in across from me.

"I invited Jameson and Michael. They get off at ten." He smiles as the bartender brushes past the vines and sets our drinks of choice on the table. "Thanks, doll. Keep 'em coming."

She winks and slips back out. I grab my scotch and take a sip, savoring the smoky flavor on my tongue. "Alright," I say. "Let's do this."

Killian grins and pulls the little bag of pixie essence from a pocket in his coat. Before he opens it, he levels a stern look at me. "Really, though. You're okay?"

"For fuck's sake, Killian. Let me get high and forget life for a bit." I roll my eyes and take the rest of my scotch as a shot, relishing the burn as it slides down my throat.

"Fine, fine." He opens the bag and pours it on the table, quickly separating it into four fine lines—two in front of him, and two in front of me. Holding one nostril closed, Killian leans down and snorts the first line, followed by the second. He shakes his head and leans back against his bench, arms spread. "You're up, Princey."

Grunting, I follow his lead, enjoying the burn as the pixie essense enters my bloodstream. The effects are immediate. I sigh and rest my head against the bench, eyes closing as the stress of my life vanishes in a haze of euphoria. Each beat of my heart, growing further and further apart, pumps the drugs through my body. As the negative thoughts plaguing me disappear, the bliss and desire rise to the forefront.

My jeans are too fucking tight, and each time I move, it sends waves of pleasure through me. "Fuuck," I groan, opening my eyes to blearily study my surroundings. Two more drinks have appeared at our table, as if by magic. I snag the scotch and down it, the burn almost nonexistent in my current state.

"Yu*p*," Killian drawls. He grabs his own drink and pushes out of the booth. "I'm on the hunt. Want me to send someone your way?"

I nod, my head feeling like it weighs a hundred pounds while also feeling like it may float away. He disappears, and I soak in my high, letting my muscles relax and my mind drift. The weight of someone settling on my lap draws my eyes open, and I find a fiery redhead straddling me, her lips pulled in a seductive smile.

"What can I do for you, My Prince?" Her voice is low and smoky, and it makes me groan.

I don't answer her, because I can't seem to make my mouth form words. Instead, I pull her face down to mine and kiss her. She rocks her hips, and I groan again. Fuck, this needs to happen now. It's been too long since I used, and the need to fuck is too strong to ignore. Seeming to read my mind, she reaches down and quickly unbuttons my pants. I lift my hips enough to pull them down my thighs, and my erection springs free, desperately seeking a warm, snug home for a few minutes.

While I lift her skirts, the redhead bites my neck and takes hold of my cock, angling it so she can slide right on. My head falls back in ecstasy as she moves her hips in a way that makes me see stars. Fuck, I'm not going to last long. I slide my hands up her arms and into her hair. Peeling my eyes open, I watch my fingers run through the red strands. In my drug induced haze, the red morphs. Deepening into a dark purple with lighter, almost pink highlights.

The image of my fingers tangling in the silky purple waves sends my orgasm crashing into me before I can even blink. My hips buck and my heart races as the pleasure rolls through my body, heat coursing through my veins. When my breathing stills, reality falls around me. The high I was just feeling drops away, leaving me sweaty and shaky.

I curse and shove the redhead off me, pushing her out of the booth. She squawks indignantly, calling me every name in the book before stalking away. I ignore her, trying to reign in my racing heart. *What the hell was that?* As soon as I saw that purple hair, I lost it. Closing my eyes, I take a deep breath. I try desperately to find my high again, but it's gone. Shakily, I shove my now limp dick back into my pants and push out of the booth.

I don't see Killian anywhere. He's probably enjoying himself in the backroom, unlike me. Whatever. I'm not waiting for him. The desperate need to run, to escape my own thoughts, drives me forward. I shove through the bodies on the dance floor and out into the winter night. Taking deep breaths of cold air, I attempt to clear my mind and head back to the palace.

I can't stop imagining my hand running through amethyst hair. My fingers tingle and I clench them into a fist, banging it on my thigh. *It was just a hallucination from the drugs.* I keep telling myself it had nothing to do with a witch currently laying in a hospital bed in the palace. But, even as high as I am, I don't believe it myself.

I slip onto the palace ground through the back gates and make my way to my room, hoping to avoid running into anyone—especially my dad or brother. The last thing I need is another lecture about how much of a fuck up I am. The previous one is still bouncing around in my skull. In my room, I head straight for the bathroom. A cold shower is exactly what I need to get my head on straight.

A moment of weakness. That's all it was. A moment of weakness combined with drugs and the possibility this witch may be the one. It won't happen again.

I Have Only One Fate

When I wake, the pain is gone. Thank the goddess. But when I try to move, I can't. Fear floods my system, and I suck in a shaky breath. *Why can't I move?* As my heart pounds in my chest and my breathing turns ragged, a small noise of fear escapes my throat.

"Whoa. Calm down, Miss Parker."

A gentle hand on my arm stills me, and I look into the kind eyes of Doctor Harmon. Then the memories come rushing back. Being captured by Tyberius. Thrown into the cell. Then the awful liquid Doctor Harmon forced down my throat.

"What did you do to me?" My words scrape up my throat, and I wince. Swallowing only makes it burn worse. I try to bring my hand to my neck, but it doesn't move. Shackles wrap around my wrists and ankles, tying me to the hospital bed. On top of that, I'm completely naked under the thin sheet. So many emotions rush to the surface that I freeze. Unable to move, think, or even breathe. Fear. Embarrassment. Anger. Confusion. It all leaves me too stunned to do anything.

A plastic cup with a straw invades my blurry vision, and I blink until it focuses. "Drink this, Miss Parker. It will help ease your throat."

I stare at the cup with distrust. There are no glittering strands of magic connected to living things. I close my eyes and reach desperately for any magic, but just as I feared, there is nothing. My heart squeezes painfully. Never have I been so defenseless. I rarely use my magic to defend myself, but just knowing that it's there, ready for me to use, has been a balm in this scary world. Now, when I need it most, it's gone.

"Miss Parker," Doctor Harmon says. "I understand you don't trust me. I know you're scared and overwhelmed. But truthfully, I have your best interest at heart. I don't want harm to come to you, so it would be beneficial if you were on your best behavior."

I huff a laugh that is definitely lacking in humor. *Trust him? After he drugged me?* He holds the straw back to my lips, and my aching throat begs for the water. Damning it all to hell, I take the straw in my mouth and swallow. Never has plain water ever tasted so sweet. The wetness glides down my parched throat, and I eagerly suck more from the straw until Doctor Harmon pulls it away.

"You don't want to drink too much too fast. It will make you sick." He sets the cup on a bedside table and stares at me. "How are you feeling?"

"I won't answer any of your questions until you answer mine." My voice is still raw, but I stare at him defiantly. It's a completely reasonable request, in my opinion.

He sighs and rubs the bridge of his nose, knocking his glasses askew. "I'll answer what I can, but some of your questions, I'm sure I won't be able to."

"Okay," I say slowly. "What did you drug me with?"

"I can't answer that one." He shakes his head and fixes his glasses.

"Why did you drug me?"

"I can't answer that one, either."

Gritting my teeth, I force myself to take a deep breath. "Then who can answer them? Because right now, those are my two most pressing questions."

"King Leander will answer them when you're ready to see him."

Taken aback, I gape at the doctor. King Leander? What does he have to do with any of this? Besides being the one to order the deaths of witches. And what does he mean when I'm ready to see him? "Um, okay." Pushing those thoughts aside, I move onto the next pressing question. "Are you going to burn me?"

"Again, that is up to King Leander."

I screw my eyes shut. "Well, you have surely been incredibly helpful. Can you at least uncuff me?"

"Do you promise you won't try to escape?"

"And where would I go? I've been sick for ... how long? I'm sure there are guards everywhere who could catch me before I made it three feet."

Doctor Harmon studies me before nodding his head and releasing the cuffs on my wrist and ankles. I lift my arms, and it takes so much effort they shake and tremble as I bring them to my face. The sheet slips, and I tug it back up, my right hand brushing my bare left arm. Bare. No golden cuff.

"My arm band!" I sit up, grabbing my bicep and looking around wildly. "Where is my cuff?" The note of hysteria raises my voice an octave.

Doctor Harmon holds his hands out placatingly. "It's here. But I can't let you wear it."

I stare at him with wide eyes, pleading with him to understand. "My mother gave it to me a year before she died." Tears blur my vision, and I rub my arm until it turns red. "I have never taken it off. Please." My voice breaks, and a few tears silently fall down my cheeks. Without that piece of jewelry, it's like I'm missing part of myself.

He studies me closely before sighing. Opening a drawer in his desk, he pulls out my golden cuff and hands it to me. I slip it on with shaking fingers, some of the nerves in me settling as it tightens around my bicep.

"How long have I been here?" I ask more quietly after a beat of silence.

"You were captured and brought to the palace four days ago." Doctor Harmon returns to his desk and jots down some notes before grabbing his stethoscope. "May I take a listen?" I sit obediently while the doctor checks my pulse, heart rate, and temperature. He also takes another vial of blood, before sitting back at his desk. "I ordered you some food. It will be brought up shortly."

I nod, but I'm not really hungry. Four days. How many witches have been killed since I was taken? How much longer do I have to live before they decide to burn me at the stake?

I can't help but run through the millions of questions floating through my brain. I don't bother voicing any of them, because I know Doctor Harmon will just say he can't answer them. How long will I have to wait before my questions are answered?

THREE DAYS. Three more fucking days of sitting in a hospital bed, eating bland food, and stewing in the constant anxiety and fear that has become my life. Doctor Harmon brought me some books from the library. I force myself to read them because I have nothing else to do, but I've never been big on reading. It does help to ease some of the anxiety, though. Sort of.

Doctor Harmon encourages me to walk around the infirmary. I'm so weak, it took me half a day to walk the twenty steps needed to make it to the other end of the room. When I became too tired to move one more step, Doctor Harmon had to sit me in a wheelchair and wheel me back to my bed

Four other beds line one wall, while a big counter and tons of cabinets line the other wall. It's white. It's all white. And if I don't see some sort of color soon, I'm going to snap.

I turn the page of the book I'm not really paying attention to, and the door to the infirmary opens. My head pops up in surprise. So far, no one else has visited this room except Doctor Harmon and the guard who watches over me at night.

"Your Highness." Doctor Harmon stands from his desk and bows deeply.

Prince Tyberius saunters into the room. He's wearing the uniform of a witch hunter—black cargo pants, long-sleeved black henley, and black combat boots. The dark clothes make his blond hair practically glow and his blue eyes shine brightly. "I got your message that the witch was well enough to visit with my dad. I'm here to take her to see him." Tyberius stares at me with disdain. His eyes narrow, and his jaw clenches so hard I can hear his teeth grind together.

The witch. He can't even acknowledge I'm a human being. I'm just a thing to him. An evil creature.

Doctor Harmon bows again. "Of course, Your Highness."

"When was her last dose of equalizer?" Tyberius asks as his cold gaze travels over my body clinically. The lack of empathy makes me shiver.

"An hour ago. She'll be good for another day, Your Highness."

"Great. Thank you, Doctor Harmon." He pulls a pair of handcuffs from his pants and motions me to stand. "Hands behind your back."

I bite my tongue and follow his commands. There's no point in fighting. Without my magic, he'd overpower me in seconds. The cool bite of metal around my wrists causes my breath to hitch. Completely helpless. I hate being completely helpless. I shove the thought aside, and focus on my breathing as Tyberius turns me around and leads me from the infirmary.

It's the first time I've ever been to the palace, obviously. I try to take it all in. The colorful tapestries, the golden statues, the insanely shiny marble floor. But it's hard. Tyberius's hand on my arm, just below my golden cuff, is unflinching. It's like a second shackle holding me back. I force my tight chest to expand, taking as big a breath as I can, and stumble. Not just because my legs are so weak they're basically jello, but because I can smell him. Woodsy and citrusy. Cedar and lemon. It's oddly soothing.

Tyberius tightens his grip, hauling me forward. A small whimper climbs up my throat unbidden as his fingers bite deeper into my skin. It only makes him squeeze even harder. I'll have bruises from him by the time this is over.

He stops in front of an unassuming door. It's dark wood with no engravings or extra flare. The reality of what's coming crashes down on me, and my stomach drops, leaving me reeling. Behind this door, my fate will be determined. And as a witch, I have only one fate.

Burned at the stake.

Tyberius doesn't knock, he just pushes the door open and shoves me inside. I stumble, but his grip on my arm jerks me back upright. A scream climbs up my throat, and I want to tear into him for this manhandling, but on the off chance I'm not about to be burned, I need to stay on my best behavior. Instead, I give him my best glare. If I get free, he's the first one to go down. He notices my glare and smirks. My fingers tingle with the need to slap that smarmy smile off his perfect face. Even though I already know it's useless, and there are no shimmery threads I can latch onto, I make a fist and reach for some magic. I can't help but try.

Nothing.

King Leander sits behind a massive mahogany desk. His head is bent over his work, his dark brown hair with gray streaks styled perfectly. I can't take my eyes off of him. This is the man who has ordered so many of my sisters' deaths. Just like his father before him, and his father before him.

The Berkshires have been ruling Rossvale for thousands of years, starting with the very first, Maximus Berkshire. The very first person to burn a witch. When they realized it was the perfect way to keep their crown, the Berkshires kept up the tradition. Protecting the citizens from evil witches, those citizens threw their loyalty at them, and they've been the ruling family ever since.

When King Leander finally looks up, all my breath whooshes from my chest as his gaze lands on me. Having the king's full attention is unsettling. Every witch knows it's a guaranteed death sentence. His blue eyes travel to his son, and he slides off his glasses, setting them on the desk.

"This is the one?" he asks, his voice deep and commanding.

"We believe so, yes." Tyberius drags me forward, and I stumble again.

The king's gaze travels over me, and he looks less than impressed with his narrowed eyes and pursed lips. But what the hell does he expect when I've been drugged, sick, and held captive for the past seven days? Not to mention the borrowed black sweatpants, rolled at the waist and ankles, and the gray sweatshirt hanging almost to my knees are way too large. And don't even get me started on my knotted hair thrown into a messy bun on top of my head.

"Sit down," he says, pointing to a chair in front of the desk.

Guess the Berkshires are men of few words. Growly commands seem to be their specialty. Tyberius shoves me into the chair, and I collapse as my legs finally give out. The prince stands behind me, an ominous, looming presence that makes me want to slink further into the seat. Instead, I lift my chin and pull my shoulders back.

"What's your name, witch?" King Leander asks, piercing me with his gaze.

I debate refusing to tell him, but as long as I'm alive, there is a chance for escape. If I piss him off, he'll send me straight for the stakes. "Neave Parker." I'll answer his questions, but I won't give him the respect of using titles.

His eyes narrow at the lack of respect, but he says nothing. "How old are you?"

"Twenty-seven."

He jots something down in a notebook before glancing back at me. I try not to squirm under his unyielding stare. "Have you heard of the witch Sybil?"

Barely containing my snort, I nod. How would I not know who Sybil was? She was the first witch ever burned by the Berkshire family.

"Do you know why she was burned?" he asks, twirling his pen in his fingers.

"I'm assuming it's because she was a witch, and people are ignorant. Instead of trying to understand the unknown, they opted to eradicate it." This time, I'm unable to keep the sarcasm from my tone. I sense Tyberius stepping closer, his looming presence intensifying.

King Leander doesn't react to my sarcasm or lack of respect. Instead, he gently sets his pen on the desk and steeples his fingers under his chin. "Sybil was King Maximus's consort. She had visions, and he used them to help raise himself to the throne. Twenty years after he was crowned, she started acting differently. Instead of visions that provided assistance in raising the Berkshire name higher, they turned deadly. Bloody." He lowers his hands to the desk to straighten the paper and line up the pen with the edge. "No one knows what happened, but she was found one morning sitting in a cooling puddle of King Maximus's blood. She was chanting, saying the same thing over and over. *She is coming. The one with the sight. She will save us. Only she can stop the threat.*"

He ends his speech and watches me expectantly. I stare back, unsure what he wants me to say or do. I had never heard this version before. The witches' version is much different from his.

"Thousands of years ago," I begin, clutching my hands together tightly. "A witch named Sybil fell in love with a young lord. They married, and he raised to kinghood with the help of her visions. One day, her visions showed her the demise of the Berkshire line, and in anger, King Maximus had her burned. Sybil's sister, Cora, murdered King Maximus in revenge. Since then, the Berkshires have taken it upon themselves to rid the world of all witches, holding a grudge that began long before the birth of most of them."

King Leander sits back in his chair and crosses his arms over his chest. A small smile plays about his lips. "I have heard that false version before. Unfortunately, it is not true."

"Okay, say that your version is the truth. Is the end any different? You have held onto a grudge for thousands of years, killing innocent witches because one of them killed your kin that lived many, many years before your birth."

A muscle ticks in his jaw as he clenches his teeth. "That is not at all what we have been doing."

"Then please, do explain your reasons for murdering innocent women who have done no harm." I wave my hand in front of me, inviting him to continue the story. Behind me, Tyberius growls softly, and I smirk.

King Leander sighs and rubs the bridge of his nose, like I'm bringing on a headache he's trying to ward off. "Sybil had drawn symbols in the puddle of blood. We have been unable to decipher their meaning. We have also studied her words closely and have not been able to determine what exactly she meant by them. It sounds as though she was warning us of a threat to our rule, and we have been diligently trying to find who this *she* is that Sybil mentioned. If this person can help us stop the threat, we will do anything to find her."

My heart thumps in my chest at the implication of his words. "You think *I* am the one mentioned in her mad ravings? Well, I hate to disappoint you, truly, because I have a feeling that means I'll be murdered, but I have no idea what any of that means."

"That is to be determined. Doctor Harmon believes you may be the one. For the time being, my son will show you to a room. We will work on figuring out what all you know."

His words make my blood run cold. How is he going to do that? More drugs? Torture? I don't have time to think about it before Tyberius grabs my arm again and hauls me to my feet. "You really aren't much of a gentleman, are you?" I mumble as he drags me out of the office.

He's silent as he leads me through the ornate palace. We pass a set of beautifully carved wooden doors I assume lead to the throne room, and climb a set of curving stairs with a golden railing. He drags me down a hallway with a deep blue rug running down the middle of the marble floor and stops in front of another plain wooden door.

Opening it, he shoves me inside. "This is your room. There will be a guard posted in the hallway, as well as below the balcony. So don't even think of trying to escape. The equalizer will be given to you every day. Someone will come for you tomorrow to begin learning what you know."

With that, he turns and slams the door behind him, leaving me gaping. That was the most I've ever heard him say. He delivered that little spiel in a bored, monotone voice with an undercurrent of hatred.

Turning around, I whistle through my teeth. For being a prisoner, they sure did set me up in a fancy room. Marble floors, light wood-paneled walls. A heavenly-looking bed shoved against the far wall, and a thankfully unlit hearth across from it, with a pair of chairs made for lounging. A set of deep blue curtains cover the glass doors that open onto a balcony.

I open a discreet door next to the bed and find a lavish bathing chamber with a shower and a sunken tub. I bet the water here is always hot. Grinning to myself, I opt to make the most of my situation. If I'm to be tortured, drugged, and killed, I might as well enjoy what's left of my time. I turn the knob on the faucet for the sunken tub and strip out of my borrowed clothes. Slipping into the delicious, heated water, I close my eyes and try to forget about what might happen tomorrow.

Without magic or weapons, there is little chance I can escape. I'm still weak from being drugged, and I don't think I'd be able to fight if I had to. My belly tumbles with nerves whenever my thoughts wander to tomorrow. *What are they going to do to me? And am I strong enough to survive it?*

King Leander's words echo in my head. I duck under the

water to try and chase them away. It doesn't work. I can't be the one Sybil mentioned all those years ago. Can I? The thought is absurd. Lungs screaming, I burst to the surface of the tub, sucking in lungfuls of air. Drowning. I think I would prefer to go that way. Anything has to be better than burning, right? Unfortunately, I'm afraid I'm about to find out.

Are Those Curtains?

It would be my luck that my dad wants me to be the one to work with the witch. I may or may not have slammed his office door shut as I left. His voice bellowing my name could be heard halfway down the hall, even through the closed door. I'm sure I'll pay for that move later, but I wasn't about to take this order sitting down.

I have no idea how long I stand in front of the witch's door contemplating my life. *If Mom hadn't died, would things have ended up this way?* When the guard outside clears his throat, I shake myself and push into her room. The sight that greets me stops me in my tracks.

"What the fuck are you wearing?" My gaze travels to the balcony doors, then back to the witch sitting in the chair in front of the fireplace. "Are those curtains?"

"If you think I was about to wear the hunter uniform that was left for me, you're dumber than I thought you were, blondie." She shudders dramatically. "I'd rather wear an outfit made entirely of living, crawling spiders."

Indeed, she is wearing the curtains. I'd never admit it to anyone, but it actually doesn't look bad. Somehow, she has managed to fold and drape it around her body in a way that looks elegant, and not bulky. However, the golden tassel rope holding it all together is a bit ostentatious. Already, a headache pulses behind my eyes, and I rub my temples. It's going to be a long fucking day.

Shoving the annoyance aside, I sit in the chair next to hers and level a stern look in her direction. "Look, witch, I don't want to be here. So I would really appreciate it if you would comply so we can get this over with quickly."

Her smile is full of vitriol, her voice laced with so much sweetness it chokes me. "Of course, Your Highness. I would never think of making this hard on you." She leans back in her chair, crossing one leg over the over, causing the curtains to split and display an indecent amount of creamy dark skin.

I yank my eyes away from her legs and bare feet and focus on the empty fireplace. "So why don't you tell me what you know?" I ask gruffly.

"Well, this should make you happy. I know nothing else about Sybil besides what I told your dad yesterday. So, looks like our conversation will be quite short." Her leg bounces, drawing my attention to it once again. "You can go ahead and leave now. I have nothing else to add. No point in taking up any more of your precious time."

I have to force my shoulders to relax. With each word out of her mouth, they steadily climb higher toward my ears as the tension in me grows. Pulling a folded piece of paper from my pocket, I toss it to her. "What do those symbols mean?"

I've studied those symbols so many times I could draw them with my eyes closed. The triple moon, Hecate's wheel, a triskelion, and a witch's knot. I've researched them endlessly, but could never determine their meaning or what they do. Why Sybil drew them in King Maximus's blood is a mystery that has plagued my family for thousands of years.

Her eyes dart back and forth across the page before she drops it on the table in front of the chairs. "I have no idea. Using symbolic magic is an older practice and one that requires someone to teach you. No one ever taught me, so can't help you there."

"But you're a witch." I barely keep the growl from my voice.

She points at me with a finger tipped in black nail polish. "You're a smart one, blondie."

Closing my eyes, I take a deep breath before releasing it, searching for any scrap of patience. "As a witch, you must know something about the symbols."

"I know their names, their general meanings. But that's it." She uncrosses her legs and leans forward, brown eyes taking on a serious light. "What exactly is it you want from me?"

"I want you to help me find whatever this threat is that is going to ruin my family."

She huffs and leans back in the chair again, crossing her arms over her chest. "Could you be more cryptic? And why are you so insistent *I* am the one who can do that? What about all the witches you've burned? What if it was one of them? Seems like you may have screwed yourself."

I need more patience. And a drink. A strong one. Running my hand through my hair, I say, "For thousands of years, we have been capturing witches and testing them. When they fail the test, we burn them to keep our lands safe from the evil you bring into our world."

She tenses, the skin around her eyes tightening as she narrows her gaze at me. "First off, we are not evil. But I already know arguing with you is a losing battle. Ignorance and stupidity are a lethal combination, and it will take more than me to drive the fear of change out of you." She runs her fingers through her purple locks, and my fingers clench as I'm reminded of the drug-induced hallucination from the other night. She breaks me out of that haze as she continues. "Second, what do you mean, you test us? What test did you perform on me?"

"Before Sybil was burned, they drained her blood. That blood was bottled and stored for years until a scientist created a drug out of it that induces hallucinations in witches that are capable of having visions. We have failed for thousands of years until you."

She gags, no doubt remembering that concoction being forced down her throat. I don't blame her, it smells god awful. "You mean to tell me, you fed me blood that is thousands of years old? How do you still have enough? I know how many witches you've murdered through the years."

I shouldn't tell her this, but I find the words pouring from my lips, anyway. "No, we don't have the blood anymore. But before we ran out, a scientist was able to extract the DNA components of it. Using that, we can produce a synthetic that creates the same results." Because that is knowledge I shouldn't have shared, I add in, "we mix it with witch blood to help make it more realistic."

She gags again and stares at me like she wishes she could curse me. I'm sure she would if she had her magic. "That's all fine and dandy, but I never had any visions. Sorry to disappoint you."

"You had dreams. Doctor Harmon monitored you while you were in the cell, and you talked in your sleep."

Her brows furrow. "Okay. How do you know they weren't fever dreams?"

I shrug. "We don't. But no other witch had the kind of reaction to the drug that you did. That's why I'm stuck with you. I have to figure out if you're the one or not."

"Lovely," she mutters.

I stand from the chair and head for the door. "Think about all of this. Tomorrow we'll begin trying to get visions out of you."

She snorts. "Good luck." My hand is on the doorknob when she speaks again. "Any chance I can go to my apartment to get my own things?"

"No."

"Then any chance I can get more curtains?"

It takes all of my self control to not slam the door behind me. I really need a fucking drink.

"WHY SHOULD I waste more of my stash on you when last time you ditched me before the high really hit?" Killian crosses his arms over his chest and leans back in the booth at Club Eden.

The bass vibrates the glasses on the table, and sounds of people laughing and singing filter through the waterfall wall and vine curtain. I give Killian my best smile and set my now empty glass down.

"I'm sorry I left last night. I remembered something I forgot to do that needed to be done before midnight." He'll see right through that lie, but he won't question it. I really have been an awful friend lately.

There is just no way I can talk to him about the existential crisis I'm going through when it's not something he's ever experienced. This is all he wants from his life. Witch hunting. And he's high up in the ranks, just under me. There isn't much else Killian desires. A strong drink and a willing woman makes a happy Killian.

That used to be enough for me. It's not anymore.

"Mmhm. If I give you some, do you promise you won't bail on me this time?" He raises one brow and purses his lips.

"I won't bail. On my honor."

He snorts. "Like that means anything. Prince Tyberius has no honor."

I kick him under the table, but he quickly lays down some lines for us. I eagerly do mine and let the haze of euphoria cloud my mind. It's that first moment the drug hits my bloodstream that I crave. The instant the numbness takes over my thoughts and sends tingles of relaxation and pleasure through my veins. The sensation of floating, of being untethered to reality, is utterly addicting.

Killian and I sit in silence and throw back drink after drink. The fog in my head mutes the sounds of revelry on the dance floor, but soon the itch to move, to rub my body against another, has me climbing out of the booth. As soon as I step foot out of the VIP section and onto the dance floor, women begin plotting their way to win their spot as my dance partner. They know where it will end—in the back room with me buried between their thighs. It's a game I play whenever we come here. It's been a long time since I've played it while high, though.

I have no idea how long I've been dancing or how many women I've danced with. Sweat coats my body and makes my gray henley stick to my skin. The brunette I'm dancing with grinds her ass against me, and I pull her closer, pleasure zinging through me. I can't help but notice her skin is the same color as the witch's, and I have to shove the thought to the back of my mind.

I've teased myself enough for the night. I'm aching and desperate for release. Leaning down to whisper in her ear, I bite her lobe before I say, "Backroom?"

She doesn't hesitate. Grabbing my hand, she tugs me toward the backroom where the club owner turns a blind eye to everything that goes down. I'm unsteady on my feet, and the hallway tips back and forth as I walk down it. How many drinks have I had tonight? Coupled with the pixie essence, it's been a long time since I've been this wasted. It feels fucking amazing to just let go.

In the back room, I lock the door before shoving the woman against the wall and pressing my chest against her back. I drop a biting kiss to her neck and shoulder as I lift her skirt and slide my fingers beneath the lacy scrap of fabric barely covering her pussy. She moans softly and rubs against my growing erection. Because I'm not a complete asshole, I play with her a bit, even though I really just want to fuck her and leave.

When she's writhing against my fingers, moaning and begging me to let her come, I finally unbutton my pants and let my weeping cock free. I grab her ponytail, wrapping the purple strands around my wrist. *Purple?* My heart skips a beat, and I blink, but the color stays. It makes me ache even more. God damn it.

With my free hand, I roughly push on the back of the woman's neck, forcing her chest down and her hips up. I kick her legs wider and dig my fingers sharply into her waist. Biting my lip, the sight of my lighter skin against her darker complexion imprints itself on my mind. This is a bad idea. I should stop this right now. Imagining the witch under my hands, my dick inside her, her body flushed and writhing from desire, is a road I do not want to go down.

I can't stop myself, though. I rub my aching length down her center before notching my dick at her entrance. She pants as I slowly slip inside, clenching around each inch. Watching myself disappear inside her—her dark skin, her purple hair wrapped around my wrist—I snap. I thrust my hips hard and fast, fucking her roughly. The combination of drugs, alcohol, and hallucination, is my undoing.

My orgasm crashes through me faster than it ever has, lightning shooting through my veins. I pump my hips until every last drop has been milked from me. With my heart racing and chest heaving, I unwrap the brown hair from my wrist and curse.

"Fucking hell," I mutter to myself, running a shaky hand down my face. I quickly yank up my pants and shove out of the backroom, leaving the unnamed woman behind without an orgasm or another word.

I can't leave, as much as I want to. I told Killian I wouldn't. So I head back to the booth in the VIP section and order two more drinks. *What the hell is happening to me?* Maybe I should stay away from the essence from now on. Clearly, it's making me see things that I really don't want to see. The high is nice. The escape from my thoughts is what I need, but it's only creating more disturbing thoughts. My hands continue to shake, and my heart is still thundering my chest when the drinks arrive. Slamming back the first drink, I try to lose myself once again, only this time, it's harder to find the bliss I had before fucking that woman in the back room.

Mistakes. The fucking story of my life.

Were You Going To Poison Me With This?

I grit my teeth and refuse to look at the damn cat perched on the balcony. *I wouldn't look like this if you had warned me of the hunter, prick.* Glancing in the mirror, I sigh. I mean, considering I'm wearing a freaking curtain, it doesn't look half bad. But I still feel ridiculous. I attempt to adjust the ugly gold tassel rope, then give up with a huff. There is no making this anything other than what it is ... a curtain wrapped around my body.

I walk to the balcony doors and peer outside. Jinx sunbathes on the railing, his gray fluffy tail swishing lazily.

Ooh, do that again. It's like you're on the catwalk. He cackles in my head.

I'm this close to going outside and shoving him off, but knowing him, he'd slip inside the door and I'd never be rid of him. "Eat glass."

I'm on the second floor of the palace and my view isn't too shabby. Most of the buildings surrounding the palace are smaller. The skyscrapers are off in the distance in the business district. With the unimpeded view, I can see the city center a few miles away. The gray stone slab with the stake perched atop. It's empty right now, only a few people passing through, but I know at night, it can fill in minutes with a crowd excited to watch the burning of a witch.

Swallowing back the nausea climbing up my throat, I tear my gaze away from the grisly sight and focus on the park to the right of the palace drive. It's beautiful. I've never been able to visit, too scared to be caught, but I've dreamed of seeing it up close. In the winter, the skeletal trees without leaves are not quite as impressive. But the fairy lights that twinkle in them at night are still romantic. More fairy lights wrap around pine trees and evergreen bushes, along with navy blue and golden garlands—the Berkshire family colors. Flower beds, void of the vibrant, aromatic flowers in the winter, are filled with fantastical lanterns shaped like various flora and fauna that glow brightly during the night. Not the same kind of beauty the gardens hold in the summer, but equally impressive.

Jinx disappears and the door to my room opens without so much as a knock. I know who it is without turning around.

"Ever hear of knocking?" I drawl, turning around slowly.

Tyberius snorts. "You're a witch. You don't need privacy."

My mouth drops open and I stare at him, completely taken aback. He's wearing his usual witch hunter gear, but this time he's holding a winter coat and a thick beanie covers his blond hair. "I ... that ..." I trail off, unable to find the words I want to describe the disbelief coursing through me at the moment.

I shouldn't be surprised. He hunts and burns innocent women. But to hear him say I don't deserve privacy because I'm a witch just solidifies his beliefs. Witches are no more than animals to him. Creatures that don't deserve even a shred of decency. It hurts more than it should.

Pushing my shoulders back, I smirk at him. "Well then. This will certainly get interesting when I run out of curtains and have to lie around naked." Tiberius's nostrils flare as he sucks in a sharp breath. My eyes narrow on him. *Why would he have that kind of reaction to my words?* Whatever. I adjust my curtains with an agitated swish. "Well, Your Highness, what are we doing today?"

He looks resigned as he says, "We're going to your apartment to get your things."

Taken aback for the second time in minutes, it takes me a moment to speak. "You're serious?"

"You look ridiculous. It's bad enough I have to be seen in the palace with a witch. I'd rather not walk around with you dressed like that." He waves a hand at my getup.

I run my hands down the curtains like they're the most exquisite ball gown in the world. "You could only be so lucky," I mutter to myself as I brush past him toward the hallway.

He grabs my arm and yanks me back into my room. "Not so fast," he growls. "You will not leave my side for one second while we are out of the palace. I will watch every item that goes into your bag, and I get the final say on what you bring. If I so much as think you're about to run or attack me, I will not hesitate to slip a knife between your ribs. Am I clear?"

"Crystal," I say through gritted teeth.

"One last thing." Digging in his pocket, he comes up with a syringe. Biting off the cap and spitting it on the floor, he raises one brow.

Sighing, I pull my hair over one shoulder and tilt my head, offering him my exposed neck. I almost can't remember what my magic feels like. The yawning, empty pit in my chest has become normal. Is this what it's like to be human? Powerless? I hiss as Tyberius jabs the needle into my neck and presses down on the plunger. Fire seeps into my bloodstream, burning all the way through my body. It slowly fades away, leaving me shivering.

"Let's go."

Tyberius walks next to me, so close his shoulder rubs against mine. As much as it makes my skin crawl, I welcome it. It's fucking freezing outside, and I'm wearing nothing but a damn curtain. The bastard never once offered me a coat. And why would he? I'm just an animal. I don't deserve to be warm.

By the time we reach my apartment, my teeth are chattering so hard I'm worried I might break a tooth. As I reach up for the fire escape, my body shivers so violently I lose my grip.

"What are you doing?" Tyberius asks, breath fogging in front of him. His hands are shoved into his coat pockets, and I'm insanely jealous.

Blowing into my hands, I look at him from the corner of my eye. "I only go through the window."

"What's wrong with the front door?"

"Nothing. As long as you don't mind being mentally undressed by a skeevy landlord. All it would take is one yank, and this fabulous dress of mine would be on the floor." Trying again, I reach up and wrap my numb fingers around the biting metal. Before I haul myself up, I narrow my eyes at Tyberius. "Don't even think of looking up my skirts."

He snorts. "Like I'd ever want to."

My fingers are so frozen it's hard to grasp and release the icy metal of the fire escape. Add to it the fact I'm wearing nothing but a curtain wrapped around my body, tied with a rope, and I'm surprised I didn't fall to my death. I didn't dare look down at Tyberius. If I saw him peeking up my skirts, I'd probably kick his face until he fell.

If being a witch wasn't a death sentence, killing the prince certainly is.

Every step to my window, Tyberius is there next to me, watching every move I make like an eagle watching its prey. I don't acknowledge him as I approach my window and the faint shimmering spell keeping people out. If there was a way to get inside without breaking it, I would. It would be the highlight of my life to see him attempt to make it through and experience the sudden urge to shit himself.

"I need a dagger," I say, holding my hand out.

"Right. And I need a million dollars."

I shrug. "Suit yourself. But you can't follow me inside then. Unless you have some kind of kink where you like to shit yourself." I turn to the window and force it open.

"What do you mean?" His words snap in the space between us like a cracked whip.

"There is a spell on my apartment keeping people out. My blood is the only thing that breaks it."

A grin spreads across his face, creating a dimple in his right cheek. "You mean I get to spill your blood? Well, why didn't you say so?" He yanks a dagger from the sheath at his thigh and holds it up, the metal glinting in the sunlight.

I hold my hand out. "Just a drop. It doesn't take a lo—"

He moves faster than I thought he could, grabbing my hand and jamming the tip of the blade into my pointer finger, harder than he needed to.

I hiss through my teeth as the blood wells ruby red. "Fucker," I ground out. He enjoyed that way too much. The spell breaks as I press my finger to the sill, the shimmery veil disappearing. I hop through the opening and suck my finger into my mouth to stop the bleeding.

Home. It's not much, but it's been home for as long as I can remember.

Plants cover every available surface, most of them now wilting and dying from lack of water. Macrame wall hangings my mom made cover the ugly, yellowing plaster walls. And colorful woven rugs hide the chipped linoleum flooring. It's chaotic, eclectic, and bright. And I wouldn't change it for the world. A pang of sadness washes through me and I rub my chest at the sudden ache. Homesick. *Will I ever return here?*

"Hurry up," Tyberius says, interrupting my moment.

Signing, I snag my bookbag from the couch, but before I can start putting stuff in it, he grabs it from me. "Hey!" I argue.

"I told you, I'm watching everything you put in this bag. That means I need to know what's in it already." He opens it and unceremoniously dumps the contents on the table.

I bite back my words of frustration because they won't do any good, anyway. He paws through my belongings, searching for anything witchy, and I hold my breath as his hand nears the book with the carved out middle. He knocks it over, and the cover falls open. I cringe.

Tyberius looks at me with a raised brow. "Well, well, well. What have we here?" His fingers close around the bag of devil's trumpet and he holds it up, dangling it in my face.

Rolling my eyes, I try to snatch the bag, but he yanks it out of reach. "I'm a witch. Of course I have plants and herbs."

He eyes the bag and brings it to his nose, inhaling the scent. "Devil's trumpet? Were you going to poison me with this?"

I don't answer because, yes. Yes, I was. "It's datura, and yes, it may be known as devil's trumpet, but it also has medicinal purposes."

He snorts and tucks the bag into his pocket. "Well, obviously, I can't let you keep that." He motions at the rest of my stuff on the table. "This is all fine. Minus the knife." He snags the knife and slips it in his pocket with the poison.

"Yeah, sure. You can have my knife. You're welcome." Rolling my eyes, I grab my bag and head to my bedroom, with Tyberius close on my heels.

I shove some clothes in—leggings, jeans, hoodies, and undergarments—before heading for the bathroom. When I grab my shampoo and conditioner, Tyberius yanks them from my hands and pops the lids, sniffing them suspiciously.

"Really?" I ask.

He shrugs and hands them back. "Can't be too careful around a witch."

Unbelievable. I toss them in my bag, along with some other toiletries. When I think I have everything I need, I head back to my room and grab some new clothes to change into. Turning to look at Tyberius, I say, "I'm changing. Are you going to watch me do that, too?"

When he says nothing, but keeps his gaze trained on me with his arms crossed over his chest, I smirk. I can work with that. Giving him a saucy little smile, I untie the golden rope and let the curtains fall to the ground. Seeing as I had no clothing in the palace, I'm completely nude under the curtains. Tyberius's eyes widen and he whips around to face the wall. *Shame. That could have been fun.* Throwing on my jeans and tee-shirt, I tell him I'm decent as I pull a hoodie over my head.

"Do you have everything you need?" He turns back around, and I can't help but notice the pink tint to his cheeks.

Did I make the vicious witch hunter blush? I nod and sit on my bed to pull on a pair of warm winter boots. "Almost." I grab my knitting needles and the blanket I was working on, but before I can shove them in the bag, Tyberius grabs them from me.

"Not a chance, witch." He tosses it to the ground, and crosses his arms over his chest.

"Seriously?" I bend down and pick it up, carefully refolding it. "It's just knitting."

"And those needles would end up in my neck if I let you bring them."

Huh. He's probably not wrong. Too bad I never even thought of that. "Fine." I put the half-finished blanket back on my nightstand. "Then I'm ready."

I'm rewarded with a grunt, and I follow him out of my room. "I assume you leave the same way you came?" He eyes the window with distaste.

"Ye*p*." I grab my coat, scarf, gloves, and hat, then hop back out the window. I debate resetting my spell, but seeing as I probably won't be returning, it wouldn't be the nicest thing to leave a spell that causes everyone who enters to experience severe stomach cramps.

It's so much easier going down wearing warm, proper

clothing. Tyberius keeps up with me, and we both land on the ground at the same time with a thump of boots.

"Let's go," he growls, and leads me back to the palace.

"YOU KNOW, if you stare at me anymore, I might start to think you have a crush on me."

When we got back to the palace, Tyberius took me to the library where we've been sitting at a table, staring at each other for the past hour. I glance around the space for what seems like the hundredth time. Ornate wooden bookshelves create a maze through the room, reflecting on the shiny, white marble floor. More shelves, and the occasional tapestry, cover the walls. Tables, chairs, couches, and chaise lounges welcome people to read and study in sitting areas scattered through the space.

Initially, Tyberius chose a sitting area by a fireplace. The flames flickering in the hearth made my blood run cold, even as sweat popped out on my skin from the heat of the fire. I shook my head and told him to pick a different place to sit. When I refused to move any closer to the fire, he reluctantly got up and chose a different spot.

"So..." I purse my lips and raise my brows at him in a silent question.

He sighs. "Just try."

Is he serious? I have to bite back my chuckle. While I know that he's not a witch and probably doesn't know much about magic, this seems like common sense. I humor him, though, if only because I know it will piss him off in the long run. Closing my eyes, I let my face relax and take on a trance-like appearance. I even sway just a tiny bit in my seat. After ten minutes of me doing this—and almost falling asleep—Tyberius finally cracks. I'm honestly impressed he made it the entire ten minutes.

"I'm getting inpatient," he growls.

"Well, so am I!" I snap. "And I'm bored shitless."

Tyberius leans down to pull something from a bag at his feet. When sits back up, he sets a crystal ball on the table between us. The clear sphere sits on a round wooden base carved with moons and stars. I blink at the ball, then at him.

He gestures with his hands toward the sphere. "Maybe this will help."

I snort and snatch the ball into my hands. It's made of glass and it's heavy. I toss it up and down, catching it with a soft grunt.

"Be careful!" Tyberius lunges from his chair in an attempt to grab it from my hands, but I stand up and dart away. "It took me forever to find one of those, and it cost me a fucking fortune."

I look at him and shake my head, pursing my lips. "So gullible. It's not real, you idiot. Crystal balls are passed down from generation to generation. They are heirlooms that are more cherished than life itself. No witch in her right mind would sell theirs. Especially not to you." I lift the ball and let it slip from my hands. The shattering glass punctuates my sentence, and I smile. Damn, that felt good.

Tyberius stares at me. His jaw is clenched so hard I'm surprised he doesn't break any teeth. Running a shaky hand through his hair, he sits back down in his chair and releases a huge breath. "Okay. Then we'll go back to your apartment and get yours."

Glass crunches under my boots as I walk back to my chair and sit. "I don't have one."

"But you're a witch."

"I'm really glad I'm stuck with you. If you weren't here to remind me every day that I'm a witch, I'm positive I would forget."

More jaw clenching. More teeth grinding. "Why don't you have a crystal ball?"

I shrug. "Must have gotten lost somewhere. I don't know."

Tyberius's fingers turn white as he grabs the armrests of his chair, like he's trying to keep himself from launching at me. "If you don't start cooperating, I'll—"

"What the hell do you want me to do?" I huff and throw up my hands, interrupting him. "I can't just make a vision happen. Especially when I've *never* had one before. Not to mention, you've blocked my magic. Pretty sure visions require access to magic." I slouch back in my chair and cross my arms. "Could you be more ignorant? No—" I hold out my hand to stop him from opening his mouth—"Don't say anything. I already know the answer. I'd hate for you to dig yourself further into the hole."

He growls and pushes up from the chair. "This is fucking useless." His boots echo in the silence as he marches to the double doors leading to the hallway. "Stevens, take her back to her room," he barks before disappearing around the corner.

I rub my eyes, trying to ward off the ache steadily growing in my head. This is a pointless task, especially if I can't access my magic. I have no clue what he wants from me or how to make it happen. I might be heading to the stakes sooner than I thought. Maybe I should start focusing on how to escape rather than trying to make something happen that probably never will.

The guard, Stevens, approaches my seat and gestures for me to stand. He apparently doesn't trust me as much as Tyberius, because his hand clamps around my arm tight enough to bruise. He practically drags me through the palace and shoves me into my room, slamming the door behind me.

"It was nice meeting you, too," I mutter to my closed door.

I strip out of my clothes as I make my way to the bathroom. Turning on the faucet, I let the tub fill with steaming water before slipping into it. The water scalds my skin, but I embrace it. It's a feeling. If only it were filling the empty hole in my chest where my magic should be. I miss the slight shimmer living things emit. Without it, everything is cold and dim. Lifeless. The heat from water reminds me I'm still alive.

I duck under the surface, holding my breath until stars burst behind my lids and my lungs scream for release. I stay under just a second longer, then shove to the surface, gasping for air as water sloshes over the sides and onto the tile floor.

I don't even bother drying my hair—just wrap a towel around my torso and pad barefoot into the bedroom, leaving dripping wet footprints in my wake.

"What the hell are you doing?" I stop in my tracks and narrow my eyes at the white fluff of fur laying on my bed.

Jinx stretches, his claws extending and retracting as he makes biscuits on the comforter. *This is so much nicer than that apartment. And look! The bed is big enough for the both of us.*

You're Going To Drug A Witch?

My boots echo as I head toward the infirmary. I already have a headache at just the thought of meeting with the witch again. I tossed and turned all night, her words echoing in my mind. Well, one word in particular.

Ignorant.

I've been called many things in my life. Arrogant. Snobby. Whore. Addict. Lazy. Hateful. The list goes on. Some of them are true. Some of them aren't. None of them have ever bothered me. But hearing the word *ignorant* from the witch's mouth raised my hackles. But my defense quickly died on my tongue when I realized ... maybe I *am* ignorant.

Shaking that uncomfortable thought from my mind, I open the door to the infirmary to find Doctor Harmon seated at his desk, glasses perched on the end of his nose. When he hears me, he glances up then jumps to his feet, offering me a bow.

"Your Highness, what can I do for you?" He straightens and pushes his glasses back up his nose.

"I had a question. About the witch." I lean against the counter and cross my arms and legs. "Would not being able to use magic impact the ability to have visions?"

Doctor Harmon puffs out his cheeks as he contemplates my

question. "I think it would be a possibility. I'm not proficient in magic use, so I couldn't say for certain. However, it does make sense."

"The witch said something to that effect. I just wondered how much of it could be a ploy to get her magic back."

"That could also be a possibility," he says as he bobs his head from side to side. "However, I've interacted with quite a few witches in my time as the doctor here, and I have a feeling about Miss Parker."

"You think it's worth the risk to let her have her magic? That could have disastrous consequences." I run my hand through my hair, tension growing in my limbs making me want to move.

"It could. But it could also be the only way to get the answers we seek."

I leave Doctor Harmon to his studies, a syringe with the antidote to the equalizer sitting heavy in my pocket. If I screw this up, my dad will strip me of my title and leave me to rot in the streets. That is, if the witch doesn't kill me first.

Taking a deep breath, I don't let myself think about what I'm about to do when I push open the door and enter the witch's room. I'm taken aback when I find her still asleep in the bed, one dark leg and arm peeking out from the tangle of blankets. Her face is relaxed, lips slightly parted, and I find myself biting my own bottom lip. She looks so ... *human.*

Shaking myself free of that thought, I let my boot thump loudly on the floor to wake her. "Get up, witch."

She wakes with a startled gasp, sitting up so abruptly her blankets fall to the floor. I can't stop my eyes from traveling over her body. Wearing nothing but a tank top and boy shorts, there is so much skin on display. I clench my hands, trying to rid the sensation of my fingers running over every inch of exposed skin.

She glares at me blearily, swiping stray strands of purple hair from her face that have escaped the messy bun hanging lopsided on the side of her head. "What the hell?" Her voice is husky with sleep, and I shove my hands in my pockets, discreetly adjusting myself.

I clear my throat, forcing the stern tone I've adopted with her. "Get up. We have work to do."

She flops back on the bed with a groan. "It's too early. Come back later." Emphasizing her point, she drags a pillow over her face, effectively blocking me out.

I fight the twitch of my lips as I walk to the side of the bed and yank the pillow away. "Stop acting like a child. Get dressed. We're trying something new today."

Grumbling and glaring at me, she finally crawls out of bed. I'm unable to avert my gaze as she walks to the bathroom, those boy shorts barely covering her ass. *So human.* When the bathroom door closes, I'm snapped out of my thoughts. *Get your fucking head back in the game, Berkshire. She's a* witch.

By the time she emerges, almost an hour later, I'm even more agitated. Mostly at myself. She's dressed in black leggings and a hot pink off the shoulder sweater with her purple hair hanging in shiny waves down her back. *Fucking hell.* I flex my hands and turn toward the hallway.

"Let's go."

I already organized everything before I went to speak with Doctor Harmon. Even though I wanted to get his opinion, I was set on this decision. As we enter the library, the witch hesitates. Guards are stationed every ten feet in a circle around the sitting area we will be utilizing. More guards are posted at every exit to the library.

She looks around nervously, hands fidgeting with the hem of her sweater. "What exactly are we going to be trying today?" Despite her obvious nerves, her shoulders are thrown back, and she lifts her chin defiantly.

I sit and pull the syringe out of my pocket, setting it on the table. "You say magic is needed for visions." I roll my shoulders, trying to ease the tension building at the thought of returning her magic to her. "This is the antidote to the equalizer."

Her eyes widen and her mouth drops open. "You're serious?" she breathes. "You're going to give me access to my magic?" She rubs her chest like it aches.

Staring into her deep brown eyes, I swallow. I'm not positive, but I swear I see the shimmer of tears before she blinks and it disappears. "There will be rules," I say as she slowly sits across from me, her gaze glued to the syringe. "Your guard will be doubled. They will all carry the equalizer, and if they ever suspect you're about to harm them or try to escape, they will use it. One misstep, and all of this is over. Vision or not, you will be sent to the stakes." I lean forward, catching her gaze. "Understand?"

She nods. "Yes, I understand." Her voice shakes slightly, and she swallows thickly.

Grabbing the syringe, I walk around her chair to stand behind her. I could let her move her hair from her neck. I *should* let her do it. But some part of me is dying to know what it really feels like. Is it as soft as I imagined in my drug-induced hallucinations? My fingers shake slightly as I brush the strands away and they flow like silk through my fingers. I take a deep breath, telling myself it's because I'm about to give a witch access to her magic, and not because I loved the way her hair felt against my skin. The needle disappears in her neck and I push down on the plunger. No going back now.

Returning to my seat, I watch her closely. It will take a couple of minutes for her magic to be released. She closes her eyes and waits, her chest rising and falling rapidly. After a period of silence, her hands clench in her lap and her eyelids flutter. A slow smile spreads across her face. I fully expected it to become twisted, a smile of cruel intent, but it's not. It's relieved, peaceful.

This time, when she opens her eyes, there is no mistaking the shimmer of tears. "Thank you," she breathes.

Unsure how to respond to that, and feeling a mangled mix of emotions, I clear my throat roughly. "So, visions?"

She signs and sits back in her chair. "Look, I know you think I'm just trying to be difficult, but honestly, I have no idea how visions work. I truly don't think you can force them. They have to come on their own, and considering I've never had one, I don't know what to say." She looks down at her hands in her lap. "If there is a way to induce a vision, I don't know what it is."

Rubbing my hands over my face, I nod. I know she's speaking the truth, even though I don't know a lot about magic. It just doesn't make sense that visions could be forced. Isn't that the whole point of them? They come when they're needed. "I guess we just have to wait then. In the meantime, let's think of ways we could possibly induce one."

FRUSTRATION RIDING ME HARD, I left the witch in the library under a guard of five men to come to my office to finish some paperwork. I fucking hate paperwork. I've been here all damn day, and I just want to go back to my room and crash. How my brother looks forward to being king is beyond me. Cooped up in this space, staring at reports, signing and filing, it makes me itch under my skin. I'm not claustrophobic, but all of *this* is too much like a cage.

Thinking of my future as more of the same—more hunting, more paperwork, more ... *nothing*—makes my heart race. The walls press in on me, and I search desperately for an escape. My fingers hover over the phone screen. The urge to text Killian and ask for some pixie essence is so strong. I stop myself, though. While the escape is exactly what I'm looking for, it's only temporary. And the effects have been making this sensation of stagnation worse. My hands tangled in purple hair, the contrast of dark skin against mine. It's unhealthy, and it needs to stop. The hallucinations are not worth it.

Hallucinations. My brain snags on that word.

Hallucinations ... that's it! I snatch my phone off the desk and send Killian a quick text. Maybe we can induce a vision using drugs! I pace the length of my office, not taking in the sights that have become just another shackle. It's starkly empty. I find no point in adding useless decorations. My desk is clear, except for a computer. Political and historical textbooks fill the shelves. Books I haven't opened since I graduated. The only bit of decoration is the tapestry. Dark blue with golden fringe and the Berkshire family crest stitched in golden thread. A diagonal line splits the shield, the top half a field of stars, the lower half a rearing lion holding a lit torch. The entire shield is wrapped in navy and golden leaves, with the words 'Veritas et Iustitia'. Truth and Justice. A reminder of the importance of my job. And my constant failure. Until now.

Killian pushes into the office and plops into the chair on the other side of the desk without any grace of his hunter nature. "You know, I'm all for this, but in the middle of the day?" He raises one dark brow, his light brown eyes searching mine. "And in liquid form? You're not getting addicted, are you?"

I sit in my chair and lean my elbows on the edge of the desk. "It's not for me. It's for the witch." I lean back and cross my arms over my chest with a smug grin. "We need her to have a vision, and drugs seem like the best way to induce one."

"You're going to drug a witch?" He stares at me incredulously. "Is that safe?"

"Probably not, but I'm running out of ideas. So far, it's been another massive failure." I run my hand through my hair, disrupting the blond strands. "I'm getting desperate, Killian."

He shrugs and reaches into his pocket, setting a syringe on my desk with a soft click, pale blue liquid shimmering inside. "Suit yourself. Just be careful, bro."

I text the lead guard on duty after Killian leaves and find out the witch is back in her room, so I make my way there. The needle is like a weight in my pocket. I'm not stupid enough to go into this without equalizer, so a second syringe rests in my other pocket. Can't be too careful with this. Giving a witch a hallucinogenic while she has access to her magic? This could backfire spectacularly.

I shove my way into her room and find the witch lounging in a chair by the cold hearth, her feet propped on the table in front of her, a book open on her lap. Her purple locks are swept to one side, and I bite back my grin. Perfect. Without giving her any time to react or move, I stick my hand in my pocket and uncap the syringe as I walk around behind her chair. In one swift movement, I pull out the needle and stick it in her neck, pressing on the plunger.

She hisses and jumps to her feet, whirling around with her hair flying behind her. "What the hell was that?" Righteous fury lights her eyes a second before her pupils dilate, darkening her already dark eyes. Her body relaxes and a small gasp escapes her lips. "What did you do?" Her words are low and quiet, throaty, with an undercurrent of need.

"I drugged you," I say simply, shrugging my shoulders. "Hopefully it induces a vision."

I can see her fighting against the high. She wants to be angry, but her body won't comply. She sways alarmingly, and I jump forward without thought, grabbing her hip to keep her upright. When she looks up at me through lidded eyes, I can't help but fall into their dark depths. They draw me in and drown me, and there is nothing I can do to fight it. If I didn't know any better, I'd assume I was the one who was drugged.

A soft gasp climbs up her throat, and she presses her body against mine. *Son of a bitch.* How could I forget about this side effect of essence? I try to step back, to pull away from the heat of her body, but I can't. Her gaze holds me captive. It's like a tether has formed between us, a current of electricity zapping back and forth. One of her hands comes up to rest on my chest and I swear it brands me through the fabric. I suck in a sharp breath when I realize my own hand has risen, without my consent, to rest on her slim neck, my thumb rubbing back and forth across her jaw.

My gaze drops to her mouth as her lips part slightly, and her chest rises and falls with her breathing. I need to pull away, but instead of listening to reason, I lean down at the same time she rises on her toes. Our mouths meet in a gentle press. When she sucks in a sharp breath, I deepen the kiss, the urge to taste her filling every part of me, driving me forward without any coherent thought. I brush my tongue against hers and she presses her body tighter to mine.

My free hand slides into her purple hair, and I groan as the silky strands slip through my fingers. This is better than any hallucination. She tastes like coffee and strawberries, and I need more. Her hands travel over my body, slipping under my shirt and tracing my skin, trailing shivers and sparks at the same time. Turning us, I walk her backward until the back of her legs hit the bed.

The witch is practically crawling up my body. Her soft curves are enticing, and I want to explore them all with my fingers and tongue. Stars burst in my vision when I rock my hips against hers, the movement subconscious. She pulls away and bites my bottom lip, hard enough to break skin. The sting shakes me out of the haze of lust. *What the fuck am I doing?* I pull back, gulping in huge lungfuls of air, hoping to clear my head, but all I can smell is her. Vanilla and chamomile.

Shaking my head, I get myself under control as much as I can. I need to get out of here. Untangling myself from the witch is proving difficult. Her hands are everywhere. In my hair, under my shirt, curling under the waistband of my pants. *Fuck.* I gently lay her back on the bed, hovering over her on my elbows. Because I'm weak—so fucking weak—I lower myself on top of her, just to know what she feels like underneath me.

Another groan slips up my throat, and I rock my hips again. *What would this feel like without any clothing between us?* She gasps, her body reacting and rubbing against mine. I take the opportunity to claim her mouth again, deep and leisurely. When I finally pull away, I'm gasping for breath. Her cheeks are flushed, and her eyes are heavy with desire. I press one last lingering kiss to her now swollen lips before slipping off the bed. Her dark eyes, pupils blown wide from drugs and desire, track over my body, snagging on my very obvious erection, and a slow smile spreads across her face. With every ounce of strength and self-control I possess, I wink at her and walk to the door. Before I leave, I turn back to see her rising on her elbows, chest heaving and brow furrowed in confusion.

"Sweet dreams, witch," I say, shutting the door behind me.

I really hope she does have dreams. That was the entire purpose of drugging her. Not that insanely hot make-out session. *Fuck.* Shoving my hands in my pockets, I adjust myself and head toward my room. The thoughts in my head make me scowl, and I notice a few servants eyeing me with trepidation and giving me a wide berth.

Why did I kiss her? She's a witch. It's like she put me under some spell, and I was powerless to fight against it. My body wanted hers, and just the memory of her hands on me, her body under mine, makes my blood simmer in my veins. And not only is she a witch, but I drugged her. She didn't even have control of her own body, and I took advantage of that. She never would have let that happen if she had been sober.

I stop abruptly in my tracks. What does it matter that she didn't consent to it? She's a fucking witch. Witches don't get that right. So why does it bother me so much that I took advantage of her?

Unsettled in every possible way, I push into my room. The grays and blues that usually calm me do nothing for my anxious thoughts. Walking through my sitting room, I ignore the stacks of books that need to be put back on the shelves and the discarded weapons that need to go back to the armory. It's a mess in here, but I refuse to let anyone in to clean it.

Closing the door to my bedroom behind me, I quickly kick off my boots and strip off my clothes, leaving them scattered on the floor with the rest of the dirty laundry. My phone beeps, and I groan as I fish it out of my pocket and silence it, not wanting to deal with anyone tonight.

The silk sheets brush against my overheated skin as I climb

into my bed, and I sigh at the sensation. I'm still sporting a raging hard on. Anytime it even starts to go away, my thoughts drift back to what just happened, and up it pops again. I rub my hand down my face, like I can rub away all the troubling thoughts floating in my brain and making me restless.

Too wired to sleep, but too exhausted to get back out of bed, I figure I have only one thing to do. Running my hand down my chest and slipping it under the covers, I take my hard length into my hand, squeezing just how I like it. Unbidden, the image of a purple-haired witch pops into my head, her mouth replacing my hand. I curse and let go of myself as if I were burned. Closing my eyes, I take a deep breath. It doesn't help. All I can picture is her. Her mouth around my cock. Her hair falling in a curtain around her head, tickling my thighs, as she bobs up and down. Her fingernails digging into the tops of my legs.

Fuck. My cock twitches, reminding me it's still there, and it wants attention. It's almost painful how badly I need release. Gritting my teeth, I take myself in my hand again, and this time, I don't fight it. I let the images flow through my head one after the other until my chest is heaving and pressure builds. I throw my head back as I come, hips bucking off the mattress, images of the witch in my mind.

I lay in my bed, heart racing, aftershocks of pleasure zinging through me. This is out of control. It's unhealthy how much my body is craving that witch. I have to do something about it, I just don't know what. We need to solve this mystery of the vision so I can send her to the stake before it's too late.

You Fucking Stabbed Me

THE IMAGE OF A CHURCH IS BURNED INTO MY MIND THE moment I wake. I groggily roll over and rub my face, wincing as my fingers find tangled strands of hair. *What the hell?* I feel like I've been steamrolled. *And why am I half naked?* My leggings and panties are gone, my shirt is half on and half off, and one breast is hanging out of my bra like it jumped ship during the night.

Thoughts come crashing into me so hard I gasp and sit up, covers sliding to the floor. Shoving my boob back into my bra, I growl. The bastard drugged me! He fucking drugged me, and I threw myself at him like a cat in heat. *Holy hell.* I kissed him. And he kissed me back! That sick mother fucker, drugging me and taking advantage of me.

I search the room and find my leggings in a pile on the bed, next to a knife. A sharp knife. I grin. Even high off my ass, I still had enough forethought to snag a dagger from his belt. The asshole was too preoccupied with shoving his tongue down my throat, he didn't notice. I chuckle darkly to myself as I slide out of bed and head for the bathroom.

Showered, dressed, and hair braided into messy pigtail buns, I finish putting on my armor—dark brown eyeshadow with a thick black winged eyeliner, enough mascara to plump and lengthen, and a medium pink lipstick with a shimmering finish. With the dagger in hand, I perch next to the door and wait.

I hear footsteps, then his voice as he says something to my guard outside the door. The guard that has doubled since he gave my magic back to me. That was a surprise. My magic flooding back through my veins, filling the hole in my chest, took my breath away. I've never not had access to it, and I'm not likely to forget the empty, cold pit inside me where my magic should have been. Now, it sits quietly, a warm ball of light softly glowing behind my ribs.

The doorknob turns, drawing my attention from my magic to the knife in my hand. As soon as the door closes behind him, I shove him against the wall and press the dagger to his neck. I must have taken him by surprise, because there is truly no way I could have managed that without the element of surprise. His eyes open wide and a small gasp slips past his lips. Lips I tasted last night. The edge of the knife braces against his neck, not hard enough to break the skin, but pretty damn close.

"Don't *ever* drug me again," I growl, shoving him harder.

He recovers, and a small smirk pulls up the corner of his mouth, that damn dimple appearing in his right cheek. "Are you flirting with me?" He raises one brow, his ocean blue eyes sparkling.

I press the knife harder, the barest increase in pressure, but the thinnest line of blood beads along the edge. "I'm not kidding, *prince*. If you drug me again, I will walk myself to the stake after I'm done with you."

The laughter leaves his eyes in one blink. He grabs my wrist and presses his thumb in just the right spot that my fingers spasm, and I drop the knife. He snags it from the air with his free hand and holds it up.

"Where did you get this?" he growls, tightening his grip on my wrist until I'm sure I'll have bruises tomorrow.

I gasp slightly at the pain. "Your belt. It's not my fault you were too distracted to notice last night." The venom dripping from my overly sweet tone makes him grind his teeth together.

He glances at the blade before shoving it into an empty holster around his thigh. Releasing my wrist with a shove that sends me tripping backward, he glares at me. "So, did it work?"

"Did what work?" I glare back at him, rubbing my wrist.

"The drugs? I drugged you to help induce a vision. Please tell me I didn't waste precious product on you." He flops into the chair he seems to have claimed as his.

I cross my arms over my chest and frown. "No, it didn't work. I passed out and only just woke up a little before you arrived."

"No dreams?" He frowns, running a hand through his blond hair.

"I don't drea ..." I trail off and scrunch my brows down. Tyberius sits up straighter in the chair. "I don't remember a dream, exactly. But when I woke up, there was an image in my mind."

He stands up so fast the chair scrapes against the floor with a screech. "What was it? Tell me *every* little detail." His hands clench and unclench, like he's trying to keep himself from grabbing my arms.

I shrug. "A church. Gray stone. Candles. It was kind of blurry. But it was definitely a church."

"That's it? That's all you can remember? There are tons of churches in the city. We need to narrow it down."

I close my eyes and try to recall the image. It's still there, but it's faint, and quickly fading. "Just lots of gray. Stained glass windows." I shake my head. "I can't make out anything distinguishable."

"Church. Gray. Stained glass windows," he repeats, thinking out loud. "We could hit up the older churches in the city. The ones made of stone rather than steel and glass." He pulls his lower lip between his teeth.

My focus drops to his mouth and I can't help but remember last night and what happened between us. Warmth grows in my stomach, and I rub my belly like I can make the sensation go away.

Tyberius nods and stands. "See?" he says with a grin. "Drugging worked."

I point a finger at him, and a thrill runs through me when he takes a cautious step back, eyes never leaving my outstretched finger. "Never. Again. I'm not playing. If you drug me again, I will unleash the force of the stars on you. Without hesitation."

He swallows and nods. "Duly noted. Now, let's go."

WE STAND OUTSIDE the church that claims to be the first church of Rossvale. I don't know if that's true, but it definitely looks old. Crumbling gray stone litters the ground where chunks have fallen from the walls. The stained glass windows are so dingy, I doubt any light can shine through.

"There is no way this building is still safe for people to enter. It should be condemned." I shove my hands into my pockets and wince as a particularly strong gust of icy wind whips down the street, stinging my exposed skin.

Tyberius shrugs and heads for the entrance. "I guess that's where faith comes in?" He pulls open the heavy wooden door and the rusty black hinges groan. Holding it open with his body, he looks at me. "You're not going to burst into flames or anything, are you?"

"You wish," I mutter.

With him standing in the doorway holding open the door, I have to walk past him to get inside the church. As I do, my shoulder brushes his chest, and my head snaps up. Our gazes lock, and for a moment it's as if time stops moving. His ocean blue eyes bore into mine, his energy radiating sex. The breath is sucked from my lungs and an electrical current passes between us, making my heart race. The moment lasts seconds, but it feels like it lasted hours.

Inside the dim church, I release a ragged breath. Fingers shaking slightly, I brush a stray strand of hair behind my ear. *Where the fuck does he get off sexily holding the door open like that?*

He clears his throat, and the door slams shut behind him, plunging us further into darkness. "Anything?" His voice is rough, and I shiver.

It's hard to focus on the reason we're here. I can't stop thinking about Tyberius and the way his looming presence makes me warm inside. But I force my gaze to take in the church. It doesn't look familiar. Besides the gray stones, nothing else is the same. The stained glass windows are different. I don't know how I know that, but they are. "Nothing stands out to me."

He sighs and turns back to the door. "On to the next, then."

By the time we reach the fourth church, Tyberius has long since lost his patience, and I'm not far behind him. "Anything?" he asks, waving his hand toward the interior of the church, his voice on the verge of yelling.

I look around, and my heart sinks. "Nothing."

"Fuck!" His booted foot connects with a wooden pew, and the entire bench scrapes across the floor from the force. He turns to me, brows lowered over his eyes and hands clenched at his sides. "Are you doing this on purpose? Do you want to burn?"

He stalks forward, and I take a step back. There is a wild light in his eyes, something I haven't seen before. He's gone beyond angry. In all of this, I've let myself forget who he is. While he hasn't hurt me, he is still a witch hunter. He will not hesitate to kill me. My back thumps against the stone wall, and I stare up at him.

"You're a fucking witch. A despicable creature that shouldn't exist. And I'm stuck parading around the entire city with you while you fuck around and waste my time." He doesn't yell, but his voice is rough with unchecked anger. "Don't forget it takes one fucking word from me and your skin will crisp and burn while I watch with delight." He plants his hands on the wall on either side of my head. Stepping closer, he growls, "Quit playing games, witch. You have one use in this world, and its figuring out this fucking vision. *Do. It.*"

That little bit of warmth I felt earlier at his closeness, turns to ice. A dagger through my heart would probably hurt less. I know what people think of witches. But the pure hatred and disgust in his voice, calling me a creature and saying I shouldn't exist, it fucking hurts. And the fact I let his words hurt me pisses me off. He's nothing. He doesn't mean anything to me. So why does it feel like a betrayal?

I stand on my tiptoes, bringing my face closer to his. Damn, he smells good, like cedar and lemon. He sucks in a sharp breath through his nose, nostrils flaring. With him distracted, I reach down and wrap my fingers around the hilt of the knife strapped to his thigh, the same one I stole last night.

"As you keep reminding me," I say, my voice low and seductive, "I'm a witch. I haven't forgotten, but it appears you have. So, I'll remind you." I lift up just a bit higher until my mouth hovers a breath away from his. All either of us has to do is move an inch, and our lips would meet.

His eyes darken and his breathing turns unsteady. I hate to admit it, but mine is just as uneven. The memory of those kisses last night is still front and center in my brain. And even as high as I was, they were good fucking kisses.

I dare to move the slightest bit closer and whisper, "I don't need this knife to hurt you. But the surprise in your eyes makes it more fun."

He blinks, and the haze of lust disappears, replaced by shock as I press the point of the blade against his thigh. A smug smile spreads across his face as he looks down. "Do it," he taunts.

I grin right back at him. "If you say so." The blade pierces through his pants and into the muscle of his thigh as I shove past the resistance with all my strength.

"Fuck!" he yells, pushing away from the wall. He clutches the dagger protruding from his leg and yanks it out. Blood seeps into his pants, glistening darkly against the black fabric. Red drops squeeze between his fingers as he puts pressure on the wound. He looks up at me from his slightly bent position, eyes glowing with anger. "You fucking stabbed me!"

I shrug. "You asked me to." And goddess above, it felt good to do it.

He growls and grabs my arm, pulling me out of the church. People stare as he drags me through the city. The prince—limping and bloodied—and a grinning witch are sure to draw attention. The entire trip, Tyberius spews curses at me, and I occasionally laugh at the creativity of some of them. It only pisses him off more.

When we get to my room in the palace, he throws me inside. "I'm too fucking furious to deal with you right now. Figure this vision shit out, before I decide you're not worth keeping around."

Before he can leave, I stop him. "So, what do I do for the rest of the day? Am I just supposed to stay cooped up in here like a prisoner? Going to the library might be helpful in finding information."

He turns around slowly to study me. "You are a prisoner. It would be best to not forget that." He frowns, then shakes his head. "As long as you don't ditch your guard or use your magic, you can go to the library. If you cause any trouble, you'll be confined to your room. And make sure you're back to your room before the sunsets."

Chills sweep over my skin, lifting the fine hairs on my arm. "Why? What's happening tonight?"

"What do you think?"

"A burning," I whisper.

He nods, staring at me like he can see through to the soul he probably thinks I don't possess.

"Who is it?" I'm finding it hard to draw in a breath. All this time I've been living in the palace and there are witches being hunted and burned. How could I let myself forget? Shame burns through me hotter than the fire will burn tonight. *It should be me up there.*

Tyberius shrugs nonchalantly. "I don't ask names. It's not part of my job." He turns and exits my room as quickly as he can with his limp, leaving me sick and unsteady on my feet.

I numbly walk to the chair and fall into it. Staring at the empty fireplace, I can easily imagine the flames licking the stone walls as the logs burn. It wouldn't take much for the fire to spread. A spark on the plush rug, fanned to life, would consume this entire room and its wooden furniture in seconds. It would consume me, just like a witch will be consumed tonight. I won't be there with her. Even standing in the back of the crowd, I was still there. It gave me comfort to know they didn't die alone, surrounded by people who hate them. I think I do it because I hope someone will do the same for me.

Having lost all desire to go to the library, I stay in my room staring at the empty fireplace and contemplating my life and how I got to where I am. In the palace, working for the enemy. *Kissing* the enemy. It's not okay. None of this is okay. I need to keep trying to escape.

THE WIND BITES into my skin, freezing me all the way to my bones, but I ignore it. I stand with my hands gripping the balcony railing, and I watch the smoke rise into the evening sky. The orange glow of the fire steadily grows as darkness falls. Flames lick up toward the wispy clouds, sparks and embers shooting off like so many fireflies.

A soft, warm body presses against my legs. *Who was it?* I ask numbly.

Abigail Williams.

I recognize the name, but I can't picture her face. That thought makes my heart race, and I wipe my sweaty palms on my pants. When I'm burned, who will recognize my name but not be able to recall my face? What if no one even recognizes my name? What if no one cares?

I shake myself, focusing on the fire blazing in the distance. The crowd in the square is large, as it always is when a witch burns. I know there are witch supporters out there, but they are so few and far between, they may as well not even care. They can't make a difference on their own. This fight of mine has never felt more impossible.

Who brought her in? I ask Jinx. Some part of me squeezing painfully at the thought of a certain possibility.

Killian Rothchild.

I don't know why I'm relieved to hear that, but the rush of tension leaving my body is undeniable. *It doesn't matter.* A witch is dead tonight, for no other reason than being born differently. I don't realize I'm crying until the chill wind freezes the wet tracks on my cheeks. Still, I stand at the railing until the last of the light fades from the fire.

Inside, I grab the blanket from my bed and sit in the chair. My limbs are stiff from the cold, and I contemplate the fireplace. A warm fire sure would feel good right now, but that will never happen. I'd rather freeze than sit before an open flame. Grabbing my journal, I open it to the most recent entry.

January 4. Eloise Matthews, 25. Burned alive. Prince Tyberius Berkshire.

I run my fingers over Eloise's name. My gaze lands on the name of the hunter responsible for her death. A wave of sickness washes through me. I can't forget what he really is. I can't let a pair of pretty eyes tempt me into thinking he is anything other than a murderer. Uncapping the pen, I write down the most recent victim.

January 7. Abigail Williams, 18. Burned alive. Killian Rothchild.

Still shivering, unable to get warm despite the plush blanket wrapped around my body, I can't stop staring at the journal. I'm ashamed of myself for not thinking about what was happening outside the palace since I've been locked away in here. I let myself be wooed with comfy beds, hot water, and confusing but distracting kisses. Just because I'm living in a cush cage, doesn't mean other witches aren't fighting for their lives. Hell, I should be fighting for my life. What happens to me after this is all over?

Escape is my only hope.

Take Your Hate, Fear, And Ignorance, And Go Fuck Yourself

I'M THANKFUL FOR THE TUNNEL THAT WAS BUILT ALL those years ago from the prison to the city center. Not only does it cut back on the amount of time to get back to the palace, but it's blessedly not windy. The winter wind cuts right through clothing, and my fucking balls are tucked so close to my body they might as well crawl inside.

In the palace, I part ways with Killian, intent on taking a long, hot shower. I'm not sure why my feet take me to the witch's room, but I find myself standing outside her door. The guards on duty look at me questionably, and I don't blame them. I'm wondering the same thing. *What am I doing here?*

I push open her door and pause at the threshold. She's asleep curled in the chair, a blanket wrapped around her and slipping down her shoulders. Her hair is still in two little buns on top of her head, ridiculous-looking, but endearing at the same time. It fits her. I step fully into her room and close the door behind me. I'm drawn to her, like a moth to a flame, my feet taking me closer and closer.

Tear tracks stain her cheeks, her makeup smeared and running down her face. I frown. *What could be the cause of that?* A little notebook sitting open precariously on her lap draws my attention away from her face. I snag it, careful not to jostle her, and scan the page. It's a list of names. Witches, I realize, with the date of their burning. And the name of the guard responsible for their death. I flip through the book. It's all the same. Name upon name of witches burned at the stake in Rossvale City. I turn to the very first name on the first page.

August 17. Althea Parker, 42. Burned alive. Edward Berkshire.

My gaze travels back to the sleeping witch. *Parker.* That has to have been her mom. I mentally calculate the dates and ages. She would have been seventeen years old when her mom burned at the stake. Looking back at the book, and the hunter responsible, my breath catches. *Edward Berkshire.* My uncle.

I let the pages of the book slip through my fingers as I fan them. Ten years' worth of burnings. There have to be almost one thousand names in this journal. For some reason, that realization sits heavy with me. My shoulders drop as I think about the sheer scale of it all. And this is only the names for Rossvale City. Every city in the country is doing the same thing.

How many witches have we burned since that first witch thousands of years ago?

I set the book on the table, but before I leave, my gaze snags on the witch again. She was clearly upset by the burning if the tear tracks through her makeup mean anything. My brow furrows. She cares about other witches. Enough to cry when one burns at the stake. An ugly emotion slithers through me as I realize something. Why wouldn't she care? Her words come back to me. *Ignorant.* Have I really been so ignorant to think witches don't have feelings?

Feelings are human emotions, though, and witches aren't human.

Confused. Disturbed. Uncomfortable. I shake myself and promptly pull my gaze away from her. I need to get out of here. I need to distract myself from this niggling in the back of my head. As soon as the door closes behind me, I text Killian. He'll be celebrating his success tonight. It sounds like exactly what I need.

THE NEXT MORNING, hung over and pissed at the world, I make my way to the witch's room. Killian plied me with so much alcohol and essence last night, I'm surprised I even woke up at all this morning. And when I did wake up, I wished I hadn't. Not only because of the incessant pounding in my head and the nausea rolling in my stomach, but the cringy things I did last night. I slept with at least three chicks—that I can remember—and all of them morphed into a purple-haired witch. Somehow, just the thought of those hallucinations makes my dick twitch. The stupid thing should've had its fill last night.

Even with the drugs, alcohol, and sex, my thoughts kept turning to the book I found in the witch's room, and the heaviness that settled in me at the sheer number of names. Every time I closed my eyes, her mascara-smeared face popped into my mind. Those thoughts were even more uncomfortable. And no matter how much I drank and fucked, they didn't go away.

Limping into her room, I find her sitting on her bed, staring at the pages of that damn book. When she sees me, she quickly shoves it under the covers. "You look like hell." She leans back against the headboard and crosses her arms over her chest. "Serves you right," she mutters. Her eyes are sad, missing the sparkle of sass and life they usually hold.

I grunt, but don't respond because I deserve it. I said some nasty things yesterday. The thing is, I wasn't mad at her. I was pissed at myself. By the time we reached the last church, I was actually enjoying myself. And when I realized that, it was like a bucket of ice water in my veins. Stupid fucking weak prince. That's all I am. I took my anger and self-hatred out on her, and she didn't deserve it. And soon as I thought that, I got even angrier. She's a fucking *witch*. Who cares if I yell at her and treat her like shit?

My head spasms painfully, and I cringe. Too many uncomfortable thoughts mixed with my hangover. "Get dressed," I say gruffly. "We're looking at more churches today."

"I woke up this morning with another picture in my head," she says quietly, fiddling with the edge of the blanket. "Seaside cliffs. They were whitish-gray, with green mossy grass on top and clinging to the sides. There was an arch branching off from the main cliffs with a spiky-looking rock formation next to it."

I stare with wide eyes, unable to believe what I'm hearing. "The Seaberth Cliffs. I'd know those anywhere. My uncle's family lives on those cliffs, and I visited many times growing up." I stop with a frown. "Why would you see an image of those cliffs, though? What do they have to do with the vision?"

She shrugs. "I don't make the rules."

"I have an idea. But I'll need to run it by my dad first." I study her for a moment before exhaling. "I think we need to go to Seaberth."

I leave the witch to get dressed and pack her meager belongings, while I limp through the palace to my dad's study. My leg aches where she stabbed me. My head fucking pounds. And my stomach is seconds away from revolting. What a fantastic morning.

I flinch as the door to my dad's office closes behind me. Rubbing my temples, I sit in the chair across from his desk, squinting against the harsh light coming in from the window behind his desk. This is quite possibly the worst hangover I've ever had.

"Tyberius," my dad says, his voice low and stern.

I groan and lean my head back against the chair, covering my eyes with my arm.

"Are you here to update me on the witch? Or are you just showing me how much of a disappointment you are?"

Fuck. "Both?" When he doesn't answer, I peek out from my arm and sigh, letting it fall to the armrest.

King Leander doesn't glare at me, he's far too poised for that, but the disappointment etched across his face is more poignant.

I attempt to straighten in my seat, but that only serves to make my stomach roll even more. Stifling a burp, I slouch back down. "I do have an update. And a request."

"Get on with it then. I have things to get done."

"The witch had a vision. Sort of."

"What do you mean 'sort of'?" He glances at me before turning his attention back to his desk.

"Well, it was more of a picture than a vision. But it was the Seaberth Cliffs."

His head pops up at that. "Why would she see the cliffs?"

I shake my head and instantly regret it as bile climbs up my throat. "I have no idea. But that is where my request comes in. I would like permission to take her to Seaberth. My thought is if she's there, maybe it will spark more visions."

My dad's lips purse as he thinks through my request. It's a massive risk. I get that, but I'm at a loss for what else to do. I find myself holding my breath. If he approves this, it will give me the chance to prove to him I'm not a complete failure.

Eventually, he nods. "Take Killian and enough guards to ensure she doesn't escape."

I exhale and push up from the chair. "I will. Thank you."

"When do you plan on leaving?" His attention has already returned to his work.

"This afternoon. I was going to take the jet."

"I'll let your uncle know you'll be coming. It would be best to keep the witch out of his house, though."

I nod, already having thought of that myself. My uncle's name in her book next to her mother's does not bode well. "She'll stay at a hotel under guard."

"Good," he says. And before I can leave, he throws in

offhandedly, "Take your brother, too. It will be good practice for him."

I stop in my tracks, hand outstretched for the doorknob. "Are you sure tha—"

"No arguments, or you won't go at all."

I recognize that tone. There will be no arguing with him. Sighing, I nod and leave the office. I quickly pull out my phone and send off some texts before heading to my room to pack. Knowing my uncle, he'll throw some kind of grand dinner or something, so I pack a tux just in case.

With my bag packed and thrown over my shoulder, I limp my way through the palace to the witch's room. Without knocking, I open the door and drop my bag on the floor just inside. "Let's go. We're leaving."

She pops her head out from the bathroom, makeup on only half of her face. Without saying anything, she retreats back inside, and for some reason, that grates on me. No greeting or acknowledgement of my presence. I stand by the door with my arms crossed over my chest and tap my foot on the floor.

When she finally emerges, my mouth dries. She's wearing the tightest black jeans I've ever seen. They accentuate her curves perfectly. A cream sweater hangs off of one shoulder, and her purple hair hangs loose in shiny waves.

Clearing my throat, I shift on my feet. "We're leaving in five minutes, and I need to check your bag before we go."

She raises one brow. "What do you think I could possibly pack? The only things in my possession are what I brought from my apartment, and you watched me pack that up."

"You had a knife yesterday." My leg aches just thinking about it, and I rub it absentmindedly.

"Fair point. But whose fault was that? You should be more careful with your weapons in the future."

I grunt and step closer to her. "Just give me your damn bag so we can leave."

She huffs, but follows my command. It doesn't take us long to reach the private hanger behind the palace. Luckily, everyone else is already waiting. I give Killian a questioning look, and he pats the small bag at his side and nods his head. Good. He has plenty of equalizer, just in case. Along with the five other guards, we should be good. Despite all the planning, nerves twist my insides. A lot could go wrong on this trip.

Julian is standing with his own personal bodyguard off to the side. I don't even bother to look at him. I know he's dressed to the nines and as pompous as ever. Instead, I grab the witch's bag and hand both hers and mine off to the guy loading the cargo.

"Let's go," I say, loud enough for everyone to hear. Pushing the witch in front of me, I prod her onto the plane.

Our private jet features an entryway with a marble floor, complete with a mosaic of the family crest. Through a sliding door is the main common room. Decked out in creams, dark blues, and golds, this space boasts plush leather seating lining both sides of the plane facing inward toward four separate glass coffee tables. A bedroom and bathroom lay beyond the common room, just as luxurious as the rest of the plane.

The witch stumbles as she walks through the sliding doors and into the common room. "Holy shit," she mutters. "This is a plane?"

I prod her into a seat in the back corner closest to the bedroom and return to the front to take my seat. Killian sits next to me while the other guards sit across from us. Of course, Julian claims the seat on the other side of Killian, and I groan. This is going to be a long fucking six hours if I'm stuck with him the entire time.

It takes another thirty minutes for everything to be organized before we finally take off. I make idle chit chat with Killian, doing my best to ignore my brother. But I can't stop my gaze from traveling to the witch at the back of the plane.

She's sitting on her knees, turned to the side so she can look out the window behind her. There is something about her expression that pulls me to her. And before I know it, I'm standing and walking back to sit next to her. She stares at me expectantly, like she's waiting for me to say something, and I realize I have no reason for being back here. I can sense everyone's eyes on me, as they no doubt wonder what I am doing. *Join the fucking club.*

"Have you ever been on a plane before?" I ask quietly, hoping to keep this conversation from traveling.

Her eyes widen briefly, no doubt surprised by my choice of small talk. "No. I've never had enough money to go anywhere else."

I sit next to her, but make sure to leave a decent amount of space between us. Even then, it's like I can sense the heat from her body, calling to me, enticing me. "Do you ... do you have a job?" I stutter over the question, unsure why I care about what she does in her free time. Not that it matters. When this is over, she has to go to the stakes. I shrug off that thought, suddenly not wanting to think about it.

"I'm a dog walker. It's not much, but considering I don't have any formal education and being around people is dangerous, I opted for a simple job."

Surprised, I ask, "You didn't go to school?"

She huffs a laugh. "Most witches don't. We're usually homeschooled by our mothers. It's safer. Especially when we're young and just learning our magic. Random outbursts aren't uncommon, and it would be a death sentence to lose control of our magic in school."

"I was homeschooled as well. For the first twelve years, at least. Then I went to university." *Why am I telling her this?* My mouth keeps moving, even as my brain yells at me to shut up. "The first portion of my schooling consisted of politics, history, and how to rule a kingdom. At least until my tutors finally realized I would make a shit king. Eventually, my training moved toward the physical and the witch hunting side of things."

"What did you study at university?" she asks, a curious light in her dark brown eyes.

I rub the back of my neck, suddenly embarrassed by this conversation. "Music," I mumble.

Her mouth drops open before she snaps it closed. "Music? Do you play an instrument?"

"Piano," I say quietly. It was one of the few lessons I actually enjoyed as a kid, and the enjoyment stuck with me. Now, it's one of my favorite ways to escape. Well, that and booze. And sex. I shake that thought away as it conjures images of my hands tangled in amethyst hair.

The witch's gaze drops to my lap, where my fingers tap a restless rhythm. Her brow furrows, like she's trying to imagine them flying over the black and white keys instead of tying a rope around the stake.

"I saw your journal," I blurt stupidly, wanting to take the attention off of me.

Her head snaps up. She gasps and places a hand on her chest. "You ... what?"

"Was Althea Parker your mom?"

She jerks backward, eyes round and wide. "You went through my journal?" she whispers.

"It was open. I just so happened to glance at it."

"Just so happened to glance at a page that was all the way in the front of it? Or do you have x-ray vision?"

"Was Althea Parker your mom?" I ask again.

She nods stiffly. "Yes."

"And the names of the hunters in each entry. They are the ones who carried out the burning?"

She nods again, eyes never leaving mine. An inner fire comes to life in their dark depths, proving to me just how strong this witch really is. Rather than cower in fear, she clothes herself in steel and determination.

"I noticed a few of the names had check marks next to them. I also realized those hunters have mysteriously been found dead."

She doesn't so much as blink. "And your point?"

"You killed them, didn't you? And you plan on killing the rest of them, too." She says nothing, but a slight twitch in her right eye gives her away. "My name is on that list. Multiple times. Did you plan on killing me?"

A muscle ticks in her jaw as she grinds her teeth together. "What does it matter? I'm going to be burned when this is all over, anyway." She looks back out the window, an expression of sadness washing over her features that makes me rub my chest.

"You know, those hunters were innocent men. They had families and friends. You took them away from their loved ones." My voice is gruff for reasons I don't want to think about too much.

She whips her head back toward me. "Are you serious?" A slight blush creeps into her cheeks, and I have a feeling it's anger instead of embarrassment. "Innocent men? They murdered innocent women. Women who had families and friends. They took them away from their loved ones." She spits my words back at me.

I scoff. "But they're witches."

"Killian is your friend, right? You care about him?" she asks with acid dripping from each word. I nod my head. "He's *innocent,* correct?" I nod again. "How would you feel if I killed him? For no other reason than I didn't like him. Simply because he's different and I don't understand his way of living. Because I'm *scared* of someone who is different from me. How would you feel?"

I don't answer her, because just the thought of losing Killian is like a knife in my gut. He's been by my side since we were toddlers. No one knows more about me than him. I trust him more than anyone else in this world. Losing him would be crippling.

She smiles, but it's not a pleasant smile. "That is how I feel. Every single time a witch is burned. One of my sister's lives is snuffed out for no other reason than hatred and fear. I watched my mom burn alive." Tears make her voice thick, and she angrily wipes them away. "I watched the person I loved most in the world *burn alive.* She never harmed a single person. Never once raised her hand or magic against another living soul. But she was murdered for no reason." The witch raises her chin stubbornly. "When you can say you've watched countless innocent people—people you care about—be murdered in cold blood, then you may judge me. Until then, kindly take your hate, fear, and ignorance, and go fuck yourself."

Such A Pleasant Asshole

I'VE NEVER BEEN TO SEABERTH. ACTUALLY, I'VE NEVER left Rossvale City. I've seen pictures of the coastal town, but I have to admit, they don't do it justice. Seaberth is built along a U-shaped cliff surrounding the bay. One side of the cliff is impenetrable grayish-white stone. The arch branching off the main cliff is massive looking at it in person, and I'm all the way across the bay from it.

The other side of the cliff is carved into switchback roads lined with white houses topped with roofs of every color. The cobblestone streets are narrow, and most people walk, ride bikes, or drive small motorized vehicles—like mopeds and scooters. Little shops, interspersed between the homes, welcome guests with colorful awnings hanging out over the cobbles. Potted plants with fairy lights decorate cafes and restaurants, and lanterns hang from posts at set intervals. The streets of Seaberth must glow romantically in soft golden light at night.

The temperature is blessedly warmer. Winter along the coast is still cold, but it's definitely not freezing. A cool breeze blows in off the ocean, whipping my hair around my head. I desperately want to walk along the beach, feel the sand squish between my toes and the water lap against my ankles. *I wonder if I'd be allowed to visit?*

Tyberius leads us through the streets to a little inn with an orange roof. "Killian, you and the guards have rooms here, along with the witch. I'm going to go meet with my uncle. I'll check in when I'm done." He turns to his brother. "Julian, you're coming with me." He sounds resigned as he turns on his heel and continues further down the sloped street.

Killian grabs my arm and pushes me through the door. A bell tinkles above my head, and I scan my surroundings taking in the sights. The smooth wooden floor gleams in the lamplight. Flowering plants sit in the corners, their aromas enticing and fresh.

Killian leads me to the desk in the middle of the room, and the tan-skinned woman standing behind it. "Hello," he says with a bright smile. It's the first time I've ever seen him smile outside of a burning. "I believe we have some rooms set aside. Under the name Berkshire."

The woman nods and scans her computer, before handing Killian some old-fashioned-looking keys. "You have rooms six, seven, eight, and nine. They are on the second floor. Everything you need should be in your rooms, but if you find there is anything missing, please call the front desk." She tucks a blond lock of hair behind her ear and smiles at Killian.

He winks at her before yanking me toward the stairs in the back. A raised section of the floor catches my boot and I trip. Killian tightens his grip on my arm, pulling me upright. I wince at the squeezing pain. At this rate, I'll have bruises on my bicep by morning. I guess I got used to being treated less like a plague when Tyberius escorted me around the palace. It makes me realize how gentle the prince really was with me. Shuddering, I push that thought to recesses of my brain.

Upstairs, the dark green rug on the floor cushions my boots. Killian stops in front of a robin's egg blue door set into the white wall, a brass number seven hanging in the middle. With the keys, he unlocks the door and shoves me inside, closing and locking it behind me. Effectively caging me inside.

"Such a pleasant asshole," I mutter as I look around the room. At least I'll have the space to myself.

As with the rest of the inn, the pale wooden floors gleam and the white walls shine brightly. A light yellow rug takes up most of the space and is soft and welcoming. And a queen-size bed with a pale green comforter juts out into the middle of the room, with a small wooden dresser against the opposite wall. The attached bathroom contains a simple sink, toilet, and shower. All in all, it's a pleasant room. Nicer than my apartment, but not as nice as the palace.

My stomach growls, and I sit on the edge of the bed, staring at the door. It's still locked, and even if it wasn't, I'm sure there is someone standing guard outside. I push off the bed and head to the window, swiping aside the yellow curtains. The view steals my breath. The bay stretches before me, with the white cliffs of Seaberth and the arch just across the way.

The rest of the city slopes down below my window, jewel toned rooftops catching my eye. Just below my room is the overhang to the entrance of the inn. I see no guard outside. *Could they have forgotten to post one below my window?* I smile at the possibility.

Returning to the bed, I lay back and try to not think about how hungry I am. I should have packed some kind of snack. Knowing Killian, he'll probably let me starve. I never thought I'd wish for Tyberius to return so quickly, but at least I know he'll make sure I have food, even if he grumbles about it.

I don't know how much time passes. There are no clocks in this room, but I'm guessing a couple of hours have slipped by. The sun is sinking toward the horizon, painting the sky with beautiful streaks of orange, pink, and purple. I'm standing in front of the window, watching the colors reflect off the water, when the lock turns in my door. I spin around to find Tyberius entering with a bag of takeout.

My mouth waters as the smell of meats and spices travel to my nose. "Please say that food is for me," I say with my hand covering my rumbling belly.

"It is." He sits on the edge of my bed and holds out the bag.

I snag the food from his hand as I climb onto the bed and dig in. A thick doughy wrap holds spiced meat and an interesting-tasting sauce. I don't really care what it is. I'm hungry enough to eat roadkill at this point.

Since the plane ride, and the incredibly strange conversation he and I had, something in me has thawed. He didn't have to come sit with me on the plane. Even if he wanted to accuse me of murdering those guards, he didn't have to make the small talk first. I feel like I was just given a small glimpse into the real Tyberius. The one most people never see. Because of that, I ask, "How did your meeting with your uncle go?" I try my best to keep my emotions from my face. His uncle is on my kill list, and I plan on trying my hardest to take care of that while I'm here.

Tyberius sighs and rubs a hand over his face. Resting his elbows on his knees, he hangs his head down. "It was fine. Political, as always. He's hosting a masked ball in honor of mine and my brother's visit."

"You sound thrilled," I say drily.

"I fucking hate these kinds of events. It's all politics and gossiping women clambering for attention."

"Oh, yeah. That sounds like something you would absolutely hate. The attention of willing women." I snort and take another bite.

He glances at me from the corner of his eye, a small smile playing about his lips. "It's the kind of women giving the attention that bothers me."

"Ah, right," I drawl. "You prefer the unnamed whores from the bars." I'm taken aback by the tinge of bitterness in my voice. I quickly swallow it down, hoping he didn't pick up on it.

His smile slips, and he pushes to his feet. "Yeah, well."

Before he can head toward the door, I stop him. "When is the ball?" I don't want him to leave my room with that sadness darkening his eyes.

"It's tomorrow night." He reaches for the door handle, but I stop him again.

"Do you think I could visit the beach tomorrow?" I ask tentatively. "With an escort, obviously. But I've never been to one, and I'd love to see it up close, just once before ... before I die."

He doesn't turn around, but he sucks in a sharp breath and nods. "I planned on walking through the city with you. We need to induce a vision. I was hoping something in the city would spark one. We can stop at the beach while we're out."

He leaves after those words, sounding so incredibly sad. Shaking myself, I change for bed and slip under the covers, excited about tomorrow and finally seeing a different city.

THE CITY WAS FASCINATING. And I loved every second walking through the cobblestone streets. The colorful sights, the scents and sounds, were all so different from Rossvale City. Even the city square and stone platform where burnings take place couldn't keep me down for long. But, it's the ocean that steals my breath.

The salty sea breeze tugs free strands of my hair from the braid I put it in this morning and wipes away the heavy thoughts that always sit upon my shoulders. Here, with my feet in the sand, and the waves lapping against my ankles, I can easily forget that I'm a prisoner and my sisters are being hunted to extinction.

I sit in the sand, dragging my fingers through the gritty substance. The waves crash on the shore, almost reaching my ass, but I don't care as it laps over my feet and exposed calves from my rolled jeans. I tip my head back and let the sun bathe me in its warmth as it tries to fight off the winter chill blowing in from the sea.

"You've really never seen the ocean before?"

I jump, having completely forgotten Tyberius was with me. Shaking my head, I turn my attention to ocean stretching as far as the eye can see. "I've seen pictures, but never in person."

"Pictures don't do it justice, do they?" He sits next to me, his bare feet digging into the sand.

"No," I whisper. I wish my mom could have seen it. She would have loved the ocean. I don't think a day went by that she didn't curse the city and tall buildings that blocked out the sun. I sense Tyberius looking at me, and I turn to find him staring with a frown and crease between his eyes. Eyes that match the ocean before me. "What?" I ask.

He shakes his head, but the frown deepens. "Nothing." After a moment, he chuckles to himself. "Actually, that's a lie. I have a question for you."

I tense. Who the hell knows what he's going to ask. "Shoot."

"The other day, you mentioned using symbols was an old practice. What does that mean? How does magic work, exactly?"

I whip my head in his direction, sure I'll find some kind of sarcastic smile on his face, but all I see is earnest curiosity. *Does the witch hunter really want to learn about magic?* I take my time thinking through my answer. I may never have another opportunity to show him we're not evil. "Hundreds of years ago, witches had affinities, and we would be categorized into a certain type of witch. There were so many different types. Green, gray, hedge, kitchen, plant, lunar, chaos. Just to name a few. Each type of witch used a different kind of magic, in a way. Runes and symbols were specialized, and that skill passed down from generation to generation."

"What happened?" Tyberius asks, leaning back on his hands and looking out over the water.

I dig my feet further into the sand. "We've been hunted so much we've lost much of who we once were." I sense him turning to look at me, but I keep my gaze straight forward. "We haven't had the opportunity to pass knowledge down. We don't have grandmothers, we don't live long enough to watch our daughters become mothers. Mothers don't have enough time to teach their children basic magic, along with the intricacies of specialized magic. All of this while also keeping us safe from a world that wants nothing more than to kill us.

"We used to be able to use magic in two different ways. Now, our only option is harnessing the magic living things offer. All living things contain magic, but by using it, we take the life from it. It's not ideal, and none of us like to do that, but it's the only choice we have now."

"What is the other option?" he prods.

"Ley lines. But the more witches we lose, the more we lose that magic. Each death of a witch causes those ley lines to dry up a little more. Hundreds of years ago, we were more powerful than we are now. Now, all witches have the same powers. No more affinities. Despite some of us being able to sense something different within us, something that may speak to an affinity we could have possessed, we're all the same."

He's quiet for a moment, taking in everything I said. "Do you know what your affinity would have been?"

I nod. "Yeah. I think I would have been a lunar witch." I don't want him to ask me how I know that. It feels too personal. But the night sky has always been a balm to my soul and my magic has always been stronger during the full moon.

Thankfully, he doesn't ask. Silence falls between us, and when he turns back to the ocean, I take the opportunity to study his profile. The strong jaw and sculpted cheeks. Lips I've tasted and know just how kissable they are. The wind tousles his blond hair, and something in me wants to run my fingers through the strands to put them back in place.

No, you don't. He's a witch hunter, Neave. He hunts and kills your sisters. He still plans on killing you! I close my eyes, the moment of tranquility crashing down around me. Hopping to my feet, I brush off the sand clinging to my jeans. "I guess we should get back," I say quietly.

His frown returns, but he stands as well, picking up both of our boots from the sand. "No luck with the visions?"

I shake my head and grab my boots, cleaning off my feet as best I can before slipping them on.

We're quiet as we make our way back up the gentle incline. The colors of the city look duller to me. They don't light the same spark of excitement they did on the way here. The entire reason for this visit was to inspire some visions. But so far, nothing. *No, that's not true.* My ultimate reason for visiting was to get to Edward Berkshire. The man who burned my mother.

The best way to do that will be during the ball. Tyberius mentioned it was a masked ball, so I could easily hide my identity. Well, except for the purple hair. But I don't have a dress. We've passed several clothing stores, some of them displaying beautiful ball gowns, but I also don't have any money. *How can I get a ball gown without paying for it?*

Tyberius leaves me in my room, and I close the door behind me. I go straight to the window and peek out. There were no guards there when we walked in, and I don't see one there now. If I'm going to do this, I have to do it now.

Sliding the window open, I climb out and twist my body so I'm hanging by my fingers. I gather magic from some moss clinging to the side of the inn, and when I let go of the sill, I clench my fingers and bring forth a wind that lowers me softly to the canopy below my window. The street below the canopy is empty when I crouch down and peer under it. Perfect.

I jump down and hurry from the inn, heading toward the area of the city where Tyberius said his uncle's estate was. If I want this plan to work, a clothing shop closest to the estate will be my best bet. The streets are filled with people going about their business, and I can't help but watch them. *What would it be like to be so free? To walk the streets and not fear being caught?*

What are you doing?

I jump as Jinx's voice echoes in my head. I was so distracted I didn't even notice him sitting right outside the dress shop. *Getting a dress. What are you doing?*

A dress? Have you ever worn a dress in your life?

I'm going to a ball tonight. I need a ballgown. And why the fuck do you care? I take a step forward, intent to get inside the shop and away from him, but he stops me.

You need to be careful going to the palace. If Edward recognizes you, you'll never be free of him. He won't make the same mistake twice.

I pause. *What are you talking about?*

Jinx shakes his head, his tail flicking in agitation. *Just be careful, Neave.*

I roll my eyes and step around him, slipping inside the dress shop.

"Hello," a dark-haired woman chimes. "How can I help you?"

Taking a deep breath, I compose myself. "Hi. I'm looking for a ballgown, for the masked ball tomorrow night."

She hums in her throat. "Leave it to Edward Berkshire to plan a ball on such short notice. We've been swamped with women trying to find dresses that don't have to be altered."

I smile. "Men just don't understand, do they?"

She snorts. "They have not a single coherent thought in those tiny brains of theirs. Come, let's see what we can find you. I'm Maria, by the way." She takes my measurements and studies me for a moment. "With your complexion and that gorgeous purple in your hair, I think black will be the perfect color. Is there a particular style you're going for?"

"Oh, I haven't really thought about that too much. Something ... distracting." The more I can intrigue people, the more likely I am to get to my target.

Maria disappears between racks of dresses and comes back with a few slung over her arm. "I have distracting right here." She grins and ushers me into a dressing room.

I try one on, a slinky black thing that leaves nothing to the imagination. While it is distracting, it doesn't scream royalty. And if I'm going to get the bill sent to Tyberius, I need it to scream royal. It's the second dress I try on that makes my heart thunder in my chest. When I step out of the dressing room, Maria smiles.

"That's the one," she says.

Glancing in the mirror, I grin. "Yes, it most certainly is."

Do You Want To Dance?

I told the witch to meet me outside the inn so we could walk through the city again before the ball. I'm not sure what else to do, except drug her, and I really don't want to do that again. As I wait, something rubs against my legs and I look down to find a beautiful white cat staring at me with the most stunning blue eyes.

"Hey there." I bend down to rub between its ears, and it lifts up on its hind legs to bump its head against my hand. "You're a friendly little guy, aren't you?" I scoop the cat into my arms and it practically melts into my touch. A soft purr rumbles from its small chest. I rub the gray ears, and its gray tail flicks lazily.

"What are you doing?" The witch's voice is strangled and high pitched, and she's staring at me in revulsion. No, not me. The cat in my arms.

"I found it. Isn't it pretty?" I hold my arms out, offering her a chance to pet the cat.

She recoils and her lip curls. "Put that down. It's not a cat."

I frown. "Um, yeah. I'm pretty sure it is. I mean I'm not an animal expert, but cat was one of the first animals I learned as a kid. C for cat. Cat says meow."

She points a finger at the creature in my arms. "That's my familiar."

"What the fuck?" I drop the cat ... familiar ... and it yowls with displeasure before hissing at me and marching away down the street.

"Yeah, serves you right, bastard."

It takes me a moment to realize she's talking to the cat and not me. Shuddering and brushing stray cat hair from my clothing, I look at her. "Aren't witches supposed to like their familiars?"

"Most witches don't get stuck with mouthy, obnoxious familiars like I did. Jinx saw you approaching me in the alley that night you caught me. He chose not to say anything because I kicked him out of my bed the night before. He's a spiteful prick. All cats are." She huffs and brushes her hair over her shoulder. "I've been trying to get rid of him since he appeared on my doorstep when I turned sixteen. I've had zero luck."

I find myself fighting a smile. It doesn't surprise me to hear she had been stuck with a familiar she hates. It seems fitting that this sassy, purple-haired witch gets a familiar just as sassy as she is. Speaking of purple hair, I glance at her roots. She wouldn't have had the opportunity to dye it recently, but I see no sign of her needing to touch it up.

"Your hair is naturally purple, isn't it?" I ask her as I take off down the street.

She looks at me from the corner of her eye. "Yes, it is."

"Huh. How did you end up with purple hair?"

She shrugs. "No idea. My best guess was the universe wanted to play some kind of cosmic joke on me. Make me a witch, then give me hair that makes it impossible to hide."

"You could always dye it," I suggest.

"Yeah, I know. But I kind of like it. It's unique."

It most certainly is unique. Just like her.

We spend the first half of the day walking the city. I point out interesting bits of architecture and give her little history lessons of Seaberth. It's so easy to talk to her, and the conversation between us is completely natural. I find myself telling her stories of my times visiting this place in the summer with my brother and Killian—before my brother turned into the priss he is now. When she laughs at one of my stories about the trouble we got into, something in my chest tightens.

I'm in serious trouble. We really need to figure out this vision so I can be done with her. Before I do something truly stupid.

At one point in our venture, she stops in front of an old church. It's the only building in the city without a colorful roof. Ancient stone makes up the structure built into the cliff side, aged and graying with moss and vines covering the facade. She stares at it with a furrowed brow.

My gaze travels from her to the church and back to her again. "Are you okay?"

Slowly, she shakes her head as if coming out of a fog. "Yeah. It just ... I just ..."

I step toward her and place my hand on her shoulder. Instantly, warmth blooms under my palm and travels up my arm. I drop my hand like I was burned. "Is it a vision?" I can't keep the excitement from my voice.

She shakes her head again. "No, I'm getting some serious deja-vu vibes." She pulls her gaze away from the church like it takes a tremendous effort to do so. "Do you think this could be the church I saw in my first vision?"

"I think that's possible. It's definitely an old church. Lots of gray." Checking my watch, I sigh. "We need to head back, though. I have to get ready for this ball. We can check out the church tomorrow."

She nods and follows me back up the sloped street to our inn. We part ways, and I don't even think about locking her door. The past two days have been incredibly weird and have left me off kilter. If I didn't know any better, I'd say some of the animosity between me and the witch has dissipated. We've had conversations, shared pieces of ourselves, and spent time together without fighting or spitting insults back and forth.

It's been almost ... normal. If I hadn't known she was a witch, I would never have guessed it. But I can't let myself forget that she is. That's the allure of a witch, isn't it? To make me drop my guard so she can curse me or slip a knife between my ribs. I shake my head as I get ready. That doesn't seem like something she would do, though.

Fuck me. I'm already under her spell. I need to figure out how to get myself free of her. And fast.

I'M SUFFOCATING. This mask is itchy, and the collar of my shirt is too tight. Tugging at the bowtie, I look around the ballroom. It's hotter than Satan's ball sack in here and sweat is already dripping down my back. A server passes with a tray of champagne flutes, and I snag one, downing it in one gulp. I grimace. I fucking hate champagne. Searching the sides of the ballroom while I fiddle with the black leather mask again, I look for something stronger. I'm going to need something much stronger than champagne to get through the night.

"Quit tugging at your collar. And leave your mask alone."

I cringe. "Go away, Julian." I pull sharply on the neck of my shirt, just for emphasis.

"You may not end up king, but you're still a prince and we have a reputation to uphold."

I turn to my little brother and smirk. He's wearing Berkshire colors, with a dark blue mask adorned with golden thread. Stubble graces his cheeks and chin. "Are you trying to grow a beard?"

He rubs his chin and a faint blush creeps up his neck. "You better behave tonight. I'm reporting back to Dad everything that happens."

I roll my eyes and turn away. "Nobody likes a rat, Julian." Not able to handle the choking any more, I undo the bowtie and unbutton the top three buttons of my shirt and sigh. It's better than nothing. But this mask will be the death of me.

A chorus of giggles draws my attention away from my annoying brother. *Great.* The simpering has already begun. The ball has only been underway for an hour, but the room is packed with the rich and elite of Seaberth. Men talk politics and sports. Women talk ... well whatever they talk about. Clothes? Makeup? Glancing at the group of women eyeing me, I'm assuming they also talk about men.

One of them breaks away from the group—a raven haired woman wearing a blood red dress and mask. Her eyes glitter as she approaches me.

"What is *she* doing here?" Julian stiffens next to me and hisses.

I turn my head, and the entire world disappears. Descending the stairs into the ball is a vision. She's wearing a black dress, like something a dark queen would wear, and the sight of her dries my mouth. As she takes a step down, the full skirts split, revealing an almost thigh-high slit that shows off an indecent amount of dark skin. Two pleated panels connect the waist of the skirts to the halter around her neck. More delicious dark skin and a tantalizing tease of her breasts are on display between the two panels of the top. She's swept her amethyst hair up on her head, with curls cascading around her face. A black lace mask that covers just her eyes tops off the ensemble. But I'd know her anywhere. Even without the purple hair.

Before I know what I'm doing, I'm brushing off the black-haired woman trying to ask me to dance, and the next thing I know, I'm standing at the bottom of the steps. My heart races as I watch her descend, like something from my dreams.

"You look ..." Somehow, I get my tongue under control before I blurt something I shouldn't. Remembering my place, I say, "What are you doing here?" My voice is gruff, and I have to clear my throat.

She smiles at me, a wicked smile. "It didn't seem fair for you to have all the fun."

"Do you want to dance?" I ask before I can stop myself.

Her smile disappears, replaced by a frown. "I don't think that's appropriate."

"Fuck propriety," I mutter and grab her hand. I tug her to the dance floor and pull her in close. The back of her dress is completely open, and my hand lands on warm skin, sending a thrill through my body. "Just one dance," I whisper in her ear.

She shivers, but she places her hands on my chest, slowly sliding them up and around my neck. This is by far the most inappropriate thing I have ever done. Not only am I dancing with a witch, I'm dancing like a commoner. My father would have a stroke if he saw this. I slide my hand up her bare back, her skin smooth under my fingers, and rest my palm on the nape of her neck. My other hand presses into her lower back, pulling her closer to me. I bend down slightly, my nose just brushing the top of her hair, and I inhale. She smells like vanilla and chamomile.

Closing my eyes, I sway us back and forth to the music. I soak in the way she fits in my arms perfectly, her head resting on my shoulder. Her fingers brush the nape of my neck, and fire ignites in my bloodstream. It's just the two of us. In a ballroom surrounded by hundreds of people, we are the only ones who exist.

"Where did you get this dress?" I ask her, my thumb rubbing back and forth against the skin of her neck.

"You bought it for me." I can hear the smile in her voice and I pull away to look at her. "I had the bill sent to you," she clarifies.

"You snuck out?" I try to make my tone disapproving, but I can't stop the chuckle from escaping. It was well worth whatever it cost. She's fucking beautiful. I pull her in again, pressing her head back to my shoulder.

"What are we doing?" she whispers.

I grin. "Dancing."

She smacks the back of my head, and I can almost feel her roll her eyes. "No shit, blondie. But we're ... us."

"Us?" I muse, contemplating her statement. The idea of an *us* is not one I can let myself wonder about for too long.

"A witch and a witch hunter." She pulls away to look up at me. Her dark brown eyes draw me in, and the sadness swimming in their depths makes my chest ache.. "When this is over, I'll still be a witch. You'll still hunt my kind. I'll still end up at the stakes."

I open my mouth to say something—what I'm not sure—but she steps out of my arms before I can do so.

"This is a bad idea," she says, her chest rising and falling rapidly, then turns and walks into the crowd. I distantly notice the tattoo of the phases of the moon on her back, but inside I'm reeling. Her quick disappearance has left me cold and empty.

I need a fucking drink. After making a circuit around the ballroom, the *only* alcohol being served is champagne. I should have brought a flask. I grab two champagne flutes, and down them one after the other, then snag two more. Grimacing, I wipe my mouth on my sleeve and look around the room. I can't see her anywhere. But the black-haired girl in the red dress is walking toward me again. I groan.

"Hi," she says shyly, twirling a curl around her finger and looking at me through lashes loaded with mascara.

It takes all my self-control to not snort at the absurdity of her act. Knowing what she wants, I grab her arm before she has time to ask and pull her to the dance floor. As we slip into the proper dance holds, I tell myself I'm not doing this to distract myself. I'm doing this because it's what is expected of me as the prince.

Raven Hair says something, I think her name, but I'm not listening. My eyes are too busy scanning the crowd, searching for purple hair. How the hell does she disappear like that? And why am I so obsessed with her? While Raven Hair prattles on, I nod and hum where needed, but my attention has turned inward.

There is no denying I'm attracted to the witch. I can lie to myself all I want, but it's becoming more and more obvious. And what does that say about me? I've trained my entire life to hunt and kill witches. They are nothing more than creatures of the night, evil beings created to destroy and harm. But the more I think about my time with the witch, the more I've started questioning those lessons.

She has never shown an inclination to destroy anything, besides that time she stabbed me. She has feelings and cares about other witches. There has never been a moment where I detected anything evil from her. She is more human than a lot of hunters I know. What if everything I've been taught is wrong?

But history has proven witches can't be trusted. My great great great whatever grandfather is proof of that. He loved a witch, and she killed him. The resulting vision that has been passed down from generation to generation is proof of that. But what if history has gotten it mixed up? What if there is more to the story than what we've been led to believe?

My inner turmoil is reaching a boiling point. I need to get out of here. I need fresh air. The jacket I'm wearing is suddenly too tight, and I can't breathe. The ground slips out from under me, and I don't know whether I want to right itself or not. I search wildly for an escape, my eyes darting around the room like pinballs.

I see my brother dancing, and when he turns with his partner in his arms, I freeze. He's dancing with the witch. And she's smiling up at him, laughing softly at something he's said.

I. Fucking. Snap.

Shoving Raven Hair out of my way, I cut across the ballroom, my heart thundering in my chest. People stare at me, but my focus is only on the woman my brother is holding in his arms. Julian's eyes widen as I yank him out of the way. He says something to me, but I'm already grabbing the witch and dragging her across the room, toward the open patio doors.

"What the hell?" she gasps. She stumbles along behind me, trying to pull her hand out of my grasp, but I hold on tight. "What are you doing?"

I don't answer. We emerge into a lush garden with tropical

flowers scenting the chilly night air. I keep tugging her behind me, her fruitless attempts to pull free getting wilder and wilder.

"Seriously, what's your problem?" she growls, digging her feet into the ground. The heels she's wearing don't comply, and she almost trips. Only my hold on her keeps her upright. "Let me go!"

I wind through a hedge maze until I'm fairly certain we're close to the middle. I know we're at least far enough from prying eyes. Yanking off my mask, I drop it to the ground and grab her face in both of my hands. She's breathing as heavily as I am, her lips parted and eyes wide. My fingers slip under her mask and I let it join mine on the pebbled path. Giving her no chance to pull away, I bend forward and close the distance between us.

This Man Can Kiss

I'm stunned into immobility for a moment as Tyberius presses his lips harder against mine. Then, before I realize what I'm doing, I lift my hands and thread my fingers into his blond hair. I stand on my tiptoes, and I kiss him back.

It's not our first kiss, but it's the first time I've kissed him while sober. And holy goddess above. This man can kiss. He steals my breath and lights my blood on fire with just the brush of his tongue against mine. Any rational thought floats away on a wind of desire. I press myself tighter against him, needing to feel every inch of his body.

His fingers trace my spine, making me shiver. I wish I could touch his skin. I want to know what he feels like under my hands. The need sweeps through me and leaves me quivering. There are too many layers of clothing between us, and slipping my hands inside his jacket does nothing but make me want more.

Tyberius pulls away, long enough to drop his head to my neck where he kisses and nips along the column of my throat. My gaze lands on the sky above as my head falls back. The stars look down on us, twinkling happily, almost like they approve of what's happening. A soft sigh escapes me, turning into a moan as his hips press against mine. I'm burning. If this is what it's like to be tied to the stake, I'll take it any day.

I've barely caught my breath when his hand slips inside the slit of my skirts. His palm is hot, burning me where he slides it up my thigh, all the way to my hip. His fingers bite deliciously into my skin as he pulls my hips harder against his. When his lips crash into mine again, it's frenzied and full of untamed passion, and something in my chest fans to life.

It's sharp and aching. And the sudden pressure pulls me from the haze of sex this man has placed on me. With an effort I didn't know I possessed, I pull away. My chest heaves as I gulp in air. Each breath clears more of the fog, but also increases the growing ache. I shake my head, placing my hand over my thumping heart.

"No," I whisper. "Stop."

He stares at me, his breathing as heavy as mine, his pupils blown and hair mussed. The moon light gilds his features in silver. How have I never noticed the gold threaded through the blue of his eyes? He opens his mouth to say something, stepping closer to me, but I stop him with a hand on his chest.

"No," I say again, louder this time. Swallowing, I turn my head to the side to clear it of the image of him. "I can't do this. *We* can't do this."

I take two steps back, and he reaches for me, but I dart to the side, avoiding his fingers. "Wait," he says, his voice rough and deep.

With one last look at him, disheveled and sexy, I turn and run from the maze. Only using my magic helps me get out of the twisting turns without getting lost, and when I burst from the hedges, I keep running. My heels slip off, but I don't stop. I need to get away. Away from him. Away from the confusing mix of emotions bubbling up inside of me. Away from the pressure building in my chest that I know will only lead to pain.

The grass is wet and cold under my feet, and I soak in the bit of magic from the ground, letting it fuel me. I round the corner of the estate and crash into something hard, sending me sprawling to the dew-dampened ground. Glancing up, I freeze. Edward Berkshire looms above me, the startled expression on his face quickly morphing into a slow, wicked smile. I scramble to stand up, heart pounding for an entirely different reason now. My magic slips from my grasp like smoke as I stare at my mother's murderer. I can do nothing but stare, and remember the flames that claimed my mom's life.

He reaches forward, and I recoil as he traces the slope of my nose with a finger. "I thought you looked familiar when I saw you dancing with my nephew. But I didn't think it was possible because I know I watched you burn at the stake," he muses, rubbing his jaw. "But no, you're not Althea Parker, are you? You're her daughter. A daughter whose existence she hid from me."

I take a step back, trying to rein in my emotions so I can do what I came here for in the first place. Where is my anger? Where is my need for revenge? *Where is my magic?*

"You look just like her, except for the hair." He reaches out and fingers one of my loose curls. I flinch, and he chuckles darkly. "Did you come here to kill me?" He shakes his head in a sarcastic, disapproving way. "Tsk, tsk, little witch. I have other pla-"

Footsteps behind me cut him short. He looks at me with such hatred I actually take a step back, before he turns and hurries away. Seconds later, hands grab my shoulders and turn me around, and I find myself staring into Tyberius's ocean blue eyes. I don't realize how cold I am until his thumbs rub back and forth on my shoulders.

His mouth opens, like he was getting ready to say something, but his brow furrows as he looks at me. "What's wrong? You're shaking."

I am? Oh, look. I am. I'm trembling so hard it's a very real probability I'll fall over.

"Did I see you talking to my uncle? What did he say to you?" There is no mistaking the edge of violence in Tyberius's tone, and it calms me just a bit.

I can still smell the smoke from my memories, though, and it clutches my lungs in a grip that refuses to let go.

Tyberius pulls me around to the front of the estate. "Come on. Let's get you back to the inn."

TYBERIUS BROUGHT me to my room, then promptly left. He was angry. He didn't say so outright, but I could tell by the way he carried himself with his shoulders tense and his jaw clenched. Whether he's mad at me or something else, I have no idea. I'm torn on whether I want him in here with me or far, far away. I have fought with myself for the past thirty minutes, debating about going to find him or staying right here. Knowing the right thing to do is to distance myself from him, I take the temptation away.

Slipping out of the dress and letting it fall to the floor, I head to the bathroom. I wish I had the big sunken tub in the palace right now, but the shower will have to do, instead. The hot water washes over me, tugging down my hair and washing away the makeup. I let it wash away the phantom stench of smoke and the shaky feeling I haven't been able to get rid of since my eyes landed on Edward Berkshire. I froze. I fucking froze as soon as I saw him. For all my bravado and anger, it was like I was a lamb being led to slaughter.

Shame fills me, and it won't wash away like everything else has. Even scrubbing my skin until it's raw doesn't work. It's like a slimy layer of grime coating me. *I failed my mother. I failed myself.*

Eventually, I give up and turn off the water. Throwing on a pair of leggings and a tee shirt, I climb into bed. I fully expect to not be able to fall asleep. I'm too wired, too hyped up on so many different emotions. But, surprisingly, sleep comes quickly.

The dreams, however, are unexpected. Gentle caresses and lingering kisses heat my blood. But the heat doesn't dissipate. It grows. Fire. Smoke. The crackling of wood. The blistering heat.

Distant screams. They chase me from sleep, and I sit up gasping for breath, only to cough as I get a lungful of smoke. I look around and realize it wasn't a dream.

The inn is on fire.

Flames lick up the walls of my room. Heat sears my skin painfully. Smoke chokes me. I fall from the bed in an attempt to climb out with the sheets tangled around my legs. There is no escape. The door is burning. The window shatters, the sound of falling glass muted in the roar of the fire. I could climb out onto the awning, but flames already crawl up the wall.

My heart thunders in my chest, beating so hard and so fast it makes my head swim. Or maybe that's the smoke and lack of oxygen. More coughing tears from my throat, my chest aches with the force of it. Tears attempt to build on my lashes, but the heat of the flames dries them instantly.

I'm going to die. I'm going to be burned alive. My time has finally come.

My terror has completely taken over. I can't do anything but curl into a ball, backed into the farthest corner from the flames, and watch as they dance steadily closer. My lungs burn, and I find myself coughing more and more, each rough inhale only drawing more of the toxic smoke into my body. I bend over and clutch at my chest, hacking until I gag.

I can't breathe. I can't make my chest expand. Darkness creeps into the corners of my vision. Was that a streak of white I just saw by the window?

Jinx?

No answer. It couldn't have been him anyway. He's too fluffy, his fur would light up like tinder. I close my eyes, not wanting fire to be the last thing I see. Instead, I bring up the last positive memory I have of my mom. The one of her smiling and tucking a strand of hair behind my ear. Just before the darkness claims me, I swear I hear her calling my name.

I'm Under Your Spell, Witch

I'm so mad, I'm shaking. After I dropped the witch off at the inn and gave Killian orders to not let her leave, I went back to the palace. I wanted a word with my uncle. Whatever happened between him and the witch absolutely terrified her. Or maybe just seeing him drug up memories of her mom's death. Either way, I need to know what he said to her.

But he was nowhere to be found. Everyone I spoke to said they hadn't seen him for some time. I searched the estate, looked in his office and even his bedroom, but he wasn't there. Giving up, I make my way back to the inn.

My thoughts are stuck on the witch as I walk through the city. That dance. The kiss. That fucking kiss. It destroyed me. I know without a doubt, there is no going back from that. My life will never be the same as it was before this night. Hell, it will never be the same as it was before I met her. That witch came into my life and blew down all the doors to every belief I've ever been taught. Every ideal I've lived she cut open and exposed the ugly truth for what it is.

Lies. Ignorance. Injustice.

Smoke rises in the distance, and a fire truck rolls past, siren wailing as it deftly maneuvers the narrow streets. I keep on walking, my thoughts quickly spiraling even deeper. My need for that witch has grown. I can't deny it. And what I did tonight, my brother will report back to my dad. I'm not sure I can bring her back to the palace without my dad deciding she's not worth it. And I can't let that happen. I've made up my mind, and I won't let her burn.

Another fire truck rolls past, and I glance at the smoke in the sky. An orange glow on the horizon peeks above the buildings. I hear people on the streets just around the curve, and my heart drops to my stomach at the same time a white cat darts up to me. It meows loudly, tail swishing rapidly, and turns around, running back in the direction it came, periodically stopping to make sure I'm following. Was that her familiar? I dash forward, the smell of smoke growing the closer I get to the inn. As soon as I see the flames licking through the roof, my blood runs cold.

I scan the group of people gathered on the streets. I see Killian and the guards, other guests, the innkeeper. But the lack of purple hair steals all the air from my lungs. Without a second thought, I run forward, holding an arm in front of my face as the heat from the fire sears my skin. Someone calls my name, Killian most likely, but I ignore it as I rush into the burning building.

The lower floor is mostly untouched. Smoke curls through the space, though, obscuring my view and making me cough. I whip off my coat and hold it in front of my nose to try to block the smoke. My eyes water the higher I climb on the stairs, the heat growing until the sweat beading on my brow dries instantly. Flames dance wildly in the hallway. The roof groans ominously and sparks fall to the ground in front of me. This building won't be standing much longer, and urgency spurs me forward.

Taking a deep breath through my coat and swallowing the cough climbing up my chest, I run through the flames, keeping as low to the ground as I can. When I reach her door, I kick it in. Wood splinters and embers fly. I waste no time darting through the opening. *Fuck, my eyes are burning.* It's so smoky I can barely see anything in her room. The fire has spread to her walls, and the bed smolders, about to go up as well. I take another step inside, and my gaze catches on a dark shape on the floor in the corner.

"Neave!" I drop to my knees and roll her over. Her eyes flutter and a cough rattles up her chest. "It's okay. I'm going to get you out." I scoop her into my arms and she hangs limply as I stand.

My heart sinks as I look around the burning room. There is no way I can make it back the way I came. Even as I think that, part of the roof collapses, sending a shower of sparks washing over us, blocking the door. I turn to the window, our only other hope. Fire crawls up the wall, but it hasn't completely caught yet.

I grab my coat from the floor, and cover Neave as best as I can before taking a running leap through the window. The roof over the entryway is still standing, and I land with enough force to pop my knees and make me curse.

"Tyberius!" I look down to see my brother rushing through the crowd, his guard hot on his heels. He stretches up his arms when he gets to the overhang. "Pass her to me."

I hesitate, but the sound of more crashing wood inside the inn hurries me forward. I kneel and gently lower Neave into my brother's arms. Without waiting a second longer, I jump down, wincing as my knees protest another jarring impact. Julian hands Neave back to me, and I cradle her to my chest. In the light of the flames, she looks uninjured. Soot covers her face and clothing, but I see no burns. Another cough rattles up her chest, and some part of me settles. She should be okay. Once I find a place for us to stay, I'll call Doctor Harmon and find out what I need to do.

I carry her over to Killian and the rest of the guards. He watches me with a lowered brow, but I really don't care what he's thinking right now. "Find us another place to stay," I rasp, forcing down a cough that tickles my lungs. He opens his mouth to respond but my cell phone rings in my pocket. Shuffling Neave causes more coughing, and I wince as I fish out my phone and hold it to my ear. "Yeah?"

"Tyberius," my uncle says on the other line. "I heard about

the fire. Why don't you come stay at the estate? We have plenty of rooms."

My eyes narrow and I purse my lips. He sounds almost excited. And how did he hear about the fire so fast? Uneasiness settles in my gut like something slimy. The last thing I want to do is put Neave in the crosshairs of my uncle. "No, thanks," I reply, my voice scratchy from the smoke. "I would hate to put you out. We'll find somewhere else to stay." I hang up before he can get another word in. I look at Killian with a raised brow.

He grumbles something under his breath, but pulls out his phone to find us another inn.

"Ty," Julian says quietly next to me.

I don't look at him, keeping my gaze on the witch in my arms. Her breath is labored and raspy, and each one makes my chest ache.

"Ty," Julian says again.

I look at him this time, brows raised. "What?"

"What are you doing?" he asks with a pointed glance at my arms.

What am I doing? I have no fucking clue, except making sure this witch lives to see another day. She almost died tonight. I know how much fire terrifies her. I've seen her reaction and aversion to it. And she almost died from it tonight. I can't imagine the fear she felt, being alone and unable to do anything but wait for the flames to take her.

"I have no idea," I answer honestly.

He looks at me, studying me, judging me, but he thankfully says nothing.

By the time we get to the new inn, a rustic place near the beach, Neave is groggy but awake. Her breathing is still labored and hacking coughs wrack her body. Each time a coughing fit passes, tears leak from her eyes and her breathing sounds even worse. More rattled and harsh.

I impatiently wait for Julian to check us in and get keys, and as soon as he does, I snag one and rush to the room, closing the door behind me. Laying Neave on the bed brings more coughing, and I wince.

"I'm sorry," I say, pulling my phone out of my pocket. "I'm going to fix this."

She doesn't answer, I'm not even sure she can, so I scroll through my contacts until I find Doctor Harmon.

"Your Highness, how can I help you?" he says when he answers.

"I need to know what to do for smoke inhalation." As I talk, I walk to the bathroom and grab a washcloth, wetting it with warm water in the sink.

"What kind of smoke inhalation and how bad is it?" he asks.

"Smoke from a fire. She was trapped in a room, and the building was on fire. I don't know how long she was in there." Back at her side, I gently wash her face of the soot, as well her neck and arms. She watches me through bleary eyes, gasping for each breath and wincing like it hurts.

"She? Who are we talking about?"

"Th-Neave."

Doctor Harmon hums in his throat. "Oxygen is the best cure for smoke inhalation." Another coughing fit interrupts him, and I hold the phone out for him to hear it better. "It sounds a little wet. Does she seem like she's in pain?"

I nod, even though he can't see. "Yes. Every cough brings tears to her eyes and makes her wince."

"I'd put in her a steamy bathroom. The steam will help clear her lungs of any foreign bodies and soothe her throat."

"Steamy bathroom. I can do that. Thank you, Doctor Harmon."

"And Your Highness," he says before I can hang up. "Watch her closely for her breathing and coughing getting worse, as well as fever. It could be signs of more serious injuries."

"Got it. Thanks again." I hang up and toss the phone to bed before heading back to the bathroom.

I turn the shower to hot and adjust the spray so it only hits one side of the stall. Then I take off my socks and shoes and pull my shirt over my head as I walk back to the bed. I scoop Neave into my arms and carry her to the shower, kicking the door shut behind me. In the shower, I slide to the floor, keeping her out of the direct spray.

It doesn't take long for the bathroom to fill with billowing steam. The longer we sit in the mist, the more her breathing seems to ease. I can't help but brush my hand up and down her arm, soothing her as the steam does its thing. With her cheek resting on my pecs, her breath skates across my bare chest and each one seems less labored than the one before it. Her coughing has stopped, and her body relaxes in my arms.

My hand rubbing along her arm goes from soothing, to more exploratory. My fingers dance over her skin, tasting and touching each inch. Every bone in her body is the same as mine. There is nothing about her anatomy that is different from a human woman's. Except the magic. And the way she entices me like no other has before.

Slowly, Neave lifts her head to look at me. Water droplets cling to her hair and lashes, gathering from the mist surrounding us. She blinks, studying me with such intensity I swear she can see straight to my soul.

"Why?" she whispers, her voice raspy from the smoke and coughing. "Why did you sa—" she cuts off and shakes her head, looking down at her lap. "The visions. You need me for the visions."

The pain in her voice, pain not from the rawness of her throat but the thought that I saved her for the visions alone, is like a knife to my chest. It's the realization I needed. She may deny having feelings for me, but that reaction tells me everything I need to know.

Slowly, I slide my hand up her arm and over her neck, grasping her chin in my fingers. Turning to her head so she's looking at me, I stare into those dark brown eyes, making sure she understands what I say. "I didn't save you because of the vision. I saved you because you have crawled under my skin, and I can't get rid of you. No matter how hard I try to fight it, I lose. Every time I walk away, I'm drawn back to you." My hand slides up to cup her cheek, my thumb rubbing along her lower lip. "I'm under your spell, witch. And I don't think I want to be anywhere else."

Her breath hitches, and my eyes drop to her mouth. Needing to taste her again, I lower my head until my lips brush against hers, just barely a feather soft caress. She pulled away in the garden earlier. She didn't want it, and I won't pressure her into something she doesn't want, no matter how much I crave her.

I brace myself for the rejection, already knowing it will hurt but willing to risk the high for the low. But instead of pulling away, she presses her lips harder against mine. My heart thunders in my chest, and I dig my fingers into her damp hair, cupping the back of her head. She shocks me when she slides her hands up my bare chest and moves to straddle my hips.

I deepen the kiss, parting her lips with mine and brushing my tongue along hers. The breathy moan she makes shoots straight to my cock, and I drop my hands to grab her ass and press her harder against me. She gasps into my mouth and rocks her hips. I'm so fucking hard it hurts. I need this witch more than I need oxygen to breathe. Sliding my hands back up, I slip them under her wet shirt and lift the fabric over her head. Not wasting any time, I lower my mouth to her nipple and suck it into my mouth. Her back arches, and she moans, digging her fingers into my hair.

Fuck. Every tiny shift of her hips against mine sends lightning through my veins. Each inch of her skin brushing against mine is intoxicating. Her body, flushed from the heat of the shower and her desire, is a fucking sight I'll never tire of seeing. I need more of her. I need *all* of her.

My fingers curl in the waistband of her shorts, and I tug them down as far as I can with her still sitting on my lap. I reach between us and slip two fingers inside her shorts, gliding down her heated skin to her core. She shudders, and her breath hitches. I release her nipple and bury my face in her neck, breathing in her scent.

"Neave," I whisper hoarsely, sliding my fingers a little lower.

She jerks back, breaking contact, and stares at me with wild eyes. We're both breathing raggedly, but she seems to gather herself together quickly. The heat disappears from her gaze, replaced by something dark and depressing.

Grasping my wrist, she pulls my hand from her pants. "No." Her voice is rough, either from the smoke or her desire, I'm not sure. "This has to stop. We're too different. Our paths cannot cross like this." She pushes to her feet, standing under the spray of water and covering her chest. "Nothing will come of this but heartbreak." Her voice cracks on the last word, and the unshed tears shining in her eyes suck the breath from my lungs.

She steps out of the shower, letting in a blast of cold air that shivers over my skin. But it's not the cold air that makes me feel frozen. It's her words, and the lack of her body against mine. It's the realization that she is correct. Nothing will come of this but heartbreak. But can I really go back to my old life when I return home? Can I tie her to the stake and lower the flame to the wood, watching as it consumes her? That thought alone makes me bend over and clutch my chest.

How can I continue hunting with her words ringing in my ears? Everything she told me about witches and how they are losing their magic because of hunters has sat heavy on my shoulders since that day at the beach. Every witch I have killed has weakened them and taken their magic away from them.

Magic. Is it evil? Is it wrong? Maybe it is. Maybe it isn't. But I know for certain, what she said to me on the way to Serberth, not all witches are bad. Just like not all humans are bad.

My body feels like it weighs thousands of pounds as I climb to my feet and turn off the shower. I have a lot to think about. My future as a hunter has never seemed so ... wrong.

What the fuck do I do now?

Lather. Rinse. Repeat

I step out of the warm shower and into the chilly air of the bathroom. Everywhere Tyberius touched me tingles, and I desperately want to jump back in that shower and continue what we were doing. Instead, I grab a towel and wrap it around myself and hurry into the room. I have nothing. Everything I had packed burned in the fire. Shivering, and not just from the cold, I rush to the door and swing it open. Julian is standing outside, arms crossed and looking pissed.

I gasp and take a step back, clutching the towel tighter to me. "Um ... I ... Is there a room for me?" I stutter. A cough tickles the back of my throat, and I bend over, hacking into the edge of the towel. *Holy shit that hurts.* Tears leak from my eyes as I stand back up. I don't know if they're from the coughing or because my heart feels like it's being torn into pieces.

His eyes, the same color as Tyberius's, scan my face. A small frown creases between his brows, but he nods. I follow him down the hall and he uses a keycard to unlock a door. Instead of shutting it behind me, he stops me just inside the room with a hand on my shoulder.

"Is everything okay?" he asks slowly, as if he is unsure if he really wants to hear the answer.

"It's fine," I say quickly, and step away from him.

But it's not fine. It's so not fine.

He doesn't look convinced, but he nods and shuts the door. As soon as I'm enveloped in silence and privacy, my knees give out. I fall to the floor, clutching the towel around me like armor. If he hadn't said my name, I don't think I would have stopped him. How can I ever look at myself in a mirror again, when I feel the way I do about a hunter. My enemy. How do I come to terms with the way he makes my body light up from just a single look?

The moment I heard my name on his lips, reality crashed around me. It was the first time he called me something other than 'witch', and I wish he hadn't. The way it sounded on his lips, like he was desperate and begging for me, it did something funny to my heart. But at the same time, it was a bucket of cold water on my desire. He's forgetting his place. He's forgetting who he is, and what I am to him. It's easy to pretend when we're away from home. It's easy to forget I'm his prey, and the end for me is a fire.

Fire. I almost burned tonight. Another shudder works through me. How ironic would it have been for me to die from a fire, but not for being a witch? A hysterical laugh bubbles in my chest, and it escapes as a raspy cough that makes me double over and clutch at my chest. *Fuck.*

A knock on the door makes me freeze. *Please don't be him. Please don't be him. Please don't be him.*

"Witch, I have some clothes for you."

I sag in relief when I hear Julian's voice on the other side. I stand, still grasping the towel and leaving a puddle of water where I was sitting, and walk to the door.

Julian hands me a stack of clothing. "Since your clothes were lost in the fire, my brother said you would need more."

I almost want to refuse them purely because it's essentially Tyberius giving them to me. But I do need clothes. I can't walk around naked, after all. I snag them with one hand, and quietly say, "Thank you."

He nods before turning and walking back down the hall. I

peer toward the room Tyberius is staying in, but the door is closed. *Thank the goddess.* What would I do if I saw him now? I'm still burning for him. His touch on my skin, his mouth on mine. The way his fingers danced under my shorts. Heat flushes through my body, and I turn around and slam the door behind me. I can't let myself linger on those thoughts.

I strip out of my wet shorts and pull on the clothes Julian brought me. A pair of olive green leggings, a white V-neck tee-shirt, and white slip-on shoes. Everything fits perfectly, like Tyberius knew exactly the shape and size of my body. With the way his hands have touched me, traced all the curves and dips, he probably does.

Unsure what to do with myself, and wanting to keep my mind distracted, I pace. I pace the room so much I'm surprised I don't wear a path on the wooden floor. It doesn't seem to be working, though. My thoughts won't stay away from Tyberius. Each time my pacing takes me to the door, my hand reaches out for the handle, ready to go search for him. But I stop myself, turning sharply and heading back toward the window.

Lather. Rinse. Repeat.

I have no idea what my emotions are doing right now. The roller coaster they're taking me on is giving me whiplash and making my stomach revolt. My mind is jumping from the dance with Tyberius, to the garden, to the fire, to the shower. Butterflies, desire, fear, hatred, confusion. It's all a swirling tornado of ugliness that leaves me queasy and jittery.

The next time my path crosses the window, I stop. Desperately needing some air, I unlatch it and climb out. I'm shocked there are no guards outside watching me, especially being on the first floor, but it's easy to slip away and disappear into the night.

The sound of the waves crashing against the shore draws me to the beach. I slip off my borrowed shoes and bury my toes in the cool sand. The moon reflects off the water, creating a stripe of white light in the rolling waves. A sea breeze blows my hair around my shoulders, and I inhale the fresh salty tang of it. More of the tightness from the smoke leaves my lungs with each exhale. Or maybe the tightness is from something else. *Someone* else.

Either way, I find myself breathing easier as I stand at the edge of the water, the waves just tickling my toes each time it comes to shore. The night sky above my head is a balm I needed badly. I'm so distracted by my thoughts, my emotions, and confusing feelings, I don't hear someone behind me until it's too late. The crunch of sand under boots filters through, and I whip around, catching a glimpse of Killian's dark skin and wind blown locs.

Then pain explodes in my head and everything goes dark.

A SLAMMING door jars me awake. The sound ricochets inside my skull, sending stabbing pain through my brain. I groan and clutch my head, squeezing my eyes shut tighter against the light trying to slip between my closed lids. *What the fuck happened to me?* Then I remember Killian finding me on the beach, hitting me on the head. Asshole. He could have just drug me back to the inn, he didn't have to knock me out.

"Wake up, witch."

I furrow my brow at the unfamiliar voice and slowly peek one eye open. The sight of Edward Berkshire sends me flying up in the bed, the motion making the room spin alarmingly. I don't have time to wonder what he's doing here before a wave of nausea rolls through my stomach and up my throat. Leaning over the bed, I heave the contents of my stomach onto the unfamiliar cream-colored rug. I'm shaking and sweating as I sit back in the bed, raising an unsteady hand to my forehead, trying to stop the room from spinning. It doesn't work.

"Well, if you've gotten that out of your system," Edward drawls, disgust pinching his voice.

I look past him toward the door, and my stomach drops to my feet. Turning my gaze to the rest of the room, I suck in a sharp breath. This doesn't look familiar. Instead of the warm colors of the inn, I'm surrounded by gray and white decor. A marble floor, wooden walls, rich opulence. This isn't right. "Where am I?" I ask shakily.

"You're at my estate, where you'll be staying indefinitely."

My attention snaps to Edward, his smarmy words bouncing around in my head, not making sense to my aching brain. I must look confused because he sighs heavily and pulls a chair up to the bed. I scooch as far away as I can; the movement causes my stomach to churn threateningly, but I swallow down the nausea, needing to focus on what's happening. There are no glimmering threads of magic attached to him, and I know before I try, I won't be able to grasp my magic. Still, my fingers clench, and nothing happens. Dread curls through me, leaving me even more cold and unsteady.

"You really shouldn't have gone off on your own. Killian was more than happy to bring you to me. He always was the better student between him and Tyberius." Sitting in the chair, he spreads his legs and crosses his arms over his chest. At the look of surprise on my face, he chuckles. "Killian was worried about how close Tyberius was getting to you. He thought the best way to solve the problem was to deliver you to someone who would make sure you were used appropriately."

I stare at this man with wide eyes. My heart thunders in my chest as the realization of what is happening finally settles within me. Tyberius doesn't know where I am. I left the inn through the window and didn't close it behind me. When he comes to get me in the morning, I won't be there. The window will be open, pointing to my escape, and he'll think I left. Maybe he'll search for me, because he can't let a witch escape, but he won't find me. No one knows I'm here except Killian, and he obviously doesn't care.

Panic rises inside me. Each breath I take is forced and shallow, not enough to fill my lungs. The room wavers. What am I going to do? How do I let Tyberius know I need help? I grip the sheets in my sweaty fists.

"Now, on to more pressing matters," Edward says, oblivious to my inner turmoil. "Obviously, I can't keep you pumped full equalizer. That defeats the purpose. I need you to have visions. However, I can't trust you with your magic. Luckily, I have a little something that will solve this problem."

Edward snaps his fingers and a guard I didn't notice steps from the shadows by the door. My gaze drops to his hands, where he idly twirls an iron band about three-finger widths wide. A chill spreads down my spine as he approaches and the band opens on an invisible hinge. Fear sluices through me as I realize what that is. A collar. An iron collar that will no doubt somehow control me.

I push away from the edge of the bed, scooting for the opposite side. The guard dives for me and grabs my foot, yanking me hard enough to pull me off the bed. Desperately, I kick and flail, reaching for magic that isn't there. I can't let him put that collar around my neck. I know with absolute certainty, I will never escape if he does.

The guard wrestles me to the ground, sitting on my chest and pinning my arms to my sides. Edward snags the collar from the floor where the guard dropped it while trying to get me under control. He kneels on the ground by my head, and wraps it around my throat. It closes with a soft click that echoes in every cell of my body.

Edward presses somewhere on the collar and a sharp sting pierces my neck, followed by a zapping burn that floods through my body and clutches my head. "There. Now you'll be compliant."

Both Edward and the guard step away. My hands tremble as I reach for the collar. It's cool and rough, and no matter how hard I pull, it doesn't budge. But each tug causes a sharp prick of pain in the side of my neck.

"I'd be careful pulling too hard. You wouldn't want to pull the prong too much. It would tear that beautiful skin something fierce." Edward smiles down at me, something evil slithering over his features.

Prong? Even as I question it, I can feel my body slipping away. A fog descends over me, cloaking me in a dull mist. My limbs must weigh thousands of pounds. My thoughts must be miles and miles away. Each one takes a tremendous amount of effort to pull from the fog. And through that haze, an almost unnoticeable current of electricity travels through my mind.

"Get back in bed," Edward barks.

Without my permission, my body obeys his command. Inside, I'm screaming. I'm fighting with everything I have to stop moving, but I can't. I climb onto the bed and lean against the headboard, looking at Edward expectantly.

A grin spreads across his face, and he rubs his hands together. "Perfect. It works perfectly." He runs a finger over the collar around my throat, and inside I flinch. Outside, I don't even blink. "This collar contains a device that will send a consistent electrical current to the nerves in your brain, causing them to disrupt the signals to your body so you will no longer be able to do anything without an express command from someone else. Basically, you will be my puppet. You will be able to access your magic so I can use you for your visions, but you won't be able to use your magic on me."

Do something, Neave. Fight him. Yell at him. Pull the damn collar off. Who cares if the prong tears through your skin? I sit compliantly, waiting for Edward to give me a command. Even the tears that burn the backs of my eyes refuse to fall.

"Excellent," Edward says, his voice ringing with excitement. "We might as well start now."

He reaches for me and yanks my arm band from my bicep. The ends scrape painfully, but I don't even flinch. Inside, I scream and writhe. He studies the band, twisting it this way and that in his fingers. Then he tucks it into his pockets.

"Do you know what that is?" He doesn't compel me to answer, so I don't. "Your mother gave that to you to protect you. It represses your visions. She used to wear it, because she too had visions. When I captured her, I did this same thing to her. I drugged her until she told me everything she saw. In the end, it was useless drivel. When she escaped, I didn't make it a priority to find her, but when I did, that's why I burned her. She was no use to me. I thought I had it wrong. That it wasn't her line that I was looking for. I didn't know she had a daughter, a daughter she had passed that armband down to. How lucky for me you ran into me the other night."

What was he talking about? I can't follow his words. They're blurring together and not making any sense. The zinging in my brain makes it too hard to focus.

Edward pulls a pill bottle from his pocket and drops one pill into his palm. "Open your mouth and swallow this pill."

Inside, I clench my jaw tight, refusing. But outside, my mouth drops open, tongue sticking out to welcome the pill. He sets it on my tongue, and I swallow without hesitation. He sits back in the chair, crossing one knee over the other, and waits.

It takes about twenty minutes before I realize what he was waiting for. My body flushes hot, then cold. My heart pounds so hard in my chest I'm not positive I'm not having a heart attack. Sweat beads on my brow and the world around me shimmers. The edges of the furniture take on a strange glowy light. He gave me some kind of hallucinogenic.

The corners of the room flicker and shadows dance along the walls. My eyes dart through the room, never settling on one thing. Fear grips my spine, and I shake from the force of it. Little creatures slowly crawl toward me, their eyes glowing red and fangs dripping some kind of venom. I curl my legs tight to my body, trying to stay as far from them as possible.

Just before one of them reaches the bed, it falls through the floor, splashing in a puddle of red. The rest of the creatures hiss and scream, turning and fleeing back into the shadows. The red puddle steams and bubbles where the *thing* fell into it, then it calms. I slowly crawl to the edge of the bed to get a better look at the puddle.

I run my finger through the ruby red substance. It's thick and cool. As I watch it, shapes form in it. No, not shapes. Symbols. Witch symbols. Ones I've seen before, but I can't quite remember what they are.

"What do you see?" Edward's voice is distant in my mind, but my body answers his question easily.

"Blood. Symbols." I tilt my head to the side, studying the vision before me. "A warning."

"What warning? What does it say?" His voice is eager and sharp.

And just like that, the vision pops like a bubble and reality slams into me. My arms are too unsteady to hold me up, and I collapse onto the bed, gasping for air. Sweat coats my skin and I shiver as the cool air washes over me. I can't move as bile climbs up my throat, but I lean over enough to spill my stomach on the floor. Inside, a part of me cackles as it splatters on Edward's boots. Outside, I slowly crawl back to the head of the bed and settle against the headboard once again.

"Bitch," Edward growls and jumps to his feet. He looks at me with disgust before turning toward the door. "We'll continue this tomorrow."

The door slams behind him, and I shrink inside myself. What am I going to do? I can't move. I can do nothing but lie in this bed and stare at the ceiling, waiting for a command. The tears that want to fall don't even build on my lashes. I try to squeeze my eyes shut, but they remain open, blinking steadily.

Oh, goddess. What have I done?

The Former Prince, Reduced To Begging For Scraps Of Food

When I finally crawl out of bed the next morning, I feel like I've aged thirty years. I spent the night tossing and turning, going over everything I said and everything I could have done differently. I probably should have just set her in the shower and walked away. A stronger man would have done that. I am, apparently, not strong. At least, not when it comes to that witch.

In the bathroom, the same features I see every morning in the mirror stare back at me. Blond hair, blue eyes, cut jawline, tattoos. But I don't recognize that person anymore. The witch hunter who spent his entire life training or out in the field doing the job. Bringing witches to their deaths. That person looks like a stranger now. And it's all because of a single witch.

Sighing, I run my hand under the water and attempt to style my hair. I lost everything I brought with me in the fire. If we stay here much longer, I'll have to get some more clothes and supplies. Neave will probably need some, too. After one last glimpse in the mirror, I head for the hall, intent on going straight to Neave's room.

A strange fluttering in my stomach brings me to a stop with

my hand outstretched for the doorknob. *I have butterflies? What the fuck?* I'm a grown fucking man. I don't get butterflies. But I'm not sure how Neave will react to seeing me after last night, and that makes me nervous. I need to keep myself on a tight leash. No letting myself get carried away with her.

I reach the door at the same time Julian opens it. We stare at each other for a moment, before he walks forward and pushes me back in my room, shutting the door behind us.

"What's going on, Ty?" He studies me with eyes that are too old for his age. I shrug and try to brush off his question, but he stops me before I can give him some bullshit answer. "I'm asking as your brother, not the future king. Not the prince, but your brother. What's going on?"

I hesitate. It's been years since Julian acted like my brother. Since he started training to be king, he's always acted like an ass around me. He seems genuinely concerned, and I cave under his stare. "I like her," I say simply.

He huffs a laugh. "Wow, you actually admitted it. I'm impressed."

I sigh and sit heavily on the edge of the bed, rubbing my hand down my face. "I don't know what the fuck to do, Julian." He sits next to me, the bed dipping slightly under his weight. "There is no happy ending for us. She's made that perfectly clear. But when this is all over, I can't send her to the stake. And I don't think I could let anyone else do it, either."

Julian nods. "Yeah, that's a problem. Dad will never let her live. And if he knows how you feel about her, I'm not sure he'd let you keep your title."

My laugh is humorless as I rest my elbows on my knees and drop my head into my hands. "No shit. Not that I really care about that in the long run. I don't think I can go back to hunting after this. It's her. It's all her. Every single thought in my head revolves around her."

He shifts, getting more comfortable. "How does she feel

about you? All of this could be a moot point if she hates you, like she should."

"She should. But I don't think she does." I shake my head, remembering last night and the disappointment she showed when she thought I saved her only for her visions.

"Then I don't see the problem," he says simply.

I turn to stare at him with my mouth agape. "How do you not see the problem?"

"You like her. She apparently likes you. Isn't that all you need?"

"Witch. Witch hunter." I point to myself, the implication obvious.

He stares at me like I'm an idiot, and maybe I am. "You just said you don't think you can go back to witch hunting. So, if you're not a witch hunter, then there's no problem."

While he's right, I still have a history of hunting and killing witches. I murdered her sisters. My family, *my uncle*, murdered her mother. I don't see how we could get past that. "Why are you trying to help me?" I ask Julian instead. "We haven't talked like this in years."

He shrugs. "I don't think I realized how far apart we've grown until I saw you at the ball. Your expression of genuine happiness when you danced with the witch was something I haven't seen in a really long time. And it made me question when was the last time we talked, really talked, and I couldn't remember." He shifts on the bed, fidgeting uncomfortably. "I think we've let a lot come between us, and I regret it."

I study his profile, his strong jaw dusted with blond stubble. When did my little brother grow up so much? When we were younger, we did everything together. Then, he started taking on my responsibilities as future king, and they went to his head. But I know I can't blame him entirely for that. I was just as much of an ass.

Sighing, I run a hand down my face. "Yeah, we really have."

He turns to me and gives me a tentative smile. "Why don't you go get your girl?"

Huffing a laugh, I stand from the bed. "Coffee first, I think. She's less grumpy when she's been properly caffeinated."

The inn has a small breakfast bar set up in the lobby, and I make my way there. Killian is sitting with the rest of the guards and I give them a nod of my head, before pouring myself and Neave some coffee. I add copious amounts of sugar to mine and leave hers black. *Like her soul.* Smiling to myself, I head toward her room, the cups of coffee warming my hands and enticing me with their aromas.

"Neave," I say as I knock on her door, careful not to spill any coffee. She doesn't answer, and that really doesn't surprise me. I take a deep breath, trying to calm my heart that is suddenly beating as fast as a hummingbird's. I should have prepared what to say. Now I'll probably make a complete fool of myself. I balance the two coffees in one hand and open her door. "I brought coffee," I offer hopefully as I step inside.

The room is empty. My breathing quickly becomes erratic. A cool breeze blows in through the open window, making the gauzy curtains dance into the room. The coffees fall from my numb fingers, lids popping off as they hit the floor, sending the hot liquid spraying through the room. I dash to the window, peering out, already knowing there is no point.

She left. Something inside me cracks open, bleeding ichor into my bloodstream. I rub my sternum like it can ease the ache, but deep down, I know the ache won't ever go away. Neave left, and she isn't coming back.

"Julian!" I yell, still staring out the window, unable to tear my gaze away.

Footsteps in the hall get louder as my brother steps into the room. "What's up? Umm, where is she?"

I turn around, and his eyes widen as they take in whatever my face looks like. "She's gone," I whisper hoarsely.

Determination straightens his spine. "Let's go find her."

How did my life get to this point? Walking the streets of Seaberth with my brother at my side searching for a witch. And not to bring her in for a burning, but because … because I want her. *Fuck.* Admitting that to myself only makes the ache in my chest grow.

"Why was there no guard outside her window?" I growl for the hundredth time.

Julian doesn't answer, just like he didn't the other ninety-nine times. Killian let his guard down and didn't post anyone outside. I want to yell at him, punish him, throw fists, but I can't bring myself to do it. We all got complacent. I foolishly thought she wouldn't leave. I let my guard down, too, and look where it got me.

The church I was planning on coming to with Neave is up ahead. I pull Julian to the front door and push inside. "She had a feeling about this place. Maybe she came here on her own." The sound of hope in my voice makes me cringe. She won't be here. I already know it. I pushed her too far last night. I freaked her out, and she took off.

It's dimly lit inside, the darkness pierced by a multitude of candles. The orange flames dance and reflect off the stone walls. She wouldn't have stayed here. As soon as she saw the fire, she would have left. I march down the aisle, anyway. Ancient pews line either side, with an old stone altar sitting under a domed ceiling in the apse. The space is empty. The only sound mine and Julian's boots on the stone floor.

"She's not here," my brother says quietly, not wanting to disturb the peace of the church.

I stop in front of the altar and turn my face to the domed ceiling. Being built into a cliff side, there are no windows, but the ceiling was painted to look like stained glass. The images don't register in my mind, but the colors swirl together as moisture builds in my eyes. Squeezing them shut, I silently throw up a prayer. I haven't been to church in years—since I decided to not pursue the crown. Even when I was going, I don't think I really believed. I'm desperate though. *Please. Let me find her. Let me...*

Julian's hand on my shoulder seems like it weighs thousands of pounds. My shoulders slump and I turn around, heading back up the aisle.

"Where to next?" he asks as we step back into the daylight.

"The beach." My voice is hollow, like the growing empty space in my chest.

We keep our eyes peeled the entire walk to the beach, but we see no sign of purple hair. There are a few people at the beach this early, most of them walking along the water's edge, a few fishing along the shore. It takes me seconds to realize she isn't here either. But I already knew she wouldn't be. The sunlight is bright as it reflects off the ocean. How can it be such a nice day when inside it feels like a storm has rolled in and stolen all the light?

"We'll keep looking," Julian says, bumping me with his shoulder.

I nod, but it's pointless. She's an expert at hiding. After living her entire life avoiding witch hunters, she won't be easily caught this time.

Did I lose her before I ever even had her?

"We can stay longer, Ty. Keep searching for her," Julian says to my back as I stride onto the private jet.

I shake my head, but don't answer. There truly is no point. If she wanted to be found, we would have found her. She made her choice, and now I have to live with it. I flop onto a couch and let my head fall against the back of it. The rest of the team follows me aboard, but I keep my eyes closed, not paying attention to who sits next to me.

"It's for the best, really." Killian says as he claims to the seat next to mine. The words make me grind my teeth together. "She wasn't helping with the visions anyway."

I snap my head up to glare at him. "She had a lead. We were going to check it out the day she escaped." I pinch the bridge of my nose. A headache has been pounding away in my skull for the last three days as we searched non-stop for Neave. "If there had been a guard outside her window, this wouldn't have happened, and maybe we would have the answers we've been looking for for *thousands of years.*"

Killian recoils at the venom in my words. His dark eyes widen for a moment before he swallows and shrugs. "I still think it's for the best." His gaze travels over me, searching and weighing.

Unable to handle Killian's judgment, I push up from my seat and walk to the back of the plane to the private bedroom. If I sit there any longer, words would be exchanged, words that I wouldn't be able to take back. Slamming the door behind me, I throw myself face first onto the bed. I've never wished I could disappear more than I do when someone knocks on the door.

"Ty?" Julian asks. The door closes behind him and the bed dips as he sits. "I know you don't want to hear this, but someone needs to ask." He pauses, and my gut churns with dread, already knowing what he's going to say. "What are you going to tell Dad?"

I groan, the sound muffled by the blankets and mattress my face is buried in. "I don't know." Sighing, I roll over. The ceiling is plain, tan with lights inset along the edges. I wish there was something more interesting to look at. "I guess the truth. That I let the witch escape. He'll probably disown me. Strip me of my title and inheritance. I'll end up on the streets. The former prince, reduced to begging for scraps of food."

Julian snorts. "You can be so dramatic sometimes."

I say nothing. The ache inside me just keeps growing, and as the jet takes off and speeds farther and farther away from Seaberth and Neave, the distance between us seems so much more finite. This really is the end. I've lost any chance I ever had with her.

Julian lays down next to me, arms behind his head, and asks quietly, "You okay?"

"No," I whisper, shaking my head. "I may be dramatic, but something about her called to me." I can't say her name. It hurts too much. "For the past few years, I've been slowly drowning. This life I've worked so hard for has been sucking the soul from my body. The joy I found in hunting was gone, and I had already been questioning my life choices when I met her. She was like a breath of fresh air, breathing new life into me. The time I spent with her made me feel alive. Now it's all gone. And I have no fucking clue what I'm going to do."

It's all just empty inside. Except for the ache. The steadily growing ache that no matter how much I rub at my chest, it doesn't go away. Maybe I was a fool for thinking I stood a chance with her. Maybe I deserve this pain for all my past sins. Yeah, this is definitely my punishment for everything I've done in my past.

Closing my eyes, I release a breath and let myself sink into the numbness. It's better than the alternative. I don't hear Julian leave, but I welcome the silence, even if my thoughts are less than welcoming. Is this what my life is going to be from here on out? It should probably scare me that I don't really care if it is.

MY DAD SLAMS his fist on the desk, making Julian flinch next to me. I don't even blink. His brows lower over his blue eyes as he glares at us.

"You mean to tell me eight men couldn't keep track of a single witch?" I've never heard my dad so upset before. And I've given him plenty of things to be upset about in the past. "How the hell am I supposed to explain that my sons lost the one thing that could save our family from ruin? The one thing you, Tyberius, have been trained for, and you let her get away." He makes a noise of disappointment in the back of throat and shakes his head. "I knew you were an incompetent idiot, but I never thought you could screw up this badly."

His words roll right through me like smoke. It's not the first time I've heard them, and I'm sure it won't be the last. Not only that, but I find that I just don't care. For the first time in my life, what my dad thinks of me is at the bottom of my list of worries. I stare at him, not really seeing the vein pulsing in his forehead or the red steadily creeping up his neck and into his cheeks.

He shakes his head disgustedly and turns his attention to Julian. "And you!" My brother flinches again as our dad points a shaky finger at him. "I thought for sure you could handle a simple job of keeping your brother in line. If he could not handle that witch, you should have made sure someone was around who could. How the hell do you intend to rule an entire kingdom if you can't even manage your brother?" I sense Julian deflating next to me as our dad pinches the bridge of his nose and exhales. "Both of you get out of my sight. I need to think about how to deal with this."

I turn on my heel, spotting Julian nodding respectfully to our dad, and stride for the door without a backward glance. In the hallway, Julian keeps pace with me, but neither of us say anything. Glancing at him from the corner of my eye, I almost say something, but I bite my tongue. With his shoulders slumped and head hanging down, I don't need him to tell me how he's feeling.

As the golden child, Julian is used to praise, not being scolded and yelled at. The feeling of being a disappointment is new for him. I know I should say something, do something, to make him realize it's not him that Dad is mad at. But I honestly can't bring myself to care enough.

We reach my room, and I open the door. Julian tries to say something to me, but I cut him off, closing the door behind me and locking it. I head straight for the cart of alcohol in the corner of my room and snag an unopened bottle of scotch. Cracking the seal, I tip it back, again and again, and let the burn slowly numb me.

I'm So Hollow Inside

I HAVE NO IDEA HOW MANY DAYS HAVE PASSED. EACH one is filled with the same thing. Haze. Fog. Drug-induced hallucinations. The only time I see Edward Berkshire is when he gives me with the drugs and questions me about what I see. It's always the same thing, though, blood and symbols. And I can never quite remember what the symbols are when the drugs wear off. Edward is becoming angrier with each day that passes that I cannot give him what he wants.

Deep down, I'm scared of what will happen when he finally snaps. But outwardly, I can't bring myself to care. Or do anything about it. I lay in my bed all day, staring at the ceiling and watching the light filter from one side of the room to the other as the sun moves through the sky. Food is brought, and I eat only because I'm told to do so. If I don't have an order to follow, my body doesn't know what to do. No one tells me to sleep, so my body fights it until it physically cannot stay awake any longer. Only then do I get any rest.

The door opens, and my gaze slowly travels to my visitor. It's like my eyeballs are moving through sludge. A young woman stands in my doorway with a hulking guard behind her. She's wearing loose black slacks and a white button-up shirt. Her blond hair is pulled into a high, tight bun on top of her head, and she's carrying a black bundle in her arms.

She approaches cautiously and nods her head at me. "His highness, Prince Edward, has instructed me to help you get ready for the evening."

If I had control of my body, my eyes would pop out of my head. Get ready for the evening? What does that mean? A distant tendril of dread curls through my gut, but the fog quickly swallows it. The woman lays a black dress on the foot of the bed and steps back.

"Please stand up," she says quietly.

I do, following the command given to me. Distantly, I realize the guard is still in my room, watching, but I don't care. The woman gives me commands and I follow them, letting her dress me. She sits me on the bed and does my hair and makeup. As she puts the finishing touches on my face, her gaze meets mine. Sadness wells in her light green eyes, and something like hope flutters inside me. It's quickly swallowed by apathy, and the realization there is nothing she could do to help without risking her life and position.

She turns to the guard and says, "She's ready."

And the next thing I know, I'm being led through the estate by a guard with a firm grip on my arm. I don't know why he feels the need to hold on to me so tightly. I can barely walk on my own, let alone try to run. Each step takes monumental effort, and it feels as if I'm wading through a pool of jello.

I catch a glimpse of myself in a piece of mirrored artwork. They've me dressed in a black velvet sheath dress that clings to my curves. It has only one long sleeve that covers my luna moth tattoo, and a slit that stops at the top of my thigh. My purple hair has been styled in an elegant chignon, and my makeup is understated sophistication. I look beautiful and classy. Something I've never said about myself. As quick as those thoughts pop into my head, they disappear in a wispy mist.

My surroundings pass by in a blur. I'm unable to focus on

anything long enough for it to penetrate the fog. It either takes hours or seconds to reach our destination. Time is strange in my current state. The guard stops at a door and pushes it open, prodding me into a dining room with a massive glass table and golden chairs. The guard leads me inside, and he pulls out a seat with a muttered 'sit'.

Once seated, a hand grabs mine, and I'm able to focus enough to recognize the golden signet ring on the pinky. I'm seated next to Edward, and he's holding my hand. Inside, my skin crawls. I recoil at his touch and pull my hand away. But in reality, I do nothing. I stare blankly in front of me while Edward absently rubs his thumb over the back of my hand. The rest of the people seated at the table chatter away, either oblivious to what's happening to me, or uncaring. Or maybe they care but can just do nothing about it.

Food is brought and served, but no one tells me to eat, so it sits on my plate growing cold. Distantly, I'm aware of my stomach rumbling and my mouth watering. Edward's boisterous laugh almost jars me out of my haze, but even that isn't enough. Conversation flows around me, but I feel as if I'm underwater. Everything is muffled and far away. And I really don't care enough to try to pay attention. It would be too much effort.

At some point, Edward leans to whisper in my ear. It takes a moment for it to register. "Open your mouth." His hot breath fans across my cheek, and goosebumps break out over my skin, but I do as he says. He places a pill on my tongue and closes my mouth with his hand. "Swallow."

No. I swallow. The pill goes down roughly without water, but I know it won't matter. In a few minutes, the hallucinations will hit, and every person at this table will see me freak out. A fine sweat coats my skin as deep inside me, the fear swells. I hate these hallucinations. The terror that floods my system, even with everything numb and dulled, is enough to make me think one of these days my heart will just stop.

My heart is beating faster now, racing in my chest so fast it's painful. The corners of the room darken first. Then shadows drop from the ceiling. I do my best to keep my expression neutral, but my gaze darts rapidly around the space, waiting for the next monster to appear. I jerk back in my seat as glowing yellow eyes blink at me from the darkness. Something slithers against my leg and I yelp, jumping up so fast the chair topples behind me.

I'm positive the dinner guests are staring and whispering, but all I can focus on is the growing red stain blooming on one gentleman's chest. His white shirt rapidly darkens as the blood spreads. I point a shaky finger, trying to yell, trying to get someone to help him, but nothing comes out. The blood just keeps flowing until a waterfall of red liquid falls from his body and puddles on the floor.

It spreads so fast; it takes seconds for it to grow into a pool. How can the blood from one body make such a large puddle? Oh, because it's also seeping down the walls and dripping from the ceiling. I step back to avoid the spread, but I trip over my chair and fall to the floor. No. It's not my chair. It's a skeleton. A skeleton with ocean blue eyes rolling in the black depthless holes. The eyes land on me and a bony arm lifts, the hand reaching for me before the entire thing crumbles to dust.

I choke on a scream and push myself backward, but the blood spreads too quickly, and soon it soaks through the fabric of my dress. It's cool and sticky against my skin. A whimper crawls up my throat, and I try to escape, but it's everywhere. I notice small swirls forming in the puddle, growing larger and larger until they suddenly stop. Symbols form as portions of the blood disappear into thin air.

It's the same symbols I see every time. And just like the other times, I can't quite put a name to them. It's on the tip of my tongue, but I just can't get it to come out. I know as soon as the drug wears off, the memory of the symbols will disappear and Edward will be disappointed once again.

It seems like it lasts hours, maybe days, but eventually the drugs wear off. My limbs shake and my body shivers violently as chills spread through me. I shake so hard, my hair falls from the chignon and surrounds my shoulders. My tongue is thick and heavy in my mouth, and I try to swallow, but my throat is too dry.

Slowly, the blood pooled on the floor disappears. The shadows creep back up into the ceiling, and the light in the room brightens. The man with the blood pouring from his chest stares at me with his white shirt pristine and blood free.

Edward kneels in front of me with a small smile. "Well, witch. What did you see? And speak loud enough for everyone to hear you."

A show. All this was for a show. To prove he had a witch in his possession who has visions. I want to lie. To tell him I saw nothing, but my reaction to the drugs made it abundantly clear I saw something. Not to mention, my body obeys his every word.

I peel my tongue from the roof of my mouth. "Blood," I whisper hoarsely. "Symbols in the blood. Just like every other time."

"What symbols?" His question is harsh, and he grabs my chin in his fingers, the pain dulled in the haze. "Tell me what they were." His patience is running thin. I can see the desperation bleeding through. The crazed look in his eyes, the clenched jaw, the tightening of his fingers on my chin.

"I don't remember," I say dully. I try. I really do try to remember, but they are just shadows in my memory. Nothing concrete. Nothing with any clarity.

Edward growls and backhands me. My reactions are too slow and I fall to the side, my head hitting the floor hard enough to make my vision blur. The fog isn't enough to block the pain, and I hiss through my teeth as blood blooms in my mouth.

"Take her back to her room!" he shouts.

A guard grabs my arm and yanks me to my feet. I'm dragged through the estate, stumbling and tripping, as I can't make my legs work fast enough. In my room, the woman from earlier is waiting. Her brow draws down when she sees me, but she says nothing. She gives me more commands and removes the dress, replacing it with soft cotton pants and a simple tee-shirt.

Before she walks away she whispers, "Sleep."

It's so quiet, I barely hear her, but my body responds. I eagerly climb into the bed and let my head hit the pillow. Exhaustion flows through me, adding to the constant pressure of the drugs, and I let my body fall into the mattress. I close my eyes and gratefully welcome the darkness.

My body aches. Every muscle screams as I roll over in the bed and my stomach heaves. There's a bucket on the floor for this very reason. Every morning I wake up and purge the drug from my system. Tears stream down my face as the bitter taste of bile clings to my tongue. I can't brush my teeth until someone tells me to, so I lay back in the bed and wait.

I'm so hollow inside. Most of the time, I don't even have any thoughts floating through my head. Right now, though, I can't help but picture a pair of ocean blue eyes and wonder what he must have thought when he realized I wasn't in my room. If only I hadn't left that night. The collar around my throat chokes me and my hands itch to grab it and pull, but my body isn't mine to command.

Panic grips me so hard I struggle to breathe. My chest constricts, and each breath in is too shallow to fill my lungs. Is this going to be the rest of my life? If so, I would welcome being sent to the stakes. Suddenly, the door bursts open, interrupting my rapidly spiraling thoughts.

Edward slams the door shut behind him and stalks toward my bed. I'd cower if I could. This man is the manifestation of my nightmares. The demon who murdered my mom. Despite my desire to choke the life out of him, he terrifies me. I'm not too proud to admit that. He does hold my life in his hands, after all.

He growls as he grabs my hair and pulls me from the bed. Pain rips through my scalp and tears prick the corners of my eyes. I'm thrown to the floor, and I'm powerless to try to catch myself. I land face first on the marble floor, my forehead cracking painfully against the cool surface. Laying on the floor gasping for breath, with pain ricocheting through my head, I pray to the goddess for all of this end.

Edward uses his booted foot to roll me onto my back. He kneels down and stares at me. "If you won't give me what I want, I will make this even more painful for you."

His threat hits, but I can't react. I can't even try to defend myself. Drugging me isn't going to make me have lucid visions that make sense. It's not my fault I can't remember what I see during those frightful hallucinations. It's all the drugs in my system. The shock waves scrambling my brain. It's the things *he* is doing to me.

"I want you to tell me what that first vision meant. The one Sybil had thousands of years ago. I want you to tell me what I need to do to make sure my brother's reign ends. What is it Sybil saw that will help keep him on the throne?"

I don't answer. Not only because I can't, but because I don't know. I have no idea what Sybil saw or what her mad ravings meant. I don't know what those symbols mean that I keep seeing, or the symbols Sybil drew in the blood. I don't know why they think I'm the chosen one when I can't have visions unless I'm drugged to do so. I just know I want it all to end.

Edward growls again and pulls two pills from his pocket. *No. No, please.* Inside, I'm begging him. Pleading with him to not give me two pills. Fear hits me like a freight train, and my heart thunders in my chest. What will two pills do to me? Edward opens my mouth and drops the pills onto my tongue. Tears stream down my face, finally breaking through the barrier in my head.

"Swallow."

A Healthy Dose Of Disappointment

Someone is using my skull as a bongo. Or maybe that's the entire bottle of scotch I drank last night. I don't even know how many days have passed since we returned home, but every night I've spent in my room with my emotional support bottle of alcohol, drinking my sorrows away. How fucking pitiful. I groan and rest my forehead against the cool wood of the desk in my office. I'm not really doing anything, but everyone knows how much I hate it here, so I figured it was as good a place as any to hide from the world.

The door slams open, the sound ricocheting in my head and making me cringe. "Buckle up, buttercup. We got a case." Killian plops into the chair across from me, his voice loud and obnoxious.

"Shhh," I whisper. "Not so loud."

He snorts and drops a file on my desk. It sounds like a ton of bricks as it hits the surface instead of the thick paper it's made of. I pull it toward me and flip it open. All the words blur together, though, and no matter how hard I try to make them unblur, it just gets worse. And honestly, I don't think I want to know what it says.

I shove it back to Killian and rub my temples. "What the fuck does it say?"

He raises one thick brow and smirks. "You should probably lay off the alcohol for a bit, buddy." I shrug my shoulders, and he thankfully says nothing more on the topic. "A group of witches have been meeting at a local shop every night. Your dad tasked us with bringing them in."

My stomach drops out of my ass. I have avoided hunting since I got back, but it looks like my time is up. Can I really do this? The thought of bringing a witch in, of subjecting her to torture and eventual burning, makes my skin prickle like it's suddenly too tight for my body. *What should I do? Do I try to get out of this? But then what?* I know if I tell my dad I quit, I'll be kicked out of the palace. I'll lose my inheritance and the only way to support myself. What would I even do with my life?

Without *her* it doesn't seem like it's worth fighting. I don't see how I'll ever overcome this. So what's more torture to an already tortured soul?

"Right," I breathe, pushing myself to my feet. "Water first. And bread."

The sun is just beginning to set as I follow Killian through the city, our team filing behind us. The bitter wind cuts right through my thick beanie. Coats are too bulky and impede movement if we need to fight, so my skin is quickly turning to ice under my Henley. At least it seems to be clearing my head of the hangover I've had all day. The closer we get to the shop, the more I regret the water I guzzled and the bread I shoved down my throat. It churns threateningly in my stomach at the thought of what's coming.

Killian stops in an alley half a block from the shop. "Okay. They've been meeting at a small library. We have reason to believe there is a hidden room or basement where the witch operates out of. We've counted anywhere from five to eight witches gathering each night." His gaze travels over the group as he relays the information he's gathered. "Berkshire is our lead on this one. Follow his command."

I stare at Killian, startled at his words. *I'm the lead? He's the one who gathered all the information.* Something sparks in Killian's deep brown eyes. Something that almost looks like a challenge. I shrug it off as he turns away. This is a pretty simple mission. We have ten hunters and the element of surprise. I don't expect we need a whole detailed plan about what's going to happen.

I march out of the alley and make my way to the library. The lights are on inside, the golden glow spilling out into the street. A closed sign hangs on the door, and all I can see inside are shelves of books and the corner of a counter in the back of the shop. I try the handle, already assuming it will be locked, and then step back to let Killian work his lock pick magic.

"We're good," he whispers and steps back.

I signal, and on the silent count of three, pull open the door. The hunters file inside and work their way through the space looking for witches. By the time I step inside out of the cold, they're all grouped before a door almost hidden in the back wall. The hinges are just a shade off from the rest of the walls making it stand out.

Killian turns to look at me expectantly, as do the rest of the hunters. It's my job to signal them to enter the hidden room. But as I stand in the library and take a deep breath, a faint whiff of plants meets my nose. Neave's words from when I found the devil's trumpet in her bag float to the front of my mind. *I am a witch. Of course I have plants and herbs.* And as a witch, having those plants and herbs is illegal. The drug was tucked inside a hollowed-out book. A smile pulls at my lips as I look around. A hidden room full of plants, and a library to hide the evidence. It's a pretty good setup.

"Ty," Killian whispers harshly.

I raise my hand, but I can't force my fingers to form the signal. If I do, witches will get hurt. Witches Neave knows and would mourn when they die. Witches that are, in all honesty, probably innocent. A cold sweat breaks out across my skin, and I glance back at the front entrance. I want to run. I want to get out of here and forget this ever happened. My hesitation costs us.

The hidden door opens and a gust of wind blows through the room, knocking us backward. Women pour from the doorway and hunters pull their weapons. *No. I don't want this.* I stand still, unable to join the fight. Unable to hurt a witch or protect my men. So I stand there like an idiot.

I see the book hurtling toward me on a stream of magic, but I'm not fast enough to avoid it. It hits me upside the head hard enough to stun me. As I'm blinking the stars from my vision, a witch throws herself at me. I let her tackle me to the floor, and she straddles my waist and presses a knife to my throat. Vines grow from the potted plants around the room and wrap around my wrists and ankles, holding me still. Not that I would have fought.

"Where is she?" the witch growls.

I blink, and my vision finally clears. The witch is older, with brown hair falling to her chin. "Where is who?"

"Where is Neave? You took her and we haven't seen her. What are you doing with her?"

My heart stops when I hear her name. "You know her?" I breathe. The sounds of fighting dim around us, as if we're suddenly thrown into a bubble. "What can you tell me about her? Tell me *everything*." I'm desperate to know every single thing about her.

The knife presses a little harder against my throat. "Like I'd ever tell you anything." The witch glares at me and bares her teeth. "I'll kill you if you don't tell me. Prince or no."

I raise up as far as I can with the vines restraining me, pushing my neck against the edge of the blade. "Then kill me," I growl.

The knife trembles slightly in her hand, biting into my skin enough to draw blood. It wells hot along the edge. "I'm not kidding, Your Highness."

I flop back onto the wooden floor and stare at the ceiling. "Neither am I," I whisper.

Before she can respond, her body jerks and she falls to the

side, the vines disappearing instantly. Killian stands above me, a sneer on his face.

"What the fuck is going on, Tyberius? You almost got us all killed!"

I sit up and scan the space. The guard has all the witches captured and equalizer distributed. A few of my men are sporting cuts and bruises, but they're all alive. I touch my neck and my finger comes away with a few drops of blood.

"You're not going soft, are you, Ty?"

Killian's words hit me like a blow. My gaze travels over the hunters in the room, and their accusation and confusion makes shame burn up my neck and into my cheeks. Pushing to my feet, I scramble out the front door, heaving a sigh of relief as the cold air hits my heated skin. My hands are shaking as I hold them out in front of me. *I almost got my men killed tonight.* I need to figure out my shit, before someone else gets hurt.

My hope that the cold winter air would clear my head and calm my racing heart is dashed as the palace comes into view. If anything, I'm even more confused and out of sorts. The hallways seem like they're closing in on me, and when I push into my room and close the door, I grasp my chest and double over. It hurts. My heart races so fast it makes my head spin.

I need to calm down, but every time I try, I picture that witch sitting on top of me with a knife to my throat. *She should have done it. She should have just ended me.* Those witches were gathering because they were worried about *her.* I can't say her name. If I do, I'm liable to completely break. That witch is under my skin. She's sunk her claws into my bones and refuses to let go.

Desperate for peace from my thoughts, I grab a bottle of scotch and tip it back. The burn doesn't chase away the turmoil, though. It only seems to make it worse. My hands are shaking so badly the bottle clanks against the full one on the bar as I set it down. Unbidden, my gaze travels to my dresser. Without giving myself a chance to change my mind, I shove it to the side, grunting at the weight. There's a loose tile in the floor, and I use a knife to pry it open.

Nestled in the space under the tile are two vials of clear shimmering liquid. I snag them and set them on the bar cart, eyeing them like they're dragons with teeth that will bite. In a way, they are. It's the last of my dragon's blood, my drug of choice all those years ago. The drug I became addicted to. The drug I OD'd on. I haven't thought of this shit in years. Now, my hands sweat as I think about taking one of those vials.

I think about my mother's voice and the words she spoke to me that fateful night. I still don't know if it was a hallucination or if it was somehow real. What would she think of me now, contemplating going down that road again? What would she think of me craving a witch? What would she think of ... *her*?

I shake my hand and snag a vial. It doesn't matter what my mom would think. She's not here. With a shaking hand, I bring the vial to my lips and tip it into my mouth.

THAT MAY HAVE BEEN a horrible idea. When I finally peel my eyeballs open sometime the next day, I'm pretty sure my brain has exploded and is now just a mushy pile of goo. I know I had at least one bottle of scotch on top of the dragon's blood, but after that, I can't remember.

Movement catches my gaze, and I slowly turn my head to find a white cat sitting next to me on the bed. I groan and close my eyes. *Great. Now I'm seeing her familiar in my hallucinations.*

"Go away," I rasp. "Leave me alone." I don't need any more reminders of her.

The door to my room bursts open and Julian scowls at me from the doorway. "Really, Ty?" He steps into my room, kicking the empty bottles on the floor and sending them scattering. "How long are you going to do this?"

I shrug and look back at the cat, but it's gone. *Fuck.* I need to get my shit together.

"It's been a week. I get that you're upset, and I don't blame you for that, but you can't let it ruin your life." His gaze falls to the empty vial of dragon's blood on the bar cart and his mouth pulls down in anger. "You're better than this, Ty."

I snort. *Am I really, though?* I'm weak. Letting a girl ruin my life. Letting my misery of missing her send me back to the drug that almost killed me.

"You better cut this act. Dad is furious about what happened last night. He wants you in his office. Now." Julian says as he heads back toward the door. With one last disappointing look, he leaves, letting the door shut softly behind him.

Huh. It's weird that his disappointment hurts worse than my dad's or Killian's. Sometime in the last few weeks, my relationship with Julian has shifted, and it's not entirely unwelcome. Too bad I'm probably fucking it all up—not that I can bring myself to care. I take a deep breath and prepare myself to stand and take a shower. When I sit up, I get a good look at my room and grimace. A week's worth of empty liquor bottles litter the floor, along with various articles of clothing. It's an absolute disaster in here.

I let the water heat before stripping out of my dirty clothes and stepping inside. The hot spray immediately helps to clear my head of the hangover, and muscles I've been holding tense for the last week relax. Keeping my dad waiting is a horrible idea, but the thought of stepping out of this shower is immensely unpleasant. I let the water run over my face and down my body, imagining it washing away the memory of *her*. Too bad it doesn't actually do it.

When I finally find myself standing outside my dad's office, all the tension I lost in the shower is back. Stretching my neck from side to side, I step in without knocking. Julian is sitting in a chair with his shoulders thrown back and head lifted proudly. The image of the future king. This is the Julian I have come to know since our mother died.

"Sit," my dad commands, his gaze hard and unyielding.

I sigh as I sit in the chair next to my brother, readying myself for the berating I'm about to get. Mentally, I make bets with myself on what this one will be about. *The mission last night, most likely. With a healthy dose of disappointment.*

"Killian debriefed me on last night's failure," he starts.

I lift my chin and say, "It wasn't a failure. They brought the witches in, did they not?" There is no mistaking the bitterness in my tone.

His eyes narrow and a vein pulses in his forehead. "No thanks to you. And the fact you almost compromised the mission is unacceptable."

I can't disagree with that, so I cross my arms and stare him down. A challenge I know will result in some kind of punishment.

The sound of his teeth grinding together is loud in the silence. He leans forward, placing his elbows on the edge of his desk. "Here's the deal." He levels a stare at me that actually makes me want to shrink in my seat. "If I catch you drunk or high one more time, I *will* strip you of your title and your inheritance. You will not be allowed under this roof, and what you do with your life after that, I couldn't care less." He sits back in his chair and crosses his arms over his chest. "Killian will run lead on all future missions, and if I get reports of you not doing your job, the consequences will be the same. Do I make myself clear?"

"Crystal," I growl, squeezing my hands into fists.

My dad turns his gaze to Julian. "You," he points with a thick finger. "You will return to Seaberth to study under your uncle. This whole thing has made it blatantly obvious we have missed something important in your training. While we focused on the politics and government aspects of ruling, we failed to actually teach you how to rule over your subjects. Edward will correct that."

Julian jerks and opens his mouth, no doubt to argue, but he thinks better of it. Instead, he hangs his head in an un-Julian like manner. Some deeply buried part of me objects to that. Like the older brother in me is slowly reawakening, and doesn't like to see Julian upset.

"What happened in Seaberth has nothing to do with Julian," I say, sitting up straighter in my chair. "You should know how impossible it is to keep me in line. If our current king can't do it, why do you expect the future king to be able to?" I don't keep the challenge out of my voice. Calling him out on his failure to rein me in all these years is probably not the smartest thing to do when he's already pissed at me, but I just can't help myself. Call it one of my favorite pastimes.

My dad's face turns an ugly shade of red, and he visibly attempts to control himself with a swallow and a deep inhale. "Julian, you leave first thing in the morning. Tyberius ... get out of my sight."

Julian and I both stand and leave the office. We know better than to argue with that tone, and even I'm not so stupid to push him any further. Julian is quiet as we walk through the palace. Once again, he finds himself on the wrong end of our dad, and it's because of me.

"I'm sorry, Julian," I say quietly.

He whips his head in my direction. "For what?"

"For getting you involved in all of this." I shrug. "You should have just went about your business. Then you wouldn't be in Dad's war path."

"It's what family does, right?"

He's so quiet, I almost don't hear him. The tentative nature of his question makes me realize how much we both missed each other, and I realize how much we've lost in the twelve years since our mom's death. I stop in the middle of the hall and pull him for a hug. He's tense at first, surprised by my actions, but then he wraps his arms around me and squeezes. *God, I haven't hugged my brother in twelve years.* When we pull apart, I blink away the tears that burn the corners of my eyes.

"I better go pack. Hopefully, I'm not there too long." Before

Julian walks away, I spot the telltale sign of tears glistening in his eyes as well.

I make a vow to myself to fix things between us when he gets back. I don't want to let any more time pass with us not talking. In my room, I grab an unopened bottle of scotch and the last vial of dragon's blood. My dad just said if he *caught* me drunk or high. So as long as I don't get caught, I'm golden.

Dripping Blood, Clattering Bones, and Tyberius's Pained Whispers

I caught a glimpse of myself in the mirror this morning after the nice young woman helped me shower, because I can't even do that on my own. I'd be humiliated, but at this point, I just don't care. Every bone in my body stands out sharply. The combination of only eating when someone remembers to tell me to, and the cocktail of drugs being forced into my system, is nibbling away at me.

Each of my ribs protrudes from my chest and abdomen. My clavicles form deep valleys where they stand out. My cheeks and eyes are sunken in. And my skin and hair have lost their luster and glow. But it's the vacant expression in my dulled eyes that startled me the most.

The gnawing ache in my belly has become a constant companion. As well as the pounding in my head from constant drug use. Every day is the same. I'm dressed in the black velvet gown, given my two pills, and paraded around Edward's guests, whether it's during dinner, a party, or simple meetings. The result is always the same. Terrifying hallucinations that fascinate the observers.

Edward's anger keeps growing as each vision is useless to him. The terror is the only thing I can remember when the drugs wear off. I know there is blood and symbols, but that is the extent of it. I should be worried about what Edward will do next, but I can't bring myself to care. If he were to give me three pills, I'm positive my heart would stop entirely, and that resulting death would not be unwelcome at this point.

Every night, while I lay awake, unable to sleep unless told to do so, I bring forth the image of ocean blue eyes. I don't know why I torture myself with them, but I can't stop it. And each night, the pain in my chest grows. I hate that I'm so consumed with him. That I care so much about what he thinks. I just wish I could tell him I didn't run away.

The guard leading me through the palace stops in front of Edward's office today, which means some kind of high-profile guest will be visiting. He opens the door and prods me forward. All I can see are the backs of the heads of the two guests. I walk numbly until I'm standing in my usual spot—next to Edward behind his desk. He turns me to face his visitors with a hand on my hip. Usually, that would make me cringe. I'd probably slap his hand away and give him a few choice words. However, in my current state, I don't even react.

Once I'm turned around, my heart stutters as much as it can. Julian is sitting in the chair nearest me. His blue eyes—so like Tyberius's—are wide as he takes me in. *Help me! Please, help me!* Of course, I say no such thing. I don't even react to seeing him, besides the slight stutter in my chest. For all he can tell, this is exactly where I want to be.

"I have a real treat for you guys today," Edward says, his fingers wrapping around my wrist. "Julian is already aware of this, but I'm lucky enough to have the witch foretold thousands of years ago. We are struggling, unfortunately, to produce clear visions, but I'm hoping having the Berkshire prince present will help inspire some."

The second guest, a tan gentleman with dark wavy hair, grins gleefully. I'm surprised he isn't rubbing his hands together. Julian frowns slightly, but says nothing. *Do something, Julian! Stop him!*

Edward turns me toward him with a yank on my wrist. "Open." I do and he drops two white pills onto my tongue.

I'm still not used to swallowing them without water, and they slide painfully down my throat, getting stuck until I swallow over and over. Inside, I claw at the barrier keeping me from my magic. I scream and rage against the electrical current keeping me contained. If I could just show some kind of reaction, I could let Julian know I don't want to be here.

It's no use.

Within minutes, the drugs take effect. My heart hammers so hard and fast against my rib cage it makes me gasp. The beats are erratic. Some of them coming so quickly on the heels of the other it may as well be one beat, while others are spaced so far apart I wonder if my heart has finally stopped. My vision wavers, everything going fuzzy, as my breath becomes harder to draw in through the tightness in my chest.

Shadows dance in the corners of the room, curling up the walls to meet the darkness dripping from the ceiling. Blood oozes out of the space where the walls meet the ceiling, and big fat drops of it splatter to the ground. The sweat dripping down my neck and back feels like blood and I whimper as I shift, trying to erase the sensation.

I drop my gaze to Julian, hoping something in my expression tells him to help me. But as I do, his form shimmers. I blink and suddenly it's Tyberius sitting in the chair instead. He shakes his head, lips pressed into a thin line, and disappointment radiates from him. I try to open my mouth, to tell him the truth, but before I can, his eyes well with tears. Only they aren't tears. It's blood, and it streams down his face, staining his cheeks and chin crimson.

I cry out as his blue eyes dull and a bloom of red spreads across his chest. His chest that now has a gaping wound. He raises one hand and points a finger at me. His mouth forms two words. *Your. Fault.*

I scream and fall to the ground, clutching at my chest as my heart skips beats. Tyberius's body disintegrates into shadows that swirl around me, and I swear I can hear his voice floating in the darkness, the pained words making me sob and gasp for air. *Why did you do it? I thought we had something special. My witch, why?*

I can't control my trembling body and I fall to my side, my cheek landing in something warm and gooey. I don't need to open my eyes to know it's blood. It's always blood. That damn puddle with the symbols I can never remember when the drugs fade. I keep my eyes squeezed shut tightly, shaking and whimpering, praying for it to end.

Something grabs my wrist and yanks. A scream tears from my throat as I open my eyes to find a skeleton with ocean blue eyes trying to drag me away. Wordless sounds pour from my lips, and I scooch myself back into a corner. Bringing my knees to my chest, I wrap my arms around my head trying to block the visions and the sounds. Dripping blood, clattering bones, and Tyberius's pained whispers.

Wetness slides down my cheeks and I wipe it away, only to find blood on my fingertips. Boots splash in the puddle before me, and I follow them up to Tyberius's now-whole body. With a knife in one hand and a torch in the other, he grins at me, and there is nothing fun or playful about this grin. Slowly, he lowers the torch to me, and as the heat from the flames kisses my face, the time between each beat of my heart grows ... until it stops.

BLEARILY, I blink my eyes open and find myself back in my room. There is no sudden need to vomit like I usually have after being drugged, but when I swallow, my throat is sore and raw, like I've already done just that.

"Here, have a drink," a soft voice says from the side of my bed.

I turn my head and find the young woman, a maid I guess, holding out a glass of water. My hand trembles as I take it and bring it to my lips. The liquid is cool and soothing as it slides down my aching throat.

"In case you're wondering what happened," she says after I hand the glass back to her, "your heart stopped. The doctor was able to get it started again, and he purged the drugs from your system."

Please, help me. I stare at her, trying so hard to force something through the haze, but it's impossible. I give up and close my eyes. Immediately, the images from the hallucination plague me. Tyberius dying. His skeleton trying to drag me away. The whisper of his words. The fire he lowered toward me. I snap my eyes open, not wanting to see any of that.

The maid peeks toward the door before turning back to me. She lowers her voice so I can barely hear her. "I'm sorry there isn't more I can do." She shakes her head and purses her lips. "I'm also sorry that I'm here to get you ready. Prince Edward wishes to see you."

Fear lights up my nervous system. Not again. Not so soon. I can't handle much more of this. My body is breaking down. My spirit is wearing thin. All hope has long since vanished. If only the doctor hadn't been able to save me. Then all of this would be over. And I wouldn't have even been burned at the stake.

The maid gets me ready in my usual black dress. It's already become baggy in places from all the weight I've lost. Once I'm presentable, the guard escorts me to Edward's office. Something like deja-vu hits me as I stand outside the door. Only this time, when I'm pushed inside, there are no guests. Just Edward sitting behind his desk, fingers steepled in front of his mouth. I'm not given the command to sit, so I stand behind the chair, swaying slightly on my feet as exhaustion presses down on me.

"I'm not sure what else to do," Edward says, adopting a bored tone. "I've brought the Berkshire prince in, and that didn't work. I've increased the dosage, and that didn't work. I've threatened you, and that didn't work." He sighs dramatically and pushes up from his seat. "What else will I have to do to make you cooperate?"

Like I'm not trying to cooperate? People and their ignorance! It's unbelievable how little people know about witches and magic. How we have lived with them for so long and still they fear and hate us. Does he think I'm enjoying my time here? That I'm purposely holding back these visions? If only I could scream at him. Inside, I'm quivering with unrestrained anger. It burns through me hotter than any fire.

Edward circles me, his gaze traveling up and down my body as he does. I want to shiver in revulsion. When he returns to stand in front of me, he trails his finger down my cheek before grabbing my neck roughly. He doesn't squeeze, but he applies just enough pressure to let me know he wants to.

"This is my last resort. If this doesn't work, you're not worth my time." He sneers and for a second, I'm afraid he is going to beat or rape me. But instead, he pulls a little yellow pill from his pocket. "A different drug. Let's see how this one works. Open."

STUPID FUCKING CAT

WHY IS IT SO FUCKING COLD HERE IN THE WINTER? THE wind whips through the streets and snowflakes whirl around like the inside of a snow globe. I tug my hat lower on my head, then shove my hands into my pockets. Each breath fogs in front of me. I'm supposed to be in the gym with Killian, but instead I'm hooking up with my old dealer. I can't bring myself to face my men after what happened. And knowing I won't be able to go back out in the field without something to numb me, this seemed like the best plan.

The Red Bridge, as people like to call it, appears in the distance through the swirling snow. The dark gray metal structure got its name from the multitudes of deaths that have happened under it. Violence and crime are at their worst in this area of the city, and the Red Bridge is at the heart of it all. The ground under that bridge has been painted in blood many, many times.

My fingers brush the cold metal of the gun in my pocket. I rarely carry a gun with me, preferring knives for their stealth and ease of use. But knowing the dangers of this part of town, especially if I'm recognized, I opted for fire power. As I slip through shadowed alleys, I keep my senses on high alert for any sign of danger.

Once I make it to the bridge, I head for the column I know my dealer liked to hang out by. I have no clue what his name is, so I always just called him Steve in my head. People watch from the darkness like hawks waiting to pounce, and my shoulders itch with the sensation of eyes tracking my every move. *How the hell did I do this when I was seventeen years old? And how the hell didn't I get jumped?* Just up ahead, I make out the outline of someone where Steve usually hangs, and I hold my breath as I approach. It's been years since I've done this. Who knows if he's still hanging around these parts. Or if he's even still alive.

"Well, well, well," he drawls. "Look who grew up. Thought I seen the last of you years ago."

Time has not treated him well. Or maybe that's the drugs. He looks like a living skeleton. Sunken eyes, gaunt cheekbones, emaciated frame. He's hunched over like he's in pain, or the cold is getting to him, or maybe he's just that weak.

"I'm surprised you recognize me," I say, shuffling behind the pillar to block most of the wind.

Steve snorts, the action almost making him fall over. "Like I wouldn't recognize the little prince."

Oh, shit. Guess I'm not that good at concealing my identity. I pull money out of my pocket and hand it over. "My usual, then."

Steve grins, displaying more gaps than actual teeth. "Anything to serve my country." He passes me five vials of dragon's blood and pockets my money. "Til next time, Your Highness." He gives me a little bow and cackles as I walk away.

I hurry through the streets, and not just because of the cold. An irrational fear settled over me as soon as I dropped the drugs into my pocket. What if my dad has someone watching me? *Fuck it.* It's only a matter of time before he finds out and throws me on my ass outside the palace. Still, the sensation of being watched follows me until I close my bedroom door behind me.

"What the actual fuck?" I groan. "I'm not even high and I'm hallucinating?" I blink my eyes, then rub them hard enough to see stars. It doesn't make the image go away.

Sitting on my bed is a white cat with gray tipped ears and a fluffy gray tail.

"Shoo." I wave my hand at it. "Shoo." The image still doesn't go away. If anything, I swear the cat rolls its eyes at me. "Why is this happening?" I moan.

Her familiar jumps from the bed and prances over to me. I grimace and take a step back. It's such a real hallucination, and I can't help but shiver at the thought of a familiar being this close to me. Witches are one thing, magic is another, but familiars? Nope. That shit is too weird to comprehend. The cat follows me until my back bumps into the wall. Its bright blue eyes pin me in place and it meows. Loudly.

"What do you want? Go away!" I wave my hands again, rather uselessly.

This time, the cat moves so fast, it's just a white blur of fur. Its claws latch onto my lower leg, piercing through my pants. I gasp and jump. The cat glares at me before sinking its teeth into my knee.

"What the fuck?" I yell, shaking my leg, trying to dislodge the demon cat. The claws dig in tighter, and a faint growl rumbles up its throat. I growl right back and reach down to grasp it by the scruff. With a firm yank, it lets go of its death grip on my leg. I lift the bastard to eye level and glare at it. "You're not a hallucination."

It huffs, and I can just imagine it saying, "No shit, blondie."

"What are you doing here? You're ... her ... familiar."

Another huff. Another goddamn eye roll. Cats can't roll their eyes, so how is this demon doing it?

Before I can open my mouth to say something impressively stupid to the cat, my phone rings. I stare the animal down as I fish it out of my pocket and swipe to answer without looking at whose calling.

"Yeah?"

"She's here. Uncle Edward has her, Ty. And it's not good."

Julian's voice filters through the speaker. His words take a moment to register.

When they do, I drop the cat, who hisses and swipes at me again. "What are you talking about?" I dodge the cat, who swipes out again. "Would you fucking stop?" I yell at it.

"What?" Julian asks bewildered.

"Her damn familiar just showed up and it's attacking the shit out of me."

"It's probably trying to tell you she's in trouble."

"What do you mean, Uncle Edward has her?" I sit on the edge of my bed, my heart pounding in my chest.

"He's controlling her somehow, through this awful iron collar around her throat. And he's giving her hallucinogens that are absolutely destroying her. She almost died last night."

The world tips precariously around me, and I have to grasp the edge of the bed to remain upright. "She's not there willingly?" My question is hoarse and broken. The hope sparking in my chest makes me rub my sternum.

"No. There is no way. She's like half of the woman she used to be. There is nothing in her gaze. No spark of life. No quick quip of her tongue. She's being forced into this, Ty, I'm positive."

"Mother fucker," I growl. Plans form in my mind, and I dismiss and rework them until one sits front and center. "I'll be there tomorrow morning. Meet me at Landon's." I hang up and glance at the cat sitting on my floor, tail swishing angrily. "Looks like we're going on a trip, asshole."

I INSTRUCTED the pilot of our smaller private jet to land in the field outside of Seaberth. I didn't want to risk Uncle Edward finding out about me arriving in the city. It would be too obvious, especially when Neave turns up missing from his estate. Luckily, when we were kids, Julian, Killian, and I would sneak out of the city for fun. So finding my way into the city and through the streets is like muscle memory.

"Stay near me, Fluffy," I say to the demon cat. "I don't want you getting—" He takes off, tearing down the street, white coat fading in the distance. "In trouble," I finish lamely. "Stupid fucking cat." Whatever that demon is up to, I don't want to know.

I creep down the winding road, my senses on high alert for any sign of being watched or followed. The sun is just rising above the horizon when my destination comes into view. They must have been watching for me, because as soon as I approach the front door, it swings open and a hand snatches my arm and pulls me inside.

"Tyberius!" Small arms wrap around me and pull me in for a hug. "It is so good to see you again."

I smile down at the top of a head full of dark hair, streaked with gray. "It's good to see you too, Shari."

She pulls away and frowns as she runs her gaze over my body. "Too thin," she clucks. "And you look tired. Are you not sleeping well?"

I chuckle. "Not particularly, no. And I am not too thin. That's just you trying to ply me with too much of your delicious cooking."

"Well, you never refuse it." Shari steps back with her hands on her hips. "How about some breakfast?"

"That actually sounds really great, thank you."

"While she cooks, you can fill us in on what brings you here so secretively."

I approach my old mentor, and he pulls me in for a hug. "Thanks for letting me come, Landon."

"Anything for my best student. Now, let's go take a seat in the kitchen, and you can explain."

We follow Shari into the kitchen. It's a small space, but homey. Landon teaches music, and he doesn't bring home a ton of money, but their house is warm and inviting. Soft shades of blue and cream fill the entire space. Bright wildflowers bloom in vases sitting atop every free surface. Landon pulls the curtains shut in the kitchen, and we take seats at the table while Shari bustles around.

"So, care to explain why my best student, whom I haven't heard from in years, suddenly calls me and asks if I'd be willing to help him? What kind of trouble have you found yourself in now?"

I shake my head. "It's kind of a long story." Rubbing my hand down my face, I launch into the tale, leaving out my feelings for Neave. Luckily, me wanting to get her back is easily explained as me needing her for the visions.

When I finish my story, Landon sits back in his chair and crosses his arms. "Is there a reason you feel the need to hide from your uncle?"

"I honestly don't know." I shrug. "Something about this whole situation is making me question his motives." And it's not just because he kidnapped Neave and is currently drugging her.

Landon studies me with a frown. I try not to shift under that penetrating stare, but it's hard. Landon has been more of a father figure to me than my own father. When I was living in Seaberth under my uncle's tutelage, I took piano lessons from him. I learned more from this man about life than I did from my dad or uncle.

He doesn't get a chance to say anything. Shari sets a steaming pile of bacon on the table, followed by a massive stack of fluffy pancakes. "Eat up, boys."

By the time we're done eating, the sun has fully risen. I'm helping Shari clean the kitchen when there is a knock on the door. Landon opens it and lets my brother in.

"Julian!" Shari rushes toward him and pulls him in for a hug. He gets the same spiel I did. "You're too thin, and you look tired."

"Leave the boys alone, Shari," Landon sighs as he sits down on the couch.

"What can you tell me?" I ask Julian. It's hard to keep the

desperation from voice, and I'm positive Landon is already parsing through my story and finding all the bits I left out. The bits about my obsession with a witch.

Julian takes a plate of leftover breakfast from Shari and sits on the couch. "I know where he's keeping her, and her basic schedule. It changes frequently, though, depending on who he wants to show her off to."

I fight down the sudden rage that makes my hands shake. Showing her off like she's some prized horse. That motherfucker will pay for whatever harm he has brought to her. "What time do you think is best for me to break in and grab her?"

"As much as I know you won't want to wait, I think our best bet is tonight."

Dread curls in my gut. "But that means another day of her being drugged." Another day where the drugs might take her away from me forever.

Julian nods with a grimace. "Unfortunately, yeah."

I chew on my cheek, contemplating everything. Another night might make it too late. But going in now will be risky. I don't think about it long. I'm this close to her. She won't suffer anymore than she already has. I push up from the couch and head toward the door.

"Where are you going?" Julian asks, his words distorted by the mouthful of bacon.

"To get my witch back."

A WHITE STREAK blurs in front of me. Fluffy, as I've taken to calling the familiar, was waiting for me outside the house. He dashed off toward the estate, and Julian and I follow.

"The back entrance we used to sneak out of will probably be our best bet." Julian says next to me.

"Do you remember any of the secret passages we used to explore?"

"Oh shit. I remember how to get into them, but I don't remember my way through them."

I fall quiet as I contemplate those secret passages. Once we're inside those, it should be easy to get her out unseen. We would just have to remember how to get through them.

When the estate comes into view, we skirt around the side, keeping to the shadows. The back door opens to a storage room. It's typically used by servants for deliveries and is currently empty. Voices sound distantly on the other side of the walls, but luckily we won't have to go out there. The secret door is in the storage room hidden behind a rolling wire shelf laden with baking supplies.

I have no idea why these passages were built, but they had to have been added when the estate was constructed. Whether or not uncle—or anyone else—knows about them, I don't know. Julian and I found one on accident when we were arguing over something as kids. I got frustrated with him and shoved him. He landed against the wall in his bedroom and a secret door popped open. It was impossible to see. Built so well into the wall, the hinges and openings were invisible.

We spent most of our childhood exploring the passages with Killian. There are at least three other secret doors in the estate—in the ballroom, the library, and a guest room. There are probably more, but some of the passages were caved in, some of the doors were locked and we couldn't get them to open, and some were just too dark and creepy for us to investigate.

Once we slip into the passage, I turn to Julian. "Which door should we go through?"

"The guest bedroom is just down the hall from hers."

The passage is dark, but we use the flashlights on our phones to light the way. Every sound echoes off the smooth concrete floor and rough rock walls, so we make our way quickly, but quietly. It doesn't take long for memory to flood back to me, and I know exactly where to go. The guest bedroom is plain and dusty. No sheets on the bed and the curtains pulled tight. Uncle must not have a lot of visitors staying overnight these days. As the door shuts behind us, I make sure the tapestry hiding the door is in place.

"I'll distract the guard," Julian says. "Give me a few minutes to get him away from the door. I'll meet you back here."

I shake my head. "Meet back at Landon's. Later, though. I want people to see you around today, so you're not accused of helping her escape."

Julian hesitates for a moment, his eyes taking on that stubborn light they usually do when he wants to argue, but he nods and slips out of the room. I wait for a few minutes before cracking open the door and peering into the hall. Empty. Creeping down the hall, I count the doors until I get to the one Julian mentioned was hers. I take a deep breath before opening it.

My heart stops as my gaze lands on her.

She's laying on the bed, staring unseeing at the ceiling. Even as I slowly make my way to her side, she doesn't turn to look at me.

"Neave," I whisper.

Nothing.

My breath catches on the lump in my throat when I get a good look at the iron collar on her throat. I don't have time to try to figure it out right now. I need to get her out of here as quickly as possible.

"Neave, look at me." My voice is hoarse, my heart thundering. So slowly, she turns her head toward me. There is no recognition in her gaze. It's completely empty. I swallow and reach out my hand, fingers shaking. "Take my hand, Neave. I'm getting you out of here."

Insurmountable Mountains

With Neave's hand in mine, I pull her to the door and push through it. The hallway is still empty, and we make our way to the guest room with the hidden passage.

"Hey! Stop!"

I look behind us to find a guard rounding the corner, his hand reaching for a weapon.

"Shit." I push Neave into the room and grab her shoulders so she's looking at me. "Wait here. Don't go anywhere."

I dash back out into the hallway, pulling two daggers from my waist. If the guard gets away, he'll be able to identify me, and Edward will know it was me who stole Neave. Not that it would be hard to figure out, but I don't want to help him connect the dots.

Before the guard can make it a few feet down the hall, I flip my dagger so I'm holding it by the blade. Knife throwing was always my favorite. I used to use it to impress girls at the bars. My steps slow, and I exhale sharply, cocking back my arm before launching the dagger forward. The guard ducks, but he's not quite quick enough to avoid it entirely. The blade slices through his shoulder and he loses his grip on his knife.

I press my advantage and dart forward, shoving my shoulder into his sternum and knocking him off balance. As he attempts to regain his footing, I shove him against the wall and slice my blade across his throat. I grimace as blood spills over my hand. His body falls limply to the ground when I step away, and I spare just one moment for regret. I hate that I had to kill him, he was just doing his job. Unfortunately for him, that job involved keeping my girl captured and drugged. He never stood a chance.

I rush back to Neave and take her hand, pulling her through the hidden passages. We make it out of the estate and into the city without further incident.

The walk through Seaberth with a zombified Neave is nerve wracking. I keep to the shadows and as out of sight as possible. Fluffy skulks in front of us the entire time, and I hope hes keeping an eye on things as well. I don't think I take a single breath until Landon's house comes into view.

I rush Neave through the front door and lock it behind me. As soon as Shari sees us, she gasps.

"What has he done to that poor girl?" She flutters around me and Neave like an agitated hummingbird.

"Sit down, Shari. Give them some space." Landon tugs his wife back and pushes her into a chair. "Take her to the spare room," he directs me.

I grip her hand tightly, lead her to the spare room and sit her on the edge of the bed. It's eerie how quiet she is. This is nothing like the Neave I have come to know. There is no sass, no attitude, no sarcasm. She's like an empty vessel. The sight makes my chest cave in, and I rub it as I look at that damn collar.

Running my finger over the surface, I look at it closely for any clasps or hinges. I can see nothing, though. It looks like a solid piece of iron. The more I look at it, the more my panic grows. *How the hell do I get this thing off of her?* Landon enters the room and grabs my wrist. It's not until then I realize I was yanking at the collar.

"Don't pull on it. Look." He points to the inside. A prong protrudes from the collar and is stuck in her neck. "If you pull too hard, you'll rip that right through her veins."

"How do we get it off?" I run my hands through my hair and notice dimly that they're shaking.

"Let me see if I have something."

Landon leaves, and I sit on the bed next to Neave. "I'm going to get this off of you," I whisper. She stares straight ahead. "Look at me, Neave."

She turns toward me slowly, and I clench my jaw, grinding my teeth together. Her cheeks and eyes are sunken in. Her clavicles protrude sharply from her chest. I'm willing to bet, if I run my hand over her ribs, I'd be able to count each one of them. She is skin and bone. Like her body has been eating itself from the inside out.

Her beauty may have been what initially drew me to her, but I quickly realized it was everything else about her that I couldn't get enough of. Most importantly, the way she challenges me to become a better man. And seeing this strong, beautiful woman reduced to this shadow of a person is utterly heartbreaking. Before I realize it, my vision blurs and wetness slides down my cheeks. I hastily wipe the tears away and clear my throat. The last thing I need is for Shari or Landon to catch onto my feelings.

Landon returns with some kind of small power tool and a wet cloth. "I'm going to need your help, Tyberius." He hands me the wet cloth. "Tuck this between her skin and the collar, away from the prong."

I do as he asks, being as gentle as possible. The prong on the other side of the collar digs deeper into her neck with the movement and I wince, even though she doesn't react. Once the cloth is where he likes it, Landon directs me to pull the collar as far from her neck as I can. When the tool powers on, a small circular blade spins with a whir and my stomach clenches.

"Do not hurt her." I don't mean for there to be such a growl to my tone, but I can't help it. That spinning blade is inches from her beautiful neck. All it would take is one slip for it to cut right into her skin.

Landon just grunts and gently touches the blade to the collar. Sparks fly as metal hits metal. Smoke curls where the blade cuts through. I feel like it takes hours, when in reality, it probably only takes minutes. Eventually, the collar snaps apart and I gently pull it from her neck, careful of the prong. I use the wet cloth to blot the little bit of blood that dribbles from the small hole in her neck.

With that collar off, the tightness in my chest eases some. "Lay down, Neave."

As she follows the command, Shari pops into the room with a tray. Steam curls from a bowl of soup, and the scent of freshly baked bread wafts toward me. Shari sets the tray over Neave's lap.

"Eat," I say quietly. I watch every bite she takes, wishing I could see the weight being put back on already. When she's finished, I remove the tray and set it on the floor by the bedroom door before returning to Neave's side. "Sleep, Neave. When you wake up, you should feel better."

Her eyes close and after a few minutes, her breathing evens out. I pull up a chair to the bed, and settle in to wait.

SOMETIME WHILE WAITING, Julian came back. He says no one followed him here, and no one suspects him of helping Neave escape. As for the escape, he says Edward is furious.

"I thought for sure he was going to have a stroke when he realized she was missing," Julian says quietly, studying Neave's sleeping form. "He's going on a rampage through the estate. Questioning and threatening everyone."

I grimace. I don't want anyone else to get in trouble for this, but when it comes to Neave, I'll do anything to make sure she's safe. Even if that means risking myself and others. "Why would he kidnap her? Do you think it has to do with more than the visions?" I ask my brother.

He sighs heavily. "I have no idea, but I'm positive it's nothing good. If he just wanted to get the vision from her like we originally wanted, why wouldn't he have just let you keep her? Why the kidnapping?" He frowns, his brows pulling into a V above his nose. "I hope she can help us figure that out when she wakes up. Maybe he did one of those evil monologues villains do in the movies."

I smirk, but it fades quickly as Neave stirs in the bed. Julian quickly excuses himself, and I sit forward on the edge of my chair. Her eyes flutter before opening. Her gaze immediately lands on me and her eyes widen.

"What ... where ...?" she groggily trails off, shaking her head.

"You're safe now," I reassure her. "We're at a friend's house in Seaberth."

Her hand lifts from the covers, and she trails her fingers over her neck, eyes widening further. "It's gone," she whispers. Tears build on her lashes, but they don't fall.

"It's gone. And I swear, you'll never be caged or collared again." My voice is rough, and I have to swallow down the emotion growing in me. When she just stares at me, I clear my throat. "Can you tell me what happened?"

Before she can respond, Shari enters with another tray of food. "Julian said you were awake. Are you hungry?"

Neave shakes her head, and I frown. "You should eat. You—"

A sob climbs up her throat, and before I know it, her shoulders are shaking with the force of her crying. Shari sets the tray on the bedside table, and quickly leaves, giving us some privacy.

"Neave," I whisper, crawling onto the bed next to her. She immediately turns toward me and buries her face in my chest. Something inside me lights up with joy that she turned to me for comfort. I wrap my arms around her and pull her close.

"I'm ... I'm so ... sorry," she says between gasping sobs.

"What are you sorry for? You have no reason to apologize." I rub my hand up and down her back, my fingers bouncing over each vertebrae.

"I didn't ... run away." She curls tighter against me, and I scoop her into my arms, settling her in my lap. "I ... just needed ... some air. I ... was going ... to come back."

More tightness in my chest eases at her words. Just knowing she didn't leave me makes it easier to breathe. She was going to return. I gently rub her back and let her tears run their course. Having her in my arms, knowing I came so close to losing her for good, has me holding her a little tighter. But just because she was going to come back, doesn't mean she wants to be with me. I still killed so many of her sisters. Maybe there is too much between us. Maybe our pasts are insurmountable mountains that will forever remain between us.

When her tears finally dry, she pulls away, but she stays in my lap. "I'm sorry," she sniffles. "I got your shirt wet."

I chuckle at the tear stained patch on my dark blue Henley. "It's no big deal. I'm just glad you're okay."

She looks into my eyes and I do my best to relay my feelings through the look. The space between us goes taut and my stomach flutters as her lips part on a soft inhale. But, she breaks the moment, turning her gaze to her lap.

I clear my throat and shove thoughts of kissing her out of my mind. She's in no shape to be doing any of the things I want to do to her. "Can you tell me what happened?"

She nods and takes a deep breath to prepare herself. "I went to the beach, just for some fresh air and to look at the stars. I wasn't paying attention to my surroundings. I heard footsteps in the sand behind me, and when I turned around..." she trails off and gasps, eyes widening. "Oh shit. Oh fuck. Tyberius, is Killian with you?"

I frown and shake my head. "No. Why?"

She swallows, and the look she gives me sets me on edge. "He's the one who knocked me out and took me to your uncle's."

Every muscle in my body stiffens at her words. A slow burning rage spreads through my veins, turning everything in its path to ash. I take a deep breath and swallow down my anger. "Are you sure?" My voice is deadly quiet, my body taut as a bowstring.

Sensing the short leash I have on my emotions, Neave turns to me and places her hand on my heart. I know she can feel it thumping behind my rib cage. "I'm positive," she whispers. Her eyes flick back and forth as she watches my face closely, and a frown pulls down the corners of her mouth at what she sees.

"It's nothing. I'll deal with it later." It's not nothing. It's huge. It means he purposely didn't post guards outside her window in the hope she'd run away so he could follow her. I asked my brother the other day if they found out what caused the fire at the inn. He said they believe it was arson, but have no leads. Something ugly curls in my gut, and suspicion swims through me. "What else can you tell me?" My voice is harsher than I intended it to be, but I'm having a hard time controlling the urge to fly home and shove a knife through Killian. Neave brings me back to the problem at hand. Uncle Edward.

"Well, he put that collar on me." She shudders, and I run my fingers over the back of her neck, reminding her it's not there anymore. "It messed with the electrical pulses in my brain, or something. It essentially made me a slave. I couldn't do anything without someone telling me what to do. Each movement, each thought, was like fighting through the densest fog."

Her voice trembles as she speaks, and I keep rubbing her back, giving her comfort. I wish I could tell her to stop. I don't want her to have to relive this so soon, but I need to know what happened and what Uncle's goal is.

She buries her face in my shirt before continuing. "He drugged me with some kind of hallucinogenic to make me have visions." She shudders again, and I give her a gentle squeeze. "It was awful." Her voice is no more than a whisper. "I saw so many horrid things, but I never remembered them after the drugs wore off. Just blood. And symbols. Occasionally ... occasionally your eyes."

I jerk back. *My eyes?* She hallucinated about me? Is that a good thing or a bad thing? "Julian told me about that. I'm so sorry you had to go through that."

"Did he tell you I was here? Is that how you knew?"

"Yeah. He called me, and I came as soon as I could."

"Thank you," she whispers. The wobble in her voice gives away the fight she's waging against her tears.

"Don't ever thank me for that. I will always save you." Her breath hitches in her chest, and she tucks her head against me. I fight the smile threatening to tug my lips up. "What about my uncle? Why was he so desperate for visions that he would kidnap and drug you?"

"It's not good. And it goes all the way back to my mom." She pulls away and slides off my lap. I immediately miss her weight and warmth. "He thought my mom was the one prophesied in Sybil's visions. She wore that armband, the one she gave me." She rubs the empty spot on her bicep where the gold band usually is. "Apparently that armband represses visions. It's why I never had any. Your uncle had my mom collared at one point. I don't know how, but she escaped. She fled to Rossvale and eventually had me. She had the band made, and then gave it to me when I turned 16 and came into my power. Edward caught her a year after that and he had her burned for escaping. I guess she never gave him what he wanted. I don't think it was her the visions were talking about."

"It was you," I whisper. We had assumed that, but with her not having any visions, I hadn't been able to confirm it.

"I think my mom knew. I don't know how, but it's why she gave me the band."

"But why does Edward want you? Why kidnap you when he could just let me get the vision from you?"

"Because he wants to know first. He wants to know what the

threat is so he can protect it. He wants your dad off the throne and you and Julian out of the picture."

"Because he wants the throne for himself," I finish for her.

She doesn't answer, but she nods. I heave a sigh and run a hand down my face. This is what I was afraid of. I never thought he was content living in my dad's shadow. I need to tell Julian. He needs to get out of the estate, and we need to find a way to gather evidence so we can tell our dad. I fall into battle plan mode, and I barely notice when Neave relaxes and slips into sleep.

I let her curl up next to me. Her purple hair splayed out behind her, and I run my fingers through the strands. I love the way it feels. Silken, soft, and smooth. I keep doing it, finding a sense of calm inside me with the motions. The bedroom door opens and Shari enters. She looks pointedly at me, then Neave. Her eyes narrow, and I know she's connecting the dots. It was only a matter of time. I sigh and force myself from the bed and away from Neave.

"I need to find Julian," I say quietly. It's not a lie, but I also don't want to hear anything she has to say. As I brush past her, she gives me a knowing look. "Not now. Please."

She nods and heads toward the kitchen while I search for Julian. Before I find him, I stumble across the music room and the grand piano standing proudly in the middle of the space. The black lacquer shines enticingly. My fingers itch with the need to touch the keys.

"When was the last time you played?"

I jump and turn to find Landon watching me. "It's been a long time. At least two years." I glance back to the piano and chew on my lip.

"Sit. Play. That's why she's here."

I shake my head. "I can't. I'm too out of practice."

"Nonsense. It's like riding a bicycle." He pushes me forward. "Don't let that talent go to waste."

My feet move before I realize what I'm doing, and then I'm

sitting on the bench, fingers hovering over the keys. It doesn't take long for me to fall into the rhythm and tune. And soon, I'm lost to everything but my fingers flying over the keys.

A Thousand Butterflies

When I wake, I sit up with a gasp. I can move. I can think. There is no collar around my neck when I trail my fingers over it. Pressure builds in my chest, growing until my eyes burn. Tyberius saved me. I take a shaky breath and let it out.

"Are you okay?"

Julian trails his gaze over my body, taking in my weight loss, and he frowns. I can't imagine how horrible I look. But I don't think on that long. Shimmering light dances over Julian and the small potted flower on the window sill. My magic is back. A knot loosens in my chest and I exhale. I feel whole again, if still tired and weak.

"Yeah," I say, wincing at the croaking sound of my voice.

"Here. This should help." Julian hands me a glass of water from the nightstand next to the bed.

The liquid is cool as it slides down my parched throat, and I drink as much of it as my stomach will tolerate. As I set the glass back down, a soft melody floats into the room. The notes are haunting and beautiful. They wrap around my heart and tug, making my breath catch in my throat. I push from the bed, ignoring Julian's attempts to make me lie back down, and slip out of the bedroom. The music leads me forward in a daze, a line drawing me from the room and bringing me to the source. I know who I'll see when I turn the corner.

Tyberius sits at a piano, his broad back to me. His head is lifted, like he's not even looking at the keys that his fingers are dancing over. I have the mental picture of him sitting with his eyes closed, letting the music pour out of him and into the air. The muscles of his back shift subtly as he plays.

It's such a beautiful song, sad and ethereal, yet the promise of hope lies in the softer high notes. I lean against the door frame, my legs unsteady and weak from lack of exercise and malnutrition. I shouldn't spy on him, but I can't make myself move from this spot. The notes dancing through the room, and the man creating them, enthrall me.

"That is an incredibly sad song," I say when the song sounds like it's winding down.

Tyberius's fingers slip as he startles, the discordant sounds making me cringe. He spins on the bench, eyes widening as he takes me in. "How long have you been listening?" Pink crawls up his neck and into his cheeks, making my stomach do a weird little flip.

"Not long," I answer. "It was beautiful. I've never heard it before. Who wrote it?"

The pink deepens to a red, and he rubs the back of his neck. "I did, actually."

"Oh, wow. That's ... amazing. It's really good, Tyberius."

He clears his throat and stands from the bench. "You shouldn't be out of bed yet."

I snort, but at the same time, my legs wobble. I grasp the door frame with one hand, and Tyberius lunges forward, wrapping his fingers around my waist to hold me steady. He quirks an eyebrow at me, as if to say, 'See? I told you so.' Instead of voicing his thoughts, he just turns me around and leads me back to the bedroom. I let him, and I climb into the bed, sighing as the stress of exertion is taken from my body.

I settle in and he covers me with a blanket, shifting

uncomfortably as he mother hen's me. Those ocean blue eyes haunted me, but as I stare into them now, I can't help but think how beautiful Tyberius is. He swallows and sits on the edge of the bed, causing me to roll slightly toward him.

"Neave," he begins.

I close my eyes and take a deep breath. This conversation is not one I want to have. I want to forget everything I feel for him and just move on. If only it were that easy. And I know this conversation will just make it even harder.

"Don't," I say quietly. "Don't make this harder than it already is."

He shakes his head, blond hair falling across his eyes. "Let me talk, please. I have a lot I want to say." He falls silent, as if he's trying to arrange his thoughts. "I know there is nothing I can say about the things I've done in my past. *Sorry* isn't a strong enough word, and those witches deserve more than that. I regret all of it, though. I regret blindly following what I was taught without ever questioning right or wrong. I regret all the burnings I participated in. I regret the way I treated you and the things I said." He clasps his hands between his knees and hangs his head down. "For a while now, I've been questioning my life and the path I've taken. But it was more because I was bored with it. It wasn't until I met you that I started to question ... well, everything else." He shifts so he is sitting facing me on the bed. "You showed me that everything I was taught, everything I thought I believed in, was wrong. Witches are as human as anyone else. You have feelings. You have emotions. You care for others the same way humans do. The more time I spent with you, I found it got harder and harder to separate the two—humans and witches. I found myself thinking, *she looks so human, she acts so human.*

"You were right, Neave. I am incredibly ignorant. And I hate that it took me so long to realize it. I hate that I hurt people. That I hurt *you*. I'm not asking for forgiveness, because I don't deserve it. But I just wanted you to know that I want to change. I want to learn everything I can about witches. I want to do what I can to make right all of my wrongs."

He falls silent, staring down at the blanket and plucking at a loose string. I don't know what to say to him. This is not something I ever imagined I'd hear come from his mouth.

"I appreciate that. And I'm glad to hear your views on my kind have changed. However, that doesn't change anything between us. I'm still a witch. You're still a witch hunter." My voice trembles, and I hate that I care so much about this. There is undeniably something between us, and even though his opinion on witches has changed, we are still who we are. The universe just loves to play cosmic jokes with me.

He shakes his head, his blue eyes drilling into mine. "No. I'm not going back to that life, Neave. I can't. I can't continue bringing witches to their deaths. That part of my life is over. And I'm glad it is."

My chest is too tight. I shove down the flutter in my stomach and close my eyes. "Your dad will—"

"I don't give a fuck what my dad does." He grabs my hand and scoots closer to me. "Neave, I've already walked away from it all. The moment I decided to rescue you from my uncle, I sealed my fate. And I'm not sorry about it. I'm only sorry it took me so long to get to this point."

I can't breathe. I don't dare let myself even think about the meaning of his words or examine the way he's looking at me. "What are you saying?" My voice is barely a whisper, and I close my eyes to hide the emotion I'm sure is shining through them. His hand cups my cheek, warm and rough. My eyes snap open, and I find he's leaned forward.

"I haven't been able to get you off my mind. You have crawled under my skin and burrowed into my bones. Every thought I have is *you*. Every breath I take is *you*. Every beat of my heart is *you*." His eyes shine so brightly, and his thumb swipes back and forth on my cheek. "And I will walk away from my title, my inheritance, my home, if it means I can keep you."

I'm not breathing. My heart isn't beating. I'm not sure I'm even still alive. "Ty," I whisper.

Something flashes in his eyes, then he lowers his mouth to mine. The kiss is gentle but firm, and my stomach flutters with a thousand butterflies. As he deepens the kiss, his words echo through my head. I don't like the tentative hope that lights in my chest. It's terrifying and uncertain, and I don't want to let myself get sucked into this grand dream that could very well be just that ... a dream.

I want to pull away, to stop this, but I can't. His mouth on mine, his tongue dancing with mine, is so addicting. My heart is beating like hummingbird wings, sending desire burning through my veins. Tyberius gently pushes me into the pillows, and I groan as he settles his weight atop me.

He breaks the kiss to trail little nips down my throat. "We shouldn't do this." His breath is warm as it fans over my neck. "You need more rest."

I open my mouth to deny it, but before I can say anything, my stomach grumbles loudly. "Oh, goddess. That's embarrassing." Heat suffuses my cheeks and I duck my head to hide my blush.

Tyberius chuckles. "Exactly my point." He doesn't move right away, though. Instead, he brings his mouth to mine again and gives me more lingering kisses. Groaning, he pulls away. "You are a temptress," he whispers against my mouth. "I'm not strong enough to fight it."

I run my fingers through his blond hair, fighting my own urge to pull him down against me again. Another rumble from my stomach stops me. "Maybe I should eat something first."

Tyberius stands from the bed, leaving me missing his weight and warmth. He turns toward the door, but stops as an older woman enters.

"Hungry?" she asks with a smile. "I heard you were awake, so I brought you some food."

"Thank you," I say quietly as she hands the tray of food to Tyberius. He settles it over my lap and removes the lids covering the dishes. My mouth waters as the aromas hit my nose. Chicken, mashed potatoes, carrots, and a brownie for dessert. "This looks amazing," I say to the woman.

"Thank you. We haven't been formally introduced. My name is Shari." She smiles warmly at me.

"I'm Neave. Thank you for the food. And bed."

She chuckles and glances at Tyberius. "It's not like I could refuse the prince, now could I?"

He snorts. "Yeah right. You've refused me plenty. Like the time Killian and I tried to get you to bake us drug brownies?" The mirth fades from his eyes instantly, no doubt remembering what I told him about Killian.

Shari clucks her tongue. "If I had provided the prince with drugged food, I'd had found myself in prison faster than I could blink."

The door opens again, and this time Julian enters. "Hey, Ty. I think I should head back to uncle's before he gets suspicious."

Tyberius shakes his head. "Not a chance. After everything Neave told me, I don't think it's safe for you there."

While Tyberius fills in Julian, Shari, and the dude I'm assuming is Shari's husband, on Edward's plans, I eat the dinner Shari prepared for me. By the time the plate is empty, Tyberius is finishing up the story.

"Yeah, I would agree with you, Tyberius," the older man says. "I don't think Julian should go back to the estate. Your uncle definitely has plans, and I wouldn't want you two to get caught up in them."

"So, what do I do?" Julian asks. "Do you want me to go back home?"

Tyberius shakes his head. "Not yet. Dad will wonder why you're home and we don't have the evidence we need to prove uncle is trying to steal the throne. Stay with us here. Help us gather the evidence and continue our vision search."

"If I go back to the estate, I can search for the evidence we need," Julian argues.

Tyberius shakes his head again. "Not a chance. It's too big of a risk."

"Ty, I'm not a child. I can do this."

"I know you're not. But—"

"I'll be careful, Ty. Let me do this."

Tyberius crosses his arms over his chest, gearing up for a fight. "No."

Julian purses his lips. "I'll pull rank," he says quietly. "You may be my older brother, but I am the future king."

Tyberius groans and sighs at the same time. He studies his brother, and I study him. There is definitely a difference between them. Before, Tyberius couldn't stand to be in the same room as his brother. Now, he's protective of him, and I hate how that makes my stomach flutter.

Tyberius studies me, biting his lower lip, then turns toward his brother. "Can we talk first?" His tone is tentative, almost uncertain, and his feet shuffle on the hardwood floor.

Julian nods, and Tyberius follows him out of the room, leaving me with these two strangers. They study me, and I sink lower in the bed, disrupting the tray of food.

"Did you get enough to eat?" Shari asks, taking the tray and handing it to the older man.

"I did, thank you. Um, would it be too much trouble to ask for a shower?" I run my hands through my knotted hair and wince. The maid helped me shower, but it wasn't the same.

Shari smiles. "Of course. Follow me." She leads me to a small bathroom with white tile floors and pale yellow painted walls. A pedestal sink, toilet, and shower fill the tiny space. She lays a couple of towels on the back of the toilet. "Help yourself to any of the products in the shower, and there is an extra toothbrush in the medicine cabinet. I'll find some clothes for you to change into and lay them on the bed."

"Thank you, so much."

I turn on the water as she leaves and strip out of my clothes, glad to rid myself of the last reminder of my captivity. Stepping into the hot spray of water, I close my eyes and release a breath. Tension seeps from my body, and I imagine all the drugs in my system running down the drain. I stand in the shower for far longer than I should, but as tears burn my eyes, I let them fall, purging myself of the past few weeks. And preparing for whatever the future may hold.

You're Good With Your Tongue

I SIT ON THE STEP OUTSIDE LANDON'S HOUSE, AND Julian sits next to me. We let the silence grow comfortably, the stars in the sky twinkling dimly above. I appreciate the quiet between us as I try to gather my thoughts and figure out what exactly I want to say to him.

"It's not that I think you can't do it," I begin. "I think ... I think my head is all mixed up. It's been so long since we actually had a relationship that all of my memories of you are from when we were kids. And the thought of sending my baby brother into the lion's den doesn't sit right with me."

Julian shifts next to me and huffs a laugh. "I'm hardly a baby anymore, Ty. Dad has taught me quite a bit about ruling, and I honestly think I can do this. This is what I've been training for. The politics and subterfuge. The spying and reading into people's words. While your battle has always been physical, this is the kind of battle I've been preparing for."

"I know. And I have no doubt you can do it," I say, running a hand through my hair. Turning to face him, I expel a breath. "I'm scared, okay? I'm scared to lose you when I feel like we've just reconnected. Everything in my life has been tossed upside down lately. I don't know what's going to happen anymore, but the thought of having you by my side again makes it easier to think of my uncertain future."

Julian nods slowly. "I'll be careful, Ty. I promise. But we need this information, and I'm in the perfect position to get it." He grabs my shoulder and squeezes. "You won't lose me again. Besides, you have someone else to keep you company now. Someone much more attractive than I am."

I laugh. "Maybe. We'll see." But the hope in my chest makes me nervous. There is so much I risk losing. So much I've already lost. But in the same token, so much I've gained and stand to gain.

Julian pushes to his feet and reaches down to help me up. "I better get back."

"Be careful, Julian."

He smirks at me and disappears into the darkness.

When I return inside, I'm immediately greeted by Shari. With her hands on her hips and her lips pursed, she doesn't look quite as welcoming as she usually does.

"I think you failed to share some information when you first told us about this witch." She raises a brow and taps her foot as she waits for me to answer.

"I, uh, yeah." I rub the back of my neck, my skin prickling with heat. What will they think of me when I admit to having feelings for a witch? It's one thing to rescue one for the purpose of the visions. It's another thing entirely for the prince of Rossvale to admit he likes one of the creatures he spent his entire life hunting and killing.

Shari stares at me, a smile slowly spreading across her face. "She has you wrapped around her finger, doesn't she?" Before I can even open my mouth to deny it, Shari continues, "Good for her. It's about time someone put you in your place."

My mouth drops open, and I gape at her. "Excuse me?"

She cackles. "I always knew the first woman to push back would capture your heart. You've lived your entire life with people catering to you. Everyone is too afraid to say *no* to the prince. It's no surprise you would fall for a woman who speaks her mind."

"Leave the boy alone, Shari." Landon sweeps into the room, pausing to kiss his wife's temple. "I think he has enough to worry about at the moment."

"Hmph." She turns on her heel and heads down the hall toward their room.

Landon gives me a look, one that a father would give their son—raised brow, small smirk, glittering eyes. "Just be careful, Ty. If you two need anything, don't hesitate to let us know. Goodnight."

I roll my eyes at that smirk and make my way to the room Neave is occupying. The thought of knocking first doesn't even cross my mind, and not because I think she doesn't deserve the privacy like I used to. Now, it just seems natural to walk in without announcing myself. I'm shocked into immobility when I open the door and find her standing in a towel, hair hanging wet down her back, water droplets sliding over her bare shoulders.

"Shit. I'm sorry. I ... you ..." I cut off before I can make a fool of myself and turn around, closing the door behind me. I lean against the wood, face burning hotly, heart thundering in my chest. My fingers itch to rip that towel away from her body and trace every inch of her dark skin. I clench my hands and bang them against my thighs. *Get yourself under control, fucker. You aren't a horny teenager anymore.*

When Neave hollers through the door that she's decent, I slowly open it and let my gaze find her. She's wearing leggings and a tee shirt that's a bit too big. Her hair has been brushed, and it gleams wetly in the dim lighting. She sits on the edge of the bed, looking down at her feet.

My face feels like a furnace, and I clear my throat. "Did you get enough to eat?"

She nods and glances at me quickly before returning her gaze to the floor. I stand by the door, tapping my fingers against my leg and looking anywhere but at her. The situation is laughable, and indeed, a small, awkward chuckle climbs up my throat. I don't know why I feel so uncertain around her all of the sudden. But the idea that I'll do something to make her shy away from me is terrifying.

"This is fucking ridiculous," I mutter and march forward, ignoring my racing heart.

She looks up, dark eyes wide as I approach. I clasp her face in both of my hands and bend down to kiss her. Her body immediately responds to my touch—her mouth opens and her hands slide into my hair. I pick her up and scoot her further back on the bed so I can push her down into the mattress.

When a breathy moan climbs up her throat, I fucking lose it. I've been craving this witch for too long, and I can't deny myself anymore. I rock my hips against her, sending pleasure shooting through my veins like a wildfire. Her fingers untangle from my hair and slide under the hem of my shirt. They trail up my back, branding my skin with her touch. I reach behind my neck and grasp my shirt, yanking it over my head.

I can't help but smirk as her gaze widens and tracks over my torso. "Like what you see?"

She rolls her eyes. "It's passable."

I growl and pin both of her hands above her head. "Careful, witch," I whisper in her ear. "You might not like your punishment."

She moans and her hips lift, grinding against mine until I see stars. I release her wrists and slip my hands under her shirt, gliding it up over her head and exposing her breasts. With each heavy inhale, her chest rises, and I bend down to wrap my lips around one of her nipples. Her back arches off the bed as I graze my teeth over the peak, then soothe it with my tongue. I pinch her other nipple between my thumb and pointer, tugging gently.

"Fuck," she gasps, fingers tangling in the sheets as her body writhes under mine.

I smile against her skin, loving the way I can make her react to my touch. Each sigh, each moan, I catalog for future reference. Learning her body and what she likes will be a game I thoroughly enjoy playing. My fingers skim down her sides, and I watch as her dark skin pebbles from the touch. I reach the waistband of her leggings and meet her gaze with a question. She doesn't hesitate. Her hips lift off the bed, and I slide the leggings down her legs.

Running my fingers over her thighs, I almost groan. Her skin is so soft and silken. I want to touch all of it. But right now, I'm more tempted by one thing. I curl my fingers to the inside of her thighs and slowly inch them up. Neave's breathing hitches and she spreads her legs wider. I grit my teeth and force myself to slow down and enjoy this. As I run my finger through her center, we both groan. She's so fucking wet it makes my dick twitch in my pants.

"God damn, Neave." My voice is rough with need, and my chest rises as rapidly as hers.

Her eyes flutter shut at the same time she lifts her hips, seeking more contact. "Don't stop," she breathes.

I let my gaze travel over her body, completely naked before me, and I swallow thickly. She's fucking beautiful, even with the weight she's lost and her bones too prominently on display. I can't wait to see her with her curves filled out. And watching her slowly come undone is going to be the cause of my own undoing. I slide one finger inside, and her inner walls clench around me. Leaning forward, I suck her nipple into my mouth again and add a second finger, curling them to hit that just right spot.

"Ty," she moans breathily, her hips jerking with each rub of my fingers.

My eyes close briefly, hearing my name on her lips like that. I know I can't wait any longer. I need to taste her. Sliding down her body, I grip her thighs roughly and spread them wider. My mouth fucking waters, and I don't wait to lean in and lick up her center. She tastes better than I ever could have imagined. As I get busy showing her what I can do with my tongue, her fingers tangle in my hair and tug at the strands. I memorize every noise that she makes and exactly what I did to bring it out of her.

I know she's getting close as her thighs tighten on my head. Her body moves against my mouth as she chases her orgasm, and I give her what she's searching for. The soft gasping moans and fingers pulling my hair make my cock ache as she comes. I keep going until her body relaxes, and she lies on the bed gasping for air.

I wipe my mouth on my shoulder and grin as I crawl up her body. Her eyes flutter open and she watches me sleepily. Brushing a stray lock of purple hair from her forehead, I lean down and kiss her gently.

"I've been dying to do that," I whisper against her mouth. "And it was better than I ever imagined."

"Same," she says softly.

I wrap my arms around her and roll over so her head is resting on my chest. Her hand immediately drops to my pants, but I grab her wrist and stop her. "You need to rest," I say, bringing her hand to my mouth and placing a kiss on the inside of her wrist.

"But—"

"Don't argue with me, witch." I try to make my voice firm, but I can't keep the smile from my face.

She huffs, her breath fanning across my chest, and she settles next to me. My fingers trace every bit of exposed skin, over the moth tattoo on her shoulder and the moon phases on her back. It's surreal thinking I have her here in my arms. No fighting. No arguing. Her head on my shoulder and her hand on my chest. Her body pressed against mine, skin to skin. I don't want to fall asleep. I don't want to miss a second of this.

"What happens now?" she asks quietly, tracing the grooves of my abs.

I sigh, reality crashing into me. "Tomorrow, if you're feeling up to it, we should head to the church. Julian is going to work on getting the evidence we need to prove uncle is gunning for my dad's throne. While he does that, we need to keep figuring out these visions."

She's silent for a moment, her hand stilling. "What happens when we return to Rossvale City?"

"Hopefully, we'll have what we need to keep my dad safe on the throne. Julian's plan is still to become king."

"What about us? Is there an us?"

Us. I want to shout to the heavens that yes, yes there is an *us.* But, I think about her questions before answering. "I told you, I'm done hunting. And that means my dad will strip me of my title and inheritance. I'd have nothing to offer you." That realization makes my stomach sink. By giving up the things keeping me from Neave, I lose everything I need to keep her.

She pushes up to look at me. "You think I like you for your money? That money comes from all the witches you've burned. I'm happy to hear you'd lose it all."

I chuckle, but get snagged on the first thing she said. "You like me?"

She shrugs. "You're good with your tongue."

Her head drops back to my shoulder, and I squeeze her tightly. Silence falls between us, and I let my mind wander toward what the future could possibly entail. As her breathing evens out and her body relaxes, I smile. The possibilities stretch before me as I close my eyes and fall asleep.

NEAVE SHUDDERS NEXT TO ME. "This deja-vu feeling is so weird. I mean, it's so strong." Her eyes are glued to the little church, unblinking. She rubs her arms, and I notice goosebumps pimpling her skin.

I thread our fingers together, a thrill rushing through me at how easy it was to fall into her like this. "Let's go check it out." Before I tug her forward, I peer at her from the corner of my eye. "You're not going to stab me are you? Should I search you for weapons?"

A wicked smile curls the corners of her mouth. "I can't guarantee I won't stab you. You should probably search me, just to be safe." She winks, and I chuckle.

As tempting as that idea is, I lead her through the wooden doors carved with a cross and roses. The last time I visited this church, I was searching for Neave. Now she's standing next to me, her hand held in mine. The interior is still dimly lit, candles still flicker as we walk past disrupting the flames. She eye's the candles with trepidation, subtly stepping closer to me. I'd blow them all out, but without windows, the church would be plunged into darkness.

We approach the ancient stone altar, and she studies the bible laying on the surface. It's so tattered, I wouldn't surprise me if it fell apart if someone blew on it too hard. Neave closes her eyes and takes a deep breath. The air is stale and musty, tinged with the scent of smoke from the candles. When she opens her eyes again, a crease forms between her brows.

"Anything?" I ask. Even as quiet as I kept my voice, it still echoes in the empty space.

She says nothing, but steps around the altar slowly, eyes scanning the apse constantly. I follow behind, watching her with an almost obsessive need. After spending so much time with her doing this exact thing, but looking at it from a different perspective, this is exciting. Before, I was cautious of her magic. I was watching her for any signs of deceit or flight risk. Now, I'm watching her just to watch her. I want to see how she works. I want to see how she interacts with her environment.

Behind the altar, Neave stops. She looks around and bites her bottom lip. "It's here."

"What's here?" I cast my gaze around but see nothing out of the ordinary.

"I don't know. Whatever we're looking for is here." She looks down at the altar. "Right here." She drops to her knees and runs her finger along the stone floor.

I kneel next to her and scan the ground. A few of the stones have scratches on them, and a couple have a mark, like a dividing line between scuffed, aged stone and unscathed newer looking stone. I stand and place my hands on the altar and push.

Grunting, I slide the altar across the floor, the stones grating and crunching.

Neave gasps. "That's it," she breathes.

I step away, and find a hidden wooden door in the floor. "I really hope there aren't rats down there."

I Will Hex You
So Hard

Tyberius jumps into the dark hole hidden under the secret door without a second thought. My heart gets stuck somewhere in my throat as I watch him disappear into the shadows before he flips on the flashlight on his phone. He sweeps the area with the beam of light, but I can't see anything from my position perched on the lip of the hole.

"It's clear," he whispers loudly, setting his phone on the ground, flashlight pointed up. He raises his arms. "Jump down. I'll catch you."

I want to refuse. Jumping into a dark hole built under a church seems like a horrible idea for a witch, but every instinct in my body is telling me to do it. Although, I'm not sure how much that has to do with witchy visions or that fact I want Tyberius to catch me. I take a deep breath to steel myself and swing my legs into the open air. "If you drop me, I will hex you so hard," I threaten right before I shove off the edge.

It's not a long drop, but my stomach lurches to my throat and an undignified squeal escapes as I free fall. Tyberius's arms wrap around me, and I crash into him. It's pure instinct when I wrap my arms and legs around him like a spider monkey. My heart is thundering behind my ribs and I bury my face in his shoulder as I breathe through my panic.

"What was that about hexing me?" he asks, his breath fanning my hair.

Realizing how close we are, I slowly unwrap my limbs and he lets me slide down his body. Every inch where we touch lights up. Our gazes meet, and it's like an electrical current zaps between us. I get sucked into those blue eyes, darker in the shadows of this secret pit. Something moves in the darkness, and we both jump.

"That better not have been a fucking rat," he whispers as he bends down to grab his phone from the floor. Shining it into the corner of the hole, the beam of light reflects off two beady glowing eyes. Tyberius curses and pulls me in front of him like a shield. "It's a rat. It's a fucking rat." His breath is raspy in his throat, and his fingers dig into my shoulders.

"What the hell?" I try to pull away, but he's stronger than me and holds me in front of him. "What kind of gentleman are you to throw a woman in front of you as a shield?"

"I've never claimed to be a gentleman. Do something," he hisses.

"What do you want me to do? Kill it?" I keep my gaze trained on the glowing eyes in the shaky beam of light. If that thing moves...

"Yes!"

"I'm not killing an innocent animal, Tyberius." Still, I glance around, finding the tell-tale shimmer of magic clinging to some storage crates. They must be wooden. I clench my fingers and pull the magic from them. They crumble to dust, their contents scattering on the stone floor. I throw the magic at the rat, knocking it unconscious. "There. It's sleeping," I huff. He shudders violently, and I can't help but smile. "Rats, huh?"

"Not. A. Word." He grabs my hand and tugs me backward toward a tunnel I hadn't noticed.

"I can't believe you threw me in front of you as a shield. What if it had been some horrible monster?"

"If it had been a monster, I'd have protected you. But when it comes to rats, all bets are off." He shudders again.

The walls are rough hewn stone and are close enough that we can barely walk side by side without our shoulders brushing. There is no light except for Tyberius's flashlight, which illuminates the mostly dirt ground. A few random stones, like someone attempted to pave the path at some point, stick up randomly attempting to trip us if we don't pay attention.

"How do we know this is the right way?" I ask, my voice echoing slightly.

"There was no other way to go. And that room was mostly empty. Just half-rotted crates and rats."

"What if the rat was the thing that is supposed to save your family?"

"Then it can have the fucking throne. I'm not dealing with rats."

I giggle. "All hail the Rat King."

"Not funny," he grinds out, squeezing my hand harder.

We walk in silence for a few minutes, the only sounds our shoes scuffing the loose pebbles in the dirt. I try to focus on what we're doing, but all I can think about is the fact I'm walking hand in hand with Tyberius Berkshire, the notorious witch hunter. What does that say about me? Does his decision to stop hunting make it okay for me to like him? Or does his past negate the change of heart he seems to have had?

"Are you getting any vibes about where we're going?" he asks, making me jump.

I force myself to ignore his fingers twined with mine, and focus on what we're doing. "Just a subtle tug in my gut pulling me forward."

"Then I'd say we're heading in the right direction."

"But toward what? Who knows what the hell we're about to walk into?" I shiver slightly, and not just because the temperature has been steadily dropping. "What if it's more rats? Or one giant rat?"

"I'm never going to live that down, am I?"

"No*pe.*"

He bumps my shoulder and chuckles. "I think we're going downhill. And unless I'm wrong, which I never am, I think we're curving around, toward the opposite side of the cliffs."

"Never wrong, my ass," I mumble.

By the time the tunnel widens into a cave, I swear we've walked miles. And if Tyberius's theory is correct, we probably have. The cave is massive. All gray stone walls and floor. I see no opening besides the one that leads to the tunnel we just exited. A beam of light from the ceiling illuminates the floor in the middle of the cave. Besides us, it's completely empty.

"Well," I say, glancing around. "This was useless." But even as the words leave my mouth, my feet carry me forward. As I pass under the light spilling from the ceiling, I look up. Way, way up is a skylight carved into the stone ceiling. It lets in enough light to keep the cave from being pitch black, but not enough to make it feel like daytime.

My feet carry me through the light to the far wall. There's something on the other side. The tug in my middle has become a fluttering butterfly. I run my fingers over the smooth stone, but there's no hidden door that I can see.

Tyberius walks along the edge and halts. "Damn. That's well hidden." He slips to the side and disappears.

I gasp and rush toward the spot he had just been standing. Hidden in the wall is an opening. Tyberius disappears ahead of me again, and I follow the small tunnel as it switchbacks. A faint sound of waves reaches my ears, and up ahead, dim light filters through. Tyberius disappears once again, and I hurry forward, stepping out of the tunnel and onto a beach.

"Holy shit," I mutter.

We're standing on the beach across from the city. The massive arch is before us, even larger up close than I ever could have imagined. White sand crunches under my shoes as I turn around.

The cliff face appears smooth. If I didn't know there was an opening there, I never would have found it.

"Did you know this was here?" I ask, turning back around to face Tyberius.

He shakes his head. "I had no idea. It's so well hidden, I bet no one knows it's there. Maybe the priests of the church?"

"What do you think they used it for?" I ask as I walk closer to the water.

Crystal blue waves crash along the shore. The surf is much rougher over on this side. The waves beat against the rocks protruding from the sand and batter the arch sprouting from the water.

"I have no idea, but I'm guessing nothing good." He steps next to me and looks out into the cove. "What are your senses telling you now?"

I close my eyes and follow the tug of my gut. An image flickers behind my closed lids. A drop-off, further out from the beach. A crack in the underwater cliff wall. A small golden box wedged inside. "It's out there." I point to the water, grimacing as it surges forth in foamy waves. "There's a drop-off and a golden box wedged into a crack in the wall."

"Of course it is," he grumbles. Kicking off his shoes and socks, Tyberius strips out of his pants and shirt. I watch, appreciating the view as he wades into the choppy water. "Holy fuck, it's freezing." He keeps going until the water is up to his chest. "It drops off here." He has to shout to be heard over the surf. "Any idea where exactly it is down there?"

"No. But you can't go in there! The water is too rough!" I'm not sure if he hears me. If he does, he ignores what I said. His shoulders rise as he takes a breath, then he dives forward and disappears into the water. "Tyberius!"

I frantically search for him, but my position on the beach limits my view. The waves thrash the rocky beach. I can't imagine how hard they smash against the underwater cliff. There is no way Tyberius can swim that strongly. I bend down and sink my hands into the icy water. It shimmers with magic and I clench my fingers, grasping as much of it as I can. Releasing it back into the water, I urge the waves to calm. The magnitude of the waves is so great, I know I won't be able to keep this up for long.

"Come on, Ty," I mutter through gritted teeth.

It seems like I wait for eons before Tyberius resurfaces. Just as he reaches the edge of the drop-off, I lose control of my magic. It slips from my fingers and it's as if the waves decide to make up for the time I held them back. They rise taller than they were before and crash ruthlessly against the shore. They slam into Tyberius, sending him sprawling into a protruding rock. His head smacks against the stone, and he falls limply into the water.

"Tyberius!" I kick off my shoes and dash into the water, gasping as icy fingers grip my lungs. Pushing myself through the waves, I reach him and pull him up. Blood streams from a gash over his right eye, and I heave a sigh as he groans. "Come on, you lug. Help me."

He's completely useless as I pull him to shore, waves pushing and pulling us this way and that. More than once, a wave sucks the sand from under my feet and I splash face first into the frigid water. By the time I get him to shore, I'm shivering so hard I can barely stand up straight.

"Ty," I gasp through chattering teeth.

He rolls over with a groan and presses his hand to his hand, hissing in pain. "Fuuck."

I wrap my arms around myself like that can keep me warm in soaking wet, frozen clothes. "Can you get into the cave? We need a fire or something."

He shivers, then groans again when that jostles his head. "Yeah, I think so."

I grab his clothes from the beach, then help him stand. Together we manage to get inside the cave, and I sit him on the floor, leaning against the wall. Glancing around, I look for anything we can use for a fire, but there's nothing. As much as I know we need one to get warm, I'm also slightly relieved.

I hand Tyberius his clothes. "Here, put these on. It will help warm you up. I don't see any wood for a fire."

He shoves the clothes back at me. "You're soaking wet. Take off your clothes and put on mine."

"What about you? You're just as cold and wet as I am." Before he can argue with me again, I take his shirt. "At least put your pants on. Your shirt is plenty big enough to keep me warm."

I peel off the wet leggings and tee shirt, wring out my hair, and pull Ty's shirt over my head. It smells like him, like lemon and cedar. I bury my nose in the collar and inhale deeply. With his pants on, Tyberius sits against the wall, panting and wincing as he prods his head.

I kneel next to him and smack his hand away. "Don't touch it." There is enough water in my clothing that I'm able to pull some magic from it. Clenching my hand, it flows toward me, and I run my fingers over the bleeding gash on his forehead. Slowly, the skin knits back together until a thin pink line is the only thing left. When I pull away, he's staring at me with his mouth agape and his blue eyes wide.

"Shit," I mutter. "I'm sorry. I should have asked you first before I used magic on you. I didn't even think—"

His mouth crashes into mine, cutting off my apology. I lose my balance and he pulls me onto his lap. "You are so fucking amazing," he murmurs against my mouth. His fingers grasp my ass under his shirt and he pulls me closer.

I gasp, hands landing on his chest, and he takes advantage, sliding his tongue against mine. His skin is freezing under my fingers, and I have no doubt mine is just as cold, but there isn't any better way to warm up than ... this. Rocking my hips against his, I grin as he moans deep in his throat, his fingers tightening on my ass.

My grin slips when he draws his hand around my waist and slides his finger between my thighs through the gathering wetness. "Oh, fuck, Ty."

He drops his mouth to my neck. "I love when you call me

that," he says against my skin, licking up the column of my throat at the same time he drags his finger up my center.

My brain short circuits, and I forget everything except rocking my hips, looking for more friction.

"That's right," he whispers darkly. "Ride my hand, witch."

My insides twist deliciously at his words. When he slips two fingers inside, I close my eyes and my head falls back, letting my body do what it wants. I chase my pleasure, Ty's encouragement lighting up my body like a fucking lightbulb. The heel of his hand presses against my clit and I bite my lip, so close to the edge. I completely lose it when his teeth clamp down on the spot where my neck meets my shoulder. Pleasure crashes through me as hard as the waves outside, and I cry out, my body shuddering. When I finally, still, Ty pulls his hand free and sucks his fingers into his mouth, his eyes lighting with desire.

That's twice now he's pleasured me, and I have yet to taste him. Gathering my shaking limbs, I slide off his lap. I trail little nips down his chest and over his abs. His pants are unbuttoned, so it's easy for me to pull them down with just a little help from him. I eye his cock with excitement as it springs free, and wrap my hand around the length. Ty's head hits the rough stone wall behind him, but he doesn't seem to mind.

I lower my head and lick up the underside of his cock. He tastes like salt water from his foray into the ocean. It's strangely addicting. I marvel at the sounds he makes when I wrap my lips around the tip and suck, swirling my tongue over the crown and slit.

His hands fist in my hair and he pushes me down onto his length. I swallow, but even then, I gag as he hits the back of my throat. But watching his reaction, his mouth lax, hooded eyes glued to what I'm doing to him, I want to do it again and again. So I do. I slowly wind him up, watching him unravel under my touch.

I don't even notice how warm I've gotten, the chill from the frigid water erased by our pleasure. I never want this to end.

Watching him like this is like seeing an entirely new side of him. A vulnerable side. The hunter mask has come off, and this is the Tyberius he really is under all the layers of training and being raised as a royal.

His fingers tighten in my hair, and I know he must be getting close. With each bob of my head, his hips lift, shoving his cock deeper into my throat. I reach between his legs and gently grasp his balls.

"Oh, fuck," he groans.

His cock pulses in my mouth and he slams his hips against my face, holding me in place as he comes. I swallow everything he gives me, watching him come back down from the orgasm. When he finally releases me, I lift up and wipe my mouth on his sleeve.

"Neave," he breathes, his chest rising and falling rapidly.

"Ty," I whisper.

He reaches for me and pulls me into his lap again. I settle against his chest and rest my head on his shoulder. We sit quietly for a few minutes as we both piece ourselves back together. His hand slides under my shirt and traces my spine, rubbing up and down gently. My eyes get heavy. I could fall asleep right here in his arms, in this random cave. But then I remember why we're here in the first place.

It's a ... Ring

"Did you get the golden box?" I push back to look at him.

His blond hair is mussed and sticking up in every direction. The blue of his eyes captivates me with the gold veins near his pupil. He smiles, and my heart flutters at the sight. "Of course I got it." He gestures next to him, and sitting on the ground is the golden box where he must have dropped it earlier.

If I don't put distance between us, I'm liable to get distracted again, so I slide off his lap and snag it from the ground. It looks like a small ring box made of solid gold. The light from the skylight glints off the surface, illuminating the seam and the golden hinges on the back.

Glancing at Ty, I say, "This is it. What your family has been searching for." I bite my lip as I think about what this could possibly be and how it will affect what has become of me and Ty.

Before I can open the box, he places his hand over it. "This doesn't change anything. I'm not going back to hunting. And whatever is in that box, I really only want so Julian can end up on the throne after my dad. Think of everything he can change during his rule."

I don't let myself think about that. It's a dangerous path to go down. The hope that possibility can bring will only end in disappointment. Taking a deep breath, I flip open the lid.

"It's a ... ring," I say quietly.

Nestled in golden fabric is a silver ring with a large, black, pear-shaped stone. Two crescent moon shaped diamonds bracket either side of the stone, while three smaller diamonds are clustered at the top and bottom. It's absolutely stunning. I angle the ring box so Ty can get a better look at it.

"Does this mean anything to you?" I ask.

His eyes scrunch as his brow furrows. "No? I don't know. For some reason it's familiar but ... not."

"That makes zero sense."

He huffs a laugh. "Yeah, I don't know. It's weird. Why would a ring be what we're searching for?"

I bite my lip and slip the ring from the box. Turning it over, I examine the black stone and the glittering diamonds. There is no engraving on the band. Nothing remarkable about it, except that it's beautiful. A tug in my gut has me sliding the ring onto my right ring finger.

I gasp and my vision goes white. Squeezing my eyes shut, I dimly hear Ty calling my name, but it's as if I'm submerged in water. All sounds are muted and echo-y. My limbs feel like they could float away at any second. I slowly open my eyes and my vision appears to have returned to normal for the most part. There is a weird glowy outline around Ty, but his words are still muffled. I can't quite make out what he's saying, but with his blue eyes wide with fear, I'm guessing he's concerned.

Motion to my right draws my attention, and I turn my head to find an apparition of a woman slowly solidifying. The wispy form becomes more concrete the longer I stare, and before I know it, a woman is standing before me. Not completely solid, light still passes through her, but I can make out her features. And on some instinctual level, I know who it is.

"Sybil?"

She smiles, her brown eyes crinkling at the corners. "I thought you'd never find that ring," she says, her voice low and warm.

I stare at the apparition before me. Sybil is a legend among my kind. The first witch to have been burned, many place her at the same level as the goddess. She looks like a normal witch, though, despite the slight transparency. Her hair is dark and long, flowing down her back in gentle waves. Her clothes are a bit odd, but I'm assuming that's what she wore in her time.

"Whoa," I breathe.

She laughs, and it sets something in me at ease. "We have a lot to discuss, and not a lot of time to do it." The long skirts of her dress flow behind her as she approaches. Without a care in the world, she plops onto the ground, arranging her dress around her. "Let's just dive right in, shall we?"

I nod, my mind scrambling to catch up to what's happening. In my peripheral vision, Ty is staring at me with his mouth agape, hands outstretched like he's about to reach for me. I don't spare him any attention, though.

"Thousands of years ago," Sybil begins, "I fell in love. It's what started all of this. Maximus was everything I could have ever dreamed of for myself. He was kind, caring, and doting. Everyone loved him. When I began to have visions of him on the throne, I knew I had to help him get there. For years, we used my visions to help the people he ruled, and everything was going well." Shadows cross her eyes and she frowns. "Then it all changed. My visions turned dark. It took me a while to figure out what they meant and what I had to do. But when I did..."

It's obvious this is hard for her to talk about. Pain etches her features, her eyes pinched and mouth turned down. I settle back on my hands to get more comfortable and wait for her to continue.

"I realized that thousands of years down the road, witches would be on the verge of extinction. Hunted until we were no more. I saw in my visions a young witch, one who would have the magic needed to save us." Her eyes clear as they focus on me. "You, Neave, are the witch that is going to save our kind."

"*She is coming. The one with the sight. She will save us. Only she can stop the threat.*" I mutter the words King Leander spoke when I met in his office. The words of the vision the Berkshire's have been trying to find the answer to. Realization dawns. "It's not about the Berkshire's. It's about the witches."

"It was never about the Berkshire's," Sybil agrees. "And they got it wrong. Or it was distorted as it was passed down. *She is coming. The one with the* stars. *She will save us. Only she can stop the threat.*"

"The stars?"

Sybil sighs. "As I'm sure you realize, with each witch's death, we lose more of our magic. Witches in your time are so incredibly weak compared to my time. The well our magic comes from is almost empty. The leylines are no longer able to be used. Once it's gone, witches will no longer exist. We will simply be human." Unfathomable sadness shimmers in her eyes, but they sharpen as she looks at me. "That well needs to be replenished. With a full well to draw from, with the leylines and our power restored, we can become what we once were. A strong collective of sisters who protect each other and the environment. You would have the magic needed to defend yourselves. You could usher in a new era."

"But how? And why me?" There is nothing truly special about me.

"Because you are a lunar witch." Sybil smiles as I gasp. "The last of them. The last of the witches to have an affinity. With that affinity, you have the power needed to refill the well."

"But ... how ... I ..." Even as I struggle to comprehend her words, a piece of me clicks into place. I always thought if I had an affinity, I'd be a lunar witch. But I never imagined I actually was one.

Sybil holds out her hands and stars glow to life in her palms, dancing and twinkling. "It's my magic that runs through your veins, Neave."

My mouth falls open. I'm related to Sybil? "You're my ... grandmother?"

"Distant grandmother, yes." She smiles. "I don't know how you got the magic after so many generations had lost it, but I'm not one to question fate."

"So, I have to refill the well? With star magic?" It sounds absurd.

"The ring will give you the power you need to draw the magic from the stars and refill the well. It will guide you. You need not worry about that."

I study the ring and quietly think about Sybil's words. "But there is still so much that doesn't make sense to me. Why did you kill King Maximus? Why did my mom have that band that restricted visions and why did she give it to me if I was supposed to find the ring? And what about the symbols drawn in blood?"

She sighs and looks down at her hands in her lap. "I didn't want to kill him," she says quietly. "I love him, with all my heart. But I needed powerful magic to place on the ring so we could have this conversation. And I needed to get the ring somewhere safe where you could find it."

Dread curls in my gut. "You killed him for the magic in his body?" Everyone knows that is the highest of evil things a witch can do. Every human has magic in their body. Drawing it from them kills them.

"As a powerful and benevolent king, Max had an unusually large amount of magic. I had to drain his blood to remove the iron from his body so I could harness it. Without it, I never would have been able to magic the ring to the cave for you to find." Her words hitch in her chest, like they get stuck. "It destroyed me. Literally. Killing him took a piece of me I never would have been able to get back. It corrupted my mind."

"That's why they found you sitting in a pool of blood, chanting about the vision," I say. She nods and tears glisten on her cheeks. "But what about the symbols in the blood?"

Sybil shakes her head. "I don't know. By that point, I was lost.

I'd used so much of my magic, and my heart was broken. That remains a mystery to this day."

My heart aches for her. Even after thousands of years, she still hurts for what she did. "Wait," I throw up a hand, clutching my throat with the other. "If I'm related to you ... you didn't ... King Maximus isn't ..."

A soft chuckle clears the sadness from her eyes. "No. You are not related to the young Berkshire sitting next to you. My dalliance happened before I met Max."

I heave a relieved sigh. How awful would that have been? With that cleared up, my mind wanders again to this situation. "So, what about my mom and the armband?"

"That I can't say for certain. If I were to guess, she was worried about someone hurting her, so she acquired that armband as protection. In turn, she gave it to you. It did cause quite the worry when you were not having visions. I had no idea how I was going to make sure you found the ring."

"Did she know? About the visions, I mean. Did she have them?"

Sybil shakes her head. "I don't believe she knew, and I don't believe she had visions. That armband was likely sold to her as a protective band. It was mere coincidence it actually blocked the visions." Her form shimmers, and when it stops, she's more transparent than she was before. She grimaces. "I'm running out of time. You must refill the well, Neave. The future of the witches relies on you."

"No pressure, or anything," I mutter. "Is there anything you can tell me to help me figure this out? Will I be able to talk to you again?"

She shakes her head. "I'm afraid not. This was all I was able to manage. I'll finally be able to rest now." A smile spreads across her face as she shimmers again. "I have every faith in you, Neave. Remember who you are and where you come from. Remember what you're fighting for."

"Wait!" I reach out a hand as if I could stop her from fading, but she's already gone. I sit back with a heavy exhale and stare at the space she had occupied. Slowly, I twist off the ring and the world rushes back to greet me.

Hands catch my shoulders before I fall over. The cave is quiet, but even then, it seems loud to me as that underwater sensation pops. Ty kneels in front of me, looking normal again, without the glowy edges.

His wide eyes scan my face. "Are you okay?" A slight tremor makes his words wobble. "What just happened?"

I place the ring back in the golden box, my hands shaking as I do so. My body suddenly wavers and only Ty's hands on my shoulders keeps me upright. It's as if I had been filled with adrenaline and as it leaves my system, I'm left weak and exhausted.

"Whoa," Ty says, pulling me against him.

I let my head fall against his chest. It's too heavy to hold up, anyway. His arms come around me, and my body sinks against his. I don't realize my eyes are closed until I feel him shuffling me around. The thought of opening them to see what he's doing is too much. So I let my body go limp and let him arrange me in his lap.

"You're okay," he says gently, rubbing his hand down my back. "Rest. I'll be here."

The last thing I'm aware of is the kiss he presses to the top of my head and the way it makes my stomach flutter.

It's Not That Hard To Imagine You Committing Patricide

"Fuck, Ty. That feels so good." Neave moans, and I bite my lip.

We're sitting on the couch at Landon's, her feet in my lap as I give her a foot massage. She still looks exhausted with dark circles under her eyes. Even after we returned to Landon's, ate food, and slept some more. She filled me in on the conversation she had with Sybil. That still blows my mind. I can't quite wrap my head around the fact she talked to the ghost of an ancient witch my ancestors burned.

I had no idea what was going on while it happened. She slipped the ring on her finger and her eyes turned white. She sat perfectly still, barely breathing, not moving, and stared blankly at the wall in front of her. It was eerie as fuck, and thinking about it now makes my skin crawl. Nothing I did snapped her out of it until she took the ring off and then she passed out.

Julian raises a questioning brow at me. "You guys just need to fuck and get it over with. The sexual tension in this room is suffocating."

"Julian Berkshire!" Shari scolds. "That is uncalled for."

I snort. Shari hasn't been able to replace our mom, but she took it upon herself to step into the role when our mom died. It's easy to forget sometimes, and it's not uncommon for us to slip up around her. He's never said it, but I know Julian feels the same way I do. I'm grateful to have her and Landon in my life. They treat us like their children, not their princes and future king. It's something we both need.

Julian ducks his head, but not before I notice the red staining his cheeks. "Sorry, Shari," he mumbles.

"So, this ring," Landon says, bringing us back to the task at hand. "You need to fill it with magic?"

Neave stares at the ring nestled in the box in her lap. "Yeah. Somehow. Sybil said it would guide me? I have no clue what that means."

"Have you tried putting it on again?" Landon asks.

We both tense. "No," she says. Her eyes flick to mine. "Should I?"

"She made it sound like that was a one-time thing, correct?" I ask slowly. "And it didn't technically hurt you. It just drained your energy. I suppose it's worth a shot?"

She stares at the ring like it might bite her, before releasing a breath. "Fuck it," she mutters, sliding it onto her finger.

Everyone in the room holds their breath. What we're waiting for, I have no idea, but when nothing happens, we all exhale.

"Well, that was anticlimactic," Neave says.

"Leave it on," I suggest. "Maybe it will spark something, a vision or a feeling. Until then, what should we do? I don't particularly want to stay in Seaberth. It's not safe for either of us."

"Is Rossvale City any safer?" she asks.

I shrug. "Probably not."

She rolls her eyes and I smirk. I'm glad to see this sassy version of her again. I missed it, and I don't want things between us to change that dynamic we had before.

"What about the cabin?" Shari asks, looking at Landon.

"That's a good idea," he replies.

"Cabin?" I ask, switching my massage to Neave's other foot.

"We have a cabin in the Chamberly Mountains near Rossvale City," Shari explains. "It's just outside a little town, Rocksberg. There is a grocery store for supplies, so you could stay there for as long as necessary."

"That sounds perfect." I can't help but get excited at the prospect of spending time with Neave in a cabin away from the entire world. "Julian, how's your search going?"

"I have a few small things, but I think I need more. I want to make sure there can be no argument against us."

"Have you tried to get a video or recording of him talking about his plans?" Neave asks. As always, when she talks about Edward, shadows haunt her eyes. I want to wipe those shadows away permanently.

Julian's face lights up. "No. But that's a great idea. Thanks, Neave." As quickly as the excitement blooms, it fades. His face falls, and he chews on his cheek.

"Everything okay?" I ask him.

He turns to Shari and Landon. "Do you think I could talk to my brother privately?"

"Of course!" Shari jumps from her seat and pulls Landon to his feet. "We'll go for a walk."

My stomach twists as they leave, wondering what he could want to talk to me about. Neave removes her feet from my lap and goes stand, but Julian shakes his head.

"I want you to stay," he says. "This kind of involves you."

She hesitates, so I pull her down next to me. Now my stomach is really twisting. I haven't had a conversation with Julian about what happens with me and Neave when this is all over. I kind of just assumed he would let it all slide. Maybe I was wrong.

He rubs his face, the scruff of his beard scratching in the silence of the living room. "So, this goes without saying, but what I say can't leave this room." He waits for both of us to nod before continuing. "Ty, you've made me do a lot of thinking lately, and I've kind of secretly been watching you two."

"That's not creepy or anything," Neave mutters.

He chuckles. "All of this"—he gestures with his hand, encompassing everything from me and Neave, to the entire situation—"has made me realize things need to change. And I want to be the one to usher in that change. But, I'm worried about what will happen when you refill the well, Neave. What kind of impact will that have on our world and how will our dad react to it?"

"What are you saying?" I ask slowly.

"I don't know," he sighs. "Things need to change. That's obvious. We can't keep hunting witches. It's barbaric and unethical. But, there is no way we can change dad's mind."

"Are you suggesting we kill him?" My voice raises an octave in surprise.

Julian rears back in his seat. "What? No! Jesus, what kind of person do you think I am?"

"I don't know," Neave mutters again, so quietly I almost can't hear, and I'm sitting right next to her. "You all hunted and burned women for years. It's not that hard to imagine you committing patricide."

Julian gives her a flat stare until she snorts and shakes her head. "Anyway," he drawls. "I don't know what to do, but I'm not sure waiting for me to take the throne is going to work. What happens when the well is filled? Will dad double down on the burnings? You know he'll retaliate. How do we stop that from happening?"

"Well, there is no way to get you on the throne without killing Dad," I say. "Like you said, he will never change his mind. And honestly, you need to stay as far away from me and Neave as possible. If you get caught associating with us at all, dad won't hesitate to strip you of your title."

He sighs and flops back in his chair, quite unkingly.

"Don't worry about the witches," Neave says. "We'll handle ourselves. There will be a fresh well of magic at our disposal."

"And I've been thinking about things as well," I add. "There have always been sympathizers among the general population. I think it's time we start contacting them." I turn my attention to Neave. "It's probably a good idea to create some kind of group or committee. Witches need representation in our government, or else you risk this happening all over again. Getting a group of witches and sympathizers together will help us fight for witches' rights ."

"I wouldn't even know where to begin," she says, tucking a strand of purple hair behind her ear. "I've never been one for politics. That shit goes right over my head."

I smile at her. "That's what I'm for. I was raised with that shit."

She stares at me in disbelief. "You'd really help me? You'd help my sisters?"

"What the hell do you think I've been doing? Of course I'll help you. I want nothing more than to make this world safer for you."

Her mouth opens, but she closes it without saying anything. She searches my gaze like she's trying to find a lie hidden in them, but she won't find one. I spoke the truth. I want her to live in a world where she is treated like anyone else. I want her to be able to walk down the street without fear of being captured and burned. I want her to be able to use her magic freely, as she was meant to do.

I want *us* to live in a world where we can be together and not worry about prejudices or hate.

Whatever she sees in my eyes, she must trust. Without warning, she tackles me backward onto the couch, crushing her mouth against mine. My arms wind around her without thought, and I tug her closer.

Julian clears his throat. "See, when I said you guys should just fuck and get it over with, I didn't mean do it right in front of me."

Neave pulls back, but ignores Julian. "Thank you," she whispers, tears shining in her eyes.

I tuck a strand of hair behind her ear and lean up to press a soft kiss to her lips. "You never need to thank me for anything, Neave."

"YOU KNOW I can carry some bags," Neave says as we climb the steps to the front door of the cabin. "I'm not helpless."

We stopped at the grocery store on the way in, as well as a clothing store, since we had nothing warm enough for the mountains. The result is about fifteen bags of supplies to unload.

"Oh, I don't know. Wouldn't want you to strain yourself. I plan on putting you to use later." I wink at her and drop the bags on the floor of the kitchen.

The cabin is a quaint little thing with one floor, one bedroom, a living room, and kitchen. A deck off the back of the house boasts beautiful mountain views ... and a hot tub. Neave notices my grin when I spot the hot tub, and she rolls her eyes.

"Keep dreaming, pretty boy. How about I unload this stuff and you can get the heat working? It's freezing in here. I wouldn't want you to complain of shrinkage."

I chuckle as I head to the thermostat. She's not wrong, it is cold in here. As soon as the heat is going, I return to the kitchen to help her unload the groceries. It's such a surreal experience. So domestic and homey. Brushing arms with her as I put something in the fridge, or helping her put something in a high cabinet. This is a dangerous trap I am more than willing to fall into.

Once everything is unpacked and we've changed into warm, comfy clothes, we settle on the couch for the evening with a big bowl of popcorn. Neave looks at me and bites her lip, and I get the feeling she's unsure how to act. All of this is so new for us, and I understand her hesitancy. I grab a blanket off the back of the couch and sit next to her, covering us both.

"What types of movies do you like?" I ask, flipping the TV on with the remote.

"Comedy, mostly. My life is full of enough drama and action. I don't need to watch it in my free time, too."

"I hear that." I scan the movies showing on the movie network and select one I think she'd enjoy. "Have you seen this one?"

She shakes her head. "Nope. I don't watch a lot of TV. Cable is too expensive."

"What do you enjoy doing in your free time?" I ask, turning to face her.

"Gardening. I don't have space for a big one, but tending to the plants in my apartment is relaxing. I also enjoy knitting."

"My mom used to knit. Or crochet. I don't know what the difference is."

She laughs softly. "Knitting you use two needles. Crochet, you use a hook."

"Then she knitted. I still have a scarf she made me before she died. I never wear it because I'm scared it will get messed up," I admit.

Neave lays her head on my shoulder, snuggling closer under the blanket. "Tell me about her."

I exhale heavily. Now is as good a time as any to give her my history and all the baggage that comes with it. "My mom was amazing. She cared so deeply for me and Julian. Unlike my dad who always thought I was never good enough, for some reason. She was the buffer between my dad and me, and when she died, we lost that buffer. My dad had no one holding him back from making sure I knew how he felt."

Neave shifts, glancing at me with wide, sad eyes. "That's terrible," she whispers.

I shrug. "I was sixteen when she died. So the majority of my life I've lived with his barbs. They roll right off me now. But at the time, it wasn't as easy. Between his words and the loss of my mom, and Julian taking his role as future king more seriously, I fell into a dark place. I began drinking and doing drugs. It started as just a way to numb myself, to not *feel* so much. It didn't take long for me to become addicted to dragon's blood."

No one knows about this, except my family, Killian, Dr. Harmon, and a few others in the palace. My dad kept it under wraps because he was ashamed. So, as I tell Neave my story, sweat breaks out over my skin. I've never been ashamed of my past, but now I am. Now that I have to admit my weakness to the woman I'm rapidly falling for, I hate that part of me. I risk a glance at her, but see no judgment shining in her eyes.

I stare straight ahead as I continue. "One night, I OD'd. If Killian hadn't found me, I would have died. I don't know if it was the drugs or if it really happened, but I swear that night I heard my mom's voice. She said she loved me and to stay strong. It wasn't easy, but after that night, I never used again. Until I met you."

She jerks back and stares at me with wide eyes. "Me?"

"I tried to wipe you from my mind with essence. It backfired horribly. And when you were captured, when I thought you'd left..." I don't want to say it, but she deserves to know. "When I thought you'd left, fell back into the dragon's blood. I'm not strong, Neave. I'm weak."

She shifts next to me, but I refuse to look at her. I don't want to see the disgust in her eyes. "Ty," she says quietly. "Look at me, Ty." I slowly face her, searching her gaze. "You are not weak. You are stronger than most humans I know. Instead of running from your questions, you dove into them. You uncovered the truth of your beliefs and realized they were wrong. That is not easy. And most people shy away from that. You didn't. That is strength, Ty."

I pull her to my side, not wanting her to see the tears shining in my eyes. Her words mean more to me than anyone else's. I appreciate that she didn't judge me or run away in disgust. She settles against my side, and we fall silent.

After a while, I notice she's gone limp, her breathing slow and even. As gently as I can, I scoop her into my arms and carry her to the bedroom. Laying in the bed with her in my arms, I decide this is how I want to spend the rest of my life. I will fight every battle that comes our way. I will do *anything* to ensure she is safe and happy. My witch will want for nothing.

I Never Want This Spell To Break

"Make sure you bundle up. It's cold out there." Ty pulls his beanie over his head, covering his blond hair.

"Is it really? I thought for sure it had warmed up since yesterday."

"Listen, smart ass, I don't want to hear you complaining as soon as we step outside."

He throws a pair of gloves at me, and I swipe them from the air. "You are insufferable." I slip the gloves on and wrap a scarf around my neck. "I hope you get frostbite."

He grins at me, and it makes my heart flutter. "If I do, you can just heal me."

"As if I'd waste my magic on you."

He snakes out a hand and grabs my wrist, pulling me flush against him, and my breath leaves me in a rush. I stare into his blue eyes as they glitter with mischief.

"You would," he whispers. "Because you can't resist me."

I want to pull away, to show him I most certainly can resist him. But he's right. I'm helpless when it comes to him. So instead of fighting it, I push up on my toes and kiss him. "It's only because you're good with your tongue," I remind him.

"I'll have to show you what else I'm good with." Before I can kiss him again, and demand he show me exactly what he's talking about, he steps away. "You ready?"

For what? You to show me how good you are in bed? Yes, yes I am. "Yeah. Let's see if this works."

We decided to take a walk at night. Since I'm apparently a lunar witch, and this ring is supposed to guide me, being under the stars seems like the first step. We meander down a dirt path lined with evergreens. The sky is mostly blocked by the trees, and I'm just about to say something when the path widens and opens into a large grassy field with a lake fed by a mountain stream.

I gasp, hand going to my throat as I take in the sight. Tall grasses wave gently back and forth in the chilly breeze. The rippling water of the lake appears black, reflecting the darkness of the sky above. Evergreens line the field, enclosing us in the space, giving the sense of privacy.

But it's the night sky that grabs my attention. Vast, never ending darkness spreads out before us, littered with thousands of twinkling stars. A crescent moon hangs above our heads, giving off the perfect amount of light to see the ground, but not dimming the stars it shares the sky with. A galaxy stretches and disappears behind the trees, the various shades of purples standing out sharply against the black.

Ty whistles softly. "Damn. You definitely can't see this in the city."

"No," I say slowly. "You certainly can't." Without thinking, I plop onto the ground, heedless of the cold or wet. I lay back in the grass, almost in a daze, as I stare above me.

I swear it's as if I can *feel* them. There's a pulsing heat deep in my veins, mimicking the twinkling lights. I close my eyes and focus on that warmth, a smile spreading across my face as it intensifies. It doesn't burn hot, but it's warm enough to make me want to remove my gloves and scarf.

On instinct, I reach out with my now bare hand, stretching toward the sky, trying to catch a star in my palm. I clench my fingers and pull. I don't know what I pull with, but I sense the magic in the stars drawing closer to me. I pull harder, and soon, shimmering white light wreathes my hand.

"Holy shit," Ty breathes, kneeling next to me. "Is that…"

"Starlight," I whisper, glancing at him. The light gilds his face in silver, making his blue eyes almost glow. *Now, how do I get it in the ring?* As soon as the thought crosses my mind, my fingers open, and the magic twirls around my hand until it finds the silver band. I watch with wide eyes as it disappears inside the black stone. For minutes, a steady stream of starlight filters into the ring.

When it stops, the clearing plunges into darkness. Except…

"Neave," Ty says slowly, "you're glowing." He reaches out and grabs my hand, tracing my palm with his finger.

Holy shit. I am glowing.

I look up at Ty, my heartbeat growing more rapid with each passing second. "How do I make it go away? I don't want to glow!" The longer I stare at my glowing hand, the more I spiral. If I glow forever, everyone will know I'm a witch. I'll never be able to hide. I'll be hunted and burned. All the peace I've found recently, all the safety I've felt with Ty, shatters. I don't realize how fast I'm breathing until my vision swims.

Ty grabs my face in his palms, forcing me to look at him. I can see myself reflected in his eyes, the glow shimmering. "Breathe, Neave. Take a deep breath. Good. Another one." He smiles at me, eyes tracking back and forth as he scans my face. "You are so goddamn beautiful." The words are whispered, but hold such a reverence I tear up. "I could live my entire life and never cease to be amazed by you."

I swallow as his words hit home. *His entire life? What is he saying?* But I can't focus on that right now. I've just crawled out of the pit of panic and I'm still standing on the very edge. A gentle breeze could knock me back down. "What about the glow?" I whisper desperately.

"I'd never need a flashlight again. Or a nightlight." He grins at me, and the panic recedes a little more. "Hide and seek might be a bit difficult, but honestly, how often will we play that? And migraines. Migraines will royally suck."

I gape at him. The panic pushed back far enough I can focus on his words. Hide and seek? Migraines? "Ty!"

His grin softens into a sweet smile, his dimple appearing, and he leans forward and kisses me. "We'll figure it out, witch. Don't worry."

꩜ ☽ ● ☾ ꩜

IT TURNS out taking off the ring makes the glowing stop. Sitting on the couch with a cup of hot chocolate warming my hands, I take the first deep breath since I started glowing. The relief that rushed through my system when Ty took the ring off and the glow faded almost made me hit the floor.

My gaze is glued to Ty. He's currently studying the ring, his brows drawn down over his eyes. The things he said in the clearing, the things he hinted at. What does it all mean? A lock of blond hair has fallen forward and my fingers itch to swipe it away so I can see his eyes.

I've long since accepted my feelings for him. The guilt and self-hate I had for falling for the enemy are gone. Ty has completely surprised me in his change of heart toward witches. He went from hunting and burning us, to supporting us. He's fighting alongside me, lending me his strength as I take on this task of saving my sisters. And he's done all that ... for me. It's a thought that is hard to wrap my brain around.

"Ty," I say quietly, twirling a strand of my hair around my finger.

"Hmm?" He looks up at me, his focus unwavering.

"What you said tonight, in the clearing..." I trail off, unsure what exactly it is I'm looking for. Do I want to know if he meant those words? Do I want to know what they mean? Is he hinting at wanting to be with me ... forever? Am I ready for that?

He sets the ring on the coffee table and turns to face me,

grabbing my hands in his own. It's hard to focus when he rubs his thumbs over the tops of my hands, but his first words ensnare me. "Every word was the truth. I don't care if you're a witch. I don't care if you fucking glow 24/7. I want to be with you no matter what." He scoots closer, releasing one of my hands so he can cup my cheek. "You are a bright spot in my life. The sass, the teasing, the laughter. It's addicting. The strength you possess inspires me. You've never let anything get you down, and I admire that so much."

Warm fuzzies explode in my chest. No one has ever said things like this to me before. No one has ever accepted me for me. No one has ever truly seen the real me. But Ty does. Ty sees all of it, and he accepts it. He ... wants it.

He casts his gaze down, letting his hands fall to his lap. "I can never make amends for what I've done in my past. And I can never thank you enough for opening my eyes to the truth. You've made me a better man, a better human, and it's still not enough. Every second I spend in your presence makes me want to do better, because you deserve the absolute best." His gaze takes on a haunted look, and something dark crosses his features. "When I thought you left, it hit me like a ton of bricks. The thought that I lost you before I ever really had you tore me to pieces. The thought that you would never know how truly sorry I was for everything, and how much I wanted to change, destroyed me. I realized during that time, not having you by my side was unimaginable. I would cease to exist without you, Neave. Every cell in my body is yours. I belong to you, body, mind, and soul. And the only thing that scares me about that realization, is that you might not feel the same way toward me."

Am I breathing? I don't think I am. Ty's declaration hangs in the air between us, and I stare at him as I attempt to comprehend his words. There is nothing but honesty and adoration shining in his beautiful blue eyes, and maybe a little bit of vulnerability. He swallows, and I know if I don't say something to his declaration, it will break him. But *do* I feel the same way toward him?

I definitely like him. He makes me laugh, and he makes my heart flutter and butterflies fly in my belly. But is that the equivalent of what he is saying to me? I look forward to seeing him, and I've found I rely on him for more than I probably should. As a witch, I've never thought of staying with one man forever. We don't do that. We have dalliances. One-night stands. Men are just a way to keep populating the world with witches. The thought of him not being in my life makes me queasy, but why?

Instead of answering him with words, I use my body to show him how I feel, because that has always been easier for me. And there is no denying I want him in that regard. I crave his touch. I'm addicted to his taste. I can never get enough of his skin on mine.

I climb onto his lap, straddling his waist, and kiss him. His hands immediately tangle in my hair and press me closer. I coax his mouth open and groan as his tongue brushes mine. He tastes like hot chocolate and the peppermint alcohol he mixed with his. It's not enough, though. I need more of him.

His hands drop to my waist and he pulls me down hard as his hips lift. "I want you, Neave," he whispers against my mouth. "I want all of you."

"Yes." I don't even hesitate, because I want this, too. We've fought each other so much. The tension between us has reached a boiling point, and if I don't fuck him right now, I may lose my mind.

Our clothing hits the floor in record time, and Ty runs his hands over my arms, stomach, and thighs. It's as if he can't touch enough of me at once. My hand shakes slightly as I grab his and tug him to the bedroom. He watches me with heated intent as I climb onto the bed. I let myself take in his body, all the hard planes and angles, sculpted muscles, and cock standing proudly at attention.

Anticipation swirls through my gut when he climbs over me, holding himself up on his elbows so we're not touching. Unable to wait, I wrap my legs around his waist and pull him down. He chuckles, and I groan. Just him touching me, his body naked against mine, is enough to drive me insane. How we've waited so long for this, I have no idea.

His mouth meets mine in a kiss that is both sweet and intense at the same time. It sends tingles over my body that settle low in my stomach. I rock my hips against his, and he moans, breaking off the kiss to stare at me with hooded eyes.

"I swear," he says, kissing the corner of my mouth, then my jaw. "You've used your magic on me." Kisses on my neck and throat. "You tempt me, witch, every fucking minute of every fucking day." Kisses along my collar bones. "I'm bewitched by your beauty, your body, your mind, your fucking sass." Kisses down the slope of my breast. "I never want this spell to break."

His lips wrap around my nipple and my back arches off the bed. He slides one hand down my chest, stopping to pinch my other nipple into a tight peak, then trailing it over my belly, and lower between my thighs. I gasp as he slides two fingers inside, stretching me deliciously.

"Oh, fuck," I moan. "Ty..." I trail off, unable to make my mouth do what I want. My body is a livewire, and I can do nothing but writhe under Ty as he draws forth my pleasure. Those damn fingers, so skilled at piano, and he knows exactly how to use them. "Ty, please." I reach for him, arms shaking. "I need you."

His smile is dark and wicked, and it makes my stomach somersault. The promise of pleasure leaves me panting. He removes his fingers and brings them to my mouth. I suck them into my mouth, tasting myself and what he's done to me.

He rubs his cock through my wetness, and he shudders. "I can't deny you anything, witch." But instead of doing what I want, he pauses. "Birth control?"

I nod. "I have an implant."

This time, when he kisses me, he lines himself up at my entrance. My heart is pounding so hard in my chest. I'm dying inside, waiting for him to fill me completely. Ty's hips move slowly in the most excruciatingly delicious thrusts. My eyes fall closed so I can focus purely on him. We're both breathing heavily when he stills. His arms shake as he holds himself above me, drumming up the need for him.

It's too much. I whimper and dig my nails into his back, urging him to move. He does, but he does it so slowly I almost combust. "More, Ty. Harder," I breathe. "Fuck me like you mean it."

His smirk makes my inner walls clench around him and his thrusts falter briefly before he picks up the pace. The pleasure is intense, but there is something about all of this that makes my heart stutter. Ty grabs my hands and threads our fingers together, placing them above my head. His gaze is latched onto mine, boring into me all the way to my soul. Something sparks in my chest. Something warm and indescribable. It grows with each thrust of his hips, each kiss placed on my lips, each long gaze.

I close my eyes to keep him from seeing the emotion shining there, but he stops his movements. "Look at me, Neave," he breathes, his words rough and deep. "I want to watch you come undone. I want to see it all in your eyes. Every emotion. Every thought. I want it."

He claims he can't deny me anything, and it would seem I can't deny him either. My eyes open, and I stare into his, giving him exactly what he wants. His hips move again, slowly, then speeding up, bringing me to the edge with each thrust until I'm barely holding on.

"Come for me, witch," he growls in my ear.

I do. Wave after wave of pleasure crashes through me, and I hold his gaze through it all. Through the stars bursting in my vision and the quivering of my limbs. He follows me over the edge, his body shuddering above mine, his eyes saying so much more than any word he's spoken yet.

We don't move when it's over, locked in each other's stare. Letting him into my innermost thoughts through my body has left me cut open and raw. And it's not entirely unpleasant. Neither of us says anything as he pulls out and rolls onto his back, tugging me on top of him.

"Neave," he breathes into my hair, my name almost sounding like a prayer on his lips. I shiver as his fingers trace lazy patterns on my side and hip.

Laying in his arms is surreal. I never would have imagined I'd be doing this, sleeping with a witch hunter. With the *prince* of all people. I prop myself on my elbow so I can look at him. His eyes are closed, a sleepy, satisfied smile on his handsome face. I let my gaze travel over his body and the sculpted muscles and tattoos inked onto his skin. This man is a masterpiece. Absolutely beautiful in every possible way.

Scars decorate his arms and torso, little slashes of silvery white that tell a story of his battles. I trace each one with my fingertip, until I get to his thigh. A bigger scar, still pink and healing, makes me pause. I did that when I stabbed him. I run my finger over it gently, and he grabs my hand, bringing it to his mouth to kiss the inside of my wrist.

"I have a lot of regrets in my life," he says quietly. His blue eyes shine brightly as he watches me. "But the things I said to you that day are at the top of my list. I didn't really mean them. When I realized I was enjoying my time with you, I got angry with myself and got defensive. I was still struggling with figuring out what I thought about witches, and ... I don't know. I felt weak and it pissed me off." He wraps both arms around me and tugs me back down to his chest. "I never should have said what I did. It was a horrible move on my part, and I'm so sorry. I deserve that scar, and I'll use it as a reminder for what happens when you let ignorance rule your life."

I bite my lip as I think about it. "You're right. It was really hurtful. But, I guess I get it, in a sick sort of way. And, what matters now is that you've learned from your mistakes and you don't repeat them."

"I won't repeat them." He kisses the top of my head, making

butterflies swoop in my stomach. "I promise. And if I do, you have my permission to stab me somewhere more painful."

A smile tugs at my lips and I drop a kiss to his chest. I squeeze my eyes shut and settle in closer to him. I wasn't ready for any of that—the sex, the apology—but now that it's happened, I don't think I can forget it. We've started down a path I won't be able to veer from. And I think ... I think I'm okay with that.

Mmm. You Taste Good Now

dream. And every time I look at her sitting on the couch, it takes all my self control to not jump her and make it happen again. I meant every word I said to her, even if she's still unsure about it all. And I don't blame her for that. She's lived her entire life in fear of me and the other hunters. She has a deep-seated fear that won't go away overnight. But I will do everything in my power to make her realize my words are true.

"Ugh! I just don't know!" Neave flops back on the couch and covers her eyes with her arm. "We've been brainstorming ideas all fucking day, and we've gotten nowhere. How the hell am I supposed to know what to do with this ring and the magic? How do I fill a well that is mostly an abstract idea?"

I rub my eyes and lean my elbows on my knees. "But is it an abstract idea? I mean, you have to pull your magic from somewhere, right?"

"Yeah, from living things around me."

"Well, where do these living things get their magic?"

"The universe?" She lets her arm fall to her side, and she gives me the best side-eye I've seen from her yet. "I don't fucking know, Ty! I'm a witch, not a goddess."

"I'm not so sure about that," I mutter.

Instead of the flat stare I expect from her, she frowns and mutters something to herself I can't hear. I debate asking her what she said, knowing it's probably not complimentary toward me, but a knock on the door pulls me away.

"Who could that be?" I ask, as I stand from the couch and motion to Neave. "Wait in the bedroom, just in case."

It's really no surprise when she ignores me, flicking her eyebrows up and crossing her arms over her chest. I sigh and head to the front door, snagging my knife from the table as I go. Cautiously, I open the door, blocking the view of Neave with my body as much as I can.

"What the fuck are you doing here?" I grab my brother's arm and yank him inside, closing the door behind us. "I told you to stay away from us."

"You are so bossy," Neave says.

Julian nods. "He really is. I think it's older brother syndrome."

I roll my eyes, even though I'm secretly happy my brother gets along with Neave. "Seriously, why are you here? You need to be careful."

"I am being careful. Relax, Ty." Julian drops into a chair, and winks at Neave.

"Don't wink at her." I sit next to Neave, and ignore Julian's chuckle. "And I've asked you twice now. Don't make me ask a third time."

Julian sighs and pulls out his cell. "I got the proof."

Neave and I exchange glances, sitting up straighter on the couch. "Seriously? Like, enough proof that Dad will believe it?"

"If he doesn't believe this, he won't believe anything we say."

I grab his phone and hit play. The video is shaky and mostly shows the grand ceiling of the estate, but I recognize where that ceiling is. I've spent a lot of time sitting in a chair staring up at that ceiling. It's Uncle Edward's office.

"Julian, have you had any contact with your brother?" Edward asks.

"None. I've tried calling him, and he doesn't answer. I even tried tracking him with the GPS, but he must have his phone off."

I smirk because, technically, that isn't a lie. My phone *is* off, and there would have been no way for Julian to contact or track me.

"I knew I should have kept a closer eye on him. His disobedience to the throne doesn't surprise me one bit. What about you, Killian, any progress finding the witch?"

I stiffen, my heart dropping straight into my stomach as Killian's voice plays over the speaker.

"None, sir. I've searched everywhere. Questioned hundreds of people. No one has seen her. It's like she just disappeared. If I were to guess, the witch and Ty are in hiding together."

So, he really has turned against me. Not that I didn't believe Neave, but I couldn't help but balk at the thought my best friend would betray me. Hearing it for myself just solidifies it.

"I've not been able to figure out how she escaped in the first place." Edward growls, and it sounds like he slams his hands on the desk. *"This put a wrench in all of my plans! How the hell am I supposed to figure out what the threat is to the throne if no one can catch the damn witch?"*

"May I ask what your plans are, sir?" Killian asks.

Edward sighs. *"Julian, you're dismissed."*

The video shifts and bounces as Julian stands and walks from the office, but I can tell he doesn't go far. Soon, the picture on the screen shows the doorframe leading to Edward's office. The voices coming through now are quieter, but it's still possible to make out what they say.

"I need to find the threat before my brother does," Edward says once Julian is out of the room. *"If I can ensure this threat comes to pass, I can use it to remove my brother from the throne and take his place. But if he finds it before me, there is no way I'll be able to take the throne."*

"You want to remove King Leander?" Killian's surprise is evident in his tone.

"He's too soft. Just like his sons. Look at how well Tyberius turned out. Given enough time, I may be able to mold Julian into the puppet I want, but this is easier. Messier, maybe, but easier. And so much more gratifying."

"You're right. It probably would be for the best."

The recording cuts off. I hand the phone back to Julian with shaky hands and walk numbly out the front door. The icy wind blasts me in the face, making my eyes water, but I welcome the cold. I can't stop hearing Killian's words, over and over, like a never-ending echo in my head.

I'm halfway down the dirt path to the clearing when Neave catches up. She wraps my coat around my shoulders, and I slip my arms inside on autopilot. We walk to the clearing in silence, but her presence eases some of the tightness in my chest. I drop onto a large rock overlooking the lake, and pull Neave onto my lap, her back against my chest.

"I'm sorry," she says quietly, her voice almost the same volume as the pine boughs rustling.

I wrap my arms around her middle and rest my head over her shoulder, sighing. "It was one thing for me to hear you say he betrayed me. It was another thing entirely to hear it with my own ears. Not that I didn't believe you," I add in quickly. "It was just easier to ignore. Plus, we were busy finding the ring and everything. It kind of slipped my mind." That, and the only thing I've been thinking about is her.

She rests her head on my chest and wraps her hands around my forearms. "I can't say I know what it feels like. I've never had any friends. Not really. But, I know you're hurting, and I ... don't like that..." Her voice trails off as if she's not sure what to make of feeling that way.

The warmth that blooms in my chest at her words only slightly thaws the ice that formed at Killian's actions. "Growing up, we were inseparable. For a long time, it was me, Julian, and

Killian. His mom was my mom's maid, and they quickly became friends. Killian was raised with me in the palace because of that. He is more like a brother to me. *Was* more like a brother to me."

"Why do you think he did it?" she asks tentatively.

A strand of her hair tickles my face as it blows in the wind, and I tuck it behind her ear. "We were raised the same way. Attended the same lessons. Trained side by side. All our lives we are taught how evil witches are. Hunting was the only thing either one of us had going for us. I wasn't going to be king, so captain of the Witch Guard was the next logical step. Killian was only a step below me. We worked hard to get where we were." A fact I hate more than anything now. I sigh. "I know him better than anyone, and I'm willing to bet he did it because he saw how hard I was falling for you. He thought he was doing me a favor by removing the temptation. And when he realized you were more than a temptation, and your loss hit me as hard as my mother's death, he probably thought there was no hope for me. I'm not sure I'd ever be able to convince him witches aren't evil."

"I'm sorry," she says again. "I feel like this is all my fault."

I shake my head vehemently. "No. Absolutely not. Do not apologize for this. None of it is your fault. And honestly, if I had known what would happen when I captured you, I wouldn't have done a single thing different. Except treat you better from the start. This is exactly how things were meant to play out. And while it sucks losing a friend like that, I can honestly say I gained so much more."

She turns, and I loosen my grip so she can face me. Her eyes swim with unshed tears. "You're an amazing person, Ty. Not many people would change their views like you did." She presses her lips softly against mine. "And another positive," she says when she pulls away. "It seems like you and Julian have mended your relationship."

I smile. "Yeah. And we have you to thank for that." We sit quietly for a few more minutes before I notice her shivering in my arms. "You're cold. We should head back."

"I'm fine. We can stay as long as you want," she says through chattering teeth.

"My ass is probably frozen to this rock." I stand, setting her on her feet. "Let's go back and get some hot chocolate."

She smiles at me, and the warmth of it melts the rest of the ice around my heart. I may have lost a friend in all of this, but I gained Neave. And there is nothing I could want more than that.

We return to the cabin hand in hand and head straight to the kitchen to make hot chocolate. Already, we work so well together. It's like we've been doing this for years instead of days.

"Are you sure you don't want a little something extra in yours?" I ask, holding up a bottle of peppermint vodka.

Her lip curls. "Positive. It should be a crime to ruin a cup of perfectly good hot chocolate with alcohol." She snags the can of whipped cream from the fridge and sprays a generous amount into her mug. "This though, I can't get enough of." She then holds the can to her mouth and sprays it straight in. Lowering the can, she smiles at me.

I grimace. "Agree to disagree. Nothing should go in hot chocolate but alcohol."

She scoffs, her eyes alight with mischief. "This will never work out. We should just end things now before it gets too hard."

I set my mug on the counter, then grab hers from her hands and set it next to mine. Her back thumps against the fridge as I pin her to it and lower my mouth to her ear. "You can just toss that thought right out of your mind because that's never gonna happen, witch."

Her body relaxes under mine, and I drop my mouth to hers. Before I can kiss her, though, I get a face full of whipped cream. Rearing back, I splutter, wiping the creamy white stuff from my eyes.

Neave cackles and sprays more into her mouth. "Agree to disagree." She shrugs and approaches with a sinister shine in her eyes. Grabbing my shoulders, she licks the side of my face, removing some of the whipped cream. "Mmm. You taste good now."

"Psh. I always taste good."

"Hey guys?" Julian calls from the living room. "Not to interrupt your flirting, but..."

I snag a towel and wipe my face before grabbing the hot chocolates and ushering Neave into the other room. "But..." I prompt.

Julians holds up the ring. "Doesn't this look familiar to you?"

I set the mugs on the coffee table and sit on the couch. "Yeah, but I can't place it. I've stared at the damn thing for hours—but I got nothing."

"It reminds me of one of mom's rings. The one that was kind of V shaped with the black stone?"

My eyebrows lift to my hairline. "Oh shit, you're right! I always thought it was weird looking because it was shaped so strangely." Snagging the ring from Julian, I look at it closer. "I bet it fits perfectly against this one."

"Do you think it's supposed to go with mine?" Neave asks. "What are the chances?"

I shrug. "I don't know. It kind of makes sense to me. Mom's ring was an heirloom, passed down among the women of our family. It's not a huge stretch to think Sybil was part of that. I bet she took this ring from the family coffers." I absentmindedly fiddle with the gold band on my thumb, another heirloom passed down among the men in our family. Technically, it should go to Julian. The kings all have worn it. Even though I'm first born, I'm not going to be king.

"Do you think both rings need to be together to work?" Neave asks.

I shrug. "Only one way to find out." I maintain eye contact with Neave as I grab her hand and slip the ring on her finger, a thrill shooting through me at the motions. As soon as it's on, she lights up like a damn glow stick.

"Holy shit!" Julian leans forward and stares at Neave with wide eyes. "Umm, you're glowing. You know that, right?"

"Kinda hard to miss," she mutters, as she stares him down. "I'm not an exhibit in a freak show. Stop staring."

"Sorry." He holds his hands up. "I've just never seen someone glow before. You would fit in perfectly at the glow parties at the clubs downtown."

"Don't forget that I'm a witch. I could hex you if I wanted to." She cracks her fingers and rolls her shoulders, the soft glow rolling off of her.

"She's threatened me before, too. I think you're safe," I say.

"Yeah, but I'm not sleeping with her." Julian sits back in his chair, and folds his hands in his lap, staring at them like they hold the secrets of the world. "Just do what you need to do. I'll sit here quietly."

Neave sighs loudly and rolls her eyes skyward. "Goddess help me."

I squeeze her thigh, and she looks at me with a smile. Seeing her happiness, and knowing me and my brother are the cause of it, sends my heart racing. I lean forward and kiss her softly. "Give it a try," I whisper against her mouth.

She pulls her lower lip between her teeth and hovers her hand over the small potted plant on the coffee table. Nothing happens. Her brows furrow and she purses her lips, hand trembling slightly. Still, nothing happens. Slumping onto the couch, she heaves a sigh.

"I don't know if it didn't work because I'm doing it wrong or it just doesn't work." With rough, angry movements, she ties her hair into a bun on top of her head. "I did what I would do if I was pulling magic from something else, except I used the ring as my source instead of something living."

I meet Julian's gaze. "I think we need mom's ring."

"I know where it is, and I can get it for you." Julian runs a hand back and forth over his short hair. "But how do we want to do this? We have the proof we need against uncle Edward. We know, theoretically, how to fill this well. The question is, what order do we do it in?"

"We need to let Neave do her thing first. I'd feel more comfortable if she had some extra protection in the form of more magic. Once we show dad that evidence, things will progress quickly. Uncle Edward won't hesitate to fill dad in on everything about me and Neave to get on his good side. I need to make sure she's as safe as possible."

Neave waves her hands back and forth. "I'm right here, you know. Stop talking about me like I'm not. And I'm not some damsel in distress."

"I know you're not," I say quietly, turning toward her. "I'm not trying to talk like you're not here. Habit, I guess. Planning with Killian and all that. I'm sorry." I shrug, a pang of loss spearing through me. "And I know you're not a damsel in distress. You're a badass. But even badasses need protection. And I won't lose you now that I finally have you." Even though she hasn't said anything about our future, I'm not giving up hope that I can convince her to stay with me.

"Alright. Let me get the ring," Julian says. "I can bring it back here in a couple of days."

I shake my head. "Let's meet up at Neave's apartment. That way we're in the city and can plan better."

Neave's head whips in my direction. "My apartment? I'm sure the landlord has rented it out to someone already. I haven't been paying rent."

I rub the back of my neck, suddenly nervous. "Yeeah. I've kind of been paying your rent." I brace myself for ... I don't know what. Anger? Some kind of push back? But that's not what I get.

Neave gapes at me, her chest rising as she inhales sharply. "What? You paid my rent?"

"I really don't know why I started doing it." I shake my head. "No, that's a lie. From the first moment I met you, I was lost. Your smartass mouth captured me immediately. I watched you look around the place before we left, and the sadness in your eyes almost brought me to my knees." Shrugging, I look at my hands in my lap. "At that time, I still planned on ... well, I didn't plan on releasing you after I got the information I needed." The thought that I was planning on sending her to the stakes makes me nauseous. "But I still decided to pay your rent. In case you ever returned there."

Her eyes shine with emotion and unshed tears. "I'll never be able to pay you back," she whispers, her lips trembling.

I grasp the back of her neck and pull her to me. "You don't have to pay me back. It's the least I can do. I know there is no way to make up for what I've done in the past, but I hope I can do *something* to make things right."

Her fingers shake as she traces my cheek before gripping my chin. "Thank you."

Her mouth meets mine, and her lips part immediately. My fingers tighten on the back of her neck, holding her in place as I leisurely explore her mouth with my tongue. My blood heats with each soft exhale of hers. The way her body reacts to my touch makes me want to tie her to the bed just so I can touch her whenever and however I want. Solely to see each and every reaction.

Julian coughs. "Yeah, well. I'm just gonna go. I'll meet you guys in a couple of days." He pauses at the door. "Have fun."

I flip him off without breaking the kiss and feel Neave smile against my mouth.

"Bedroom?" she breathes.

I shake my head. "Hot tub."

You're Not Going To Stab Me Again, Are You?

CLIMBING THROUGH MY APARTMENT WINDOW, I CAN'T help but stop and stare. It's the exact same. Nothing has been touched. Nothing moved out of place. The plants are dead, of course. And a thin layer of dust coats everything, but it's the same. I close my eyes and take a deep breath. Stale air hits my nose, and I grimace. Despite the cold, I'll have to leave the window open to freshen up the space.

Ty pokes me in the ass. "You gonna let me in or make me freeze to death out here?"

I move out of the way so Ty can climb through while I scan the apartment for any sign of life, besides Ty and myself. A spider in the corner of the kitchen shimmers in my vision. Using animals and insects doesn't sit right with me, but I need these plants.

"Sorry little guy. I need your magic." I draw his magic to me. Not waiting to watch him fall lifelessly to the floor, I head to a potted plant.

The monstera was my mom's favorite. I hover my hand above the brown, wilted leaves. The spider didn't give me a lot of magic, but it's enough. Clenching my fingers, I give the magic to the plant, feeding it to the roots. It's just enough of a boost to lift the leaves and turn the stems green. The leaves are still brown and curling, but with some water and fertilizer, I should be able to get it back to the world of the living. Then I can use it to bring back the other plants.

"I don't think that will ever get old," Ty breathes behind me.

I turn to him. "What?"

"Watching you use your magic." He wraps his arms around my waist and tugs me against his chest. "You are so amazing."

Looking into his bright blue eyes, it's impossible to not believe him. The way he looks at me, like I'm the most beautiful thing in the room, like I'm ... a goddess. My heart suddenly feels heavy, but not in a bad way. It struggles to beat under the realization that this man would do absolutely anything for me. This ex-witch hunter would go to the ends of the earth to keep me, a witch, safe.

Standing on my tiptoes, I brush a kiss to his lips. "Ty..." I don't know how to say what I want to say, but he deserves to know exactly what I'm thinking and feeling. I tug him to my worn down blue-green corner couch. Dead leaves litter the surface, and I brush them to the floor before we sit. The hanging plant above the sofa might not be salvageable. Turning to Ty, I swallow and take a deep breath. "I'm a witch, and we don't have significant others. We have one-night stands to keep up the witch population." Something passes across his eyes. Pain, maybe? And I rush to get out the rest of what I want to say. "I'm telling you this, because I want you to know that this is weird for me. It's not bad, and I don't hate it. I just don't know how to do it."

He looks a little nauseous as he settles back on the couch. "What exactly are you trying to tell me? Is this your way of telling me to stop pursuing you? Because I'm not going to do that."

I laugh and groan at the same time, rubbing my eyes. This man is so infuriating. "That's not what I'm saying. But if it was, I would be thoroughly annoyed with you. No. I'm trying to tell you, I need time. Time to process this, to figure it out, to ... I don't know." I shake my head, frustrated with myself for not being about to find the words. "I like you. And I want this. But it's going to take time for me to settle into it." I exhale and look down at the couch, snagging a leaf and crumbling it in my fingers. "I just thought you should know exactly where I am and what I'm thinking."

He brushes the crumbled pieces of leaf from my lap. Cupping the side of my face, he turns my head so I'm looking at him. "I have to disagree. I think you're settling into this extremely well. But thank you for telling me. I won't push you into anything you're not ready for."

How did this man come into my life? I lean forward and kiss him. Putting all the emotions I can into my actions, showing him how I feel without using words—because that's hard for me, apparently. He tugs me onto his lap so I'm straddling his waist.

"Please tell me we can still have sex?" he asks, gently biting my neck.

Fuck. Even if I didn't want to have sex with him, I wouldn't be able to say no. He lights me up inside. Sets me on fire with just a single touch. The more time I spend around him, the more I crave it. In answer, I slip my hands under the hem of his Henley and pull it over his head. "There is nothing I want more," I say, rocking my hips against his.

"Thank fuck." He tugs off my shirt, then unhooks my bra, letting it slide down my arms. His mouth wraps around my nipple and I gasp.

Tangling my fingers in his blond hair, I hold him to my chest, tipping my head back as he builds my pleasure. I wasn't lying when I said he's good with his tongue. He knows exactly what he's doing with that thing. I drop my hands to the waistband of his pants and unbutton them, but that's as far as I can get with both of us sitting.

Growling, I stand from his lap. "Take off your pants." He chuckles, but complies. I slip my legging and panties down as fast as he steps out of his pants and boots. Pushing him back onto the couch, I straddle him again, grinding against his cock, making us both moan.

He tugs my hair away from my face, wrapping it around his wrist and pulling sharply so my head is forced back. My scalp prickles, but the pain only fuels the fire burning in my veins. Ty bites the spot between my neck and shoulder, and I cry out, grinding harder against him. This is different from the first time. Less sensual, more rough. And I'm here for it.

Bending my head down to kiss him, tugs on my hair even more, and he doesn't let up. I scrape my teeth against his lower lip before biting it hard enough to draw blood.

"Oh, fuck, Neave." Ty's hips buck up, and I grin, licking away the bead of blood. "This is happening. Now."

I raise on my knees, and he reaches between us to angle himself for me. I bite my own lip as I sit on his cock, slowly drawing out the stretch and pleasure. He fits me perfectly, and I try not to think about how that makes my heart thump and my breath catch. When his hands land on my hips and he squeezes his fingers hard enough to leave bruises, I start moving. Lifting myself up and down, the need building in me each time his cock slides out then back in. My thighs burn, but I don't stop.

"Harder, Ty," I rasp. "Fuck. I need more." I'll never get enough of him.

He stands, lifting me from his lap and spinning me. His hand on the back of my neck pushes me down until I'm bent over the armrest of the couch, ass in the air. He doesn't give me any warning. Just re-wraps his hand in my hair, tugging sharply at the same time he slams back into me. I cry out as stars burst in my vision. My fingers curl around the armrest and I struggle to keep myself in place as Ty thrusts his hips harder and faster.

I'm high on the euphoria building in my system. He moves exactly how I need him to. I clench around him as he uses my hair to tug me up until my back is against his chest. The sounds we make are erotic as fuck and tip me closer to the edge. His sharp breaths against my ear, skin slapping, the wetness as he slides in and out.

Ty glides his freehand down my chest, pinching one of my nipples hard, before moving down my stomach. He slips his finger between my folds and rubs my clit. "I want to feel you coming on my cock. Now, witch. Come for me."

There is no way I could stop it. My orgasm barrels through me, and only Ty's hand wrapped in my hair keeps me upright. Stars burst in my vision and my breathless scream echoes in the apartment. Ty keeps fucking me, drawing out every last bit of pleasure until his thrusting falters, and his hips slam against mine one more time before he stiffens and finds his own release with a groan.

Ty wraps his arms around me and pulls me backward with him as he collapses on the couch. It takes tremendous effort for me to roll over and lay my head on his chest. We're both sweating. Both heaving for breath. My limbs are like limp noodles, and I can't make them do what I want.

Ty presses a kiss to my sweaty temple, brushing my hair over my shoulder. "Thank fuck we can have sex," he breathes, repeating what he said before this all started. "I can't get enough of you."

I hum my agreement, my brain still not functioning properly. As our breathing slows and the sweat dries, we lay on the couch, tangled together, putting the pieces of ourselves back where they belong.

Ty rubs his hand down my back, squeezing my ass. I feel him harden under my stomach and I grin. "Round two?" he asks, lifting his hips.

I push up and straddle his waist. "If you can handle it."

"THIS IS STUPIDLY DANGEROUS," Ty mutters for what must be the thousandth time.

I don't reply, because he won't listen, anyway. Instead, I pull my hood lower, ensuring my braid is hidden in the dark folds. From my vantage point in the mouth of the alley, I can see the entire city center. Stone platform, stake, and all. A familiar figure emerges from behind the platform, most likely having used the tunnel from the palace. Julian makes his way toward us, head turning left and right as he checks for danger.

"Why doesn't the idiot have on a fucking hood?" Ty groans.

He's right. Julian is completely recognizable as he slips into the shadows of the alley. "We need to work on your stealth skills, Your Highness." He gives me a questioning look, and I roll my eyes. "The entire point of this is to remain hidden. Ty doesn't want you involved in this. If anyone sees you, they'll know exactly who you are and wonder what you're doing skulking in the shadows."

A faint blush creeps into his cheeks. "Sorry. I didn't even think of it."

"Were you at least cautious about getting the ring?" Ty asks, exasperation clear in his voice.

"I didn't have a choice. You know Mom's shit is under a tight lock and key." He digs in his pocket and pulls out a small white ring box.

I take it from him and open it. Nestled inside is a silver ring that looks like it would sit against mine perfectly. A smaller oval shaped black stone rests at the point of the V, with a cluster of three diamonds around it. Pulling it from the box, I slip it on my right ring finger, somehow not surprised to find it fits perfectly. I don't fail to notice the emotion shining in both Ty's and Julian's eyes. This was their mom's ring, after all.

I hand the box back to Julian and creep up to the edge of the alley again. There's no sign of any guard in the city center, so I cautiously step out into the open.

Or at least, I try to. Ty grabs my arm and pulls me back with a hiss. "What do you think you're doing?"

My attempt to shake him off fails. He's got a death grip on my bicep. "Relax, blondie. This is going to be a piece of cake." I stand on my tiptoes to kiss him. It's a quick peck, and before he can grab me again, I dart into the city center.

"Goddamnit, witch!"

His boots thump on the ground as he catches up to me, then slows to a walk. We don't want to draw attention to ourselves, so he grasps my hand and we stroll to the center of the square. Stopping in the middle, we turn to face each other. Hopefully, the few people crossing the city center will just see us as a couple in love, and not look too closely.

"Are you sure you have to do this right here?" Ty asks, his blue eyes shining with concern.

I nod. "It feels ... right. So many witches have died here. Their magic snuffed out in this very spot. Something just tells me this is where it has to be done."

"And you don't think you should practice first? In the safety of your apartment?" He steps closer to me. "So much could go wrong."

I don't answer him, because he could argue with me all day about this. Instead, I pull my ring from my pocket and slip it on my finger. It sits perfectly against Ty's mother's ring. Nothing happens, except I start glowing. This is why we chose to do this in the middle of the day when the sun is shining. Hopefully, no one will notice the glow. Still, I tug the sleeves of my hoodie over my hands and yank the hood lower.

I take a deep breath and pull the magic from the ring before bending down. I place my hand on the ground and shove. Nothing happens. I try again, and still nothing happens. I yank the ring from my finger and stand.

"What the hell?" I stomp my foot like a petulant child, but frustration rushes through me, and I need to get it out somehow. "What am I doing wrong?"

Ty bites his lip, and we both stand thinking through our options. I pour through Sybil's story in my head, dissecting every word. And suddenly, it hits me.

"I need a knife." Excitement bubbles in me as I realize this is exactly what I need to do.

He pulls his dagger from the sheath at his thigh, and hands it over. "You're not going to stab me again, are you? Like some sort of sacrifice?"

I can't help but give him an evil grin and a wink. But instead of stabbing him, I slice the blade across the palm of my hand. I hiss, but the pain is distant as the blood wells ruby bright. I kneel down again and scoop blood onto my pointer and middle fingers and begin drawing. This is less inconspicuous, so I hurry. In just a couple of minutes, I have painted the four symbols I saw in all my hallucinations on the ground in my blood.

Slipping the ring back on, I press my hands to the ground again and push. The magic swells inside of me, and I'm distantly aware of Ty cursing, but I don't pay attention to him. My body feels like it's expanding to the point where it will burst like a balloon. The pressure inside me grows until my eardrums pop. I grit my teeth, sweat beading on my brow, even in the freezing cold. Suddenly, magic rushes from me like water over a waterfall. It flows from me to the ground, spider webbing as it tunnels down, deep into the earth.

In my mind's eye, I follow it. A glowing path that leads to a giant empty chasm that slowly fills with swirling luminescence. I push harder, and the chasm fills more quickly, the shimmering magic spreading from the well and into the ley lines that invisibly criss cross the earth. The pressure inside me abates. My body no longer feels like a balloon. I tremble hard enough that I fall over, but I can tell the ring is depleted. The magic no longer flows through me into the earth.

"Shit," Ty says, his arms coming around me. "Are you okay, Neave?"

I have no idea. I'm still trembling. Hard enough that I knock Ty over. Glancing up, my mouth falls open. "What...?"

I'm not trembling. It's the ground. It shakes and rumbles. Buildings sway alarmingly around us. A crack forms in the ground under us, and it slowly spreads outward, hundreds of tiny fissures reaching for the edge of the city center. As soon as they reach the edge, the shaking stops. The cracks cease growing. Everything is plunged into silence.

Ty pulls me to my feet, and we run across the square, back into the shadows. I yank the ring off as we run, shoving it into my pocket. Julian is still in the alley, ducking as a few loose bricks tumble to the ground from the building above him. Without thinking, I throw out my hand and a bubble appears around him just as a brick would have knocked him in the head. Instead, it bounces harmlessly off the bubble and tumbles to the ground.

I come to a screeching stop, and I gape at Julian. No, not at Julian. At the bubble around him. I didn't pull magic from any living source when I did that. I just threw out my hand in a desperate attempt to protect him. Slowly, we walk to Julian, and as he stands, he runs his hands over the surface. It's glowing a pale silver light, with little flecks of sparkles throughout.

"Is that ... starlight?" Ty asks, mirroring Julian's movements.

I peek at my hand, making sure I actually took off the ring. The only one still on my finger is Ty's mom's ring. I gape at the bubble and poke it with my finger, imagining it popping. And that's exactly what it does.

"Holy shit," Julian breathes, running his hands over his body as if making sure he's still alive. "I thought I was a goner."

"Your welcome," I breathe, still staring where the bubble had been.

Ty grabs my face and forces me to look at him. "Neave, are you okay?"

I nod slowly. "Yes?" His fingers tighten on my face and the slight pain helps me to focus. "I think ... I think that just got rid of the need to use living sources. I think I pulled straight from a leyline."

Ty rips the bottom of his shirt into a strip and ties it around my still bleeding palm. "You sure you're okay?"

"Yeah. Yeah, I'm fine."

"Okay." He turns to Julian. "You ready to go talk to Dad?"

Julian's eyes pop wide. "Now?"

"That earthquake will have distracted everyone. It will be easiest to slip in and get to his office undetected."

"Yeah, okay. What's the plan?"

"I want you to escort me in, like you found me and are bringing me to Dad for him to deal with me. Send me the video, so it's on my phone. I'll show him only the half where you're standing in the hallway. I don't want you to be incriminated in any of this in case it goes badly." While Julian sends the video, Ty turns to me. "Stay here. And be careful. If someone finds you, run. I don't care what you have to do, just stay safe. I'll find you when this is all over."

He pushes me against the wall and kisses me. I don't like this kiss. It feels too final, like he's memorizing the way I taste. Like he doesn't think he'll be coming back from the palace. He pulls away, his eyes shining in the shadows. "I love you, Neave."

Before I can even comprehend what he just said, he disappears with Julian. My breath gets stuck in my chest. Wrapping my hand around my throat, I lean against the wall and replay his words in my head. *I love you, Neave.* He didn't even give me a chance to respond. Not that I know what I would have said. Do I love him? Are witches even capable of loving men?

I push off the wall and shove all of those confusing emotions and questions to the back of my mind. My fingers shake as I pull my hood lower and step to the edge of the alley. People are standing in the square, studying the cracks in the ground. I can just barely see the bloody symbols I painted on the concrete.

A footfall behind has me whirling around. All I catch is a glimpse of a dark silhouette. Then pain explodes in my head and the world goes dark.

The Question Is, Who Do I Burn First?

It was too easy getting into the palace. Even with Julian 'escorting' me. Even with the panic over the earthquake. I expected some kind of guard presence, someone to stop us and ask what we were doing.

I haven't been back here since I left to rescue Neave. I don't know what my dad knows or what he thinks. Which is why I'm using Julian to get me in. If my dad knows about me and Neave, I never would have made it into the palace without getting caught and thrown into the cells.

But something itches under my skin. I don't like the lack of people in the halls. Usually, servants and guards fill the palace at the very least. I figured with the earthquake, people would be running around like chickens with their heads cut off.

"Something isn't right," Julian says next to me, echoing my own thoughts.

"Agreed. Keep your guard up."

Outside our dad's office, Julian turns to me. "Ready?"

I take a deep breath and nod. He pushes open the door and we step inside, my heart sinking to my stomach. Dad's not alone in his office. Uncle Edward is standing next to his desk, a smarmy smile on his face. My hands go to my knives, but they aren't there. I gave them to Julian to perpetuate our ruse.

"Well, isn't this just perfect," Edward says, his voice dripping with glee. "I was just talking to your father about you, Tyberius."

"That's funny. I came here to talk to him about you." I glance around, but it's only the four of us. "Dad, I have proof that Uncle Edward is scheming against you. He wants the throne from himself."

My dad scoffs, and the first bubble of fear grows in my gut. "Like I would believe anything a witch lover has to say. You have always been a selfish, disrespectful excuse of a son. You would do anything to save yourself, including throwing your own flesh and blood under the bus. Disgusted doesn't even begin to describe what I'm feeling right now." His cheeks are red and vein pulses in his forehead.

I've heard my dad angry plenty of times. He's said hateful things to me my entire life. But something about his tone and posture is different this time. He's fed up with me and the bullshit I've put him through. It didn't take anything for Uncle Edward to spin this tale and make my dad believe it. Although, it's really not a tale. Everything is true.

"If you would just give me a minute, I can sh—"

Dad's hand slams onto his desk, silencing me. "I don't want to hear another word out of your mouth. Out of respect for your mother, I have put up with your shit for too long. But it ends now." He turns to Julian. "Thank you for bringing him in, Julian. At least I have one son I can rely on."

I turn to face Julian. *Did my brother betray me?* He won't meet my gaze, but I notice his first two fingers tapping on his thigh. We may not have had the best relationship lately, but I still know my brother. He's thinking, trying to find a way out of this. The fear eases. I wasn't prepared to deal with my brother betraying me. That sharp stabbing pain in my chest took me by surprise, but it was unfounded.

He nods to our dad. "Of course. Anything for the crown."

I smirk, despite the situation. That's the Julian I've come to know the past few years. Pompous, arrogant, ass-licker. Two guards enter the room, and one attempts to grab my arms. I'm not about to go down without a fight. My elbow smashes into his face, and I laugh as it crunches, and warm blood coats my sleeve. I whirl around and use my momentum to throw a right hook at the second guard. He goes down instantly like a sack of potatoes.

The first guard has recovered, and I face him, blood still pouring from his nose. I'm distracted with making sure he doesn't get the jump on me, and I don't expect Uncle Edward to get his hands dirty. But I quickly realize my mistake as he wraps me up in a bear hug, trapping my arms at my sides.

"The question is, who do I burn first? You or the witch?" he asks, mouth next to my ear.

His words freeze the blood in my veins. "No," I whisper. My gaze shoots to Julian, and I meet his wide-eyed stare. "No!" They can't have her. She has to be safe. I throw my body forward, trying to knock Edward off balance. Unfortunately, this is the man who has taught me everything I know about fighting. I'm not able to surprise him. "Don't fucking hurt her!" I writhe and fight, but it's not enough. "Neave!"

The guard raises the hilt of his knife and brings it down on my head. The last thing I see is Julian's concerned eyes, the same color as mine, the same color as our mom's. Then darkness.

MY HEAD THROBS to the beat of my heart. Each thump causes my stomach to churn threateningly. Groaning, I clutch my head and beg for the agony to cease. I'm too scared to open my eyes, knowing the light will probably be the thing that makes me vomit. By the hard ground underneath me, I think it's safe to assume I'm in a cell, and as soon as I realize that, I remember why I'm here.

"Neave!" I sit up so fast my head swims. The world tilts

alarmingly from side to side, and I have to plant my palms on the ground on either side of me. I squeeze my eyes shut, and swallow repeatedly until my stomach settles. "Neave!"

Cautiously, I open my eyes and look around. I'm definitely in a cell under the palace, but the rest of them are empty. She's not here. Hope lights in my chest. Maybe Uncle Edward was just messing with me. It's exactly the kind of thing he would do. I hold on to the hope that she is safe and far away from here.

The door opens, the sound echoing in the silence, and Uncle Edward steps into the room. A grin spreads across his face when he sees me awake. "Nephew." He tsks and shakes his head. "How disappointed we all are. I always knew you were weak, but falling for a witch?" His lip curls in disgust. "Even I never thought you'd stoop that low. Then again, when you're desperate, I guess you'd stick your dick into anything."

I clench my teeth and swallow the growl that climbs up my throat. I'm not going to give him any satisfaction at getting me riled up. Slowly, I scoot backward until I'm leaning against the wall. Resting my arms across my bent knees, I stare at my uncle.

He leans his forearm against one the bars. "When your brother turned up missing, I figured he had found you and was bringing you in. I knew I had to get here before him to make sure your dad took care of you properly. Imagine my surprise when you said you had proof of my motives. I searched your phone but there was nothing on it. So, what exactly were you planning on showing your father?"

Nothing on it? I'm careful to keep my expression blank, and still I say nothing.

He huffs an annoyed breath. "You don't want to talk? I bet I can find something to make you. Like, say, your little witch? She's currently tied to the stake in the city center. We're just waiting for nightfall to light the bitch up."

My vision swims as the blood drains from my face. I hold on tighter to the hope that he is lying and Neave is safe. I have to clench my fingers to keep from launching myself at Edward, despite the bars in my way.

He chuckles. "I see you fighting to control yourself. You never were good at concealing your emotions." He steps back from the bars. "That's fine. You don't have to talk. She's going to burn either way. And so will you. Then once I remove your brother and father, nothing will stand in my way of the throne, and I can rid the world of witches once and for all."

I cave. "You're no better than our ancestors. Holding a grudge because someone hurt you. And *I'm* supposed to be the immature one of the family," I snort. "And were you desperate? When you fucked a witch, were you desperate?" His eyes bulge and his face turns an angry shade of purple. I laugh. "Oh yeah. I know all about that. I know years ago a witch used and discarded you like the piece of filth you are. I only hope her attempts at getting pregnant failed. We don't need more of you in this world."

Edward growls and throws open the cell door. Prepared for this, I jump to my feet. Still off balance from being hit in the head, the world tilts, and I grit my teeth as I get my feet under me. Edward throws a punch that I just barely avoid, and I step back to give myself time. Banking on him being clumsy in his anger, I smirk, trying to taunt him to make him even more careless. It works. He charges forward, and I lower my shoulder and level it into his chest, shoving as hard as I can.

Pressing my advantage, I throw a couple of jabs, hitting him in the jaw and making his head snap back. He stumbles backward and I jump forward. Throwing an uppercut at his jaw throws me off balance, my head still not liking the sudden movements. Edward dodges the punch and sweeps his foot out, connecting with my legs and knocking me face first into the ground. I curse and flip over. If only my head wasn't still spinning. We're a fairly even match. Being younger than him, I would probably have the upper hand, but with the fog still clinging to me, he has a clear advantage.

Before I can attempt to push to my feet, Edward's boot

presses down on my chest, pinning me to the ground. My ribs crack, threatening to break under the weight. All the air in my lungs is squeezed out, and my head spins even harder.

"You can't even put up a good fight," Edward shakes his head. "A disappointment all the way around."

As if someone pressed slow-mo on a video, time seems to stop. Edward leans down and raises his fist. I know I won't be able to move in time. With his foot still on my chest, I'm pinned to the ground. I close my eyes and send my desperate plea into the universe. *Please let Neave be okay.* Pain explodes in my skull, the same spot I was hit earlier, and I'm plunged into the dark.

Yeah, Keep Smiling, Blondie

My shoulders scream, and fine tremors work down my arms. I've lost track of how long I've been tied to the stake. At least three hours. When I came to and I realized where I was, the panic hit me so hard I almost puked. Now, the longer I stand here, the angrier I become. Killian stands watch next to me, and if looks could kill, this man would be long dead.

Apparently, the equalizer also blocks access to the ley lines I refilled. I had hoped it wouldn't, but when I woke up, the first thing I tried was to access it. No go. The longer I stand here, the more I'm able to come to terms with my imminent death. As soon as the sun begins to descend, they'll light the flame that will take me.

I scan the crowd, searching for a familiar face. Any familiar face. I see none, though. My fear of dying alone is looking like a real possibility. Although, I won't truly be alone. By tying me here earlier than usual, the crowd has had time to grow exponentially. I even spot people selling glow sticks and food. My death is being turned into a massive event.

I can't stop looking for Ty in the crowd. I've had too much time to think while I've stood here, and I've found I have no regrets in my life. Except one. Ty told me he loved me, then he ran off before I could even let his words sink in. They've sunk in now. And the warmth they create in my chest has been the one thing to keep me calm as I wait for my death. Imagining those blue eyes, that kissable smile, and his seductive chuckle brings tears to my eyes. I'll never experience that again.

I'll never again get to bask in his attention or the warmth his smile brings me. I'll never walk into a room again and feel immediately at home just because he's there. Even tied to the stake, with Ty nowhere to be seen, I feel protected just knowing he loved me. I know my memory will live on, even if it's just with him.

And the pain that sucks my breath from my lungs when I think of leaving him alone would make me fall to my knees if I could.

I just want to tell him how I feel. I don't know if this is love, but it's definitely something special, something that could very possibly turn into love. And he'll never know. A single tear falls from my eye, the only one I'll allow to fall. And it's for him.

Killian shuffles next to me. He pulls a walkie-talkie from his pocket and steps away. I don't hear the conversation, just the crackling of voices. He points to another guard. "Watch her," he barks, then jumps from the platform and hustles around toward the secret door in the back.

The sun is sinking lower to the horizon, darkening the sky. The crowd is becoming restless. In just a few moments, their entertainment will begin. My eyes are constantly scanning now. *Where is he? Why isn't he here?* I'm not expecting him to save me. That's asking a lot. But I had hoped I could at least see him one last time. Stare into those eyes that always make my heart flutter and calm at the same time. I hadn't realized how nice it must have been for the witches to have at least one person with them. Being alone is ... heavy.

A flash of white catches my eye, and I turn my head to see Jinx sitting on a window ledge. His blue eyes bore into mine, sad and regretful. Guilt burns through me. Not only am I dying today, but Jinx will as well. When a witch dies, their familiar just ceases to exist. And his life has not been easy. I've done nothing to make it good for him. Just because he bothered me, doesn't mean I should have treated him the way I did. He nods his head, as if he knows every thought that just passed through my mind, and he understands. I swallow back the tears burning my throat.

A commotion to the side of the platform snags my attention. The crowd parts, gasps and shocked sounds coming from them. My blood turns to ice and my heart drops to my feet. Killian climbs onto the platform, Ty thrown over his shoulder. *No.* I yank at my bindings, trying desperately to free myself. I reach for the magic I just released into the world. Nothing works. I watch in horror as Killian and another guard secure Ty to a second stake. His head lolls forward and blood trickles down his face, dripping onto his shirt.

"Ty!" His name tears from my throat. Pain and terror like I've never experienced courses through me. My heart is splintering into thousands of tiny pieces. I can't even think of Ty dying. This beautiful soul, who has had such an amazing change of heart, who has done *everything* for me. His life can't be snuffed out.

Tears spill down my cheeks and I scream and rage. I yank and pull and tug, doing everything I can to free myself. *Not Ty. Please! Anyone but him.*

Killian turns to me, a smug smile on his face once Ty is properly secured on the stake. "My orders were to make him watch you burn first. But I think it will be more entertaining for you to watch him." His smile turns into a sneer and he steps closer to me. "And while he burns, you can think about how this is *all* your fault. If it weren't for you, Ty would never have gone down the path he did. He wouldn't be tied to a stake, being *burned alive.*"

I gasp, sucking oxygen into my lungs. I didn't think my heart could hurt any worse, but his words pierce it sharper than any knife ever could. *He's right. Ty is going to die because of me.* My fight leaves me, draining from me like water down a drain. I'm left heavy and numb. My gaze latches onto Ty, and I'm struck with absolute certainty.

I love him. I love Tyberius Berkshire, and it's my fault he's going to die.

Ty stirs, and a soft groan climbs up his throat. His head turns slowly, eyes opening even slower. But when they do, they land on me without err. Even through the haze of pain and confusion, the sadness swimming in those blue eyes steals the breath from my lungs.

I'm sorry. I mouth the words, tears streaming down my cheeks.

He smiles, that adorable, kissable smile with the damn dimple, and my heart fractures even more. Even though his eyes crinkle in pain, he shakes his head, as if he's telling me not to be sorry.

Killian steps between us, a lit torch in his hand. I notice it shakes slightly, almost as if he doesn't want to do this. He's murdering his best friend, and I hope he rots in hell.

"Wait!" Julian's shout halts the lowering of the torch. He pushes onto the platform, chest heaving as if he ran the entire way here.

Killian stiffens and steps between us and Julian. "Don't do anything stupid, Julian. You'll meet the same fate as your brother."

Julian shakes his head and skirts around Killian. He reaches for Ty's hand and the guards around us pull their weapons. Not just knives this time, but guns. Julian only slips the gold band from Ty's thumb. "Family heirloom. Wouldn't want to lose it."

The guards relax, and Julian steps past me. As he does, he brushes against me, and something sharp pinches my leg. I glance down to see a needle in my thigh. I blink and it disappears. Julian climbs down the platform and pockets something in his black pants.

Hope flares inside me and I hold my breath. *Did he just give me the antidote to the equalizer?* My hope bursts as Killian approaches Ty with the lit torch. *No. I need more time!*

Ty lifts his head, breathing heavy from the exertion. "Don't do this, brother." His voice is raspy and strained, but the pain is evident. And not pain from his head.

Killian's shoulders stiffen, but he doesn't stop his approach. "Should have thought about all of this before you jumped into bed with a witch."

The torch drops onto the wood, and I scream. "Ty!" He meets my gaze again, a sad smile spreading across his face. *No. No, no, no! More time. Just a little more time!* The tingles of magic returning are spreading through my limbs, but it's not enough. Still, I close my eyes and focus, not on the threads of magic shimmering in the people of the crowd or the trees in the garden behind us. No. I focus on the well of star magic I just filled, the ley lines coursing through the world around me. The magic swells and churns deep underground, and I pull it toward me, holding on with every bit of strength I have. The magic burns through the lingering equalizer, the antidote making a way for it to slip into my bloodstream.

Calm descends upon me. The roar of the crowd, the crackle of the fire, disappears. I imagine the ropes securing me to the stake withering into dust, and when they do, I grin. Jumping from the pile of wood under my feet, and I throw as much magic at the fire slowly climbing toward Ty. It sizzles and hisses, fighting against me, but the flames die down to glowing red embers.

Killian charges me, and I jump backward to avoid him knocking me down. I need to get Ty free, but I need to get these guards away from us first. The crowd roars, and I can't tell if they're cheering or screaming in fear. Maybe both. But I don't have time to think about it. Killian faces me with two guards flanking him. There are only five total on the platform, and I've lost sight of the other two.

My breath saws in and out of my chest, and I hurl the magic forward. It collides with Killian and the other guards, knocking them backward and sending them sprawling across the platform. Spinning around, I search for the other guards and find them already on the ground, gunshot wounds to their heads. *Holy fuck. Who did that?*

I rush to Ty and quickly disintegrate his ropes. He hits the smoldering wood and a puff of embers erupts from the charred logs. He keeps his feet under him, barely. I dart forward and wrap my arm around his waist.

"We have to get out here," I gasp, eyes scanning for an escape. The crowd is too thick, and I don't think they'll stand idly by while we make a run for it. Gritting my teeth, I thrust my hand forward and a blast of magic pushes people out of the way, creating a path for us. "I'm sorry!" I yell as they topple over one another.

The ones touched by the magic are already up and running in the opposite direction, pushing and shoving others out of their way. It won't be long before the square descends into complete chaos.

I pull Ty toward the edge of the platform and shove him off. He hits the ground and collapses like a rag doll. I wince and jump down next to him. "Shit. I'm sorry." Hauling him to his feet, we slowly work our way through the surging crowd. The path I created has already disappeared, but we're able to slip into the frenzy easily, blending in with upheaval.

"Where are we going?" Ty asks, his breathing wet and labored.

"I know of a place. We just have to get there." I'm already tired. Ty is heavy, and he's not doing much to help me. "I know you're hurt, but I really need you to help me here," I grunt. "For fuck's sake, you're heavy."

He barks a laugh that quickly turns into a groan. "Sorry. The world is currently spinning like a carousel, and I'm trying my hardest not to puke on you."

I gag. "Oh, goddess. Please don't."

The crowd thins as we exit the square onto a side street. I quickly check behind us, but it's too chaotic to tell if we're being followed. With the smaller crowd, we're more at risk of being spotted. I haul Ty forward and into an alley.

"We're not going to make it," I breathe. My sides are heaving, and Ty has turned an alarming shade of green. "Please hold it together, Ty. We need to get to safety."

"Tying my hardest, witch." Sweat coats his forehead and slides down his temples despite the icy wind cutting through the alley.

"Fuck, fuck, fuck," I mutter on repeat as I attempt to pick up the pace. "Useless. You are absolutely useless. Stupid, arrogant hunter." Each ground out insult I throw at Ty makes him smile, and if I had time to stop, I would slap him across the face. "Yeah, keep smiling, blondie. I'll laugh when they catch you again."

The alley ends and I check the intersecting street before pulling Ty with me. The sound of boots on pavement echo throughout the city, ricocheting off the buildings. I can't tell where they are. Are they behind us? In front of us?

Jinx sprints past, a blur of white fur. *Don't stop. They aren't far behind you.*

I curse and pull Ty along, while Jinx dashes forward to check the path ahead. With his guidance we make it three blocks to the pet store I was aiming for. It's in the bottom corner of a skyrise apartment building. We go around to the side of the shop, to a small door typically used for deliveries. I double check our surroundings before banging my fist against the metal door.

My heart pounds so hard in my chest while we wait. I shiver in the cold as the sweat cools on my skin from lugging Ty through the city. When the door cracks open, and a pair of bright green eyes peer through, I heave a sigh of relief. The eyes widen, then the door swings in.

"Quick. Get inside." The blond witch ushers us in and closes the door behind us, sliding the lock into place. She instantly moves across the floor to a shelf of cat toys and shoves it to the side. "They'll be searching everywhere for you. You'll have to remain quiet." Bending down, she lifts a hatch in the floor.

I grimace, looking down into the black pit before us. "How the hell am I going to get you in there?"

Ty groans. "Just push me. I'm sure you're dying to do it, anyway."

A laugh slips from me before I can clamp my mouth shut. "You're not wrong about that." I lead him to the small ladder descending into the gloom, and he clumsily climbs down. I hear a distinct thud, then cursing and a groan. Wincing, I step onto the ladder. "Thank you, Millie," I say, my heart full of gratitude..

She nods and waves her hands. "Hurry. There is water, food, and some medical supplies down there. Just remember to be quiet."

I give her one more grateful smile and climb down the ladder, careful to not step on Ty sprawled at the bottom. "Come on, you lug. Get up." I haul him to his feet and try to peer into the dark, but the space is pitch black, so I stand with Ty leaning on me for a minute until my vision adjusts. In the corner, I can just make out a cot, so I drag Ty to it, and plop him down. He immediately lays down and grabs his head, groaning.

"Holy fuck," he whispers, pain lacing his words. "I think I have brain damage."

"You had brain damage before you got hit in the head." I move his hands and brush his hair out of the way. It's difficult to see the extent of his injuries in the dark, but running my fingers over the spot, I can tell there is a significant bump. And it hurts, because Ty curses at my touch.

"I got hit twice," he mumbles. "In the same spot."

I purse my lips and take a deep breath. I've never been great at healing. Small cuts and bruises have always been the extent of my abilities, but that was before I had all this magic at my disposal. As gently as I can, I place my fingertips to the bump and push magic into him, imagining it healing the injury and making him whole again.

A soft sigh escapes his lips, and he smiles. "That's much better," he says, slurring his words. With tremendous effort, he opens his eyes, blinking owlishly at me, then they slide closed.

I press my hand to his chest, heaving a sigh as it rises and falls rhythmically under my palm. I leave it there for a moment, his heart thumping steadily, a reminder that he's okay. When my shaking stops, I find a bottle of water and a clean cloth. I gently clean the dried blood from his face, then cover him with the blanket folded at the foot of the cot.

I sit on the floor next to the cot, the hard concrete cold on my ass. But I don't care. Ty is okay. We're safe. For now. Leaning against the wall, my head falls back against the cold surface. I idly run my fingers through his hair, needing to touch him somehow. As the adrenaline leaves my body, it leaves me weak and shaky. Exhaustion seeps in, and I find it harder and harder to keep my eyes open.

Instead of fighting it, I lay my head on the cot next to Ty's. It's wildly uncomfortable, but I'm too tired to care. As soon as my eyes close, I'm asleep.

PRINCE OF THE WITCHES

I wake with no ache, no twinge of pain. Raising my hand to my head, I feel for the lump that should have made my eye swell shut. Nothing. No bump. No blemish. My eye opens fully. Then it hits me. Neave used her magic to heal my injuries.

I look to my side and find her sleeping with her head on the cot next to me, her back bent at an angle that will surely pain her when she wakes. My heart swells. Not only did she heal me, she saved my fucking life, then sat on the floor while I slept.

I run my hand over her head. Her braid has mostly fallen out, and strands of hair lay tangled over her face. "Neave," I whisper.

She shoots up with wide eyes, only to wince and grab the back of her neck. "Ow."

I scoot back on the cot so I'm leaning against the wall and pat the open space between my legs. "Come here." As she climbs up, I angle her so she's facing away from me, and I swipe her hair over her shoulder. "Why did you sleep like that?" I ask, keeping my voice low. I dig my thumbs into the soft muscles of her neck, and she groans.

"I didn't know what else to do." There is a soft tremble in her voice that strikes me right in the heart.

"Thank you. For saving me and healing me. You didn't have to do that."

"Yes, I did."

I can barely hear her response, it's so quiet. We'll have to have a conversation at some point. I saw the guilt in her eyes when she mouthed she was sorry, and I need her to know she has nothing to apologize for. If I had died, it would have been because of my own choices. Choices I would make again in a heartbeat. But now is not the time for that.

Slowly, her body relaxes under my hands, the knots in her neck and back releasing. She exhales, and her body melts back into mine. I wrap my arms around her and hold her close. Faint tremors shake her entire body, and each one makes me hold her a little tighter.

"Neave. We're okay. Both of us are okay." I press soft kisses to her temple and murmur words that make no sense. I just want her to hear my voice, to feel my touch, to know that we survived. So far.

When her shaking lets up, she turns to face me, her eyes wide and dark. "Ty," she whispers. Her mouth opens, but she hesitates and closes it, instead, leaning forward and kissing me.

It takes seconds for the kiss to turn from soft and sweet to desperate and needy. A sense of urgency spurring both of us into action. It doesn't go any further than roaming hands, tangled tongues, and gasping breaths. But it's enough to settle the unease in my chest that has been there since I first discovered she might be in trouble. With her in my arms again, I can think straight. Well, sort of. With her lips against mine, I can't think of anything else.

She pulls away, her fingers trailing over my cheeks, rubbing against the stubble that I haven't been able to shave. "It's going to be okay," she says, almost to herself, and rests her forehead against mine.

I don't know how long we sit like that, just taking in each other's presence, but eventually, scraping above pulls us apart.

Neave tenses and flexes her fingers, no doubt readying her magic. The trap door in the ceiling opens, spilling light into the space that temporarily blinds us. But we both relax when a soft female voice calls down.

"Neave? It's safe to come up."

Once in the storage room of the pet store, I smile as the witch who saved us gapes at me. "Thank you for risking your life to hide us," I say.

"You're welcome, Your Highness." She smiles hesitantly at me.

I shake my head. "Please, call my Ty. I'm not a prince anymore."

"Prince of the Witches," she mumbles under her breath.

Neave chokes on air and splutters as she gapes at the blond witch. "What?" she screeches.

"I went into the city earlier to get a feel for the vibe. Everyone is calling you Prince of the Witches." The blond witch wrings her hands nervously.

I chuckle. "I'm guessing they are not doing so in a complimentary fashion."

She shrugs. "It's hit or miss for the humans. The witches, though. They see you as a hero."

Neave stares at me with her mouth agape. "Hero? *You're* the hero?" Her voice raises an octave. "I'm the one who saved your useless ass!"

The blond witch whose name I can't remember, stares at Neave with disbelief. If I had to guess, she's not used to being around so-called royalty and seeing Neave treat me like she is, is probably startling.

"Don't be jealous just because I'm cooler than you," I say to Neave, laughing as her face scrunches with anger.

"Next time, I won't save you. Let's see how well you fare without me."

"Oh, I have no doubt I wouldn't survive a day without you." And I mean that with my entire heart.

She pulls her gaze from mine with visible effort and looks at the other witch. "Seriously, Millie. Thank you. I'll never be able to repay you for what you did."

Millie waves her hands. "Don't mention it. It's what we do. Now, the safe house is ready. Someone delivered food and supplies already."

"Safe house?" I look back and forth between the two witches.

"We have a safe house that can be utilized by any witch who needs it," Neave replies. "We all help supply it at some point in our lives. It's one way we work to keep each other safe."

"Wow. If only more people could see inside the inner workings of your sisterhood. There is no way you could be considered evil or dangerous." I glance at Neave from the corner of my eye. "Except for you. You're a spiteful witch."

She glares at me. "And you're an ignorant ass."

Grinning, I turn to Millie. "Is there any way you could get a message to Prince Julian? I don't want to risk using my phone." When she stares at me with fear-filled eyes, I clarify. "I just need you to tell him the location of the safe house in passing. He'll understand."

She swallows and nods. "I can do that, Your Highness."

It's no use trying to correct her again, so I let it go. Turning to Neave, I hold out my hand. "Ready?"

THE SAFE HOUSE is more like a cottage tucked away along the coast. With sloping roofs, white stone walls, and blue shutters, it's a charming little place. During the warmer months, the windows can be opened to let in the salty sea breeze and the sound of crashing waves. If the dead plants lining the walkway and in the window boxes are any indication, colorful flowers must bloom during the summer.

By the time we reach it, we're both starving. I hop out of the borrowed car and head straight to the front door. "I'm fucking starving."

Neave mumbles her agreement, and rushes past me to type in the code to unlock the door. It swings open, and I spare one moment to search the small space for danger. It doesn't take long, as the bedroom and bathroom are located to the right of the main living room, and the kitchen to the left. That's it. Another cozy space to be stuck in with Neave.

"Everything looks good," I say, walking back into the kitchen. Neave is at the counter pouring cereal into two bowls. I reach around her and tip the box higher, causing it to spill out faster. "I need way more than that measly amount."

We don't even waste time sitting down. Standing at the counter, we shovel the cereal into our mouths until our bowls are empty. When we've finished our dinner of champions, Neave sets her bowl in the sink and looks at me. "I know it's probably not safe, but can we walk to the beach?"

"You're right. That's probably a horrible idea. But because I can't say no to you, I guess we'll risk it."

She beams at me and my heart skips a beat at the beautiful sight. As soon as we step outside, she takes a deep breath, inhaling the salty air. Grabbing her hand, we walk the twenty feet to the beach and kick off our shoes. Neave heads straight for the water and lets the freezing waves lap over her toes.

"I would love to live near the beach," she says, head tipped back to soak up the warmth of the sun.

I stand next to her and when the next wave washes over my feet, I yelp. "Jesus, that's freezing! You're nuts."

I step back, and Neave laughs, turning to face me. The wind blows her hair around her face, and she tugs a hair tie from her wrist to pull it back. She stands on her tiptoes and kisses me. But before I can pull her closer, she steps away.

"What happened back there?" she asks.

I sigh and sit down in the sand, leaving plenty of space so the cold water doesn't reach me. She sits next to me, our shoulders touching. "When we got to my dad's office, Edward was already there. Luckily, he still doesn't suspect Julian, so he thought Julian left the estate because he found me and was bringing me in to face my dad. He thought it would be best if he were there to make sure my dad punished me accordingly." I'm surprised at the bitterness in my voice. I thought after all these years, I'd grown used to my family's opinions of me.

"What happened when you showed your dad the video?"

"I didn't get a chance. My dad wouldn't hear anything I had to say. Edward had already poisoned his mind, although I'm sure it didn't take much to do so. My dad's opinion of me was never very high." And, yes. I know some of that is my fault, but a lot of the problems in my past are due to my dad's thoughts about me. "I don't know what happened, but when Edward searched my phone, there was no video on it. Which is lucky, because if there was, it would have proved Julian was the one to take it."

"So your dad was going to burn you at the stake?" The disbelief in her voice only makes the little kid in me wish for a different dad ... again. "That's insane, Ty."

I nod. "Yeah. Well. It's on par with everything. He's pretty fed up with my shit. This was the last straw for him." She turns to face me, and I sense her intent before she even opens her mouth. I hold up my hand, stopping her. "Don't say it," I say, looking into her deep brown eyes. "I don't want to hear an apology from you. Nothing that happened was your fault. I made my own choices, and I would make each one of them again." I cup her face in my palm. "The risk is worth it, Neave. *You* are worth it. I'd burn at the stake for you in a heartbeat."

Tears fill her eyes, but they don't spill over. Her throat works on a swallow, and I can practically sense her nerves. "I had a lot of time to think while I was waiting to die. A lot of time to work through my feelings."

My stomach flips. This is it. She's going to tell me there will never be anything between us. I hide my shaking hands by turning to face her, one leg bent and the other tucked under it.

"I realized what it is you make me feel. When you look at me, I feel like the most beautiful person in the world. When I'm in the same room as you, I feel safe and protected. When your arms are around me, I feel cherished and loved. And when I saw you tied to that stake and I realized I was going to lose all of that, all of … you, there was no denying it." She scoots closer, her gaze drilling into mine. "I love you, Ty," she whispers, her words shaky. "And I don't want to lose you."

My heart soars at her words. I spread my legs in the sand and a smile grows across my face. "Come here," I say to her.

She crawls the short distance to me and I pull her on top of me at the same time I roll us so she ends up under me, pinned to the sand. Her breathy exclamation turns into a moan when I kiss her deeply. With the surf crashing next to us and the seagulls crying above us, not to mention I'm completely lost in Neave, I don't hear the footsteps crunching in the sand.

"You're both idiots," Julian says, making us jump. "Anyone could have snuck up on you." He stands above us, a fluffy white cat in his arms.

I grin sheepishly as Neave squirms out from under me. Julian tries to set Jinx on the sand, but he refuses to be put down, clinging to Julian's leg with his claws.

"He says he hates sand," she says, prying him off by the scruff of his neck. He dangles in her grip, growling softly as she wraps Julian in a hug. "Thank you," she says. "We never would have escaped if it hadn't been for you."

"I'm just glad you didn't believe my act," he says to me. "I didn't know what else to do, so I played into it."

I hop to my feet, and Neave steps out of Julian's arms, settling Jinx on her shoulders. I pull my brother into a hug. "It was smart and exactly what I would have told you to do. I knew you wouldn't betray me. Not after everything we've been through."

"Oh, here." He hands me the gold band.

I bounce it in my palm and frown. "It's yours," I say, handing it back. "You're the future king. You're still part of the Berkshire family. Keep it."

"Ty, you're still part of the fam—"

"I'm not, and I'm okay with it," I say, interrupting him. "I just have one request that we can talk about later."

He nods, albeit reluctantly. "You shouldn't be out here like this," he says. "Aren't you the one always yelling at me for not being careful? Put a pretty girl in front of you and you lose all common sense." His blue eyes glitter with amusement as he shakes his head.

I shrug and laugh, because it's true. When it comes to Neave, she completely invades my mind and takes over every thought.

"Come on," Neave says, turning toward the cottage, Jinx's tail swishing lazily across her chest. "I think there's a frozen pizza we can make."

My Beautiful, Magnificent Witch

I did it. I freaking did it. And while it was terrifying to admit my feelings to Ty, it settled something inside me that had been unsure for a while now. I may not be sure what my future holds, or the future of the world I live in, but I'm sure about this. *I love him.*

"What I don't understand is how Edward didn't find the video on my phone," Ty says as we sit in the living room eating pizza.

"It didn't send," Julian answers. "Either the earthquake or the surge of magic did something to the cell towers. We had no service, so the video never went through, and we were too distracted to notice you never got it."

"Damn, that was super lucky." Ty sets his empty plate on the coffee table shaped like driftwood.

"Who killed those two guards?" I ask Julian.

"One of my personal guards."

Ty's eyes widen. "They know?"

"One of them does," he shrugs. "Don't worry. I trust him."

"So what happens now?" I ask, looking between the brothers.

"Well, we still need to convince dad of Edward's betrayal and work with him on changing the laws regarding witches." Ty says, leaning back on the couch.

Julian swallows his last bite of pizza. "Give me some time. I'll work him down and get him to agree to meet with you."

Ty frowns. "We need someplace secret, or some way to meet without Edward finding out. Otherwise, it will be a repeat of what just happened."

"I'll figure that out." Julian stands and drops an old-school cell onto the coffee table. "I'll call you on this when I get things figured out." He heads for the door, pausing with his hand on the knob. "You two just stay hidden. No sex on the beach." He levels a stare at Ty with a small smirk. "Do you guys need anything else?"

"Besides sex on the beach? Nah, I think we're good."

Ty walks his brother outside and I scoop up the empty plates, taking them to the garbage in the kitchen. When I turn around, Ty is standing behind me.

"Son of a bitch!" I jump and slap a hand over my heart. "Did you sneak in on purpose? Gah. Don't do that."

He chuckles and steps closer, pinning me to the pantry door. "Sorry?"

"You are not," I say, breathlessly. Not sure if the lack of oxygen is from the scare or Ty standing so close. "Do you think Julian can convince your dad to meet with us?"

He reaches out to wrap a strand of my hair around his finger, his knuckle brushing the side of my neck and sending goosebumps across my skin. "Yeah, he'll make sure it happens. I haven't given him enough credit over the years. He's not as useless as I thought."

I snort. "High praise coming from you, who's also useless."

A dangerous glint appears in his blue eyes, and a slow smirk spreads across his face. "Useless, huh?"

A thrill runs through me, and I shrug, taunting him. I expect him to attack me, to throw me over his shoulder and carry me to the bedroom to prove how *useful* he is. Instead, he kisses me softly, hands slowly traveling up my arms to brace either side of my neck. His thumbs press into my chin, lifting my head back.

When his lips part mine and he sweeps his tongue into my mouth, my legs turn to jelly. The slow sensual kisses are intoxicating, and only his body pressing mine to the pantry is keeping me upright. He keeps up with the slow, deep kisses until I'm gasping for breath and desperate for more.

His hands slide back down my arms and over my hips. He gives my ass a squeeze before lifting me up. My legs and arms wrap around him on instinct. Never breaking the kiss, he carries me to the bedroom and gently lays me on the bed, right on top of Jinx.

"What the fuck?" I screech, at the same time Jinx yowls. "Get out of my room!"

He jumps from the bed and glares at me. *Technically, it's not your room, hag.*

"Rat," I growl, but my mouth tugs into a smile as he saunters out. It fades instantly as I look at Ty, staring at me with adoration.

His chest heaves as he takes deep breaths. "Did you mean it?" he asks, his eyes a darker blue than normal. "What you said on the beach? Did you mean it?"

I climb to my knees and grasp the sides of his face. "Yes. I love you, Ty."

His eyes close, and he smiles. "I'll never get sick of hearing that," he rasps.

His fingers curl around the hem of my shirt, and he lifts it over my head. I unclasp my bra and let it slide down my arms while he removes his own shirt. My fingers tremble slightly as I unbutton his pants and push them down his thighs. Biting my lip, I wrap my hand around his cock and stroke from base to tip, rubbing my thumb over the crown. His head falls backward, and he groans.

I watch a bead of precum form and I dip my head to lick it up. His hips jerk forward, so I open my mouth and swallow him down. I love the way his fingers thread through my hair, tugging the strands as he holds my head gently and thrusts his hips forward. He hits the back of my throat and I swallow.

"Shit, Neave," he grunts.

I slide my hands around his thighs and dig my fingernails into his ass. He groans and pulls out, rubbing the head of his cock along my lower lip.

"Lay down."

I love the gravel in his voice when he's aroused and trying to control himself. The sound settles deep in my bones and warms me from the inside out. I scoot back and lay down, letting Ty remove my leggings and panties. He wraps his hands around my thighs and spreads my legs. His eyes darken further and he doesn't wait to lower his head and lick up my slit. Heat courses through me with each swipe of his tongue.

He hums and the vibration almost sends me over the edge, but he pulls back. "Not yet, witch," he says, wiping his mouth on my thigh. Slowly, he climbs up my body, his cock nudging my entrance, but he holds himself still. "Say it again," he whispers, his eyes boring into mine.

I gently cup his cheeks in my palms. "I love you."

His body shudders above mine, and he holds my gaze as he presses in. Each inch stretching and filling me perfectly. When he's fully seated, he kisses me softly. "I love you, Neave."

My heart soars, and I wrap my legs around his waist to pull him closer. Even connected as we are, it's not enough. I need him closer. His upper body presses mine into the mattress while his hips keep thrusting, slowly at first, then faster. Our gazes stay locked on each other, and as my pleasure builds, so does the overwhelming lightness in my chest. It's like my heart could fly right out of my body.

Ty buries his face in my neck. "Together, Neave." His breath fans over my neck and I whimper, the pleasure building to a crescendo. Ty thrusts harder, and I bite my lip hard enough to draw blood. "Now, Neave. Come with me."

I hold him tightly, and he does the same to me as we crash

over the edge into the euphoria of our orgasms. Stars erupt in my vision, and my body shakes as the waves roll through me. Ty shudders, his fingers digging sharply into my hips as his breath leaves him in harsh puffs.

When we've both come down from the high, Ty pulls out and rolls us over. I have no control over my body, my limbs limp and uncoordinated, but I don't care, so long as I'm tucked against Ty, skin to skin.

"Neave," he breathes against the top of my head. The way he says my name, like a prayer, makes my heart thump madly in my chest.

I curl against him even tighter. If I could, I'd crawl inside him and never leave again. I've never experienced this before. The lightness inside me, the warmth and contentment. Fear briefly flashes through me, but I squash it. I won't think of the possibility of losing this. It's not something I can worry about. He's here now, we're together now, and that's all that matters.

As my eyelids close and I drift off to sleep, I swear I hear him whispering.

Don't ever leave me, Neave. I need you more than I need air to breathe. My beautiful, magnificent witch.

THREE DAYS later I find myself in the borrowed car with Ty, heading back to the city. I can't stop my leg from shaking as Ty drives us to meet with his dad. Julian called this morning and gave us a time and location. The butterflies in my belly haven't let up since Ty hung up the phone.

He reaches across the car to place a hand on my thigh. "Relax. We'll be okay."

"How do you know? Last time, it all went to hell. Who's to say it won't again? "

"We were idiots last time. I should have suspected something like that, but I didn't. This time, we're prepared. We won't let them get the jump on us."

He squeezes my thigh, and the shaking stops, only for me to bring my thumb to my mouth to chew on the skin around my nail. He peers at me from the corner of his eye and sighs. Grabbing my hand, he threads our fingers together and rests them on my leg. Determined to let my anxiety out somehow, I resort to chewing on the inside of my cheek. He can't do anything about that.

"My dad has a private dining room at an upscale restaurant in the city. Julian was able to convince my dad to meet with us. He said they posed this as a father-son dinner for him and Dad to do some bonding now that I'm out of the picture." He snorts at the idea. "Like my dad would ever try to bond with us. But we'll sneak in the back in case Edward is watching for us."

My stomach is revolting against the coffee I drank before we left. Groaning, I thump my head back against the headrest.

Ty taps our hands on my thigh. "Chin up, witch. We got this."

As much as Ty complained about the piece of shit car Millie let us borrow, it does help us remain incognito as we drive through the city. No one would suspect the arrogant prince to drive a run down beater that is days away from crapping out. With a hood over my highly recognizable hair, and a ball cap pulled low over Ty's blond locks, hopefully no one realizes it's us.

He pulls the car into an alley and kills the engine. Turning to look at me, he smiles. "Ready?"

"No."

He leans forward and plants a smacking kiss on my lips. "That's the spirit!"

Ty parked the car a block away, and we slink through the dirty alleys like the rats that infest them. The only bright side to all of this is Ty jumping every time a rat scurries in front of him. His muttered curses would make a sailor blush, and each one brings a smile to my face. I'm pretty sure he's laying it on extra thick to distract me, but I'm not completely positive.

"This is it." He nudges a box out of the way, and a rat scurries from underneath it. He jumps, and an entirely unmanly squeal escapes him. "Son of a bitch!"

I chuckle, because I know that was not a show. "Such a baby."

He squeezes my hand almost painfully, and approaches the back door. A royal guard is standing just inside, wearing the witch hunter uniform with the royal crest, signifying his rank. I stiffen and prepare myself to run while also pulling up some magic. Ty doesn't react though, at least not how I expected him to. Instead of running or fighting, he cocks his head to the side.

"Huh," he says under his breath, brows furrowed under the bill of his ball cap.

"Ty," I whisper, tugging on his hand.

He looks down at me and shakes himself. "It's okay. It's one of Julian's guards." He returns his attention to the guard. "How's it going, Luca?"

Luca nods, his face a mask of indifference. Turning, he weaves his way through the busy kitchen. No one spares us any mind, as if random people walking through is commonplace. Then again, the dark glare Luca gives anyone who glances our way would make the bravest of people look away.

The kitchen door opens to a short hallway. One end of the hallway leads to the main dining room. The other, the direction we turn, leads to a dark oak door with the word *PRIVATE* etched into the wood. Luca takes up guard outside the door, and Ty pushes into the room. His head turns left and right as he scans the space before pulling me in behind him.

The private dining room is lavish. It takes all of my control to keep my jaw from hitting the floor. An elegant red rug covers the marble floor. A chandelier hangs from the ceiling, the crystal beads casting shimmering rainbows over the shiny wood-paneled walls. Sitting at the glass dining table, Julian smiles at us, but his dad sneers.

Ty pulls out a gold chair cushioned in white fabric for me to sit in before taking his own seat across from his dad and brother. "Thanks for meeting with us."

King Leander snorts. His dark blue eyes crease as he frowns at Ty. "I'm not doing this for you."

"I don't care who you're doing it for. I'm just glad you're doing it. We have a lot to discuss."

Conversation falls silent as a server enters and pours water into the crystal glasses. When he leaves, King Leander leans back in his chair, crossing his arms over his chest. "What do you have to say?"

"First, I have proof you'll want to see regarding Uncle Edward wanting to take the throne from you."

Leander scoffs, but takes the phone Ty slides across the table. Pressing play, I watch his expression as the video unfolds. Ty cropped it to just show the portion recorded in the hallway, and Leander's face goes from annoyed, to slack, to angry in the span of a few seconds.

"There is more to that video, but I'm not comfortable sharing it with you yet." Ty rests his elbows on the table, leaning forward. "But I think that's all the evidence you need to show he's gunning for your throne."

Leander drops the phone onto the table with a clatter. He rubs his eyes and sighs heavily. I swear it's like he ages five years in the time it takes me to blink. The creases at the corners of his eyes deepen, the frown on his face pulls lower, and the gray in his neatly trimmed beard looks more prominent.

"Do you have any other proof?" he asks.

"Yeah, but none that you would take seriously. He admitted all of this to Neave."

Ty's right. His dad doesn't even blink at this statement. "I always worried about him doing this, but I never thought he'd actually go through with it." He grits his teeth. "Thank you for bringing this to my attention."

Ty barks a laugh. "Wow, don't hurt yourself with that gratitude."

"What else do you have to say?" King Leander growls.

Ty reaches under the table to grab my hand. He squeezes it before saying, "I want to propose a change to the laws regarding witches."

His dad laughs. "Not likely." He stands as if he's going to leave, but Julian stops him.

"Dad," he says. He raises his brows, and when King Leander doesn't sit back down, Julian sighs. "Fine. If you don't listen, I'm walking." He removes the slim silver crown from his head and sets it on the table. It clinks softly, the only sound in the room.

Ty's eyes are wide, and I'm not sure I'm breathing. *Is he really threatening to walk away from the crown to help the witches?* Leander grinds his teeth and sits back down.

Ty takes a deep breath. "I understand why all of this started thousands of years ago. They were scared and angry and did what they thought they had to do. We followed their choices because we thought we had to, and we had the vision to figure out. Well, that's no longer an issue. The mystery behind the vision has been solved and taken care of. There is no longer a need to keep hunting witches."

"You figured out the vision?" His dad leans forward, interest sparked.

"Yeah, and it was never about us. True to the Berkshire theme, our ancestors were arrogant and thought everything was about them. It wasn't, though." He glances at me and nods.

I pick up where he left off, the butterflies in my belly making me want to vomit. "Sybil's vision was about the witches. She saw the downfall of her sisters and knew she had to stop it."

Leander's face is pale and pinched. "How do you know this?"

I hesitate. He's not going to believe me. "I ... talked to Sybil. My visions led me to a ring that was infused with Sybil's magic. When I put it on, she was able to manifest long enough to explain everything."

Ty, sensing his dad about to say something stupid, leans forward. "It doesn't matter. We did what Sybil told us to. And in doing so, we saved the witches. That's not the point."

Face turning a bright shade of red, Leander sputters, "Not the point? What the hell is the point, then?"

"There is no reason to continue hunting and burning witches," Ty says, his voice ringing with authority I haven't heard before.

"Except to keep our people safe?" Leander scoffs. "You've forgotten yourself, Tyberius."

He shakes his head. "When was the last recorded crime committed by a witch?"

"I'd have to look. I don't remember off the top of my head."

"You don't remember because it was over twenty years ago. Twenty-three to be exact. And it was an act of self-defense. Before that, it was fifteen years. Now, when was the last recorded crime committed by a human?" He doesn't wait for his dad to respond. "Two days ago? A week at most? There is no evidence that witches are evil. If you look at the records, you'd see the opposite. It's humans causing all the problems."

"Witches are naturally inclined toward non-violence," I say quietly. "We are drawn toward nature and peace. We want nothing more than to use our magic for good."

"Think about it," Ty adds. "Neave has used her magic to heal me twice. What could happen if a witch was free to use her magic to heal people? Or grow food? Or protect us? Our country would flourish. We've spent so long destroying it. It's time to change our ways."

I clutch his hand so hard his bones grind together. A bead of sweat slides down my back, making me want to twitch.

King Leander sighs. "I need to deal with your uncle. There is a lot I need to think about. But in the meantime, I will pause all hunts and burnings. Once I've taken care of the threat to my throne, we can talk some more."

It's Not A Magic 8 Ball

Neave and I walk to the car in a daze. I can't believe my dad has agreed to talk to us more. And he paused all hunts and burnings. Inside, I'm screaming with excitement. The possibilities for our future stretch wide and unending before me, but I can't let myself fall into the dream. There is still so much that can go wrong.

As soon as the doors close, Neave turns to me. "Did that just happen?" Her dark brown eyes are wide and glossy, like she's holding back tears.

"I think it did." I laugh. "Holy shit. I can't believe my dad just agreed to that." I lean forward and kiss her. "We won't stop fighting," I say when I pull away. "I won't rest until you can walk down the street without fear."

Her lips wobble, and she presses them together. "What now?" she whispers through her fight to contain her tears.

"We return to the cottage and wait for Julian's all clear. My dad will have to make an announcement, and he won't do that until Edward is in custody."

She nods and settles in for the drive back to the coast, but I spot the smile on her lips, and it doesn't fade the entire trip. When we reach the cottage, she gets out and looks longingly at the beach.

Snagging her hand, I lead her to the shore. "Let's go for a walk." The sand squishes between my toes, cool and rough. A chilly breeze blows Neave's hair around her head. "I'll never understand your obsession with the beach when it's cold. It's miserable out here. The sun isn't even shining today."

She laughs. "It's nature. There is so much magic shimmering around me. It's ... invigorating."

Looking at her face, I can see it. She's shining from the inside out. Her smile is contagious, her eyes radiating happiness. This is what I want for her. For the rest of our lives. Happiness, peace, joy.

"Can't we hang out at a greenhouse or something? It's warm, and there are plants. Same concept, right?" I brush my hair from my face, only for the wind to blow it right back into my eye.

She giggles and darts out of my grasp, straight for the water. I watch as she lets the waves crash over her legs, soaking her pants. She raises her arms in the air and spins, head tipped back, purple hair brushing her back. Like a magnet, I'm drawn toward her. Ignoring the cold water, I stop her spinning so I can kiss her.

"I love seeing you like this," I whisper against her lips. "We could always get a little place on the beach. For the summer. I refuse to live there in the winter." My breath catches. I didn't mean to say that out loud. We haven't really talked about *after*. I assume she wants to stay together, but with Neave, you never know. She's a free spirit, and I'd hate to be the one to tie her down.

"That would be nice," she says. A small smile blooming on her face.

I lean down to kiss her, but she ducks. Before I can figure out what she's doing, she's bent down and splashes water at me. I gasp, the cold drops soaking through my clothes immediately. She darts away again, laughing and looking back at me.

I take off after her, chasing her through the crashing waves. "Fucking witch!" When I catch her, she'll regret doing that. She squeals as I wrap my arms around her and throw her over my shoulder. Grinning, I carry my witch to the cottage, her insults and laughter a warm blanket wrapped around me.

Julian meets us at a small cafe just off the city center. Neave rushes forward and pulls him in for a hug. I smile. Seeing my brother and my witch get along makes my heart happy. And having my relationship with Julian repaired makes it even happier.

"You know, I'm starting to get jealous," I say, hugging him. "If I ask her one more time who she's texting, and she says your name, I'll throw the phone across the room."

He grins. "It's not my fault I'm the more handsome brother." The grin fades, and he bites his bottom lip. "I can get you in to talk to Killian, if you want. Dad has him imprisoned. He's going to question him before he makes any decisions regarding his sentencing."

The lightness inside me seeps away. I think about meeting with Killian, finding out when it all went wrong, but I shake my head. "No. I think I'm good. He made his choice and I'm over it. I don't need him in my life anymore." Not with Neave and Julian by my side.

We walk together to the city square. The stakes are still there, but there is no wood piled under them waiting to be lit. One day, I will see those stakes torn down. One day, the crowd gathered here won't be jonesing for a death. Today is not that day, though.

We stop front and center of the platform. I want Uncle Edward to see me and Neave before he loses his head. I want him to know we won. Julian hops up on the platform where he's expected to stand next to our dad while our dad removes his own brother's head. A few months ago, that idea wouldn't have phased me. Now, I look at Julian, and the thought crushes me. We lost so much time not getting along. And it all changed because of a witch.

Uncle Edward is led onto the platform, more guards surrounding him than would typically be used. I watch Julian catch the gaze of one of the guards. Luca. I can't believe I never noticed that before. I snort as a faint blush creeps into Julian's cheeks and he looks away.

"What?" Neave asks, looking up at me.

I smile down at her. "Nothing. Just laughing at Julian. Pompous ass."

My dad reads through the charges against Edward as the guards secure him to the iron rings on the platform. Rings that have been there for thousands of years. Some things never change. The crowd falls silent as my dad unsheathes the ancient sword at his hip. Another relic from our ancestors. One that has been maintained and is still sharp enough to ... well, sever a head from a neck.

As he raises the sword, the metal catching the light from the sun and glinting, Neaves turns her face into my arm. I watch, though. I stare into those brown eyes as he stretches his neck forward, and I smile. The fear shining in his gaze turns to hate as soon as he sees me and Neave, and a sneer pulls one side of his mouth up.

The sword comes down, and Edward's head hits the stone with a thunk, the sneer frozen on his lifeless face. Neave shudders, and I place my hand against the back of her head, pressing her face against the fabric of my shirt. My dad bends down and picks up the head, lifting it high so the crowd can see what happens to traitors. When he tosses it in a burlap sack, I release Neave.

"For such a civilized world we live in, we can be incredibly uncivilized in our actions." She stares at Edward's limp body as the guards remove it.

"I'm sorry you didn't get your revenge." I know my uncle was at the top of her list for burning her mother.

She shrugs. "It's okay. He got what he deserved. Besides, I

think we've learned what happens when people make revenge their priority."

I kiss her forehead and turn her from the platform. We walk the short distance to her apartment and climb up the fire escape to the window. She hauls it open and presses her bloody finger to the sill before she climbs in, stopping just inside.

I smack her ass. "Seriously. Why do you always stop just inside the window? It's fucking freezing!"

She steps to the side and points to the coffee table. "Where did that come from?"

I look past her shoulder and grunt. "Is that..."

"I think it is," she breathes.

Sitting on the coffee table is a crystal ball. The glass sphere is completely see-through and sits on an ancient-looking gold base. The three legs sprout from the base and form claws that sit on the table.

Neave walks slowly to the couch and sits down. Her hand hovers over it and her fingers shake.

"Ask it something," I urge. "Is Tyberius the hotter brother?"

Her hand drops to her lap, and she glares at me. "That's not how it works, dumbass. It's not a Magic 8 Ball." She lifts her hand again, and this time she runs one finger over the smooth surface. A golden glow pulses from the orb and she jumps. "Holy shit," she breathes. "It is. It's Sybil's. Where did it come from?"

"Magic."

She heaves an exasperated sigh. "Ty."

"I would think you'd be used to magic. You are a witch, after all."

"Like I could forget. You won't stop telling me."

I grin and tug her to her feet. "You're my witch. And I'll say it however many times I want. Now, ask it which Berkshire brother is the sexiest." I nod toward the crystal ball.

"I don't need to ask it that. I already know. It's your dad." She cackles and darts out of my grasp. In my moment of being too stunned to move, she makes it to the bedroom before I can start to chase her, and she slams the door, laughing the entire time.

"Fucking witch!"

Epilogue

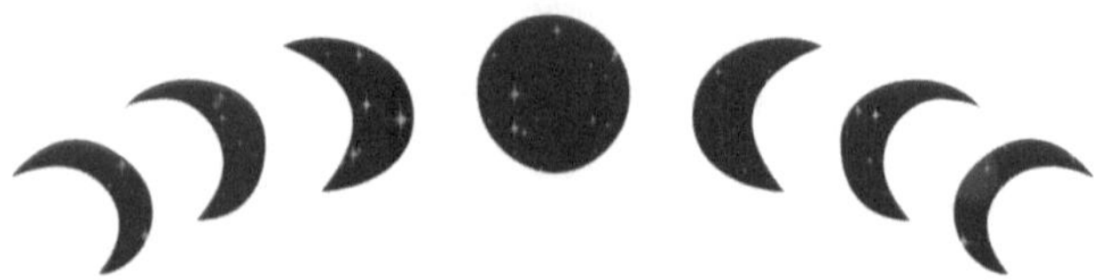

We exit the palace and I can't feel my limbs. Or my face. Or my body. I'm completely numb. "We did it," I whisper. "Holy fuck, we did it!"

Ty lifts me up and spins me around, right in front of the palace doors. "I told you I wouldn't stop fighting until we won."

Tears stream down my face, but for once, they're happy tears. He wipes my cheeks and kisses each one. For four months, we have been in non-stop negotiation with his dad. Ty has become the spokesman for the witches. We have met with almost every witch in the city, listening to their wants and needs, and we brought them to the king. We have worked with him to change the laws, and put new ones in place.

No longer will witches be hunted and burned. We will live under the same rules as every other human. Ty has agreed to take up a position on the governing council, and he will act as the voice for all of us. Prince of the Witches, indeed.

Change won't happen overnight. I know prejudices are deep-seated and it will take time for people to come to terms with this. But we're on the right path, and it wouldn't have been possible without the man by my side.

"Thank you, Ty. I truly cannot express what this all means to me. And the fact you have jumped in willingly and taken on such a huge role, I'll never be able to thank you enough for that."

"I thought by now you'd realize there is absolutely nothing I wouldn't do for you. All I want is to see you smile every day, and I'll do *anything* to make that happen."

Before I can respond, he threads our fingers together and tugs me from the palace. "Where are we going?"

"There are a couple things I want to show you."

He leads me to the city center, skipping the tunnel so we can enjoy the warm spring breeze. The platform is still there, and the stakes, although no wood is piled beneath, and no witch has been burned in the last four months. The ground is still cracked from when I refilled the ley lines. Ty stops at the base of the platform.

"You wanted to show me the stakes?" I ask, raising my brows.

"No, I wanted to show you this." He pulls his phone from his pocket, and hands it to me.

I scroll through the pictures, my heart speeding up with each new picture. "What is this?" I ask, my voice shaking.

"I've been working with a contractor. We're going to turn the city center into a park." He steps behind me and points to one of the pictures. "The platform will be torn down, and in its place we'll build a stage for concerts and shows. There will be a lot of green space and plants. This corner will have a playground for kids. And here," he points to a corner in the southwest part of the square, "Will be a monument for all the witches burned in the past. I'm still working with a designer, but it will have a fountain and a place for people to sit and reflect. I wanted you to be part of that design."

My eyes water, blurring the drawings. I can't believe I have this man in my life. How he went from the most prominent witch hunter at the top of my revenge list to this man who loves me and my sisters so deeply, still amazes me. I turn and wrap my arms around him. There are no words I can say to tell him how I feel, but I know he doesn't need those words. He hugs me tight and kisses the top of my head.

"Thank you, Ty."

He pulls away and smiles. "That's not all." With our fingers laced together, he leads me back toward the palace. "You've always wanted to see the gardens, right? Spring is the perfect time for that."

He tugs me past the towering hedges and into the gardens. I can't look everywhere fast enough. Flowers of every imaginable shape and color bloom brightly, their fragrance perfuming the air. Birds chirp from the branches of trees just starting to get their green leaves. A fountain bubbles from somewhere, the sound making me want to follow it to find the source. Arches covered in flowering vines dot the pebbled path, and it's under one of those, with big drooping white flowers, that Ty stops.

He turns to me, blue eyes shining in the sunlight. "I know traditionally witches don't have relationships. But there is nothing traditional about you or us." Grabbing my hands in his, he gets down on one knee and looks up at me.

My breath catches in my throat, and I gasp.

"Neave, ever since I met you, I have been nothing short of amazed. You tore down every belief I had and set it on fire. You have opened my eyes to the truth, and I will forever be grateful for that. Not a day goes by that I don't realize how lucky I am to have you in my life, and I want to say that every day for the rest of my life."

He reaches into his pocket and pulls out a black box. I'm positive I'm not breathing as he opens it and holds it up. Nestled inside is a beautiful silver ring with a square cut stone the same color as his eyes. The ring blurs as tears fill my eyes for the third time this day.

"Neave Parker, will you marry me?" His voice is rough with emotion, and through my tears, I see the ring box shaking in his hands.

I force a breath into my lungs and swallow. "Only if you

promise to get me a house on the beach." My voice shakes as much as his hands.

He huffs a small laugh. "Is that a yes?"

I nod my head, tears spilling over, and clasp his cheeks in my hand. Against his lips, I whisper, "Yes."

Acknowledgments

This book almost didn't happen. It was a last minute decision in July, to write and publish a witchy book before Halloween. The two months that followed that decision were pure chaos and anxiety. But with the help and encouragement of my publishing family and street team, I did it.

Thank you to my husband, and I'm sorry. I know I wasn't much help around the house while I was getting this book written, edited, and published. I promise, I'll never do something this crazy again. I think.

As always, thank you to my Midnight Tide Publishing family. Elle and Lou, you have made this all possible, and I can't possibly thank you enough for everything.

To my street team, Whitney's Whimsies, you guys rock! I appreciate all of your support and cheerleading! And a special thank you to Kirsten for helping me pick names for the cities in this book!

And of course, the biggest thank you goes to YOU! My readers are the reason I keep doing this thing. So keep reading!

About the Author

Whitney L. Spradling is a full time Occupational Therapist and autism mama, who has had a dream to write and publish a novel since she was a little girl. She lives outside of Cincinnati with her husband, son, and two cats. When she is not writing she can be found in her craft room making custom tumblers, or curled up with a good book and a cup of coffee (or glass of wine).

Also by Whitney L. Spradling

The Obsidian Artifacts

The Obsidian Sword

The Obsidian Crown

The Cursed Realms

Of Flames and Curses

Of Smoke and Betrayal (coming 11.2023)

Fates

These Dangerous Fates

These Deadly Dreams (coming 1.2024)

Standalones

Those We Couldn't Burn

See the full catalog at:

www.midnighttidepublishing.com

***

The Hex Next Door by Lou Wilham

What's a little necromancy between family?

For the Crow Witch, Icarus "Rus" Ashthorne, Moondale seemed the perfect hiding place. But like they always say, you can't go home again, and Rus finds out quickly that nothing is how she remembered, while at the same time very little has changed. Then she comes face to face with the only woman she's ever loved, Az Elwood, and... well, things get messier than she thought they ever could.

The Elwoods are a staple of Moondale, respected, feared, powerful, and Azure Elwood was always happy with her place amongst them. Happy to play the part of the good little witch, until Rus Ashthorne. Eleven years ago, Rus got on a bus and left Azure behind, but she's back, with two little girls trailing her like ducklings, and enough unspoken things between them to drown the town.

Now witch hunters are knocking at their proverbial door, the council of magic is being a real pain in the ass, and Rus wonders how much magic it'll take to protect the people she loves from herself and the danger following her.

A LGBTQ+ cozy urban fantasy novel for fans of The Ex Hex, and October Daye.

www.ingramcontent.com/pod-product-compliance
Lightning Source LLC
Chambersburg PA
CBHW050752190726
48285CB00005B/1626